Praise for C

G000150921

The Baby

"Definitely recommend this ~~~ ~~ a fan of murder/mystery stories." ~The Reading Café

"This is a wonderfully written story that has a plot filled with suspense, intrigue and mystery that had me turning the pages as fast as I could." ~Sharon

Skinned

"A murder mystery book, but more!! It's the first time I've read a book like this, and not been able to put it down." ~The Reading Café

"This story is paced beautifully and grabs the reader from the start." ~InD'tale Magazine

"The storyline was interesting and unusual and the action fast paced. In short it was unputdownable and I finished it in a couple of days - as my frequently shushed husband will confirm!" ~ Ysyllt Rabey

The
Baby Contract

The
Contract
Series

Book Two

by
CeeRee Fields

The Baby Contract
Book Two
CeeRee Fields

Warning
This story is intended for adults, 18+. Characters portrayed are 18 or older.

Dedication

Have enough courage to trust love one more time and always one more time."

~ Maya Angelou

Acknowledgment

To Amber Daulton and Daryl Devoré a huge thank you for helping make sure that Rafe turned out to be a good guy worthy of Elizabeth's love.

Thanks to my mother for always being there.

I couldn't have done this without you all!

Chapter One

Excitement bubbled in Elizabeth Sutherland Martinez as she left the balmy California night air and slipped through the front door of her stepfather's home. The mansion was not to her taste, ostentatious in the extreme with expensive marble, gaudy antiques, and flashy paintings. Nothing of her mother's elegant touch remained after her death.

Her sandaled feet slapped against the pure white marble tile of the foyer. The grand staircase split into two sections that ran on either side of the entrance and swept to an arc that met on the second floor of the house. A small balcony overlooked the foyer and the great room where Harold held lavish parties. Large dangling crystals set in the chandelier took up half the room, clinking when the air conditioning kicked on, breaking the oppressive silence in the house.

This wasn't her home, never had been. Harold and her mother had moved here after they'd married. Even though her mother had passed several years ago, Elizabeth still considered Harold Moore part of her family. The only family she had other than her husband, Rafael. Heading for the great room, she stopped when she heard nothing in that direction.

Turning back to the foyer, she took a right at the foot of the stairs toward Harold's office. Giddy at finally being able to deliver her news, she skipped a few steps over the plush cream carpet as she passed a door that led to a cream-and-beige parlor on the left. Hearing Rafe's deep, sexy baritone, she stifled a giggle and took a sharp right down the only other hallway.

With Esther, the housekeeper, gone for the evening, surprising Harold and Rafe would be a piece of cake. But she froze as her name was ground out between clenched teeth. Loathing coated every syllable, confusing her because she had never heard that tone in Rafe's voice had never spoken before. Worried, she crept to the door on silent feet.

"No! I agreed to a year, and I've given you a year and two months."

Elizabeth flinched at Rafe's harsh tone. Her best friend, Megan, would have stormed into the meeting, yelling and screaming at the two of them until they provided answers. Elizabeth had never been that bold, preferring to soothe tempers and downplay arguments.

"Elizabeth's not pregnant, Rafe. Therefore, the contract is null and void."

Her heart felt as if it had stopped beating. Peeking around the crack in the door, she quickly pulled away and pressed her back against the wall. So much anger and rage were painted across the faces of both the men she'd thought cared for her—considered family.

"No! My lawyers and I read it. The agreement stated I had to do everything in my power to get Elizabeth pregnant, and I have. I have fucked her every night. You can ask Megan if you don't believe me. Elizabeth shares every damned detail with her." He all but spit the words out, as if taking her to bed were revolting.

"Oh, I'm sure you've more than done your nightly duty in the bedroom," Harold stated acerbically.

"If she's not pregnant, it's not my fault." Rafe's voice lowered.

"But it is. That was the only thing I asked of you—"

Tears fell as her heart twisted in her chest. Was Megan in on this as well? Why? Elizabeth's mind flew through all the nights Rafe had made love to her—no, not love. Sex. Seen in a new light, what she had mistaken as a passionate claiming was just a fuck. Everything she had thought to be true was a lie. But why?

"That wasn't part of the contract. Hell, I didn't want any part of this. All I ever wanted was my grandfather's cabin, which you bought out from underneath me like the sneaky, conniving bastard you are."

But that was another lie. Rafe had asked her to marry him. Granted, he hadn't actively pursued her except to ask her out the first time they met. After that, everything spun from there. The accidental meeting at a friend's birthday party after a week of silence, as if their first date had gone badly. Another few dates squeezed in around his busy schedule. Then he had asked her to marry him.

Had she wanted him?

Yes, she had been more than obvious about that. However, she had never pursued him, would never have done that. Her mother had raised Elizabeth better than to chase down a man who had expressed no interest in her after that first date. She had assumed Rafe—no, he was not, had never been, Rafe—Rafael had been stressed about his work. When his big project was completed, it was as if he finally noticed her. Pursued her. Captured her.

Only he had never chosen her.

"I'm filing for divorce tomorrow and will finally be rid of you and your manipulative daughter."

"I still can't understand why you won't wait a few more months. The timeline won't change—"

"Chloe's ready to be married. She wants a family, and my entanglement needs to be severed." Rafael's venomous tone softened at the mention of Chloe.

"Oh. Well then, I'll have my attorneys discuss this with your attorneys. However, do not think you'll get off that easily. Elizabeth wanted a child out of this, and as long as there is breath in my body, she'll have it. So, you might have to leave a few deposits—"

"Whatever. As long as I get the damned cabin and my divorce."

She realized then Rafael was at the door, his hand that had touched her so intimately holding the knob. Not wanting to face him with a tear-stained face and a shattered heart, she fled the way she had come and rounded the corner where the main staircase was. Elizabeth moved so fast she hit the tiled floor only to lose traction. She slid across the marble and skidded into a wall. Pushing away from the wall, she clutched her purse to her heaving chest, trying to calm down.

When she met Rafael again, she wanted it to be on her terms. Calm and composed, so he never knew how much he had hurt her.

A sob passed her lips, breaking through the silent room, alerting her to be quiet if she wanted to avoid her husband. Soon to be ex-husband. Pressing a hand to her mouth, she needed to clean up before she confronted Harold. Shore up her mental defenses because if he saw a hint of weakness, she would never get the answers she so desperately needed. Instead, he would be protective and try to shield her.

Spinning on the ball of her right foot, she headed to the small bathroom under the stairs.

She quietly shut the door and turned on the light. The crinkling of the plastic bag reminded her of the reason she had come. Looking down, she set the innocuous bag with its equally mundane contents on the side of the pedestal sink. The bright pink stripes shone like a beacon, all but making the pregnancy test glow. Positive.

Stupid. She had been so stupid, wanting to rush over as soon as she had seen Rafael's calendar with a meeting scheduled at Harold's house tonight. She had wanted to share the news with both of them; this was the first time they had been together since Christmas. They were the only family she had left. Elizabeth had felt like they should know before she even told her best friend. *Boy is the surprise on me.*

Shoving the plastic bag deep into her purse, she lifted her face to the mirror. She looked the same, except for the runny mascara and red-rimmed eyes.

She had been called plain her entire life. The merging of her gorgeous mother and handsome father had misfired in her genes. Instead of platinum blond hair like her mother's, she had gotten muddy brown like her father's, but instead of the piercing green eyes that set him apart, she had received her mother's deep navy-blue orbs.

Her features were even, but not breathtaking. Her mother, Lillian Sutherland Moore, only had to walk into a room and men would stop to watch, to lust for what they could never have. Maximillian Sutherland had had the same appeal. Women threw themselves at him, but with Lillian, he never strayed. Nor had she ever looked at anyone but Maxim. After several years of mourning her lost love, Harold Moore was the man who'd captured Lillian's attention.

Allowing herself one last shuddery breath, Elizabeth looked around for a rag before she remembered this was the water closet. Nothing except guest hand towels graced this bathroom since it was mostly used for the elegant dinner parties Harold threw. A handful of tissue from the box on top of the commode handled the majority of the cleanup. Mascara that had left black smudges under her eyes was mopped up with a bit of hand soap and water. She reapplied her blush and powder, slicked more lipstick on, and ran a brush through her shoulder-length hair.

When she felt she had done all she could, Elizabeth stowed everything back in her purse, washed her hands, and stepped out of the small bathroom. Taking a minute to gather the rest of her courage, she slipped around the corner and froze at the tableau in front of her.

Megan was plastered against Harold. His lips ground into the smaller woman's, and his hands gripped her ass. What. The. Hell?

Shocked, Elizabeth didn't know what to do. She wanted answers, wanted to know why Harold had bribed Rafael to marry her, why Megan had told him so many personal details, and she really wanted to know why he wanted Elizabeth pregnant. At least one of the answers presented itself. Her best friend was obviously sleeping with her stepfather, so of course, pillow talk would be involved. Those talks must have led to personal details of Elizabeth's life. Why would they discuss her instead of their own relationship? She hadn't a clue.

And why are they keeping their affair a secret? How long has it been going on? Obviously not while Mom was alive. No one would cheat on her.

Elizabeth was so lost in her thoughts that she jolted at Megan's vibrant voice. "So, he's actually leaving her?"

"Yes, it seems Chloe is ready to get her claws into him."

There was that name again. Who was Chloe?

"So, what do we do? How do we get our hands on the trust?" Megan's question, one after the other in rapid succession, filled in a few more blanks.

However, the blanks they filled in made Elizabeth's stomach churn more as she huddled deeper in the shadows.

"I'll pay someone else, though Rafael said if it got him out of the contract faster, he would be willing to make a sperm deposit."

"She'll jump on it. She fancies herself in love with him, and she wants his baby." Megan's mocking tone made Elizabeth want to curl up and hide. Had her friend always hated her? "Just remember our deal, Harry-hon. I took care of Lillian for you, and I'm helping you with Elizabeth, so I expect my cut of that trust or you and I will have issues—"

He grinned down at her, his smile hard and cold. "As if we would ever have problems. But as soon as she has that baby, we'll have to kill Elizabeth to gain control of the child and open the trust. Which means—"

"I know what it means." Megan flashed a diamond ring that graced her third finger. "Only marriage will do to knit up your broken family."

When had they gotten engaged? The hateful words they spewed slammed into Elizabeth like a fist to the face. They planned on killing her after her baby was born. Her hand moved to her stomach as if to protect the small life within her. Was Rafael in on this as well? Had they all been laughing behind her back as they plotted her death? Had any of them ever been on her side? Shivers raced over her skin; she needed to leave without being seen. All thoughts of confronting any of the serpents flew out of the window now that she realized they intended to kill her and take her child.

Thank God she'd parked in front and not in the garage the family used. She hadn't wanted anyone to catch her before she'd sprung her surprise. But now, Megan and Harold stood between her and freedom. The front door was so close, but the obstacle between her and it was insurmountable. Elizabeth wasn't stupid, though the past year might speak otherwise. If Harold and Megan even suspected she'd overheard them, they would kill her now and take their chances in court trying to get what they wanted.

The trust had to be the one her grandfather had set up as that was the only one tied to her baby.

Cowering in the meager shadows the stairs provided, she struggled to remember what she could about the trust. Her father's estate had automatically defaulted into it upon his death. Lillian hadn't needed the money; she had more than enough to take care of Elizabeth and herself. So, she'd included Maxim's estate in the trust.

Elizabeth hadn't needed the money either; her mother had left her enough to live on for a lifetime. Then she had married Rafe and had her mother's estate invested. Thank God, she hadn't put it into the trust.

Because now she would need that money to run.

She couldn't fight. At least not yet. Protecting her baby was more important. For her and it to survive, she needed to leave this house without anyone knowing she had ever been here.

After what felt like hours, but couldn't have been more than a handful of minutes, Megan laced her fingers with Harold's and led him up the left staircase.

"How about we continue these negotiations in bed?"

"Lead the way," Harold growled, making Elizabeth shudder in disgust as the sound echoed through the downstairs. Their footsteps trailed away as they reached the upstairs.

She couldn't relax even with them out of sight. Her imagination ran wild. They could come back down and find her. With Harold's resources, they could hold her until she had the baby and then make her disappear. Her heart pounded in fear.

Swiping a trembling hand over her face, she forced herself to calm down.

Being a writer gave Elizabeth insight into how to get out of this situation. She needed to tread carefully if she wanted to live. Anger churned in her. She wanted to survive, if for no other reason than to rain hell on these assholes for screwing with her.

She was glad now she had some sort of experience to fall back on. Otherwise, she probably would run straight to the police, and that would be a mistake.

One, because she couldn't prove any of this as Harold and Megan would deny everything. And two, with Harold being an attorney, he would have contacts that would tell him about his whacko stepdaughter trying to send officers on a wild goose chase.

So, she needed to lay low for a while until after the baby was born. Elizabeth counted to fifty, slow and measured. Time slipped away as her nerves twisted tighter and tighter, urging her to hurry. But hurrying would put her in danger because if she rushed, she was sure to make mistakes. And with her and her baby's lives on the line, she couldn't afford any errors.

Even if her gut was screaming at her to get home before Rafael, she forced herself to be calm. It didn't matter if she was there before him as long as he was the one who mentioned the divorce first.

Then any questions she had would seem natural as well as any shock. Elizabeth didn't know where she could run, but she would figure it out after she escaped.

Shaking her head, she raced for the front door and was out and in her car in seconds. She needed to focus on her first step, which was getting home and confronting Rafe.

Frustrated, she frowned. That place was not her home. Nor was it safe, but it was the first step. The next would be to leave without anyone noticing her fleeing.

Then she would make her own home—one where she and her baby would be loved.

~ ~ ~ ~

Elizabeth's mind spun and her stomach filled with so many butterflies at the sight of Rafael's car already in his spot in their garage. Opening the car door, she stood and grabbed her purse and the few shopping bags from behind her seat.

Elizabeth opened the door between the garage and the hallway that led into the kitchen. The beeping of the alarm pulled her from the fog her mind had descended into on the way home.

She growled at her lapse. *This isn't my home.*

Rafael's house was the polar opposite of Harold's lavish mansion. Warm and welcoming with a Mediterranean flavor, Elizabeth had loved it at first sight, at least when she saw the outside. However, inside was another story altogether. Most of the rooms held only the barest of bones in furniture as if waiting for someone to breathe life into them.

She thought it would be her placing the intimate touches throughout their home. Pieces that represented their combined lives, but the few times she had tried, Rosa, Rafael's housekeeper, had picked it all up and dumped it into Elizabeth's office.

After finding the items piled on her desk for the third time, Elizabeth had asked Rafael about it. He had told her she needed to coordinate with Rosa. So, Elizabeth had tried to befriend the woman. It had never worked. Now, she wondered if Rafael wasn't behind her things being removed, as if he didn't want her to get comfortable since she wasn't staying.

"Elizabeth, is that you?"

She froze, rooted to the tiled floor as if it had wrapped itself around her ankles and held her in place. The bags she clutched in each hand rattled as she trembled. Clearing her throat, she answered, "Yes, it's just me."

"Can you come to my office, please?"

The bags shook harder as terror gripped her limbs. Was this it?

A hysterical giggle bubbled up, and she slapped a hand over her mouth. The bags banged against her side, pulling her out of her spiraling panic. *Get it together, Lizzie. He can't know you're pregnant, not yet. You haven't even been to the doctor.*

He couldn't know unless he was a mind reader. Lucky for her, she was sentimental and had wanted to go to the doctor together. With this being their first child, she had wanted to do all their firsts together. In her naive mind, she had thought it would bring them closer.

So, unless he had been in that drugstore with her when she bought the test, or in the restaurant's bathroom stall where she had taken her test, so excited she couldn't wait for the results, he couldn't know.

She could do this. Especially since she already knew what was coming, there wouldn't be any surprises. She gathered her roiling emotions and shoved them into the darkest corner of her mind to deal with later.

Passing through the sleek kitchen with so many professional touches even she didn't know what everything did, she skirted the open-plan living room and dining room to the front of the house. A staircase led up to the five bedrooms and three baths plus the master suite.

Dropping the bags on the floor near the staircase so they wouldn't give away her nerves, she walked on unsteady legs to the office, mentally chanting that he couldn't know until she told him. She swiped her sweaty palms across her calf-length sundress before pushing the door of Rafael's office open and stopping to drink him in.

Even with everything she had learned about him tonight, he still had the ability to steal her breath. God, she loved him. It pissed her off and brought her out of the numbness of shock as she realized she still loved the asshole. Had loved him the first time she set eyes on him. It seemed she was like her mother in that she'd found the other half of her soul. However, unlike her mother, Elizabeth had chosen unwisely because there was no way Rafael had ever loved her if he was willing to let her die and allow Harold to raise their child, all for money.

Shaking off her depressing thoughts, she clutched the straps of her purse as a lifeline and took the chair opposite his desk. He was as gorgeous now as he had been the first time she'd met him a year and a half ago.

Black hair brushed the collar of his blue button-down shirt. Combined with his broad shoulders and sculpted chest, it kept him from looking like a tame businessman.

Instead, he resembled a jungle cat dressed in business attire. Lithe and sleek. But it was his eyes that showed his true nature as they held a glistening, predatory gleam. The same gleam Rafael had had when their eyes had first met almost two years ago. If she hadn't been introduced to the truth, she would think he wanted sex. But now that she knew he didn't want her, she saw the look as more calculating—processing how to bend her to his will so he could get what he wanted.

Lean fingers raked through his hair, pushing the thick strands away from his sharply angled face. It wasn't handsome, would never be handsome, not with the intensity that poured from him like an alchemist poring over a formula.

He stood and came around his desk. His presence was formidable as he towered over her before leaning against the desk. Folding his arms over his chest, he crossed his ankles, giving him a casual look. However, the stance showed he was closed off to anything she had to say. It was his *lecture* pose whenever she and Rosa, the housekeeper, had butted heads. He rubbed the indention of his upper lip. "I know you and your father will be hashing out the details of the contract in the next few days."

She bit her cheek to keep from correcting him. Harold hated being referred to as her father. He'd been ten years younger than Elizabeth's mother and felt that was entirely too young to have children Elizabeth's age. So, she had always referred to him as Harold. When she remained silent, Rafael continued.

"Anyway, you know I like to be straightforward as well as get my say in."

It was the trait that had made her trust him. Fool that she was, she still trusted him—at least more than she trusted Harold. "Of course."

"It's been a year and two months . . ." he began.

She tuned him out, not needing to hear the words. Instead, she imprinted every nuance of him into her soul. This would be the last time she would ever be with him.

Her gaze jumped to Rafe's face at the mention of her child, but his stony expression never changed.

"First, if you have a child, I will be in its life. I know we agreed to custody in the agreement, but I wanted you to know that if you or Harold give me any issues, I've already retained a family attorney to make sure my rights are met."

She nodded, unwilling to chance opening her mouth. As if she would ever allow her child near him or Harold after screwing her over. She hadn't signed any agreement except the prenup, and as she had gone through that with a fine-tooth comb before they married, she knew there wasn't anything about children or custody.

"You're not pregnant yet, I know that," he held up a hand as if to ward off any comment about children. "But I'm donating sperm so you can keep trying after we separate." He leaned toward her. "And we will be separating."

"Why now?" She couldn't help but be curious.

"Because I'm tired of all the games you and Harold are playing with me. I'm not a toy to be grabbed off a shelf and forced into a happily-ever-after role where all the power is one-sided. And the contract I signed only stipulated we had to be together for a year." His gaze narrowed on her. "I gave you an extra two months hoping you would get what you wanted, but it looks like it didn't work."

Elizabeth flinched. She had thought they were happy, and she didn't know anything about their marriage being one-sided. At least she hadn't until tonight. She rubbed her temple as it pounded with stress. "And you found someone who doesn't play games?"

"Yes, which is why I want this farce ended." A joy-filled smile crawled across his face. One she had never seen in their entire marriage; it made her heart clench in her chest.

"Who is she?"

His black furrowed as his lip curled in warning. "An innocent."

"Of course, I was just wondering her name." She craved to know who had brought such happiness to this man when Elizabeth had only garnered lukewarm fondness.

"Chloe Ellington."

Elizabeth bit her cheek again. He had to be kidding. That bitch was the furthest thing from innocent, and talk about a game player; she was a master manipulator.

Elizabeth met Rafael's gaze, and every word she wanted to utter died on her lips. He wouldn't believe her. He would think she was jealous.

And she was.

But she was the only one who had been innocent in all of this. Hell, even their wedding night, she had come to Rafael as a virgin. Not that he had known, as drunk as he was, and not that he had cared to be all that gentle.

Elizabeth countered his question with one of her own as she tried to get all the answers she could. "Does she know about the contract?"

"Hell, no. Do you think I want anyone knowing that I willingly sold my dick to the highest bidder?" Rafe snarled.

She flinched as anger rose in her. "How long have you dated her?"

"Three months, not that it's any of your business."

"But why?" She meant to ask, *'why her and not me?'* But she couldn't open herself up that much. She didn't trust him not to mock her for allowing her heart to be involved when, for him, it was nothing but business.

"Because I want a damned family and a warm home. I want to be wanted for me and not because my wife wants access to her mother's money." He shoved his angry face into hers. "Because I want to have a marriage built on love."

The mother's money comment confused her, but knowing Harold as well as she did, he must have led Rafael to believe it was her mother who had set up the trust. "And Chloe thinks we're divorcing, why?"

Rafe straightened and crossed his arms. "Everyone knows you're an ice queen. Chloe assumes that transfers into our sex life, and I'm letting her continue to think that."

The pain in her heart urged her to stand up and flee, but she refused to be a coward. Elizabeth shuddered. Jesus, she couldn't believe he had fallen for a woman who screwed anyone that caught her interest, and sometimes several at the same time. Elizabeth didn't care what people did in the privacy of their own bedroom as long as they didn't expect her to join in. Bile rose to the back of her throat, and her hand moved to her mouth. "You haven't slept with her yet, have you?"

"That's none of your damned business," he snarled.

She would need to be tested. *Oh, God, what if I caught something from him and passed it to my baby.* Pushing her luck, she scowled at Rafael. "Well, it would be awkward as hell to try to explain a pregnant fiancée and a pregnant ex. If I come up pregnant at my next appointment."

"I used a condom with her," he bit off between clenched teeth. He raked his hands over his face. Eyes filled with pain and regret met hers. "I'm sorry."

Her gaze delved into his, and she knew in that moment he had been lying about sleeping with Chloe. Probably to piss her off or hurt her she didn't know. Even though Elizabeth felt she could read Rafael, she couldn't relax her guard there was too much at stake to put her child at risk by telling him about the baby. "For cheating?"

"For lying about cheating." Bitter anger twisted his face into an ugly mask. "I wanted you to hurt the way I have been for the past year but you're as icy calm as ever."

She almost relaxed at hearing he couldn't see into her as she could him. But hearing that he cheated, she had known deep in her gut that wasn't him. Rafe would never break his vows in that fashion. She startled when his hands slammed on the armrests on either side of her, trapping her in the chair.

"You won't mess with her, Elizabeth. If you do, I'll make you sorry you ever set eyes on me." His face contorted into a mask of resolution. "Do I make myself clear?"

"Crystal." She recoiled from him as much as the words he spat at her.

He straightened and smoothed his expression.

Her mind swirled at the ramifications. She needed to see a copy of this contract, one that she'd certainly never signed, but how to ask for it? "What do you get?"

"I don't understand."

Why had he agreed? Why had he given her hope of a future with him only to rip it from her in the cruelest way possible? She could never ask Harold, since he was behind this whole mess, but she was counting on Rafael not being in on all of it. Especially her death, since he was talking as if he expected her to be in their child's life. That gave her enough courage to ask some of her questions before she fled.

And she had to escape. She couldn't fight them while she was pregnant. Not that she was much of a fighter, but no one was taking her baby. And she would be damned if she sat back waiting for them to kill her to get her child.

"I'm asking what you got for marrying me?" she asked, needing the truth of why this had happened to her.

"Seriously?" Rafe pinched the bridge of his nose. "Did you not even read the contract before signing it?"

"No, I never read it." Her throat constricted as she forced the words past her lips. What had he gotten for this unholy alliance? What was more important than her? More important than their child?

"My grandfather's cabin. The one I visited every summer, where Mom sent me to live after Dad died."

Confused, she frowned. "But you owned that—"

"No, there was some kind of mix-up with taxes, and the bank foreclosed on it. They sold it to Harold before I could do anything about it."

It felt like the Middle Ages. Elizabeth had been betrayed for a piece of land. How screwed up was that? Needing to be out of the room, now, she jerked to her feet. She needed out. Out of the house she had hoped to make into a home, out of this state that held dreams of what could have been, and out of her life. Because if Harold tracked her down while she was pregnant, he had the resources to make her disappear until the baby was born, and Elizabeth would be in an 'accident' or reported to have died in childbirth.

"Elizabeth, are you okay?"

She leaned against the doorjamb before straightening. Why was Rafael talking to her as if he were worried about her? She reminded herself he had made a deal with Harold, that he didn't give two shits about her or her feelings.

"You're not saying anything." A frown pulled across his features. "I thought we could at least part as friends."

Friends? He wanted to be friends? Friends didn't go behind someone's back to accept payment to marry them for a cabin. Nor impregnate them under false pretenses. Cold crept into her. A friend wouldn't conspire to kill her, leaving their baby defenseless. "Why would we remain friends, Rafael?"

Surprise replaced his frown as he straightened from his slouch. "Why wouldn't we at least remain cordial to one another, Elizabeth? We go to the same clubs, attend the same events, support the same causes, so of course, we'll see each other. And we were married for a little over a year."

"You're right. Sorry, I didn't think of that. I'm not feeling well." She grimaced and rubbed her temple again, not needing to lie about how bad her head was hurting. "I'm willing to remain cordial in public, Rafael, but I doubt you or I will be inviting each other over for dinner."

She forced a curl to her numb lips. The expression felt as false as her life had been. However, she hoped none of her heartbreak and fear showed through. She would be damned if he ever saw how badly he had hurt her.

Not that there would be any charity dinners in her future. Rafael didn't realize that they supported different causes. She helped at the homeless shelters and the hospice programs while he focused on cancer research in memory of his grandmother and Alzheimer's for his grandfather.

They led two disparate lives.

Elizabeth didn't go to the club, Harold did. She didn't go to social events, Harold took Megan. That fact seemed so small in the grand scheme of things, and it had made sense at the time. Harold and Megan both dealt with the same people in their jobs. Elizabeth did not.

Now, Harold taking Megan became part of a larger picture.

One where Elizabeth would be dead and her child acclimated to Megan as its mother.

"Listen, I'm staying with Chloe for the week, and I've sent Rosa there to help get her packed up—"

"Rosa?" Rafael's housekeeper went to Chloe's? That didn't make sense since the woman hated being parted from Rafael.

Not that Elizabeth could blame her. She hated being parted from the man as well, but after all the blows dealt her tonight, she was over that craving. At least she hoped she was. She just wanted to be alone to put the pieces of her heart back together.

"Yes, Rosa volunteered."

Of course she did. Elizabeth would have snorted at the irony of how much Rosa hated her but was tripping over herself to help Chloe. Instead, she raked her bottom lip with her teeth. "Okay, I thought she could help me pack up—"

"Where will you go?"

Like he gave a rat's ass where Elizabeth ended up, but she answered as he would expect. "Harold's house. He has a wing set up for me."

He didn't, but she had no qualms about lying.

"That's good. Okay, well, I'm off. I'm sure your attorney will call me when everything is ready to be signed."

She gulped in a breath of air, needing to make sure she wouldn't be tricked into popping her head out of her hidey-hole anytime soon. "The deed?"

"Oh, I got the land after our one-year anniversary. Harold signed it over to me." He shoved the papers in the top drawer of his desk and locked it with a snap of his wrist.

"Do you happen to have a copy of the contract?" Might as well go for broke. She crossed her fingers.

He frowned at her as he shut down his computer. "Of course I have a copy."

"Okay, just wanted to make sure in case Harold tries anything underhanded—"

He snorted in derision. "As if the entire sordid thing isn't underhanded." He grabbed his leather jacket from where it hung on the back of his chair. "Now, I need to go. I'm picking up dinner for Chloe and myself."

Elizabeth nodded numbly and fled to the stairway leading up to the second floor before pausing. Her foot hovered over the first step as Rafe's heavier tread moved closer. There was one last question she needed answered, or she would never be able to move on with her life. Gathering her courage, she laid a hand on Rafe's arm to stop him from moving past her to the garage.

"Now, what?" he asked, annoyed.

"Did you ever care for me?"

His laugh was acidic, and his face twisted into disgust before he scowled at her. "You're serious."

"Yes."

He shrugged her hand off as he took a step away from her. "The first month we went out, I thought we could build something. I thought you were the one." He snorted with derision. "Fool that I am, I thought you actually gave a shit about me. But then your father—"

"Don't call him that." she snarled, her hands curling into fists.

"Whatever. In the beginning, yes. But after that meeting, I realized you were just feeling me out since you'd told dear old Harry that you wanted kids and my name was on the list of *approved* donors."

She shook her head and reached for him again, but he was already gone.

She'd never had a list of approved donors. Her only list was one of dreams. At least that month had been true even if the rest of her marriage was a lie. It relieved her to know that she hadn't misread his interest in her, only the love she had tried to cultivate and grow. That had been a lie. She hadn't had a chance at Rafael's heart. The irony was he'd had hers from the second she had agreed to marry him.

Her heart shriveled as the last of her blind innocence was ripped from her. Rafe hadn't been the fool. No. Elizabeth had been for believing she'd had a chance at the kind of love her parents had.

Chapter Two

Within seconds, Elizabeth was in her room, bags tightly wrapped in her hands and the solid wood door the last barrier between her and any more emotional pain. A temporary slice of safety and a small haven she had claimed in the last year.

Seeing the bed Rafael had had sex with her in, but never slept in with her, she realized she was an idiot.

After their wedding night, he'd slept in his own room, leaving her each night. But not until he'd screwed her into the mattress. She saw now that he didn't sleep in the master suite alone because he was a restless sleeper and didn't want to keep her awake, as he had stated early in their marriage. No, the truth was, he couldn't stand being in the same room as her for more than a few hours at a time.

Memories of the last year poured into her. No anniversary dinner because Rafael had been in Canada, neck-deep in a startup. No nights snuggled in front of the television. No date nights after they were married.

Was I really that blind?

She knew he worked long hours. Knew he traveled all over the world wheeling and dealing. He always seemed to have a legitimate excuse for why he didn't include her in any of his travels, and she had never questioned him.

She'd been in love with him. Happy with whatever scraps of attention he tossed her way. Snorting, she still loved him.

She made herself face that truth and let it go. No doubt she could move past it eventually, but the baby would always be a reminder of her happiest moments, right before her rose-colored glasses were ripped away and she was forced to see everything she believed to be true was actually nothing but a fairytale.

How screwed up is it that I still love my husband?

Her back pressed against the door, she released the bags to fall where they liked while she sunk to the thickly carpeted floor Shock slowly left her as the pain of betrayal broke through the numb wall she had erected. Pushing the heel of her hand against her lips, she did her best to stifle the sob threatening to escape. If she broke down now, she would never stop crying.

She couldn't think about Rafael without breaking down completely, and it wasn't safe yet for her to lose control. So, instead she pushed the pain down to the pit of her gut and circled back to the conversation between her stepfather and her best friend.

They had killed her mother. Why? Based on what she'd heard, it was for money. Which made no sense. Harold was wealthy in his own right.

As for Megan, the woman wasn't in their income bracket, but between her inheritance and her investments, Megan technically never had to work again.

The chirp of her cell jerked Elizabeth back into the present. So lost in her head she didn't think about checking who the caller was, she automatically answered it.

"Hey, girl. How's things?" Megan's light tone drifted through the speaker.

Elizabeth flinched, unsure if she should be impressed with her so-called friend's acting ability or worried she would hear through any lie Elizabeth now spun. Because she was going to have to lie. Reminding herself the woman on the phone *wasn't* her friend, she allowed some of the emotion she was feeling out. "Not so good. Apparently, I'm the first of us to get a divorce."

Had that been the right tone? She hoped so. Resting her heated cheek against her upraised knee, she tried to remember everything from that drama class Megan had dragged her to in college.

The first lesson had been about drawing emotions from personal experience. Elizabeth didn't need any coaxing to pull up sadness and betrayal. They were already right beneath the surface of her skin. She only needed to make sure none of her secrets slipped out by accident.

"Damn. Are you serious?"

If Elizabeth hadn't been in that foyer earlier and heard Megan and Harold herself, she would never have believed her friend capable of planning her death. She would think the woman was sincere in the sympathy and disbelief that coated her voice. "Yes."

"Do you need me to come over?"

"No." Her voice rose in panic. It took her several breaths to calm her racing heart. "I mean, no. I'm trying to wrap my head around everything." Thank God she was a solitary person when things hit her.

When her mother had died, Elizabeth had left for a month-long trip to Alaska. She'd rented the most remote cabin she could find to decompress and sort her thoughts. A light went off in her head. She could do the same now.

If she could find someone to help her get out of this mess, Elizabeth could get lost in the wilds of Alaska. Or make Harold and Megan believe that's where she was, anyway.

"I hear you. How about we go to the spa tomorrow—"

"I think I need some space, Megan. I mean, the love of my life basically told me he only fucked me because of a contract—"

"He told you that?"

There was a distinct growl to Megan's tone that alerted Elizabeth to danger. So, the contract was something she wasn't supposed to know about. She needed to see that contract, but Harold's attorneys would never give her a copy without alerting her stepfather, and she could *not* ask Harold for one. However, she did have a few nefarious skills thanks to researching her heroes for her books. And one contact she'd used a lot was a safe cracker. Hopefully, Casey was in town and available for a rush job.

However, she couldn't tip Megan or Harold off before she left. And her gut was telling her to play the contract off as something Rafael was lying to her about.

"I think the contract is bull."

"You do?"

Elizabeth ran her fingers through her hair and tugged at the ends in panic. "Yes. He's probably trying to drive a wedge between me and Harold so he doesn't have to take responsibility for dating Chloe while he was still married."

"You heard about that too?" Megan's tone relaxed, telling Elizabeth she had been right to lie.

"Yes, Rafael filled me in. Wanted to make sure I didn't stir anything up with her." She wanted to curl up in a ball as pain tore into her heart.

"Chloe?"

"You know Chloe," Elizabeth teased, falling into the camaraderie she had always had with Megan. "Chloe Ellington. The one we caught screwing her masseuse in the mudroom at the spa."

"I remember that." A snorting laugh drifted down the line. "If there's any drama, she'll be the one to start it, not you. That man doesn't know you at all, does he?"

The question sobered Elizabeth like a glass of cold water tossed at her, reminding her that not only did Rafael not know her, but she didn't know Megan any better. This wasn't her friend. Megan had killed her mother and was planning to kill her. Every survival instinct Elizabeth had sprung to life as she did her best to hurry Megan off the phone. "No, and I'm beginning to think I didn't know him either. But I'm going to hire movers later this week, then I can leave Rosa with a list of things to pack and I'll bail for a while. Harold can handle the rest."

"Yes, he can. Let him deal with all the fallout, and you go get your head back together. Then we'll see about a cruise around the Bahamas or somewhere warm when you get back."

"Sounds great. I'm off. I want to be gone as soon as I can so I don't run into Chloe if she tries to come here."

"Okay, text me when you settle," Megan replied before hanging up.

Shaking at how close she'd come to having Megan barrel down here, Elizabeth released a hiccupping laugh of relief. She might be able to fool her friend over the phone, but she was not a good enough actress to bluff her way through a face-to-face. She glanced down at her cell and jolted to her feet. Six-forty-five. Racing to her office across the hall, she woke her computer up. No time to wallow.

She had to get out before Megan discovered Rosa wasn't here. Before Harold called Rafael about why the divorce papers weren't at his attorney's office. And before they all figured out Elizabeth knew more than any of them realized. She shouldn't have mentioned the contract. That would be the tipping point. If Megan brought it up to Harold, he would definitely say something to Rafael. If Harold asked Rafael at the club, or if Chloe taunted Megan if they crossed paths, the small lies Elizabeth had spread would unravel.

She knew she was acting and not dealing with any of the churning emotions she kept burying. Hopefully, she would be in a safe place when the box she was shoving every feeling she had into broke and she fell apart. Because when that happened, she would have a meltdown of epic proportion. Already, she felt bubbles breaking through the numbness that surrounded her.

She just needed to focus on her escape one step at a time, just as she had her characters do when they were in dangerous situations. Then she could fall to pieces.

Searching through a list of moving companies, Elizabeth groaned as she continued to scroll down. The first five closed at six on weeknights and ten on weekends. Being that it was Wednesday, well after closing time, she began to panic until her eyes fell on the tenth choice. Not in the best part of town, but it was open until eight.

Thinking about everything she had in the house and in the storage unit, relief twined into her. This place would work. It wasn't necessary for her to have movers as much as a rental truck. And as she didn't have any furniture, only knickknacks, decorations, and clothing. She could fit that into a pickup. She would need the truck anyway, since even the car she used was one Rafael had purchased.

She wanted nothing tying her to him when she left.

~ ~ ~ ~

Thirty minutes and many U-turns via the GPS later, Elizabeth parked in the gravel lot in front of the business. She hopped out of her car and raced to the nondescript brown brick building flanked by a variety of bright blue moving trucks. From massive trailers that attached to trailer hitches on vehicles to eighteen-wheelers to pickup trucks based on the selection, this place would have exactly what she needed even if all of them were in blinding blue.

Slinging her purse over her shoulder, she opened the door and stepped into the building, exchanging the humid summer heat for the ice-cold interior. It was organized. Packing boxes in various sizes hung from the pegboard to the left with larger boxes flattened on the bottom shelf. Masking tape, labels, and shipping paraphernalia hung on racks to the right. Across from her was a gray and blue counter manned by a man with gray peppering his close-cropped dark hair. The closer she drew, the more relaxed she became as his tanned features crinkled into a smile.

Something about him told her she could trust him. He was solid, and his brown eyes were kind. Considering the hell she had just been through, she could use some kindness and understanding. Her mother had always told Elizabeth if a person could meet her gaze head-on without flinching, they could usually be trusted.

She should have listened to that piece of advice before she married Rafael. Because he hadn't been able to meet her gaze for longer than a few seconds at a time since their engagement. As if he couldn't bear to look at her. As for Harold, he rarely met anyone's gaze, too focused on his cell, or whatever was going on around him, to bother with what was right in front of him.

The man's bright blue shirt had *Matthew* stitched on the left side. Matthew had been her grandfather's name. Maybe it was a sign.

"Hi, can we help you?"

Elizabeth took a deep breath and tried to organize her thoughts. "I need to move. Tonight, preferably, but—" She cleared her throat as tears threatened to overtake her. "—I need to keep the move quiet."

"Domestic violence?" Matthew asked, his brow furrowed as he straightened, his gaze moving behind her as if looking for danger.

"Not exactly."

His eyes narrowed as he crossed his arms, muscles straining the short sleeves. To be pushing fifty, he was in good shape. "Look, if you're in trouble, we can get you out, and my husband can handle the legal end of things if needed. He does pro bono work for several women's shelters."

Her watery laugh sounded unhinged to her before she broke into sobs. She bit her lip, hoping the pain would stem the flood. Embarrassed, she smacked her purse on the counter and hid her face in it on the pretense of looking for a tissue as the tears continued to fall.

"Jeez, Uncle Matt, what did you do now?"

The voice jerked her from the depths even as the new person slapped a box of generic brand tissue on the counter. A wide-eyed panicked look crossed Matt's features before they settled into a frown. "Nothing. I think she's dealing with a domestic but doesn't wanna say."

"You better not let Uncle Jessie hear you say 'wanna,' nor that you made a lady cry." The man looked like a younger version of Matt.

"Shut it, Ellis," Matt growled before turning back to her. "So—"

"It's not domestic violence," A hysterical laugh burbled forward and immediately changed to a hiccupping sob. "It's complicated."

Oh, God, I cannot fall apart yet. She couldn't stop the flood no matter how hard she tried to bring up the numb wall she'd had earlier.

She snatched several tissues from the box and proceeded to mop her face up for what felt like the millionth time tonight. For some reason, these two made her feel safe. They showed her compassion. That urged her to lower her guard. To top that off, they weren't set on killing her.

"Complicated, right." Matt's eyes scrutinized her as if trying to find the truth.

"Well, what else would you call a husband who was paid by your stepfather to screw you for a year to get you pregnant, a stepfather who wants to kill you and take the baby after it's born, and a best friend who's not only sleeping with your stepfather but also might've killed your mother?" Twisting the tissues between her fingers, she gave another watery chuckle that held no amusement. "And that's all within the last three hours."

Looking back at the two men, both wore shocked expressions. Matt's arms now hung at his sides, and Ellis looked like a gaping fish.

Panic flooded her, making her heart race. She took several steps back as she slapped a hand over her mouth. "Oh, God, forget I said that."

Matt's eyes narrowed. "Why? Were you lying?"

She meant to nod, but for some reason, she shook her head instead. It was as if her mind and her body weren't on the same wavelength as she began to tremble. The longer Matt scrutinized her, the more she felt the need to run.

"Holy crap, Uncle Matt, we're going to be in a movie." Ellis's comment broke the tension that wrapped around her and had her laughing hysterically, which turned into sobs as she slid to the floor in a boneless heap.

"Don't mind Ellis, he won't tell anyone." Matt smacked Ellis on the back of the head. "Go get Seth. You and him are going with her to make sure she stays safe."

That statement drew another sob from her. These strangers cared about her more than her own family. But could she trust them with her safety when they found out what was on the line? She met Matt's gaze and saw a resolve that reminded Elizabeth of her father. This man would stand by her. Going with her gut, she relaxed for the first time in hours as Matt darted around the counter and awkwardly patted her shoulder. The comfort relieved more of the terror that had been riding her since hearing so many revelations.

Instead of arguing, Ellis spun on the ball of his foot and darted through the door on the back wall.

"It really does sound complicated, so here's what we're going to do. Ellis and Seth will help get you packed up. And you'll stay with me and my husband tonight so we know you're—"

"You believe me?" To be honest, if she'd heard the story from someone, she would think they were feeding her a line of crap.

"Yes, you told me you weren't lying." He patted her shoulder again. "'Sides, I've trained new recruits for the Navy, so I've been fed a lot of bullshit in my time. I can tell when someone's lying or trying to hook me. You're definitely not lying, and you don't look like you need to hook me for anything based on that fancy

purse and thousand-dollar sunglasses." He pointed to
the sunglasses that lay on the counter next to her purse.
"We're not going to do any paperwork. Instead, we'll
get your things, and you can stay with us until you find
a place."

"Oh, no. Thanks, but that's not why I told
you—" She didn't know why she had blurted everything
out, honestly.

"Look, I'll be worried about you if you're at a
hotel. Besides, do you even have any cash on you to pay
for one?"

Surprised, Elizabeth stood and rushed to her
purse. With fumbling fingers, she opened her wallet.
Her black American Express Harold had given her
years ago was nestled in the left pocket with a few local
cards interspersed for gas and shops. But all were tied
in with Harold, none with Rafael. "No, I don't have
cash."

"I watch a lot of spy shows, and you don't want
them to track your movements using your credit cards,"
a new voice chimed in.

The blond-haired boy looked to be barely out
of high school. Violet eyes peeked through hair that
hung long in the front and was shaved close in the back
and sides. "I'm Seth, by the way, Ellis's boyfriend."

"She's staying with us, Ellis."

"Us?" she asked, her eyes moving from the two
young men back to Matt.

"Seth was kicked out when his parents found us
together back in high school." Ellis's gaze filled with
love when it landed on Seth.

"Will that be a problem?" Matt asked, his voice
lowered.

"What? Being gay?" she asked, confused.

"Yes."

Relief poured into her, and she shook her head in jerky movements. "No, I was just surprised. Living in California; I thought families were more accepting."

"I'm originally from Texas," Seth said.

Matt turned to the young men. "You two go with her. Get her stuff and bring everything back to the house. We'll get her sorted in no time."

Ellis shifted from one foot to the other, his gaze bouncing from her to Matt before landing and staying on Matt. "Is that such a good idea?"

"Letting her stay with us?" Matt's brow furrowed.

"No, going to get her stuff." He bit his lips as his eyes met hers. "Look, if you're in enough trouble you need to hide—"

"Yes." She knew that much. Of course she needed to hide. That was why she was here, to get her things and hide.

"You're not hearing what I'm saying." Ellis leaned toward her, both hands braced on the counter, expression intense. "You don't go back and get things. If they're trying to kill you, they might do it now, when you're not thinking straight. I mean," Ellis looked to Seth. "Back me up here. You've watched all those scary movies—"

"You mean when the main character goes back to their house for some memento they just can't live without, and the bad guy is there to get them?" Seth's head bobbed so hard his hair flopped around his face. "It's true. That's where they always get the good guy and either kill them or kidnap them. I mean, it's in all those thrillers—television, movies, and books."

The conversation gave her something to focus on instead of her spiraling emotions. Was it a good idea to get her things? Her mind churned, and she voiced her reasoning. If they heard it and thought it was stupid, then she would just run, but if her reasoning was sound, they would support her, right?

Gulping, she pushed her hands through her hair and tugged at the ends. "They need my baby, so they would more than likely kidnap me and then kill me."

The three men gaped in shock. Matt was the first to snap to attention. "Forget that. You don't go back. Instead, we'll hide you—"

"No, wait." She held up a hand. "If I just run, my stepfather will turn over every stone to find me, and he's swimming in cash. My baby is worth a fortune. The money it stands to inherit could buy a small island with just the interest and never touch the principal."

"Jesus," Matt scrubbed a hand over his close-shaven hair. "So, what was your plan?"

She shrugged and shook her head.

Ellis gasped. "You don't have a plan?"

"My plan is to make it look like I don't know anything and go off to lick my wounds. Then come back and try again."

"They don't know you know about their plans?" Matt asked, a sly smile curling the edges of his mouth. "Oh, that is sneaky."

"Well, they'll suspect something when I use a different lawyer for the divorce, but I can play it off." Elizabeth nibbled her bottom lip, trying to look at her idea from every angle. "If I just run, they'll search for me."

"But if you call them regularly and act like you had to get out of town. . ." Seth trailed off, a bright grin stretching across his face. "It'll work. If we get your stuff and get you gone."

"It's not perfect, but it will keep you safe enough until we can put our heads together and find a more permanent solution," Matt stated.

"My solution is to come back and somehow make them pay. But—" She placed a hand on her stomach. "—I need to make sure my baby is safe first."

"Then let's do this." Ellis turned to Seth. "You ride with her, and I'll follow in one of the larger—"

"I only have a few rooms to pack, so a pickup or a small truck would work."

"Got it." Matt rounded the counter. He chose a set of keys from one of the pegs and tossed them to Ellis.

With that, Ellis darted away and Matt pointed at Seth. "Don't rush any of this. Slow and careful, and make sure you aren't followed."

"Like I said, I've watched a lot of spy shows. I know how to dodge a tail." Seth nodded.

Elizabeth pushed everything back into her purse as she found her first smile at Seth's words. *Dodge a tail . . . too funny.*

"Jessup's not due home until midnight because of that fundraiser thing, so I'll pick up some Italian from Petrocelli's on the way home," Matt added.

Seth nodded sharply and headed for the door.

"Let's go," he said, holding the door open for her.

Gathering her things, Elizabeth prayed she could trust these men. She had met enough backstabbers to last her a lifetime.

Chapter Three

Seth's and Ellis's eyes widened when Elizabeth showed them to her office. "If you two could pack this up, I'll go meet Casey to get the safe open."

She had explained to Seth why they needed in the safe, and he had filled Ellis in when they came in.

Seth's hands trailed over the spines of the books. "Lucy Stridell." His gaze tangled with hers, excitement sparkling in the violet depths. "Do you know her? I mean, you have every one of her books and several of her framed covers." He pointed to the wall above her computer. "Are you like a super fan?"

Sighing, Elizabeth rubbed her pounding head. "I *am* her."

"Oh, my God. She's amazing . . . uh . . . I mean *you, you're* amazing. That one with the killer stuffing his victims in safes to suffocate them as payback for trapping his mom in a safe during a bank robbery—"

"Yeah." Uncomfortable, Elizabeth backed into the door and fumbled behind her, searching for an escape route.

Ellis smacked Seth on the back of the head. "Calm down, hon. If I remember right, Lucy has never been seen in public."

"That's true," Elizabeth twisted her fingers together. "Everyone in my life considered my writing a joke, so I never talked about it. I'd appreciate—"

"Our lips are sealed," Ellis said, and then he began putting together the boxes to pack up her office.

Elizabeth saw the disappointment in Seth's eyes as he looked at her books. Taking a chance, she patted his back. "I'll sign a full set for you, but you can never, ever tell anyone my real identity."

"Deal." His bright smile returned.

"You're not taking any of the furniture?" Ellis asked. His finger circled to encompass the expensive desk where her laptop perched, the ragged couch with several broken springs, which had followed her from her home office, and her worn and frayed captain's chair which she had planned on replacing later this week with a pregnancy chair for more support when she wrote.

"No." She looked at the uncomfortable furniture. Of everything, only the couch had come with her from her previous life, and she rarely used it due to the springs digging into her back and ass.

"Got it." Ellis met her gaze. "So, where will you be?"

"Across the hall, packing up my bedroom."

It would take Casey a good hour to get there. Elizabeth could have most of her room packed before he arrived, and maybe Ellis or Sam could help her search Rafe's office after she had Casey pop all the locks. It was a good idea to triple check that Rafael didn't have any other paperwork with her name on it.

Before she began packing, Elizabeth called her friend who had been instrumental in helping her write the book about the serial killer using safes to kill his victims. Casey assured her he would be there within an hour, and Elizabeth trusted the man, so she tucked her cell away and tackled the packing.

The closet was straightforward and took up two medium-sized boxes as she crammed everything together. She left only the extravagant gowns and empty clothes hangers from the clothing she did take. The dresses could be donated after she left since she wouldn't need them in her next life. A plan had been forming in the back of her mind now that she had a safe place to stay. A place no one would ever think to look for her.

Within five minutes, she had her dresser emptied into another box, and the few breakables on top of the dresser were cushioned in her clothing. Next, she cleared the makeup table and settled that into her suitcase with her shoes stored in the largest piece of luggage. The bathroom was last and filled a small box.

Stepping into the bedroom, she ran her eyes over the antiques. The light-colored dresser, the matching makeup table with its gray poofy chair tucked under it, the two empty nightstands, and the perfectly made bed she had slept in alone. None of the coverings on the bed were hers, so she left them. Every item she could claim fit into a few boxes and the two pieces of luggage all piled next to the door. Tears she refused to allow to fall pushed at the backs of her eyes. There was so little, when she had had so many dreams about her married life. All of it was nothing but ashes now.

But if she could make it through the fire of betrayal, she would be stronger for it in the end.

The first step was knowing what her enemy knew. She needed a copy of that contract. She dusted her hands off and popped her head into her office.

"I've packed up everything in here. The boxes and luggage are by the door if you can get them loaded next."

"That was fast. Don't you have tons of shoes and stuff?"

She laughed. "I did, and I dumped them all into the largest piece of luggage. I'll go through them at your uncle's house."

Surprised, the boys both froze and looked at her with wide eyes. It was Ellis who broke the silence, "You really want out of here, don't you?"

"Yes. I need to grab a few things from downstairs—"

"One of us will go with you."

She waved them off. "No, seriously, no one will come tonight. Tomorrow, maybe, but not tonight. We just need to get out of here tonight, so keep packing. I'll be right back."

"We'll keep our ears open." He pointed to her. "If you get in trouble, don't hesitate to scream. Waiting to see if you imagined something is how all the characters in the movies get in trouble."

She chuckled and shook her head, enjoying the two young men's protectiveness. It was like a balm to her jaggedly torn soul. "I know. As you've discovered, I write those kinds of books."

"Yeah, so no going out in the dark or down in the basement to investigate anything without one of us."

"Promise," she said, making a cross over her heart before stepping from the room and turning toward the stairs. A frustrated oomph made her turn back to her office.

"No." Ellis was at the door, shaking his head at her before pointing at Seth. "Keep packing the boxes, then load the truck. This shouldn't take long, and I'll be back to help."

"Kay." Seth continued to stuff the boxes full of not just Elizabeth's books but her research materials that littered the shelves as well.

She searched Ellis's gaze and found resolute determination.

"I know I joke, but really, you're running as fast as you can like a scared rabbit." He scrubbed at his hair. "If you're that terrified, then you shouldn't be left alone, just in case. Even if you think it's overkill. It might not be, this time, so why take the chance?"

When he put it like that, Elizabeth caved and motioned for him to follow her.

This was the first time she'd entered Rafael's office with his overwhelming presence missing. Stepping into it, she froze when the scent of him overwhelmed her. His expensive aftershave and masculine scent dominated the space. Ellis gently urged her into the room.

"We're not breaking and entering, right?"

"Nope, this is my husband's office, and he's invited me to make myself at home in here numerous times." She didn't add that it was always when he was present, but that was just semantics. "You look through the file cabinet, and I'll check the safe."

When Ellis tried to open them, they were locked. Elizabeth had hoped maybe Rafael had at least left them unlocked, but no. Just as she resigned herself to wait for Casey, the doorbell pealed through the house, causing Elizabeth and Ellis to jump and break into nervous laughter.

"I'll wait here," Ellis said. "Check the peephole before you let anyone in, and if you need me, just scream." He hefted the heavy paperweight of a monkey covering its mouth.

"Calm down, Ellis, it's just going to be my friend."

"We don't know that." Ellis made a shooing motion toward the office door.

Elizabeth rolled her eyes but followed the silent demand.

Casey Ackerman was nothing like what anyone would picture as a jewel thief. No debonair smile or lithe build.

Nope. Casey came across as a retired military man with his buzz-cut brown hair, stocky build, and a face better fit for a pugilist than one of the most notorious jewel thieves in the world. Though retired, the man still had another ten years before the statute of limitations was up on the last of his crimes.

Not that Elizabeth would ever turn him in. She had been introduced to him by a mutual friend. A friend who was one of her shadow contacts, those she used to research the complicated, less-than-legal aspects of her books and give them a realistic feel.

Taking a step forward, she hugged the taciturn man. "Casey, it's so good to see you."

"How're you doing?" He stepped inside, and she closed and locked the door behind him.

"I'm good. Tracey said to thank you for that trick with the spaghetti." He fell in behind her as they headed for the office.

"Oh? So, the kids haven't discovered she's adding carrots into the sauce yet?" Elizabeth smirked as she refrained from teasing the man yet again for marrying a woman named Tracey even if they had been high school sweethearts.

"Not yet." He bumped her shoulder, and his cheeks reddened. "We also wanna thank you for putting my name into the hat to work with the cops."

"Oh?" Elizabeth halted outside Rafael's office door. "Did they call you?"

"Yeah, needed some advice on the safe cracking stuff, and being in the locksmith trade, they assumed it was a hobby."

Elizabeth shrugged. She'd wanted to help the man since his business needed a boost, and even though he was wanted by the police in several countries, none had his fingerprints nor his face, only his build and that he targeted the exceptionally rich. As Tracey's father was their fence before he passed years ago, they never were caught.

Instead, when the man was diagnosed with cancer, Casey retired and took up the locksmith business Tracey's father had owned. And as they still had ten years for those pesky limitations to fly by, Casey made a living with his father-in-law's business and hadn't touched his cash yet.

"So what'd'ya need?" He stepped around her and into Rafael's office.

She followed him. "Ellis, meet Casey. Casey, this is Ellis."

"Nice to meet ya." Casey held out a gloved hand that was long and slender, his one elegant feature as he cared for them more religiously than his lock picks. Ellis took the offered hand with a smile before they both faced Elizabeth, waiting for their instructions.

"I need all the cabinets unlocked and the safe opened."

Casey grunted and smiled. "My pleasure."

She loved how he didn't pepper her with questions, just believed there was something important or she wouldn't have called him to crack a safe. When the first cabinet was unlocked, she pointed to it. "Ellis, can you look for anything that has my name or Harold Moore's name on it?"

Ellis began flipping through file folders, a frown digging a deep V between his brows. "I'm not sure what I'm looking for."

"Legal documents, letters, emails. Rafael would have kept a hard copy of any correspondence between him and Harold."

"Got it. Oh, good. He has everything organized by date, so that will make things easier." Ellis closed the top drawer and opened another. "Do you know the exact date, because he's got a lot of files in here."

She flinched but steeled her resolve. "November fifteenth."

"Nothing on that date. But I have a file for November twentieth."

"Pull it and let me see."

Ellis pulled the nondescript hunter-green hanging file and handed it over. Elizabeth flipped it open, shook her head, and passed it back. "No, that's a contract for one of his startups."

"Okay, I'll look at the rest then." Ellis settled the file back into the drawer and began flipping through the ones after it.

"So, your husband made a deal with the devil?" Casey asked as he finished unlocking the desk and moved on to the credenza.

"Yeah," Elizabeth rubbed the back of her neck, trying to get the tension to loosen with no luck. "You were right about Harold all along."

Casey shrugged his massive shoulders. "Didn't want to be, but I've run into a lot of those kinds of people."

"What kinds?" Ellis asked, his face still buried in the file cabinet.

"The ones who give you that oily feeling while making all the hairs at your nape stand on end." Casey eyed the safe and rubbed his long finger across his bottom lip. "Gonna take me a few on this."

"Okay." She should have known Rafe wouldn't have an easily cracked safe. "I'll start on the desk."

Ellis reached the bottom of the file cabinet with an annoyed huff. "There's nothing in here that I can tell. Mostly spreadsheets and project names. The only contracts are between Rafael Martinez and someone listed as a co-owner by the name of Tristan Barrett and a company. Each company changes but not Rafael or Tristan."

Elizabeth nodded. "Tristan's his partner for investing in startups. Do the credenza; it's probably filled with the same, but I'd like to be sure."

"On it." Ellis bounded over to the long, squat cabinet behind the desk and began riffling through the folders.

The deep click of the safe opening drew her attention, and she caught the triumphant smile as it spread across Casey's face. He loved safe cracking. It was too bad he didn't get called to do much of it in his line of work. Hopefully, the police would use him more now that they had his name.

Casey took a careful step back and packed his tools away. "I'll hang around until you're done here."

"Thanks," Elizabeth said.

"Everything's packed upstairs. I'm going to start loading it on the truck," Seth said from the doorway.

"How about I give you a hand? Elizabeth and Ellis can finish up in here." Casey clapped Seth on the shoulder. "And you can fill me in on what's going on."

Seth met Elizabeth's gaze, and she tipped her chin to let him know it was fine to share everything with the man.

"Okay, follow me." Seth hurried out of the room.

"Why didn't Casey stay and help?"

"Because he knows this isn't wholly legal. Otherwise, I wouldn't need him." Elizabeth shut the last drawer in the desk and moved to the safe.

"Why not? I mean, how does he know it's not legal?"

Elizabeth grinned at Ellis's naivete. "Because I would have had the combination to the safe, and I would have the keys to the locks in here."

"Huh, I never thought of that." He shut the bottom drawer of the credenza. "Nothing. The same as the file cabinet, but these ones stretch over five years instead of broken down in months. Not sure why he would have two different kinds."

"One is for long-term investments. The other is startups he's probably looking at tracking the cash flow of on a shorter scale, so he knows where every penny of his investment will be going." Elizabeth pulled several file folders, a brown envelope, and an accordion file out of the safe before patting around to make sure it was empty.

"How do you know so much about his business?" Ellis asked, taking the items from her as she handed them over.

"Research. One of the businessmen in my books was mirrored after my husband." Elizabeth turned to the desk. "That's everything from the safe."

With trembling hands, Elizabeth flipped quickly through the accordion file but only found personal tax records for the past ten years.

Ellis's crow of triumph made Elizabeth grin and hold out her hand. A file was slapped into it. Not thick but not thin either. With trembling fingers, she opened it and found not only the contract but several emails between Harold and Rafael as well as the transfer of the cabin referenced in the contract.

"That's it, isn't it?" Ellis said, and at Elizabeth's nod, he did some weird victory dance.

"I need a copy." Ignoring him, her gaze bounced around the room and settled on the multifunction printer.

Ellis flipped the printer on, and she fed the pages into it. Her hands shook the more she scrutinized each official-looking page. Her initials were alongside Harold's at the bottom. Coming to the end, she gasped. "My signature's at the bottom—"

"I would expect so, since it's the infamous contract you told us about," Ellis teased.

She knew he was trying to lighten the mood,
but he didn't understand. The papers she had
supposedly signed but didn't actually held her signature.
No hesitation marks, no squiggles out of place. This
was her actual, honest to God signature on a contract
she had never seen.

Was I drugged? Or maybe drunk?

But again, the signature didn't have any odd
flourishes or wiggles denoting something like that. So
how had Harold gotten it there? Because if it was a
forgery, it was a damned good one.

After Ellis flipped the printer off, he pointed to
the door. "I'm going to help Seth and Casey."

Elizabeth forced herself to set the copy of the
contract on the desk. "Can you send Casey in here to
lock up?"

"Oh, sure." Ellis spun and headed out of the
office, calling for Casey as he went.

Casey strode into the office and had everything
locked up within minutes. Done, he faced her,
expression set in a deep scowl. "You need to
disappear."

"I know." God did she know that.

"But even if you hide, you're gonna be looking
over your shoulder forever."

She stacked the copied pages together and
shrugged. "I don't wanna hide forever, just long enough
to have my baby." Fierce determination settled into her
bones. "Then I'm going to come after Harold with
everything I have."

Casey tipped his chin, and a sly smile curled the
edges of his lips. "You know, if someone steals your
identity and uses your social, you're entitled to a new
one."

Dumbfounded, Elizabeth shook her head. She hadn't known that.

"Yep." Casey clapped her upper arms. "So how about I get Hank to work on that for you? He still owes you for the whole Turkish prison thing."

Elizabeth shivered. "I only helped him because he's your brother."

"I know."

"I mean, he's a hitman—"

"Never been proven."

"Whatever."

"And he's retired from his job, whatever that was." Casey teased, though to look at him, you had to know him well to see the mirth dancing in his gaze. "So, we'll get your identity screwed up so you can get a new social, and Harold the lying sack of shit won't be able to track you that way."

She didn't want to take any favors from Hank, but technically it wouldn't be a favor since he was paying back what he felt was his debt to her. Not that she had asked her CIA contact to get Hank free because of Hank but because Casey had asked. And Casey, well, she liked him and his family. She was godmother to his youngest daughter Adelaide. And Adelaide had deserved her uncle to be at her christening. Swallowing her pride, she nodded. "I would appreciate the help."

"Good deal, now for some pointers on how to disappear," Casey said and began to lay out several suggestions for Elizabeth to consider in order to not only hide but turn into a ghost so her baby was protected.

~ ~ ~ ~

The large colonial style house with a circular drive was a welcome sight after everything Elizabeth had endured. As soon as Matt opened the door, he led Elizabeth into the kitchen to throw together a sandwich. A few minutes later, Matt had her late night dinner plated in front of her with a glass of milk.

While Elizabeth ate the bacon, lettuce, and tomato sandwich, Matt left to help Ellis and Seth unloaded the truck. Then Matt had waved Seth and Ellis out with the order to take the truck back to the rental office and pick up Ellis's car so it wouldn't get stolen. Bone-weary exhaustion pulled at her limbs and made her eyes water as they begged to close. But first, she needed to eat for the little bean, and second, she needed to meet Matt's husband. Though she doubted she would be able to put two words together, let alone form a coherent sentence.

Then between one blink and the next, a vision that should grace the sides of billboards strode into the room and kissed Matt hello. The soft whap of the tomato falling out of the bottom of her sandwich and onto the plate drew both Matt and Jessup's attention.

Jessup freaking Sawyer. She should have known when Matt referred to Jessup. There weren't many of those in California. The house should have set off another alarm in her head. Her only excuse was exhaustion. If she hadn't been so blessed tired once the adrenaline had worn off, she would have caught the clues.

"I didn't know you were gay." She set her sandwich on her plate and took the napkin next to it to wipe her fingers off.

"I don't advertise my personal life—"

"Because you're gay?"

He huffed, spun, and opened the fridge behind him. After some rummaging, he shut it and faced her with a bottle of water in his hand. "No, not because I'm gay. Because I'm a very successful family lawyer, and that means my clients win and the opposition loses." He twisted the top off the water and clicked it on the counter with an audible click as it landed. "That doesn't make them happy, so they threaten, and I refuse to ask my husband to stop working at his business. Which, if you were there, you would know, isn't in the safest part of town."

"Oh, that makes sense." She sipped her water, giving herself time to try to wake up.

Jessup's cold gaze froze her to the spot. He looked like he was trying to decide if she was a danger to his family. She had seen the same cold, calculating look when they had served on boards together. His pale eyes held the barest hint of blue, making them look frigid and unwelcoming when he was pissed. But he wasn't angry now, just very annoyed. If not for his eyes, he would be gorgeous with his raven's wing black hair, broad shoulders, and sharp features. He was what she pictured a jewel thief to look like.

When his gaze left her and settled on Matt, she sucked in a startled breath as the ice in them warmed and melted. "So, you're the waif Matt wants to give sanctuary to," Jessup tipped his bottle of water toward her as he met Matt's gaze. "You do know this is Elizabeth Sutherland. As in Lillian Sutherland-Moore's daughter."

Matt shrugged. "I don't know who that is. She introduced herself as Elizabeth Martinez."

"I had forgotten she married." Jessup drank his water in a gulp and tossed the plastic in the garbage under the sink. "She's only been with the guy for about a year, right?"

She pushed her plate away, losing her appetite as Jessup ripped all the barely healed wounds open. Half the sandwich still lay on it with the tomato underneath, and Elizabeth felt bile rise in her throat at the thought of trying to eat it.

"I can leave and get my stuff tomorrow," she said.

"Please, you're swaying where you sit," Jessup retorted in his calm upper-crust tone that soothed all the board members of every non-profit they sat on together. The same tone that filled those groups' coffers with money at any charity event he attended. But to Elizabeth, it grated on her nerves like nails on a chalkboard.

"I'm not weak," she whispered. Then in a firmer voice, "I'm not weak."

"I didn't say—"

She stood, swaying as she slammed her fists on the table. "I'M NOT WEAK," she roared, all the rage and betrayal finally having a target. Her gaze lifted to tangle with Jessup's, and she found sympathy filling his. It made her angrier. She didn't need his sympathy nor his pity.

"I never said you were weak."

"Lies!" She might not be able to confront Harold or Rafael, yet, but she could damn well stand up to this man. "I heard you tell Penelope Mitchell that I couldn't argue with a fly even if it was dead for fear I'd hurt its feelings."

Jessup tipped his head to the side. "I did say that, but then you fought for the shelter to get the garden as well as a daycare so the parents could get to their jobs. So, I took it back."

She shook her head and looked to Matt, but his wide-eyed gaze bounced between her and Jessup. Slumping in her seat, she burst into tears as her emotions bombarded her. "I didn't argue in the beginning because my mother had just died. Harold left for two weeks after cremating her. Before he left he ordered his staff to pack up my mother's things and send them to storage. I didn't want that so I had to pack all my mother's things alone."

"Jesus," Matt whispered, darting around the kitchen island to hurry to her side and gather her in his arms.

She leaned into him, unable to stem the flow of anger, hurt, and—most of all—terror. Where Jessup was cool and deliberate, Matt was a bulwark of warm strength and caring. Her stomach churned at the thought of being forced from what she had begun to think of as a refuge until she could get her divorce finalized and disappear.

She jerked to a stand and slapped a hand over her mouth as she felt her stomach give a sickening lurch. She dashed down the hall to the bathroom she'd used earlier, and as she emptied everything she had eaten for the day into the toilet, Matt came in and rubbed her back. He asked her something, but between her pounding head and raw throat, she just nodded, and he left her alone.

What did it matter if he wanted her to leave? It was his and Jessup's house, so it wasn't like she had a leg to stand on. When she felt as if she were done turning herself inside out, she stood and shuffled to the sink. A clean washcloth and toothbrush still in its package sat on the vanity.

Shivering with dread and worry, she cleaned herself up and brushed her teeth. Done, she squared her shoulders. She refused to show any more weakness to these men if they were going to kick her out.

When she returned to the kitchen, she faltered. Jessup was in navy-blue loungewear. She had been gone longer than she thought.

He pointed to the chair she had vacated earlier. "Sit."

Tentatively, she took a seat, glad to see the food had been cleared when her gut gave an unsettling roll.

"We are *not* kicking you out," Jessup stated. "We're going to help you."

Matt nodded his agreement as he took the chair next to her. "I told Jessup everything after you said it was okay in the bathroom."

That was what he'd asked? Her muscles, poised for flight, had relaxed at Jessup's statement. Now, the twisting in her abdomen finally calmed.

Jessup poured her a glass of ginger ale and plopped it in front of her before taking the empty seat next to Matt.

"Matt gave me the paperwork dealing with the contract, and I glanced through it." He settled a pair of wire-framed glasses on his nose.

She sipped the ginger ale, not tasting a drop. "Is it legal?"

He snorted. "It would be if you had actually signed it." He peered at her over his wireless frames. "Are you sure you didn't sign it?"

She thought back to the past year. "It would have come from the attorneys via Harold, and the only thing I signed was a prenup. Which you have in the file folder on your left. Otherwise, the last time I signed anything was three years ago when the last of my parents' estate was released."

"Then it's not legal, and we need to—"

She jolted. "No, no legal action on the contract."

"We need to get this dealt with, Elizabeth. If for no other reason than this attorney is writing up fake contracts."

"But you said the contract was legit. And his signature isn't one of the witnesses. So, he did his job as he was supposed to."

Jessup sipped from his glass, his gaze set on the far wall. "That's true."

"Can you explain how this contract even exists?"

"It's a sperm donor contract, basically. Except with a—"

"Not that. I mean, how could Rafael be held accountable for it? And if say I was on birth control almost the entire year—"

"You were on birth control?" Matt, who had been silent, chuckled. "I bet your husband and stepfather never thought of that. That's hilarious."

"Not so much, since I stopped taking them and now, I'm pregnant." They were the first people she'd told. Nerves roiled through her.

"Well, that explains the no wine thing. I thought you just didn't want to lose your faculties while in a strange home with strangers."

"That too." She drained her glass, wishing it was something stronger. "Tell me how I can get out of this mess."

"First, we should look into getting you a new identity."

She grinned. "I might have forgotten to mention that I write mysteries."

"How does that help us?" Matt asked.

"I have a friend who made a lot of suggestions. He's calling in a favor to get my identity stolen." Her smile broadened as Jessup's eyes popped wide, then narrowed as if hunting prey.

"Tell me everything."

Elizabeth laid out what Casey told her. "I'm not sure how to find someone to be my twin in Alaska, but everything else is pretty easy."

"I have a firm I can call to set that up." Jessup tapped his finger against his lounge pants. "The rest should be easy. It's just a matter of keeping you hidden here until all the paperwork gets sorted."

"As long as you don't get sick of me. I'm game to hide out in my room. I've got so much work to do."

"Work? Writing?" Jessup asked.

"Yes. My last book is slotted to become a film. I've been working on getting the two sequels finished before negotiations begin." She still couldn't believe she was in his home, and seeing him in anything other than his bespoke suits was surreal.

Jessup pointed at her. "I'll be helping you with those. Once we get you to safety, we can't have any kind of paper trail leading Harold, Megan, or Rafael back to you. Not until we're ready for them."

"I'm with you on that. I won't endanger little pinto." She cradled her stomach while the two men laughed.

"Little pinto?"

She shrugged. "It's just a collection of cells right now. Not much bigger than a dried-up bean. Anyway, in my research, I've made quite a few contacts, and one of them happens to be a judge in Oregon."

"We have to give your friend time to steal your identity, but I can get all the paperwork filled out and ready to go." Jessup grinned. "Oregon would actually come in handy. If we can get the paperwork filed in another state, it will help hide the trail that much deeper. Washington would be better since Seattle is a large city."

The knots in her stomach finally unwound. "We can ask, but not until tomorrow."

Jessup nodded. "How about we head to bed? Tomorrow is going to be a long day."

She stood and hurried around the table, grabbing both men in a hug. "Thank you so much. When I showed up to rent a truck, I didn't know what to do or who to trust. I'm so grateful Matt opened your home to me and that you're willing to help me."

They patted her arm. "I'm just glad Jessup could help you. I knew something was wrong, but I had no idea how to help except to get you out of there."

She sighed and let them go. A jaw-cracking yawn let her know it was well past her bedtime. "I'm going to get some sleep."

"Good night," Matt called out as she left the kitchen.

Chapter Four

"No, seriously, go. I promise I'll be right here when you get back." Elizabeth smoothed a hand over her barely-there baby bump. "I would never do anything to hurt the little bean."

"First, I think your kid is bigger than a bean now, and second, we're in Vegas." Seth bounced next to Ellis, his hands clasped to his chest. "So, please, can we go? I've never been to Vegas or Reno or Atlantic City. And I've never seen a real casino with all the flashing lights."

Ellis's narrowed gaze warmed and softened as it landed on his partner. "You just want to blow on the dice."

"Well, yeah." Seth turned a playful grin on her. "It's in all the movies and television shows I've seen that take place in casinos."

Ellis's gaze was hard as it met hers. "No shenanigans."

She held up her right hand. "I swear."

Elizabeth hoped he couldn't tell she was lying through her teeth.

"Just because Uncle Jess got you a new identity and just because there's a decoy up in Alaska doesn't mean Harold and Megan aren't still trying to track your movements. Especially since Jess handled your divorce instead of Harold."

She winced at the memory of the firestorm that decision had created. Harold had been livid, but she had stuck to her guns. It helped that Jessup was the most sought-after family law attorney, and his law firm handled big names in divorce cases. Whereas Harold's dealt in corporate.

Jessup had also helped Elizabeth change her name the second the divorce was finalized. Though it had taken three months to get everything settled, the wait had been worth it. Now, it was time to implement the second part of the plan Casey had suggested, one she had not shared with Jessup.

Seeming to find whatever he was looking for, Ellis sighed. "Fine, let's go."

Seth raced out of the room, and Ellis followed at a more sedate pace.

Elizabeth waited twenty minutes before leaving. It was reckless, what she planned, but dammit Rafael had acted like she knew about the contract. Even during the divorce, Jessup had gotten several emails from Rafael about the contract and making sure he delivered his sperm to the appropriate clinic.

How could he think Elizabeth had been involved in that farce? What concerned her more was that, in their entire year of marriage, it had never come up. There was something fishy about that.

But if Rafe was really going to try to make a go of it with Chloe, did Elizabeth want to interfere? Did she have the right to screw up his chance at happiness? Especially after Elizabeth's pseudo-family had already brought such misery to the man?

She didn't know, but she wanted to be prepared. Her curiosity always got the best of her; being a writer, she always wanted to know how something worked or how a person's story played out. This was no different. She would eventually ask Rafael what the hell happened but on her terms.

So, she needed to prepare.

Smoothing a hand over her baby to help soothe her nerves, she watched the elevator's panel as it descended to the lobby. Her skin broke out in goosebumps the second the doors of the elevator slid open. To make herself a target set her teeth on edge.

It didn't matter that her name had legally been changed. Harold had resources. If he thought for a second Elizabeth wasn't in Alaska, he would scour the country for her. Jamming her hands into the pockets of her hoodie to keep from smoothing them across her stomach again, she made a beeline for the desk where a man with hair more gray than brown handled the counter by himself.

She hung back while he took care of a few guests, and when the last guest headed for the main doors, Elizabeth walked the last few steps to the counter.

Scanning the area one more time, she saw they were alone and leaned across the counter. "Do you handle odd requests?"

It was something Casey had suggested to ask at the main desk of a hotel in a busy city. Vegas had to be the busiest city she'd ever been in next to LA or New York. And she had waited until after nine before suggesting Seth explore the city at night.

His gaze narrowed, and his lips flattened. Elizabeth wanted to groan at her nerves getting the better of her and making her sound like an idiot. "Not drugs or illegal things, but . . ."

Maybe she should have gone to a shadier hotel as Casey had recommended. But she didn't want to chance getting mugged because then she would have to explain to Ellis and Seth what she had been doing. Explaining it to Jessup was a whole other thing; he'd agreed she should get a few burner phones if she had the funds so she could call the decoy in Alaska without compromising her own number, but she hadn't told him she wanted one to talk to Rafael.

Jessup would strangle her if she set one toe in a shady section of town, so she refused to add wood to the inferno that was going to rage when she confessed what she'd done to the man who now acted like her big brother. He and Matt had both adopted her, and Elizabeth soaked up their affection. No way would she jeopardize it.

The desk manager arched a brow, reminding her more of her father and making her flinch at how guilty she sounded. *I'm a damned mystery writer for Chrissake. I should be able to know how to pull off subterfuge.*

Huffing, she went with the story Casey had told her to use. Even though it painted Rafael in a bad light, to Elizabeth he was already an asshole for ever agreeing to that stupid contract.

She smoothed a hand across her stomach before she could catch herself and saw the stern expression on the hotel worker's face lighten.

"Look, I'm running from an abusive ex, and I just found out I'm expecting."

The frosty look in his eyes warmed the more Elizabeth explained.

"I want to stay in touch with the family I'm leaving behind, but I need to do it in such a way it can't be traced—"

He held up a hand, and a smile curved the corners of his lips. "Normally, I wouldn't know where to send you, but my brother bought a large storage unit earlier today, and I think he might have what you need."

She straightened, hope blossoming in her chest. "Really?"

"Yes, but you'll need to talk to him because he'll want to vet you." His tone turned serious.

Elizabeth nodded. "I can have him talk to my lawyer, the one who helped me with the divorce."

Jessup would vouch for her. Hopefully. All she had to do was make him understand the need for this.

The man passed her a piece of paper with "Joe's Pawns and Antiques" and an address scrawled on it. He tapped the paper. "Ask for Steve. I'll give him a call now to tell him you're on your way."

Elizabeth smiled and grabbed the piece of paper before he could change his mind. "Ask for Steve. Joe doesn't own the pawnshop?"

"Joe's our granddad, and no, he doesn't own the pawnshop anymore. He passed a few years ago and left it to my brother and me." The man shook his head. "I hate trying to find deals for the shop and haggling. So, I'm a silent partner while Steven and his wife are front and center."

Elizabeth tucked the paper into the back pocket of her jeans and held out her hand. "Thanks . . ."

"Paul."

"Thanks, Paul." She pumped his hand twice before releasing it and hurrying out the double doors to find a cab.

Being just off the Vegas strip, cabs were easy to come by, and within a few minutes, she was tucked into the back of a yellow cab and on her way to the shop. Dialing Jessup's number, she prayed he wouldn't be upset she had left the safety of the hotel.

"Jessup."

"Hi, Jess, it's me."

"Colby, I'm hearing traffic. And I know the boys are sight-seeing, so what gives?" Jessup had started using her new name the second she had it so she could get used to hearing it. It still sent a jolt through her before she realized he was talking to her.

Her skin felt tight as she scanned the area around her but only saw tourists and other cars. "I waited for them to leave because . . ." Her breath caught, and her skin tingled as her gaze narrowed on a man that looked like Harold. Her vision blurred as she lost her breath. But when a petite blond ran into his arms, she gasped for breath.

Jessup's strident voice dragged her back to the cab.

"Sorry, Jess." Straightening her shoulders, she gripped the cell tightly as guilt churned through her stomach, making her nauseous. "I'm getting a burner like we talked about. But. . ."

"You want to use one to talk to Rafe."

How did he know?

"I know because I've gotten to know you, as has Matt, and Matt warned me you'd do this." Jessup groaned. "And now I have to go to a damn Lakers game with him."

She grinned. Jessup was a hockey fan and tolerated basketball for his husband. "Sorry?"

He sighed. "Are you at least being safe?"

"Yes." She plucked at the zipper on her hoodie. "I'm sorry, I just wanted to talk to Rafael without giving him my cell. I mean, Harold bought us changing my number to quit getting so many calls from people when they heard about the divorce. And as my new cell is a direct line to Harold and Megan, I don't want to use it for Rafael too."

"I get it. So, where are you getting them?"

"A pawn shop."

"I still can't believe you know what a burner is."

"Jess, I'm a damned mystery writer. Of course I know what a burner phone is."

"And you just happen to have a contact in Vegas?" Disbelief coated every syllable.

"Hell no, but I asked at the front desk—"

"Jesus."

"Shut up and listen. I told him I was fleeing an abusive ex, and I'm pregnant and want to stay in touch with my family."

"And he bought it?"

"Yes, with the caveat that I'll need someone to vouch for me but if there is more than one."

He heaved a heavy sigh. "That's why you called me. Just in case there's more than one, and if the pawnshop owner mentioned the number of burners, you didn't want me limiting it."

She wanted to say "Duh" but bit her cheek instead. Dammit! She hated how he knew her so well. Instead, she said, "Yes, and I'm planning on buying them all."

"Fine. But no more gallivanting on your own."

"The boys would have stopped me." Elizabeth cringed at that half-truth because with how innocent Seth was, he would have given everything away. He wouldn't have meant to, but he couldn't lie for shit.

"More like Seth would have looked guilty and ended up giving you away, but I get it. And technically you are fleeing . . ." He paused. "Harold's checked to make sure the cabin in Alaska is occupied."

"How do you know that?"

He snorted. "Because Kennedy cloned the property manager's cell to keep tabs on who asks about that cabin."

Elizabeth was never so glad as to have employed the security company Jessup recommend. Kennedy was a godsend, tracking Harold's movements while also impersonating Elizabeth in Alaska. All so Elizabeth could stay under the radar.

"Why are you getting the burner phone to call him, Colby?"

Elizabeth nibbled her nail, trying to come up with a good enough answer to derail Jessup.

"You're still in love with him?"

She flinched before shouting, "No, I'm not."

"Right."

"Dammit, why do you have to always ask the hard questions." She took a breath to calm her racing pulse.

"I'm a lawyer. It comes with the job description."

"Yes, if you have to know, I'm still in love with him." Her heart gave a lurch, and the blood heated in her veins. "But that's not why I want the phone. I just . . ."

"If it makes you feel any better, I think he still cares for you."

"What makes you say that?" Her arm curled protectively around her stomach. Could he still care?

"He said some things at the divorce signing."

That was news to her. She hadn't gone since she was supposed to be in Alaska, but Rafe's friend Tristan had been there as had Jessup, representing her. "What things?"

"Look, I wrote most of it off as bitterness—"

"What. Things?" She bit the words off through clenched teeth.

"Like how he wished he hadn't fallen for you that first month you two dated—"

"I wish that too because to find out he sided with Harold hurts." She rubbed her hand over her heart where the slashing pain felt like a gaping wound. "Why did he do that, anyway? Did he say?"

"Not really. Just that Harold approached him after you two had dated a while and explained you wanted to get to know Rafe before presenting the proposition."

"And he didn't confront me?" That would have been what she had done. She would have tossed the damned contract in his face.

"No, and before you ask, I don't know why." Jessup huffed. "If I had to hazard a guess, I would say he was angry and figured he would get something out of the bargain at least. He did say if he had seen your true colors earlier, he would have dumped you. Instead, he was blindsided."

She cringed. "I always showed my so-called true colors."

"He claimed you cheated on him."

"What?" she gasped, clutching the phone. "I was a damned virgin on our wedding night, and let me tell you, that first time was the most horrendous experience I've ever had. If he hadn't screwed me again before we left the hotel room, I would have sworn off sex for life." She shivered at the memory. "Though, in his defense, he was drunker than a skunk when he finally came up to the suite."

"Jesus, I did not need to know this. And he made up for that lousy experience during the honeymoon, I'm sure."

"No honeymoon." She laid her head on the window as they rolled forward another inch before stopping again. "I got food poisoning the next day. Three days after that, I was in the hospital, and Rafe was off to Canada for some big deal closing thing."

She had hoped they would eventually get around to the honeymoon, but one thing had led to another, and it never happened. Now, it never would. "Oh, my God."

"What?"

"He mentioned the contract on our wedding night." Elizabeth's heart raced as she replayed that horrible evening.

"He what?" Jessup sounded on edge. "So, you did know—"

"No, like I said, he was drunk, and he made some weird comment about him needing to follow the contract."

"And that didn't ring any alarms?"

"Hell no. I was a nervous wreck, Jess. It was my wedding night, and I was a damned virgin. I thought he was actually talking about our wedding night. As if he was as nervous as I was and that was why he was drunk."

"I doubt that."

She did too, now. But as they said, hindsight was twenty-twenty, and hers was spouting off all kinds of truths. How had she not remembered that?

"Well, he thinks you cheated on him every time he went on a business trip. He swears you had men, and yes I'm using the plural term here, at the house."

She snorted and then laughed, though there was little humor in it. The accusation was absurd. "He thinks I brought men back to the house? With Rosa there? The woman loved nothing more than to run to Rafe and tattle over every little thing I did wrong."

"Rosa's the one who told him."

"Figures. Probably didn't think to get corroborating witness accounts."

"His mother confirmed it."

Ice flowed into her veins, and she shook with rage. "Are you kidding me?"

"No, I wouldn't do that. His mother backed up Rosa's allegations, and she got her information from Chloe."

"His mother hates my guts, and I mean that literally. She actually told me she would do everything in her power to get Rafe to leave me."

The cab had traveled no more than an entire block, but Elizabeth was tempted to step out and walk to the pawnshop to try to burn off some of her anger. But a second look at the crowded sidewalk and she stayed put. She had some privacy here, whereas out there, it was as jammed as the bumper-to-bumper traffic was, only with people. "Jessup? You still there?"

"Yes." His voice was a mere whisper. He cleared his throat. "It was Harold—"

She scoffed. "No, it sounds like it was Rosa and Mrs. Martinez."

"No, I mean, it was Harold all along." The squeak of leather from his chair carried over the phone, breaking up the silence. "Do you remember when Harold married your mother?"

"Yes." *How could I ever forget?* Lillian was so happy, and Elizabeth had been elated with the man who'd brought so much joy to her mother.

"It took a month for you two to move here."

"Yes. We had to pack and sell the house, and Mother wanted a different house than the one Harold had . . . I don't understand. What's that have to do with the rest?"

"Mrs. Martinez hates you because she thinks you're a gold digger."

She shook her head, then roared with laughter. "Bullshit."

"No, seriously. Harold came back after he got married and talked about you two constantly. Except he said your mother's dead husband had lost her inheritance and now you two were dependent on Harold."

"You're joking." Elizabeth straightened, enraged. She wanted to find Harold and gut him like her father had taught her how to do with their fish. "My mother could have bought and sold Harold several times over. Hell, I could do the same."

"I know that now, but back then, we didn't know you, and our social group did know Harold."

"Oh, that makes so much more sense."

Her head spun as the blanks filled in. Little things like the private school telling her mother they would need to confer with Harold before allowing Elizabeth to enroll. The shelter Elizabeth wanted to help fund being put on hold by the bank president until he talked with Harold.

All of Elizabeth's funds had gone through Harold's corporate law offices until two months ago when she'd had Jessup shift everything to a small out-of-state bank with no ties to Harold. That had been a singularly unpleasant phone call between her and Harold. But after she pointed out that Rafael and his mother used that bank and she wanted to be damned sure her money was safe, he had backed off.

It wasn't the truth. She wanted her money safe from Harold, but again, she couldn't say that yet. As many lies and half-truths as she was telling, she would need to start keeping notes so she could keep her stories straight.

"Exactly. We all thought you were like the Beverly Hillbillies, only not rich anymore. And only the ones who worked closely with your mother knew the truth." Jessup tugged her from her spiraling thoughts.

"Because everyone gossips, and it's easier to believe the bad than the good—or in our case, the normal." She slumped in her seat. "That explains why Rafe's mother hates me, but why would she lie?"

"Because she wants Chloe for Rafe, and you were in the way."

"Christ." Chloe's family was in a higher social class than Rafe's, and Elizabeth could easily see Mrs. Martinez using them to climb that ladder. Hopefully, those spiky heels would stab Chloe in the eye when Mrs. Martinez used her as a stepping stool. And if there was any justice, both of them would lose their footing. Damned social climbers.

"But now we know, so you can come back and win your man—"

"Jessup, you forget three things, hon. One, Harold is trying to kill me. Two, I'm pregnant with the baby Harold wants to kill me for. And three, Rafe is with Chloe." And if he was genuinely happy, Elizabeth didn't want to screw with that. Not after everything Harold had put the poor man through. Because yes, she still cared what happened to Rafe. Even after all this, he had been played just as much as she had. Maybe more.

"Dammit, Eliz—I mean Colby, you need to fight for—"

"No," she snarled. "I need to keep this baby safe. Once it's out of me, then we fight. Once we have a plan, we fight. And when Rafe sees Chloe's true colors, maybe I'll give him a second chance."

"Maybe?"

She saw the pawnshop two blocks ahead on the left. "Yes, maybe. It depends on how much he knew and how deep his ties are with Harold. And it also depends on if he even wants one."

"I'll go to the club for lunch more. Maybe run into Rafe while I'm there."

She rolled her eyes as she tapped on the plasti-glass divider between the back and the front of the cab. "Here, I'm walking the rest of the way."

She pushed the cash and a hefty tip toward the driver and stepped from the vehicle.

"Did you hear me?"

"Yes," she said, jogging across the street. "Look, befriend Rafe if you want, but until he's free, I'm not doing anything with him. Because unlike him, I don't cheat."

Jessup huffed. "He didn't either. He swears he and Chloe only met up at events and a few dinners. He refused to break his wedding vows just because you were."

"Mighty big of him, considering he was my first and only." She tried to let go of the bitter anger that burned through her at Rafe's betrayal, at his even thinking she would do something like that. Maybe she would get to set the record straight with the asshole but she knew cheating wasn't in his nature. She wished he had the same faith in her. It was too bad her stubborn heart was still set on him. But Elizabeth couldn't dwell on what she yearned for. She needed to get settled and take care of her baby. The rest would work itself out. "Look, I'm at the shop, so I gotta go. But can you make sure the deed to the cabin is definitely clear? I don't want Harold pulling something."

"I can do that. Take care and send me a text letting me know you got back to the hotel safely."

Her heart warmed at having Jessup in her corner. "I will." Hanging up, she tucked the phone into her purse and pulled open the door.

The store was like most of the pawnshops she had visited for research for her books, whether to find a certain item to better describe it or to find out how different pawnshops operated. They all had a musty smell that permeated the stores. Cluttered shelves spanned the length and width of the left side of the store while large arrays of glass cases took up the center and acted as a counter for the cash register. The cases held all sorts of jewelry, from watches and rings to bracelets, necklaces, and even barrettes. There were even a few trays of cigarette paraphernalia like lighters and gold embellished cases, even a few fancy holders like Elizabeth had seen in the black and white movies she loved to watch.

"May I help you?" a young blond woman smiled brightly behind the cash register, and Elizabeth headed toward her.

"I'm looking for Steven."

"Sure, hon. You must be the woman Paul called about." She waved Elizabeth behind the counter. "Come on back, he's in the office."

Elizabeth caught the woman's name tag as she turned to face her, "Lorie" was scrawled across the slender gold-colored plaque pinned to her shirt. Stepping into the hall, Lorie pointed. "It's the second door on the right."

"Thanks."

She was in and out within half an hour. Steven had been ready to go home and eat dinner with his wife and kids before coming back and relieving Lorie for the night. Slipping out the door, she headed for the strip.

Now that she knew the pawnshop was only a few blocks from the hotel, she decided to walk. Granted the blocks were much larger than standard city blocks since the Las Vegas casinos could house small cities inside them, but Elizabeth didn't care. She had five new burner phones. Never been used.

That was why Steven was so paranoid about not just selling them willy-nilly. It had been his first foray into dealing with burners as he refused to buy just any old phone from Joe Blow off the street. But because he had purchased the storage unit without being able to go through it, he hadn't known about the phones.

The second he learned what was in the box, he'd notified the police just in case the cells had been used before. They had not, but now Steven's name was tied to the phones, so he wasn't going to just toss them or sell them to just anyone. All of this worked perfectly for her as it gave her a clean way to contact Rafe, Harold, or Megan if she needed to since her primary cell was with Kennedy—with calls being forwarded to Elizabeth so she could stay on top of Megan's daily chatter.

Just as she had put one block between her and the pawnshop, Elizabeth's cell rang. Dragging it from the back pocket of her jeans, she flicked answer. "Elizabeth."

"Thought you were supposed to go by Colby now," a gruff voice stated.

And that was another reason she needed the burners. If they rang, she knew to answer them as Elizabeth and she could finally start answering her primary cell with her new name.

"Mac, have you seen the places?"

"Yep."

Pulling words from the man was like pulling teeth. Slow and onerous. "Did you find one that would work for us?"

"Yep. The last one." Mac had worked as the foreman on her father's ranch in South Carolina. After her parents there was no one Elizabeth trusted more than him.

She sighed. "And? What about the buildings? Can you fix up the bunkhouses before the winter? Are the bunkhouses even winterized? How does the main house look?"

He sighed deeply. If she had been standing in front of him, it would have felt like a warm breeze passing her face smelling of peppermint from the sugar-free candies he always chomped on since he quit smoking years ago.

"Bunkhouses are gonna need a lot of work. We'll have to stay in the main house with you, but there's plenty of room, so it shouldn't be a problem."

"We? Did you pick up a woman on the way up there?"

"Nope. Brought a couple of fellows with me from Virginia."

Huh? "Why didn't you say anything?"

He sighed again, and she knew it was because she was forcing him to speak and not because he was pissed. "Because. Iff'n you don't want them, you're gonna lose me too."

"Mac, you know I trust you. If you brought them there, it's fine. Why did you feel the need to keep it a secret?"

"One's a friend who was getting a rash of shit on Ebner's ranch when Ebner's sons took over, and the other was kicked outta his foster home when he hit eighteen. I found him on the road with only a backpack and not even a decent pair of shoes. Pissed me off."

Elizabeth dodged between two groups who had stopped in the dead center of the sidewalk, their voices loud as they all debated which show to see after dinner.

"Jesus, girl, where are you?"

"Vegas. Listen, have you told them about why I'm running?"

"Some, not all. Ain't my story to tell and thought it would be better coming from you."

"Fair enough. Okay, get the main house set up for all of us. I'll feel safer with you all near me anyway, especially being pregnant. Make sure you get plenty of linens, so we don't freeze to death at night. North Dakota winters are not anything to sneeze at."

"Okay."

"Also, Mac, make sure you and those boys you brought have enough clothes. Winter and summer. There isn't any shame in them getting them, and we can take it out of their pay over the next several months. Let them know that."

"I sure will."

She could hear the appreciation at her caring about the boys Mac thought enough of to bring with him. They must've impressed him in the short time he'd known them because Mac didn't take to too many people, and he never put his reputation on the line for just anyone.

Chapter Five

Six Months Later

Colby Harrison took her ginger and lemongrass tea to the bay window in the great room. North Dakota was vastly different from California in December. Colder, crisper, and more rugged. That one night, six months ago, had changed everything. Walking into Matt's rental place had been provenance. Meeting Matt's husband had been life-altering. Jessup Sawyer was an attorney everyone wanted, but not many got. A shark.

The second the divorce papers were signed, Jessup had immediately handed in the documents to have her name changed. A judge Colby knew was more than happy to help and promised to be discreet with the paperwork. At that moment, Elizabeth Sutherland Martinez ceased to exist, and Colby Harrison was born. Colby had been taken from her father's middle name and Harrison from her mother's grandmother. A grandmother who was fond of reminding her group of friends of the two presidents in her family's line.

Rubbing her hand over her distended stomach, trying to soothe the twins who were overly active in the mornings, Colby sipped the tea. She smiled when she saw Mac, her foreman, stomping through the snow toward the front porch. The tromp of boots as he wiped them clean, then the squeak of the screen door gave her a brief warning before the bitter cold swirled into the room.

"Hey, Mac. I started some coffee."

She took his grunt as a "thank you" and hid her smile in her tea mug. Downing the rest of her tea in a few gulps, she followed the taciturn man into the large kitchen. "Charlie and Russell heading over soon?"

Another grunt as he inhaled his first cup of coffee.

"Then I'll get breakfast started." She bustled around the kitchen, pulling the carton of eggs out along with her skillet and other cooking ingredients. The biscuits were pushed into the oven, eggs whisked while Mac slowly unfroze from his morning inspection.

The quiet clink of silverware and dishes relaxed her. She finally had a home. Not a museum showcase and not a place where she'd never felt welcome, but one that hugged her every time she entered a room.

The stone and wood exterior felt rustic as did
the large great room with the fieldstone fireplace that
separated the dining room and kitchen from the great
room. She fallen in love with it at first sight, picturing
herself snuggled in front of the fire with a dog at her
feet while she wrote her next mystery. Add in the seven
bedrooms and four baths upstairs, and it fit her soon-
to-be small family perfectly. Enough room for the
young men Mac had unofficially adopted to each have a
room, the twins to have separate rooms when they were
older, Mac's room, and two guest rooms. The master
suite was beyond the great room. Mac had added two
additional rooms down the same hallway when he
discovered she was expecting. A nursery and an office
for her so she wouldn't need to climb the stairs later in
her pregnancy.

Jessup and Matt had been surprised when she'd
told them she wanted a ranch, but she had been born
and raised in South Carolina on a horse farm before her
dad died. She had missed the bustle of ranch life.
Missed the quiet wickers of the horses, the soft snorts
of the hounds, the rough voices of the men that worked
the stock. Voices that could be raucous and loud unless
they were calming a skittish mare or a rambunctious
foal bent on mischief.

"You figure out what you're gonna raise here?"
Mac's slow drawl was a taste of her original home, his
Carolina twang a welcome addition.

She grinned, dishing up the last of the grits into
a bowl and setting the pots and pans in soapy water to
clean after breakfast. Picking the last two platters up,
she joined the rest of her motley crew at the table.

"Boss lady has a wicked smile, Mac. Got a feelin' we're 'bout to get a surprise," Russell said, his honey-colored orbs danced with mischief.

Russell had been somber and serious the first time she'd met him. It had taken months for him to let down his guard enough to tease her and even more time before he was comfortable enough to be himself.

Charlie was alternately bouncy like Seth as he helped the other two men around their new home and quiet when he was thinking.

Then there was Mac. The grizzled, not overly friendly bear of a man was someone Elizabeth counted as family. And even though Jessup had told her not to contact anyone from her old life, she'd needed to check on Mac. He'd been her surrogate father, her father's closest friend, and someone she called whenever something in California threw her for a loop.

"What's got you smiling so big, boss?" Charlie asked, his dark eyes twinkling with a teasing light.

"She's figured out what we're gonna be raisin'," Mac replied, his gruff voice rumbly like boulders rubbing together.

Surprised expressions turned on Mac.

"She did?" Russell asked.

"What is it?" Charlie asked over him in an excited tone.

"Iunno, but whatever it is, it ain't horses." He slurped his coal-black coffee.

"Nope, not horses. I originally thought angora—"

Mac's fork clattered to his plate. The grits on it landed on the table. "Rabbits? You're gonna have us raisin' *rabbits*?"

Russell's face mirrored Mac's in pinched disgust while Charlie's looked more thoughtful.

"I thought angora came from goats." Charlie frowned in confusion.

"Oh, I can do goats." Russell nodded, shoveling more food in his mouth.

"It comes from both, but I don't know much about either, so I talked to some friends who raise alpacas."

"Those are camels, right?" Charlie looked to Mac for the answer.

She forgot how young the man was, barely eighteen. It still pissed her off that his foster parents had tossed him out the day after his birthday. Though they were now paying the price since Jessup had dug into the situation. Come to find out, the foster parents had been paid an extra stipend to help Charlie attend job fairs and college campuses so he could figure out the next part of his life. Unfortunately, they'd never let Charlie off their farm until they kicked him out with only a backpack.

The county was suing the foster parents for the money back, and the police had arrested them for fraud. Sometimes karma doled out the sweetest of justice. Too bad it hadn't done anything to Harold or Megan. At least not yet.

Mac huffed. "No, they're closer to llamas iff'n I had to pick one."

"Llamas? Like on Diego?" Charlie scratched at the back of his head, making his longish strands of light brown hair stand up in the back.

She made a mental note to take him for a haircut. Russell kept his head shaved, so his thick beanie adhered to his head and let him wear a bomber hat over it. As he had let them know every day, he was not built for the cold.

Before the conversation could get too far out of hand, Colby cleared her throat. "Anyway, a couple from the Netherlands is coming over next year in the spring to help get me started. They breed the animals, so I bought three of each kind from them." She met Mac's cobalt blue eyes and asked, "Do you think we can do it?"

"Well, Alpacas don't need much room like cattle. About an acre for a hundred of them, I think, and if we can grow the hay on those three fields me and Russell looked over when we got here last summer, then that'll cut down a lot of the cost."

"You've worked with them before?" Russell quizzed, his plate empty.

"Yeah, before I came to land on the Sutherlands' farm. Weren't too bad. You gettin' the long-haired ones or the curly ones?"

"Both. I want to try crossbreeding eventually and seeing about varied colors. But both interested me."

"Kay. I'll take the boys with me and start looking at the paddocks and such. Winter gets pretty cold up here, so as long as we got them a warm shelter and plenty of shade in the summer, they'll be fine."

"Make sure there aren't any acorn trees, poppies, or buckwheat anywhere," Colby replied, pushing her empty plate away.

Mac nodded absently.

"Why's that?" Charlie asked.

"That stuff's poison to the animals," Mac answered, his face creased in a frown of concentration.

Colby wouldn't be surprised if he was pulling up everything he knew in that brain of his from the brief time he'd worked for the farm in Alabama. He wasn't there long, said the summers were too hot.

"Good to know. I think I've seen some acorns in the north pastures," Russell murmured.

"We'll go do some research, check the pastures real good just like we would iff'n it were cattle, horses, or sheep and clear out what we need to," Mac said, standing and taking his plate to the sink. "Charlie, it's your turn on these here dishes."

"Yessir." Charlie jumped up and began to clear the table.

Colby stood to help but was waved away.

"I got it, boss. You go put your feet up."

"Thanks, you all." She smiled at her small family and made her way to her office. There were calls she wanted to make about the alpacas as well as her upcoming book release. She paused when one of the twins kicked and petted her stomach where the fluttering was. The babies were another reason she'd settled on alpacas. They were kid-friendly, playful, and adored attention. They would relate well with the little ones as they grew older.

~ ~ ~ ~

Rafe popped the top off his beer and propped his feet up on his coffee table. It was nice to relax in the comfort of his own home in silence for a change. Rosa was at her niece's helping with a new baby and wasn't due back for two weeks.

He wished Chloe had opted to at least move in with him, so the house wasn't empty when he returned from his business trips. But he got it.

She wanted to wait until they were married to merge their lives so she wasn't painted with the same brush as Elizabeth. Rafe didn't care about the living arrangements, but he wished he could have convinced her they didn't need to wait to make love. But Chloe always pointed out how promiscuous Elizabeth had been and how she wanted to prove to Rafe that she was different. It was refreshing to have someone want to show Rafe how trustworthy they could be.

The one thing he had done was open a bank account with his and Chloe's names on it so she could begin decorating their house. Elizabeth's room was the first Chloe had tackled. The furniture was due to arrive the week after Christmas, and Rafe was glad. He hated being reminded of his ex-wife.

Taking a sip of his beer, he relaxed into his couch. But now, even with everything finally settling into place for him, he was on edge.

He expected Elizabeth to pop up and ruin it all.

Chloe, her parents, and his mother had all said Elizabeth was a drama queen and would definitely make a scene. That was another reason Chloe hadn't moved in. It was also the reason Chloe continued to attend the social events with her parents, in case Elizabeth tracked her down and cornered her.

All the warnings they'd given him came back the longer he thought about his ex: How Elizabeth would stalk them at their social events. How she would fight tooth and nail for every piece of Rafe's life. How she would take great pleasure in making everyone in his realm miserable.

She had done none of those things.

Rafe didn't understand what was holding his ex back. And it wasn't as if the divorce was finalized yesterday; it had been nine months. If Elizabeth was going to act, wouldn't she have done it by now?

But there was nothing. No contact at all. Not even to say he owed child support after dumping his sperm at that bank—nothing but silence.

He should feel relieved, but he mourned the life he had wanted. He wished he had chosen more wisely the first time, but it was over and done with. Thank God there were no innocents tying him and Elizabeth together.

Now he had a chance to have the life he wanted with Chloe and her warm personality.

His stomach growled. Having skipped lunch, he opened his restaurant app and placed an order for Thai. Lifting the beer, Rafe drained it, stood, and tossed the bottle in the recycle bin in the kitchen before grabbing a second one. Three was his limit, and as he preferred iced sweet tea with his Thai, he'd take the second beer while he waited for it to be delivered. Returning to the den, he settled back into his leather sofa.

Jessup was another oddity linked to Elizabeth. He was one of a few men Rafe admired. An ethical attorney. As mythical as a unicorn. But Jessup was one. His clients were in the elite top one percent. To keep them at the top, Jessup was a shark. There were two things the man despised: vodka and Harold Moore. Yet, he had represented Elizabeth in the divorce.

The doorbell pealed through the house, and Rafe rolled to his feet. After paying for dinner, he opened his contacts. Selecting one of his best friends, he put the call on speaker as he set everything out on the coffee table.

"McCord." A deep voice drifted through the speaker, commanding attention.

Being a Sheriff, Jackson McCord was always in control. Being Rafe's friend, the man was as loyal as the winter day was long.

"Hey, man. It's Rafe. You on duty?"

"For another fifteen minutes. Pulled second shift for the next few weeks. One of our guys is a newly minted dad, so we're taking turns covering for him." His cool tone warmed and relaxed. "So, why are you calling? You've got your divorce. You didn't lose a dime, didn't lose the house, and aren't a baby daddy. Unless Chloe's knocked up—"

"No, we're waiting so she isn't compared to Elizabeth." It was more Chloe holding him off than Rafe wanting to wait, but he got it. After Elizabeth's infidelities, he appreciated Chloe's craving to prove she was better. To prove Rafe could trust her. He took a bite of the Pad Krapow Moo Saap. The beef was tender, the spices balanced to perfection. Spicy foods were his weakness. Again, something he and Elizabeth didn't have in common. "You know you and Tristan are my best men. Like standing right there next to me when I say 'I do' to Chloe. So, you better be ready for that."

"Yep, me and Brianna are looking forward to some fun in the sun whenever you give us the date. And with me, you, and Tristan together again, it'll be like old times."

"Don't say that. I feel ancient compared to Chloe some days." Rafe winced at the reminder of the fifteen-year age difference.

"Well, as much as I enjoy catching up, based on your tone you didn't call to chat. What's up?"

"I'm not sure." Rafe huffed and drank some of his tea to settle his thoughts. "Everything I was told about Elizabeth said she'd tear me to shreds in the divorce. Hell, even her attorney is a bastard who's all but taken the skin off a person's body. Yet, she didn't fight for anything. Didn't take any of the custom furniture in her room or the junk she brought with her in her office. Even Harold didn't balk at signing the cabin over to me. Though, leaving a sperm donation for him and his viper of a daughter was disgusting, I still haven't heard anything."

"It's odd considering how much she wanted that baby. Maybe they want to wait to make sure it takes before alerting anyone."

Rafe tipped his head from side to side even though Jackson couldn't see him. "Maybe."

"I ran background on her and Chloe." Jackson fell silent.

"You did? Wait. On Chloe too?" He should have been surprised, but knowing his friend like he did, he wasn't.

"Yes."

"And?" His curiosity was piqued. He waffled over how ethical it was having his friend do a background check on his ex-wife and his current fiancée.

Jackson cleared his throat. "Look, do you really want to know?"

What the hell could Jackson have found on Elizabeth? Did he want to know? Yes. Especially if she turned up pregnant. Chloe, he wasn't worried about. She wouldn't have anything in her background. She was too sweet to get into much trouble. "Yes. You know I prefer having all the—"

"Facts. I remember." Jackson hummed. A tell he'd had as long as Rafe knew him.

Something in the background check was going to be bad. What could Elizabeth have done? With Harold in the mix, there was no telling. Robbing grandmothers of their money, kidnapping babies and feeding them to trolls, he wouldn't put any of it past Harold.

"I already know Elizabeth was sleeping around—"

"Wait. What?" Jackson asked, surprised.

"Rosa told—"

"Okay, so the facts. Before I get started, let me call in so I'm off the clock. I swear, one in the morning is quiet as hell over here."

Rafe heard the high-pitched squawk of Jackson's CB radio as he called in a shift change. A few minutes later, he was back on the line.

"Back."

"Do you need to head home?"

"No, I don't drive and talk. That shit's dangerous, and this isn't something Brianna needs to hear. She already doesn't like Chloe—"

Rafe's hackles rose in defense of his fiancée. "She doesn't even know her."

"Brianna's been following her on social media to get a feel for your new lady, and from what she's seen . . . She slots the woman in the 'spoiled rich girl' column."

Rafe laughed. "That's not Chloe. She's with one of her best friends now spending the night watching romantic comedies."

Jackson snorted. "Man, you have got your head buried deep in that sand . . . or up your rear. I'm not sure which yet, but we'll see in a second. Chloe is not over at her friend's house."

She wasn't?

The glass of tea he'd been lifting almost fell from his grasp before he carefully set it back on the table and sat back. "How do you know?"

"I'm looking at her social media posts, and right now she's doing body shots off some guy who's only wearing a jockstrap."

Rafe flipped his phone open and looked, but the only pictures he saw were of Chloe's toes, as if she'd just polished them, and a big pitcher of margaritas. He shot the photos off to Jackson.

"She must have two accounts because the one Brianna follows shows Chloe at a rave doing body shots off some almost naked guy."

Rafe rolled to his feet, wondering who he could get the address of this rave from.

"Before you race out trying to rescue your lady love, you need all the facts. I think all those rumors about Elizabeth are a crock of—"

"Why didn't you tell me?"

"Because it was just a gut feeling. I didn't find anything in her background check either. And without proof, you wouldn't believe me." A frustrated huff. "You could give a donkey lessons on stubborn when you've made up your mind, and your mind was made up the second Harold entered the picture—who I hate, by the way. It wouldn't have mattered if Jesus himself came down from the sky and told you Elizabeth was an angel in disguise. You wouldn't have believed it." Jackson chuckled. "You'd probably try to have me commit Jesus to the psych ward. But your mom's a different matter. She's the one who told you Elizabeth was cheating, right?"

"Yeah."

"So, yeah, I don't know because your mom doesn't have a reason to lie to you. And with Rosa backing her up. . ."

"Exactly." Rafe felt vindicated in his opinion of Elizabeth when Jackson pointed out his mother and Rosa catching Elizabeth cheating.

"And then there's Chloe. That woman knows how to work her body and what buttons to push to get men to drop at her feet." Jackson paused. "Here's the thing. You've been traveling a lot more the last six months, getting the new startup off the ground in Seattle. And let me just say, I'm so glad I didn't go into investments."

"Maybe not, but you know I manage all your savings. And you're invested in that startup too."

"I'm glad you're managing it. It lets me relax, knowing someone I trust is handling my money. But you've been traveling even more than when you were married to Elizabeth, and trust me when I say, Chloe has taken full advantage."

"What's that mean?"

"It means I don't like Chloe," Jackson stated, flat out with no waffling.

"You liked Elizabeth?"

"Doesn't matter if I liked her, Rafe. It mattered that you did until you discovered Harold was her stepfather and that contract was given to you. Everything went to hell after that." Jackson hummed again before continuing. "If Chloe's staying at a friend's house, I'd give her a few hours to get back there, then pay her a visit."

"You think I'll find her screwing around on me?" Rafe shook his head at the thought. Chloe wouldn't do that. She might be sowing her wild oats at that rave, and they would discuss it like adults, but she was loyal.

Unlike Elizabeth.

"My gut says you need to go and find out, preferably before you tie the knot with her." Jackson snapped his fingers. "Oh, if you catch her in something, I would highly recommend getting a video or pictures just in case so it's not *he said, she said.*"

"Shit." Rafe's stomach churned harder.

"Sorry, man. Call me if you need me."

After saying goodbye, Rafe gathered everything up and put the leftovers in the fridge.

Jackson was right. He trusted his friend.

As if the man knew Rafe was thinking about him, a video link popped up in their chat. Clicking it, he saw his fiancée licking a line of salt across chiseled abs. The man was laid out as if on a buffet or a bar with two lemon slices leading down to his naval.

Chloe bent over and slid her mouth perfectly over the shot glass, her hands tucked behind her back as she arched her head back and took the shot. Catcalls and whistles followed as she scooped the lemon up with her nimble lips and teeth.

It would take him at least five to six hours to get from his home in Woodside to Sabrina's house in LA. Sliding his shoes on, he grabbed his keys and headed out. He knew Jackson was careful in gathering all the facts before sharing them.

However, Rafe also knew Chloe. She couldn't have fooled him for almost a year.

The video was probably her having fun, and worried Rafe would judge her for still being young. Their fifteen-year age gap had never felt insurmountable, and he wouldn't let her need to party start putting up barriers between them now.

This would be the one time Rafe would prove Jackson wrong.

Rafe could not be so cursed as to have two women he thought he loved turn around and cheat on him. Because for as bad as everything had played out between him and Elizabeth, in the beginning he had loved her enough to sign that damnable contract and try for a future. And unlike her, he had never broken his vows.

Chapter Six

The drive to Sabrina's took an eternity with how fast his thoughts spun.

A little after two in the morning, Rafe finally took the turn into the drive and parked. When he had visited before, he hadn't realized how impersonal Sabrina's house was. Chrome, concrete, and glass with rock gardens bracketing the stairs. No flowers spilled across the expanse, and no burst of color could be found anywhere in the sea of gray, white and silver.

Stepping from his sedan, he strode up the walk to the side door. One he'd entered a few times at various events Chloe had brought him to. Rafe raised his hand to knock but saw the door hadn't been fully shut. Stupid. What if he were there to rob them? He made a mental note to remind Chloe and Sabrina to take better care next time.

The mudroom and kitchen were both dark as Rafe navigated his way toward the voices. A left put him in the doorway to the great room with its floor to ceiling windows. But it wasn't the breathtaking view that froze him. It was his fiancée.

He should have listened to Jackson.

With shaking hands, he fumbled his cell from his pocket. Three swipes and he was recording. If he wasn't here seeing it with his own eyes, he would never have believed it. That must've been why Jackson had pushed.

As his gaze raked Chloe's naked form, rage coiled tighter and tighter within him. Disgust wasn't far behind.

She was flawless. Her waist-length blond hair was fisted in a tight grip by the man who'd been laid out in the video Jackson had sent him. Esthetically, the two fit, Chloe delicate and fine-boned to the man's muscled brawn. Muscles that tensed and released as he rammed into her. Not to be outdone, another man was in front of Chloe receiving a blow job from her. From the same mouth that had whispered the sweetest of lies to him.

Disgust won as he snapped the video off and shoved the phone back into his pocket. Leverage created a strong position; as a businessman, he had learned that lesson the hard way.

He raised his hands and slow clapped, pulling a startled shriek from Sabrina. Rafe had missed her being pounded into the couch on the right, too betrayed by the treacherous woman in front of him.

"Well, done, hon."

"Rafe?" Chloe scrabbled back, then her eyes narrowed on him. "What the hell are you doing here?"

Arching a brow, he smirked. "It seems I'm preventing myself from making another huge mistake. Thank God we're at least not married."

She smiled. It was sharp and held edges Rafe didn't understand. "Oh, we're getting married, lover."

"No, we're really not." He tucked his hands in his pockets to keep from wrapping them around her throat. *Was I ever in love with her? Or was I blind because I wanted a family?* "I expect you to explain to your parents that this farce is over. I'll be canceling everything I'm supposed to pay for in terms of the wedding." He didn't add that he would be closing every joint account they had. It was his money, so he didn't need to justify why she wouldn't have any further access to it.

"Daddy won't like this. He's—"

"Of no concern to me." Rafe's mask was firmly in place. He'd dealt with CEOs who had more bite than Chloe or her father. Hell, he'd dealt with scarier grandmas when he lived in Chicago. "We don't do business together. I have no contracts with him. He's been pumping me to help him with financing on an investment. So, if anything, I have *his* balls in a vice, so to speak. Not the other way around."

"We can work this out." Her haughty expression turned meltingly sweet.

"No."

"What the . . . You cheated on Elizabeth with me for almost a year, and now because I have one indis—"

"I never cheated on her. You and I never had sex, and if Elizabeth had ever bothered to check my calendar, she would have seen I was with you at various events. She never did. So, I also didn't lie to her." Though he had lied in the end, allowing Elizabeth to think he had slept with Chloe. Hell, he had purposely made his ex believe he was leaving her to pack her things while he stayed with Chloe that week. In reality, he had left for an extended business trip abroad. Why had he done that? In the hopes of hurting her as deeply as he'd been hurt. And now he was walking the same damned path again.

He rubbed his pounding head but didn't let a shred of the pain Chloe was causing him show. She didn't deserve to see the suffering she caused him nor the doubt she'd put into him about being enough for any of the women in his life. "You, however, have done both. And let's be honest, you've done it more than this one time. You were too much of a pro sucking that guy's dick without gagging for this to be your first time. Not to mention doing it while getting pounded from behind. Those are some straight-up porn skills there."

Chloe's roar of rage made Rafe find his first smile. "Oh, now you're angry?"

"You will not back out of our wedding. We're supposed to be married next month. What will people think?" She was wailing by the end.

It hit him then, the age difference between them. Not only had Chloe never claimed to love him, she'd always couched their wedding in terms of what others would think. God, he was done. Done with her. Done with his bad choices in women.

Just done.

"Well, nothing. We can say our age difference created a rift, that is if you want to be mature. If you don't and want to drag my name through the mud . . . well, let's just say a certain video of you being spit-roasted might be called into evidence."

Soul-deep exhaustion ate at him that he would have to play hardball in order to dig her out of his life.

She gasped, falling into a chair. "You wouldn't."

"Not if you let me go without a fight. Just chalk it up to irreconcilable differences." Rafe pulled his keys from his pocket. "Needless to say, you will end this relationship tomorrow. Or I'll explain to your parents and my mother in great detail why we're no longer together."

He spun and strode back the way he had come, refusing to seem as if he were fleeing. He wasn't the one in the wrong, so he wouldn't be made to feel guilty for catching her.

"You're too funny with your judgmental bullshit," she growled, trailing behind him.

He raised his middle finger and flipped it over his shoulder.

"No, fuck you, Rafe." She laughed, but it was filled with acid so caustic he was shocked the hallway didn't have holes from it. "I can own my sexuality. I wonder if the savvy businessman you are can own his gullibility."

"What's that mean?" He froze just on the threshold to the kitchen. Turning, he knew he shouldn't let her get to him, but he was unable to stop himself.

"It means, lover, that you believed Elizabeth was unfaithful to you." She leaned in. Her rancid, alcohol-soaked breath made him wrinkle his nose. "It means you fell for all those lies. And you did it so easily. All because your mother hated Elizabeth and wanted you out of that marriage. She wanted us to be together." Chloe waved a finger between them.

That wasn't possible; his mother never would have lied to him.

He spun on his heel and called over his shoulder, "I'm not gullible, Chloe. I just seem to trust the wrong people."

When he reached the middle of the kitchen, he thought he was home free, never anticipating the crazy naked chick landing on his back and pummeling him in the head with her fists.

Shaking her off, he swung around and jabbed a finger at her as he snarled, "If you do not end this tomorrow, I swear on my father's grave, I will post that video on so many sites you'll never see the end of it. Fifty years down the road, it'll still haunt your ass."

He left her cursing him from the kitchen floor while he cursed himself for bringing another cheating whore into his life.

~ ~ ~ ~

Colby's bladder jolted her from her reverie, and she took the few remaining steps to the bathroom.

She'd just opened the door when the muffled sound of her cell's ringtone reached her. Jessup's ringtone. Colby hurried as fast as she could from the small bathroom back to the kitchen as her cell trilled.

"Jessup," she greeted, out of breath.

"Were you running again?" he asked, exasperated worry in his voice.

"Only a few steps from the bathroom to the kitchen. I didn't want to miss your call." It was always hard to get her friend on the phone. Normally, she would chat with Matt, Ellis, or Seth. "What's up?"

"I went to the club for lunch today and ran into Rafe . . ." He trailed off as if there were something she was to infer.

"Was Chloe with him? Married or engaged? Is that why you're calling?"

"No." He emitted a weighted sigh, so unlike Jessup. "He saw me and came over. Ended up joining me for lunch, and he asked about you."

"Me?" She snorted. Her ex had never asked after her. "You must be mistaken. Maybe he wanted to triple-check that the divorce was final so he could move on to his true love."

She would need tea to calm her nerves after this conversation. She heard the quiet hum of the dishwasher and saw Ben had left the counters spotless, just the way she liked them.

"No. I'm an attorney, for God's sake. I can read a person backward and forward, and I'm telling you, the man was asking because he cared."

"Bullshit. Since you bought that convertible, the sun has fried your brain. If that's it . . ." She filled the tea kettle with water.

"He wanted to know if you'd gotten what you wanted out of that contract."

"Oh, he's fishing to see if I turned up pregnant. The answer is no."

"But you will in a few months . . ."

"No." Slamming the tea kettle onto the stove, she forced herself to calm down. "I cannot alert Harold to my babies, or he'll stop at nothing to find me and kill me. You know that."

"What're you gonna do, Colby? You've changed your name and your location, but your parents wanted you to have that money. It's not right that Harold gets a stipend after everything he's done. For all we know, he could be skimming the money in other ways."

"And I'm the only one who heard him and Megan, Jess. Me. The police won't believe me. Not after all this time. Or have you found the evidence to prove they killed my mother?"

"I have not." His quiet words barely made it through the line.

A few deep breaths and the fine tremors in her hands calmed enough for her to finish making the ginger and lemongrass tea that would help to settle her stomach. "Look, I'm sorry I snapped, but Harold *bought* Rafe. The man turned me into a broodmare. No sane person would do that. I can't chance something happening to my babies when Harold finally comes for me." She cradled her stomach. "After I have them, we can figure something out."

"How about adoption?"

"What?" Her mind reeled. *Adoption?* "You want me to give up my babies?"

"What?!" he almost shouted. "No! I meant *you* adopt. I've combed through the trust thoroughly, and adoption frees those funds up just as much as the babies."

She nibbled her thumbnail. "But it's the same thing. I'd still be putting a child at risk."

"No, you find someone older, like a sixteen-year-old. Maybe someone who's been on the streets for a while and would be able to protect themselves."

"No. I can't do that, Jess." But now that the idea was in her head, Colby knew some of the kids she dealt with at the shelter could handle this if she was upfront. They were street smart and knew how brutal people could be, how desperate. But to put some unsuspecting kid in that position would be just like putting her babies in the same predicament.

"I'm not saying keep them in the dark, Colby. Those are streetwise kids; if you're straight with them, they'll be straight with you, and most are running from situations harsher even than yours."

"Jess, that's like painting a target on someone's back."

"No, because in order for him to get that money, it'd mean doing something to you. At the moment, he doesn't know where you are, but if you can get that trust open, we can use it to lure him out in the open. If nothing else, we need to move it to a different bank and have someone else looking at it. Right now, it's just Harold's people because your mother trusted them."

She rubbed her pounding head, worry winding through her. Did she want the trust? Yes, simply because she didn't want Harold to have it. He'd killed her mother, and there was no way on this earth Colby wanted him to be rewarded. "You think he's really done something with it."

"I don't know. It depends on how much oversight Harold's been given. If his inner circle hasn't kept an eye on it, he's probably siphoned a good chunk off."

"But then he wouldn't need the kid."

Jessup fell silent. "I didn't think of that. That means Harold doesn't have access to it. But we need to take that money out of the equation."

She agreed. But she also knew she couldn't put anyone else in danger. After pouring the boiling water into the insulated carafe, she took it with her to her office. "Let me think about it. Maybe we can brainstorm when you come up for Christmas." She froze. "Unless you're calling to tell me—"

"Don't be dramatic. Of course we're still coming. Matt would make me sleep on the couch for a month if we didn't."

"Oh, good, then I can tell you all about the alpacas."

There was a moment of silence before he replied. "Alpacas?"

"Yep." She did a quick dance step in glee at the shock in his voice. This man was hard to fluster.

"Those are like camels, right?"

"Not really. Though Mac did say they spit at you if you piss them off."

"Okay, so I'll stick to the horse side of the barn when you get them. Just make sure you research everything and send me any contracts."

And he was back on track. Not much fazed him, so when she did get to him, it was even more rewarding. "Will do. Now I need to go kill someone."

"Please, tell me it's a new book."

"'Course, I wouldn't hurt a fly unless it comes for my family." She plunked the carafe on her father's tigerwood desk next to a large mug.

"I'll see you in a week."

"I can't wait to see you all."

~ ~ ~ ~

Colby reread the last sentence she'd typed and
groaned when she realized she'd replaced the hero's
name with Rafe—again. Ever since she had hung up on
Jessup, her thoughts kept circling back to Rafe.
Normally, she would talk to Megan, but as Megan was
trying to kill her, Colby didn't think it would be a good
idea to ask her ex-friend for advice.

Leaning back in her plush office chair, she
sipped the last of her tea. Murder mysteries, intrigue,
spies, all the action she could cram into her books along
with romance had made her aware of certain security
risks. What she didn't know, Casey had been more than
happy to educate her on. She couldn't email Rafael and
ask why he was quizzing Jessup about her, and she
didn't know if she wanted to hear his voice.

His voice was what had drawn her to him in the
first place. The outside package was nothing to sneeze
at, but she had seen many a gorgeous man. Most had a
snide or entitled tone to their voices.

But Rafe hadn't. He'd been self-deprecating and
down to earth. Even his laugh was sexy, rich with
mirth, and drew a smile from those around him even if
they hadn't heard the joke.

Colby would cave if she heard him, she knew it
with every particle of her being. Rolling her head to the
side, she opened the top drawer of her desk. The five
burners she had purchased in Vegas lay innocuously
next to her pens, paperclips, and a yellow legal pad.
Three of the cells had masking tape with names
scrawled across them: Casey, Kennedy, and Hank. Each
had their own cell.

Colby had thought not to use them when she found the burner app, but Casey had talked her out of setting it up. It was still new tech, and he didn't fully understand how it worked. As she wanted to remain safe and hidden, she had listened to him and used the burners. Her fingers trailed across the two that had no tape. It would be so easy to pick one up and call Rafe. But did she trust him?

Her hand smoothed over her now-huge middle. She withdrew her hand and shut the drawer—no sense in chancing it. After the twins were born, then she would see how deep Rafe was in all this mess. And she needed to keep one clean in case any of the others in use were compromised.

Hank and Casey, she trusted with her life as Casey had trusted Colby with his brother's life when he'd landed in a Turkish jail. Luckily, a CIA agent had owed her a favor—he had used her author name as cover while he was abroad on a mission. It had gotten him out of several tight spaces by claiming to be her research assistant and allowed him to travel through several countries without raising any flags.

God, had she had to send the agent a lot of signed copies of her books, covers, and goodie bags. He had helped free Hank for her, though Hank could never return to Turkey, seeing as he was a fugitive. Instead of standing trial, her CIA contact had arranged his escape.

Colby had, of course, had them tell her everything, and she had used the method, heavily edited, in one of her books. And yes, Hank was a killer, and Colby was leery of him. Casey was not. Neither were Casey's kids. Watching the way the kids interacted with Hank showed Colby the man wasn't as cold and hardened as he liked to pretend to be. So him, she would trust with not only her life but her family's lives as well.

Kennedy, Colby didn't know, though the woman had come with a high security clearance and Hank had dug into her background. But as Colby had only talked to the woman on the phone, she couldn't make a determination until she spent a little time with her.

Snorting, she huffed in frustration as she realized how adroitly Megan, Harold, and Rafe had played her. Maybe meeting the woman wouldn't shed any light on whether Kennedy was trustworthy or not.

Absently rubbing her big as hell belly, Colby glanced out the window and saw the men she'd come to think of as family move around the yard from the fully restored bunkhouse to the barn that still needed a lot of repairs and back to the corral. Snow was piled on either side of the paths they walked. Mac gestured to the fence and held his hand several feet higher while Russell yanked a tape measure off his tool belt and Charlie took notes.

These men were her future, so why was she still drawn to her past?

The trust Harold wanted access to didn't matter in the grand scheme of things. The money didn't matter. At least not to Colby. It was the principle of the thing. She would have happily shared it with Harold. But for him to just try to take it? No.

Jessup was right. Harold wouldn't stop coming for her until he had his grubby hands legally on all the money. The millions in that trust were life-altering and would entice even the most righteous to murder. Harold could never be compared to an honest man.

Pushing her hand through her shaggy hair, she realized she was putting off the decision to call Rafael. It'd been hard that first month away from him.

She had missed his deep, whiskey-smooth voice flowing over her like the warmest sunshine. Missed seeing those jaguar-colored eyes that flickered to a deep forest green in the throes of passion. Missed his steady presence those few times when they'd gone out together.

There were so many things she missed. His quiet groan as he pushed into her, as if he didn't want to feel anything but couldn't help himself. The vaulted control shredding as he drove into her repeatedly, making her lose her mind, hurling her over the edge. The cultured sound of his voice turning into a rougher timber, gravelly and dark, as he finally lost control and took her. But most of all, she missed him holding her those nights after he'd fucked her.

She forced herself to use the more vulgar term her mother would flinch from to remind herself it was a business transaction. However, she was positive the deal hadn't included him pulling her against his chest and holding her until she fell asleep—more like feigned sleep. She'd craved his tenderness so much. It was rare for him to treat her with kindness near the end. She knew why now. But then, she had ached for the closeness to the point that she never slept as long as he was with her. Of course, when he thought she'd finally dozed off, he would slip from the bed to return to his own.

If it weren't for the masculine, spicy scent he left behind, she would have sworn it was all a dream.

Yanking at her shoulder-length strands of hair, she growled. He wasn't hers. Never had been.

But why is he asking Jessup about me? And why do I care?

She still loved him. Even after everything, her heart yearned for him, dammit. She could dodge the feelings when Jessup, Mac, or Matt asked, but she couldn't escape them when they swirled in her own head.

Shoving awkwardly to her feet, her stomach bumped into the desk, knocking the notebook into the empty teacup and sending both to the carpeted floor. Colby looked at them, angry that she would have to figure out how to crouch down and pick them up.

Sighing, she left it. One of the men would need to deal with it because, in her overly large state, she would end up lying on the floor next to the overturned teacup.

She gathered up the empty teapot and headed for the kitchen. They were going to have roast tonight with sourdough bread. If she couldn't wrestle her emotions for her stubborn ex-husband into submission, she would take her frustration out on the bread dough.

And maybe she would use one of those burner phones. But it wouldn't be today. She needed a bit more time to pick her way through the emotional minefield Rafael had left in his wake.

Chapter Seven

It took Rafe a little less than a week to untangle himself from Chloe. The deeper he dug into their joint account, the more he cursed himself for his blindness.

It was almost as if she had tried to spend him into debt—a five-million-dollar condo on the beach in Santa Monica that hadn't yet been closed on trumped the rest.

He had canceled everything. Explained that Chloe was no longer his fiancée, and he'd never been aware of the purchase no matter what she had told the real estate agent. Granted, he'd been forced to waive the earnest money, which was a hundred thousand, but Rafe chalked it up as punishment for a lesson learned.

His cell warbled as he finished dealing with the last of the ties that'd bound him to Chloe. Grinning, he answered. "So, I guess you're calling for an 'I told you so' moment?"

Jackson laughed. "No, but now that you mention it, maybe I should have a set of T-shirts made."

"I don't think so." Rafe leaned back in his office chair and plunked his socked feet on his desk. "Maybe you and Tristan can move your travel dates up since there's no wedding."

Jackson cleared his throat. "About that . . ."
There was silence and a quiet shuffling sound as if the
man was nervous. "Brianna's pregnant."

"Oh, my God! That's great news!" Rafe shouted
over the line, happy for his friend even as a twinge of
envy hit him.

It was what Rafe had always wanted, whereas
Jackson had been more of a love 'em and leave 'em
type. At least before his friend had met Brianna.

Rafe ruthlessly stomped the jealousy away and
focused on giving his friend a hard time. "And you
don't want to travel now? You do know women work
right up until their water breaks," he teased. Now that
the possibility of seeing his friends had been floated, he
realized he wanted it more than he thought.

"Her parents are still making ripples here, so I
don't want to leave her behind, and the doctor doesn't
want her to travel." Jackson's nerves all but vibrated
through the open line.

"Why not? She's not that far along.

"Her mother had six miscarriages that Brianna's
aware of so we're being—"

"Careful. I can't say as I blame you on that."
Rafe took a steady breath, his teasing mood shifting to
concern, and a thought came to him like a bolt of
lightning. "How about next summer I come to you?
You have horses, and I've been wanting to go riding
again. I set my schedule up for three weeks' vacation to
take Chloe on an engagement tour . . ."

Jackson released a whoop. "We'd love to have
you. I'll see if Tristan can rearrange his schedule too.
He's going through a messy divorce. When I talked to
him yesterday, he was at his wits' end."

"He hasn't mentioned that at all to me, and I talk to him weekly. The little shit is going to get an earful." Rafe dragged a hand through his hair.

What kind of friend did that make him? With his head so far up his own ass, he hadn't seen Tristan dealing with the same issues. He would put a call in to Tristan as well. Whether the man came to Jackson's place or not didn't matter, Rafe needed Tristan to know he was in his corner.

"So, we'll get the group back together, and Brianna can see how crazy I can be compared to her insane friends."

Rafe laughed. "I don't think anything can top the bedroom decorated as a porn set."

"You'd be surprised."

Rafe's landline buzzed. "Look, that's my other line."

"Take care, man," Jackson said before ending the call.

Snatching up his office line, Rafe propped his socked feet back on his desk. "Rafael Martinez."

"*Mijo*, finally."

"Mama, why are you calling on my landline?" Rafe's day brightened at the sound of his mother's voice.

Marisol Martinez was the one woman he could count on to be wholly in his corner. "I tried your cell, but nothing but voicemail."

"I was talking to Jackson." He grinned. "He's going to be a papa."

"Oh—"

"I congratulated him for both of us." He quickly interrupted her.

Though from his mother's cool tone, Rafe knew the hatred she harbored against Jackson hadn't dwindled.

"Not from me. He killed your father."

"Mama, Jackson was twelve. You know as well as I do, he had no part in killing Papa." Rafe slid his feet to the floor and braced his arms on his desk as the memories from that time assaulted him. "He lost his parents just as surely as I lost my father. Worse, because Jackson not only turned them in to the cops but was a witness at their trial."

"Bah, I didn't call to talk about that man. I called to discuss you ending your engagement with Chloe."

He let the old argument go, knowing he would never convince her that if Jackson hadn't called the police the second he saw his mother shoot Rafe's father, no one would have been the wiser.

The murder would have been chalked up to a home invasion gone wrong. It was happenstance that Jackson had run inside to use the bathroom. He wasn't even supposed to be at Rafe's that day, but whatever Jackson was supposed to do had been canceled. So, he'd hitched a ride to Rafe's to check out Rafe's new treehouse.

Rafe had blamed Jackson in the beginning until Detective Ray McCord had pointed out Jackson's innocence. Not only innocence, but how Jackson was just as much a victim as the people his parents had conned. Especially since they'd used the child to facilitate many of their more lucrative cons.

"Well?"

Rafe was jerked back to the present by his
mother's strident tone. Unlike Elizabeth, another
person his mother hated, his mother adored Chloe.

Rafe cursed at having to be the one to shatter
his mother's affection for the woman, but Chloe had
brought it on herself.

"She cheated on me, Mama."

"What?" His mother's voice was whisper soft.
"Are you sure?"

"I saw it with my own eyes and have a video in
case she tries to drag my name through the mud."

A gasp was followed by a growl. That was his
mother, always protective of her boy, and Rafe soaked
it in.

"I just can't believe I'm that bad at judging a
person's character. I mean, Elizabeth cheats on me and
now Chloe. Thank God I never slept with Chloe.
There's no telling what diseases I'd have had by now,"
he said, laying his pain on his mother. Even through the
phone line, she was a comfort.

"And you were tested after Elizabeth?" his
mother asked briskly. "Because she was with many men
trying to get that baby—"

"I know, mother," he snarled before biting off
his anger and stuffing it away.

It wasn't his mother's fault Elizabeth had
screwed anything that moved, nor was it his mother's
fault that Chloe was cut from the same cloth. He was
just thankful his mother had been willing to tell him the
truth. He had loved Elizabeth, heart and soul, and it
had nearly killed him when he had learned she had
screwed one of the waiters at their own wedding
reception.

Even with the contract, Rafe had wanted to try to have a future with Elizabeth. It was too bad she'd never wanted the same.

Taking a calming breath, he released those memories and leaned back in his office chair. "And yes, I was tested after Elizabeth left—and again three months later to be safe. I'm due for another test next week. After that, I'm in the clear."

"You might not be if Chloe was as promiscuous."

It was like a dash of cold water to his face to be so wrong not once but twice.

How could he show his face after this? It was a blow to his ego not to be able to have any sort of fidelity from the women who were supposed to be faithful. Scrubbing a hand across his face, he shook his head. "Like I said, I never slept with Chloe. First, I refused to break my vow to Eliza—"

"Why not?" his mother growled. "She did it to you."

"Because of Father." So many nights, he remembered hearing his parents railing at each other because his father had cheated again. So many nights, he went to bed to the sounds of his mother crying softly in the next room. It didn't matter if Elizabeth hadn't been loyal. Rafe wasn't cut from the same cloth and absolutely refused to turn into his father. Rafe had endured his own marriage for his grandfather's cabin and ended it the second he had a chance at happiness.

His mother's quiet, "Oh." said it all as she no doubt relived the same memories. "But after the divorce, you were free to—"

"Chloe wanted to wait. She said she wanted our wedding night to be the first time, and since we had waited this long . . ." He sighed deeply, exhausted to his bones with all the drama. "Anyway, I thought she wanted to prove how different she was from Elizabeth, so I agreed."

"I'll see about booking a flight home tomorrow."

"You will do no such thing," Rafe ordered. "You've been dying to see Italy."

"But you need me."

He smiled. "I always need you, Mama, but you don't need to come home. You've been planning this trip for two years. You wanted to spend Christmas in France. Between the Eiffel Tower's lights, the outdoor markets, and the ice skating, you've been talking about going there for the holidays for ages.

"Then you wanted to hit England for New Year's and Tokyo before you land in Shanghai to celebrate China's New Year. If you cancel, not only will you lose all that money, but it will be years before you can plan it all again.

"So, I'd better not see you home before February, and I'd definitely better not hear you blew this trip off just because of Chloe's crap." Rafe hardened his tone to let his mother know he not only had this handled but meant business.

"Okay, *mijo*, if you insist, but I will be listening to make sure that girl doesn't cause trouble for you." His mother stated in her mama bear mode.

"I expected nothing less. Besides, I have Rosa here and several meetings lined up, so I'll be fine until you get back." He didn't add that Rosa was actually in Arizona helping her niece with her new baby. But Rosa would be back by the end of next week, and he was sure she would make all his favorite foods to comfort him.

"Okay, as long as Rosa's there to take care of you, I'll stay." Her tone frosted over. "But if you need me, you better call me immediately."

"Yes, ma'am."

"Such a good boy."

"*Te amo*, Mama."

"*Yo tambien te amo, mijo.*"

His mother's whispered words of love carried through the distance as Rafe placed the phone back into its cradle. Now, he had the strength to triple-check that everything between him and Chloe was severed.

~ ~ ~ ~

Colby reveled in the love and laughter filling her house this Christmas. It was so unlike the cold Christmases with Harold and his lavish parties, or the one impersonal Christmas she had passed with Rafael. She shuddered at that awful farce of a family Christmas.

Colby had bought him a new briefcase, a rare brandy, and socks to keep his feet warm around the house since he never wore slippers. Nothing personal as she didn't know him as well as she had thought she would by then.

The presents she'd received were worse. Several gift cards to stores she didn't frequent and a week-long spa package in Arizona. Nothing that spoke of her love of reading and writing. Nor her charity work. None of the black and white movies she loved. Watching Cary Grant as he tried to wrangle his serial killing family in Arsenic and Old Lace was what had turned her on to writing murder mysteries. She loved the twists and turns in the movie and the many layers the characters presented.

But Rafe knew none of that about her.

Here was the warmth, joy, and family she had always craved even if they weren't blood. Ellis, Seth, Matt, and Jessup had all come out. She had invited them the second she'd discovered that Matt only had his sister who was on a cruise. Jessup had no immediate family as he was raised by his grandmother, who had passed several years ago. Jessup and Matt usually took a trip or a cruise.

It was no way to spend the holidays.

So, Colby had put her foot down and told them they were expected at her house. Matt, Ellis, and Seth mixed seamlessly with Mac, Charlie, and Russell. And the laughter of the men going out to chop their own Christmas tree would be memorialized in one of her books.

They had left a roaring fire for her to enjoy, to which she added the peel of the orange she was in the process of snacking on.

Between bites, she and Jessup discussed her various business contracts. The movie deal took an hour to dig into. The television one was pretty standard. Then they tackled the smaller contracts regarding her latest books.

Jessup set the paperwork aside and took off his reading glasses. "I have some news."

"About Harold?" Worry tightened Colby's gut.

"No. It's Rafe . . ." Jessup cleared his throat as his fingers stroked across the arms of his glasses.

"Just spit it out."

"He and Chloe are done."

Surprise filled her, followed quickly by satisfaction as Colby rubbed her distended belly. The Braxton Hicks contractions helped keep her from chuckling with glee. "Do you know why?"

"I've heard a few rumors about him catching her cheating, but nothing concrete." Jessup set his glasses on top of the papers and picked up his lukewarm tea. "It would explain why he was asking about you a few weeks ago."

She shifted as a sharp pain grabbed hold of her back. Maybe it wasn't false labor? But the pain was gone as fast as it had snuck up on her.

"Christ, please tell me you aren't in labor." Jessup's face was drawn in a frown of worry. His gaze darted to the picture window as if looking for rescue.

"Not in real labor, just fake labor. And quit looking outside, you know the guys are going to be a bit longer getting that tree."

His heavy gaze landed back on her, and he sipped his tea.

"You think he wants me back?" Her heart lurched at that thought. *Do I want to go back to him? No, I love my new life.*

But if he were willing to move here? She didn't know. His harsh words and cavalier attitude, tossing her aside for Chloe, had sliced her to the bone. To top that off, she had no idea how enmeshed he was with Harold.

But no matter how many arguments she gave herself, her heart yearned for him. It was him she dreamed of each night, and his name on her lips the few times she had used her battery-operated boyfriend.

And though she tried to forget him, her mind continually circled back to him.

Maybe if she understood why he had turned on her, or why he went through with the contract in the first place. But she didn't have any of those answers. She still had two free burners and would only need one to contact him. But no matter how much she tried to justify calling him, she knew it was the wrong thing to do. At least for right now.

Not until the babies are safely born. Then I'll tackle Rafe and the tangled mess I ran from.

"I have no idea. But if you want, we can test the waters after we deal with Harold."

"I bet Chloe was screwing in their bed and Rafe came home early and caught them." Colby really shouldn't gloat or find so much joy in Rafe's pain. What could she say? She was human, and he had cut her deep, deeper than Harold and Megan combined. Elizabeth had given Rafe her heart, and he had ripped it from her chest and stomped on it. She hoped he felt half the pain she had.

"Quit gloating," Jessup smirked as he wagged an admonishing finger at her. Her friend knew her too well. "Like I said, I have no idea what actually happened, I just know they're over." His eyes brightened when the sound of the ATVs reached their ears. "Sounds like the men are back."

He helped Colby to her feet.

"I'll make the hot chocolate if you want to see if they need help getting the tree inside," she said. Jessup hurried to put his brand-new boots on. Colby chuckled. "I still can't believe you bought cowboy boots."

"This is a ranch. Of course I'm going to wear cowboy boots. I have to fit in," Jessup said, lifting his feet up one at a time so she could appreciate the boots. "Matt got them for me. They're gorgeous, right?"

"Just gorgeous." Colby shooed the exasperating man out the door and headed to the kitchen to make hot chocolate and gather the Christmas cookies she'd made yesterday.

They spent the afternoon and evening decorating the tree, eating popcorn, and watching Christmas movies. It didn't matter. With Christmas a week away, all her wishes were finally coming true. She had a new family, Rafe was getting payback, and she and her babies were safe. What more could she ask for?

Several hours later, Matt helped Colby up from the couch.

"Night, hon. We'll see you in the morning," Matt said as he released her.

It was impossible for her to get up from the couch in the den anymore without help. Thirty-seven weeks in and she was bigger than the barn outside. After hugging her guests goodnight, she waddled to the master bedroom in the back with Mac hovering like a mother hen. "I can do this, Mac."

"Let an old man help, Colby. It don't hurt you none, and it puts my mind at ease."

"Fine, but I draw the line at you coming in the bathroom with me."

"No worries, I'll settle right here." He pointed at the rocking chair tucked beneath the picture window and next to the large bassinet. "You said you've been getting pains all day. It might be that you've overdone it."

"Or I ate too much of that spicy dip you and Ellis made." Colby huffed in exasperation. "They're just false pains or indigestion, Mac. I'm not due for another three weeks at least. And all the books I read said the first one takes a while to even come out."

Closing the bathroom door, she shoved the toothbrush in her mouth and brushed, then cleaned up and got changed for bed. She flipped the bathroom light off, stepped into the bedroom, and shut the door. "Are you staying here or going to the bunkhouse?"

"Me and the boys are staying here. We're all keeping an eye on you."

"Great." She climbed into bed. The soft glow of the nightlight, which Mac had insisted on, reassured her that she could find her way to the bathroom without any trouble.

She snuggled into her massive bed. The king-sized monstrosity was entirely too big for her alone. But she had bought it with the picture of weekend cuddles with the twins dancing through her head.

It'd reminded her of her parents' bed where she'd felt safe and loved. She wanted the twins to have that same feeling, so she'd purchased it on the spot.

Mac tapped the doorjamb on his way out. "Night, Colby."

"Night, Mac." She sighed softly. "Thanks for taking care of me."

"That's what family does." His broad back disappeared into the blackness of the hallway.

~ ~ ~ ~

Colby felt like she hadn't closed her eyes. Squinting at the green numbers on her clock, she groaned. Two a.m. With a few grunts and an unladylike yelp, she scrabbled from the bed and waddled into the bathroom to pee for what felt like the fiftieth time that night. After washing her hands, she took a step to the door only to feel yet another sharp pain that wrapped around her entire abdomen. Before she could gasp her way through the false contraction, her water broke.

Clenching the side of the vanity, Colby took a deep breath and released a blood-curdling scream.

Loud thumps from next door reassured her that Mac had taken the daybed in the twin's nursery.

Her bedroom door banged open; she flinched, thinking of her abused wall, and wondered if it had a hole in it now. The bathroom door was the next to be wrenched open and filled with Mac's worried face.

"My water broke," she whimpered as another pain shot through her like a fiery wave.

Mac raced away, shouting for the others. Then
he was back with Jessup.

"Jessup, grab her bag from the closet. It's the
bright ass pink one."

Jessup chuckled as Mac helped her dress and
slide her shoes on.

"Where's Matt?" she asked.

"Gettin' your seat in the car ready." Mac guided
her out the door to the front porch. "The boys will
follow us—"

"They don't have to—"

"They're part of your family, so they're coming,"
Mac stated.

She reached Matt's side next to the SUV to see
a beach towel with a brightly smiling sun draped over a
garbage bag. "Thanks, Matt."

"My pleasure, hon. Now, up you go." Matt
gently lifted and deposited her into the seat.

She had forgotten that even though her water
broke, she would continue to leak fluid until the baby
was born, and no way would she ask Mac to put a pad
on her for the drive to the hospital. That would be too
embarrassing. Thank God Mac had remembered those
details and knew how to handle them. She would have
hated to ruin her brand-new SUV.

Mac climbed behind her with Jessup at the
wheel as they'd decided so Mac could help Colby focus.
Within a few minutes, everyone was buckled up and
headed down the road toward town and the hospital.

Between contractions and Mac's instructions to
breathe, Colby almost missed seeing the bright red
cloth lying half on the road. It wasn't until Jessup
swerved to keep from hitting it that she yelled, "Stop
the car!"

"You must be out of your ever-loving mind," Jessup growled.

"That was a body, Jess."

"I know, but I'm not stopping this damned car. Matt, call the boys and tell them to check it out," Jessup said.

"Jess—"

"No. If you were having one baby, then yes, I'd stop. But not with twins. And not when you're three weeks early."

Frowning, she did her best to breathe through the next pain. When it subsided, she asked, "What does it matter if I'm having one or two?"

"Because Mac could deliver one—"

"Excuse me?" Mac rumbled.

But Jessup talked over him. "I mean, he's delivered horses, cows, sheep, and a mule, so your baby wouldn't be any different."

"Did you just compare me to a bunch of barn animals?" Colby snarled, unable to believe the eloquent man driving had compared her to a bunch of animals. Then it dawned on her what animals he'd used. "Oh, my God. Did you compare me to a cow?" she screeched. "You're a damned attorney with more wins under your belt than Muhammad Ali, and you just compared me to a cow!"

Matt cleared his throat, and Colby swung her narrow-eyed gaze on him. "What? Are you going to defend him?"

"No, and quit shooting daggers at me with those eyes. I wanted to let you know the boys said they found the body. Charlie swears kid is about his age."

"Tell them to stay with him." Colby panted, working to push the words out between the pain.

"No, I told them to load him up and bring him to the hospital." Matt pinched the bridge of his nose. "The kid is still alive."

"Seriously?" Colby groaned as another pain hit her. Crap! The contractions were closer together than she'd thought. Gritting her teeth, she prayed she would not have babies in a damned car.

"Yes. I have no idea where he came from, and Seth said he only had on canvas tennis shoes and a hoodie. He'd been beaten to a pulp, and his hair had been cut off in clumps."

"Had to be King's ranch," Mac growled, rubbing Colby's shoulders. "Nothing else on this stretch of road but King's ranch. The Cutters are north of us going the opposite way from our place."

"I thought he only had his girl."

"Has foster kids. Charlie mentioned wanting to talk to Jessup about it while he was here," Mac rumbled.

"Why me?" Jessup asked. "I have nothing to do with foster kids."

"No, but Charlie said King takes 'em in for labor, and some of them are beat. But when the kids tell their social workers, no one believes them because King's a pillar of the community or some shit."

Jessup's fingers tightened on the leather steering wheel, causing it to creak under his grip. "I'll talk to Charlie, and if the kid makes it, I'll talk to him too. Then I'll tear King a new asshole if he's hurting kids."

Colby patted Jessup's shoulder before curling into herself with a loud groan. "We need to be at the hospital now. I need drugs because this shit hurts." She was wailing by the end and couldn't bring herself to care how much of a crybaby she sounded like.

Another contraction swallowed her as Jessup hit town. Focusing on Mac's voice, she made it through the other side and panted.

Finally, Jessup roared up to the Emergency Room door. While Matt and Mac helped Colby inside, Jessup pulled out to park.

Minutes, hours, or days later—Colby wasn't sure with no clock in the room—she pushed, grunted, and groaned her babies into existence. The pain was forgotten the second the precious bundles were laid in her arms. Dark hair coated the top of both babies' heads. "Mac, take one. I want to check their fingers and toes."

He grinned and lifted the baby wrapped in a yellow blanket while she kept the one wrapped in lavender.

The baby was immediately cooed over by her uncles. Big strapping men passing around the yellow wrapped bundle brought a smile to Colby's lips, and she wished she had a camera.

Just as the thought passed through her mind, a flash lit the room. Her gaze jumped to Ellis, and she laughed to see him snapping several pictures of Jessup, who couldn't do anything except scowl with the baby in his arms.

"What happened to the injured kid?" she asked.

Jessup gave the baby to Matt and sat in the chair next to her bed. "The kid was beat pretty badly—"

"How old?"

"Seventeen, and he was one of King's foster kids," Jessup growled.

"Was?" Mac asked, joining them.

"I put in for Colby to foster him and to get the others from King's custody, not to be returned until after they do an extensive investigation."

Curious, Colby looked up. "Do you know why he was beaten?"

"Again, this is hearsay, but Charlie said the kid told him that King's daughter took a shine to him—"

"Jesus, you don't have to say anything else." Colby yanked her messy ponytail.

King doted on his sixteen-year-old daughter and gave her whatever she wanted. Spoiled didn't begin to cover how utterly self-centered and narcissistic the teenager was. If she'd set her sights on one of the foster kids, then she'd basically aimed a missile at the kid. King would end anyone who even thought to touch his baby.

Shifting, Colby pushed the heels of her hands into her eyes. "If there are more kids who need placing, we'll take them, Jess. It's almost Christmas. I don't want a bunch of kids tossed into a group home with no thought."

"You just had your twins—"

"I don't give a shit. Russell, Charlie, and Mac will help me and you and Matt and the boys too. And if the kids are still there when you leave, I'll hire someone. I'm not having kids lose out on Christmas." She looked at the sleeping angel in her arms and thought about the babies losing their home just before the holidays. Her resolve firmed.

"I'll go see what's what now," Jessup said, stepping into the hallway with his cell in his hand.

"You know they won't just hand over the kids like that," Mac said, gently placing the sleeping baby in the bassinet labeled Baby One Harrison. As the sheet and label were in yellow, and the second bassinet held shades of the softest purple, she assumed the nurses had color-coded the twins to make it easier to tell them apart.

"With Jessup in the mix, they damned well will."

"King will have left some kind of trail. I don't think he expected the boy to live."

"Duh." Colby had to refrain from rolling her eyes. "Quite obviously he wanted the kid dead, and I'm so sick of all these pompous ass jerks doing whatever they—"

"It's time for Mommy to feed her little ones," a bright, cheery voice sang out ahead of the nurse who entered Colby's room.

Mac gripped Colby's shoulder. "You feed the girls. Me and the men will meet up with Jessup. We'll see what we can do to push things along. Or, if they're in a home already, we'll wrangle up some presents for them."

Before he could leave, she called out, "Mac."

"Yep."

"You okay with me saying you'd help?"

"Iff'n I wasn't, I'd have said so." He gave her a rare smile.

Colby tipped her head in thanks, and he stepped from the room. Then the nurse walked her through how to breastfeed her baby, and Colby lost herself in the sweet innocence of her newborns.

Chapter Eight

It took two days before the hospital released Colby and her girls. Two days for Jessup to set Colby up as a foster parent so Tanner could come and stay with them. Tanner was placed in the hospital room with Colby so she could keep an eye on him while he recovered. And when Colby left, Tanner was able to walk out with her and into their new family.

A soft tap on her door frame had her swinging toward the opening. Expecting to see Mac, she was surprised to find Tanner filling the doorway.

"Can I come in?" Black and blue marred every visible inch of his torso, and his cast-wrapped wrist cradled his ribs.

"Sure, but why are you up? Aren't you supposed to be taking it easy?" she lifted one of the girls from the bassinet before her fussing could turn into howls of discomfort.

"I needed a shower. But I couldn't re-wrap my ribs, so I followed the noise."

"Let me guess, everyone else is asleep," she said, snagging the pre-made bottle and heading for Tanner.

"Have a seat there." She pointed to the rocker. "You can feed one baby while I get the other."

"Still haven't named them yet?" he asked, settling into the chair she had indicated.

"Not yet." She knew what she wanted to name them, but Elizabeth wished she could ask Rafe. Shaking away the thought, she gently transferred the baby to the teenager. After showing him how to hold the baby correctly, she turned her attention to the other one. With both twins occupied, she met Tanner's gaze. "Besides your bandage, what else is going on?"

"I wanted to ask about Ricky and Becky. Do you know what happened to them?" Tanner ducked his head as if she would admonish him for checking up on the two kids.

"They're with a nice couple in town. By the way, I meant to ask Jessup, but with you here, I can just ask you. Are they twins?"

He snorted and shook his head. "No, siblings, but Becky's a year older."

"Okay, well, they're with the Petersons in town, and Mac and Jessup took over presents, so they'll have a nice Christmas."

"Thank you for looking after them."

"Known them long?"

"Nah, a month or so. King was gonna have them moved before spring because they were too young to do some of the heavier chores."

Colby bit her cheek to keep the snarl of rage from slipping past her lips. The baby she held helped calm her. She lifted the baby to her shoulder and rubbed her back until the little one let out a hellish burp. She quickly swapped the calm baby for Tanner's girl to do the same. "I know you didn't track me down just to ask about the kids from King's place. So, want to tell me what the real deal is?"

"I had an idea on how to catch Harold. But I wanted to see for myself what kind of person you were." He grimaced and ducked his head before snapping it up and meeting her gaze.

"And what kind of person am I?"

"You care. You could have told your men to screw off with Becky and Ricky. Or just let them do their own thing." He tipped his head from side to side. "But instead, you offered to help them. And all of them have nothing but good things to say about you."

"It seems my men gossip like a gaggle of hens." She frowned as she changed the baby's diaper. Then it hit her why he was sizing her up. "They told you *everything* about Harold?"

"Mac did, yeah. He felt if I was living here, I needed to know so I could keep an eye out." He tipped his chin up. "Besides, Harold can't be any worse than that asshole King is—"

"Language," she said.

"I'm almost eighteen." He puffed his chest up, then slumped back with a gasp.

"I don't care about your mouth, because you're almost an adult, but I won't be explaining to a kindergarten class what those curse words are. So, you'll watch it around the girls." Based on the information she'd received from Tanner's social worker, he would be eighteen in four months, so she didn't want to crack down on monitoring him. Besides, overall, he was a good kid. She knew because he cared about Becky and Ricky. He was proving he cared about her and her girls as well. And his hero worship of Mac was there for anyone to see as he tried to emulate the cantankerous man. Mac had seen it as well and gave Tanner one of his old cowboy hats and told him when he healed up, Mac would take the boy for some new boots.

"Oh," his eyes darted to the two babies. "Yeah, probably should start early so I don't screw it up when they do start to understand."

"Exactly, especially since Mac is counting on you to help come spring." She hid her smile by nuzzling her baby girl. When she had her mirth under control, she turned back to Tanner. "Swap with me again. I need to change her diaper."

After changing her, Colby placed both babies in the bassinet. Turning to Tanner, she picked up the elastic wrap and wound it around his midriff. *It wouldn't hurt to hear him out.* "Tell me your idea."

"Does the kid who opens the trust have to be yours?"

Confused, she tried to sort out what he meant. "Mine like how?"

"Like blood. Or can you adopt a kid and open the trust?"

She froze, the bandage dangling from her numb fingers.

"I mean, it's probably a stupid idea. It has to be your blood—"

"Not necessarily."

"So, if it doesn't, we could use me as—"

"Hell, no! I'm not using you as bait." Her mind rejected putting this kid in danger. He was already beat to hell, and even though she had said no to Jessup all those months ago, the idea was hard to shake loose. Everything in her said it was wrong to use a kid as bait, but she knew her babies were in danger the second Harold discovered their existence.

Tanner grabbed her shoulder with his good hand. "At least I have a chance to defend myself, or if kidnapped, I could figure out a way to escape or alert you where I am." He waved to the bassinet. "They wouldn't, and from what Mac said, this Harold guy is going to come. Maybe not today or tomorrow, but soon."

The words echoed Jessup's fear too. Everyone knew Harold wouldn't wait forever. She had been lucky he'd waited nine months. But he was getting restless. Colby felt it in her gut since she had been fielding calls daily from Megan. But Megan and Harold traveled between Christmas and New Year's Day, so Colby had until the first of the year to form a plan.

"I can do it, and if you're with me, we can do it." The weight in his eyes made him look older than his seventeen years. It spoke of strength and perseverance. "Talk to Jessup. Maybe we could take a security team to trap them."

How could this kid have come up with the same plan Jessup suggested when she had been scrambling to find another solution? "I'll talk to him."

"It might be mute anyway if the trust is for your blood kids."

"Moot," she corrected absently as she finished wrapping his chest.

"Huh? What the hell is moot?"

"Moot is the word you need, not mute. Mute means silent. Moot means that the subject is too uncertain to allow a decision."

"Oh." He grinned. "I didn't know that. I always thought it was mute. Cool. With you being an author, is what you say copyrighted like what you write?"

She had no idea where he was going with this as he seemed to hop subjects like a dog chasing after squirrels. "No, what I speak isn't copyrighted, why?"

"Because I can so use that to impress the ladies."

"Oh, God," she whimpered. "No ladies. You can impress the *young* ladies, but you are not to even side-eye anyone my age or older."

"I like you."

"Like me all you want but no romantic thoughts."

"Ew. I meant I like you as a sister, not as a girlfriend."

"Great, now is that tight enough?" She waited while he shifted around with the bandage on. Some days she felt older than dirt, but having Tanner and Charlie in her life reminded her to smile.

"Yep, seems good." He stood slowly.

"Though you do move like someone Mac's age," she teased, unable to help herself. He felt like her little brother, just as Charlie did. Mac had always felt more like a father figure. Russell was harder to pin down, as he was quiet and watchful, but Colby couldn't wait to get to know him enough for him to lower his guard. Instead of prodding him for information, Colby knew she would need to wait for Russell to open up and give her his trust. Luckily, she had a wealth of patience.

"Ew." He wore the most disgusted expression with his lips pursed and nose scrunched up. "I'll show you how young and spry I am when I'm cleared—Oh, God, I used spry. Mac uses that." He made gagging noises. "I sound like an old person. Quick, say something cool."

"The square root of pi is—"

"No." He tipped his head to the side, and his stomach growled. "Now, I want pie."

She huffed in exasperation. "Go get a slice of apple pie. It's in the fridge. Then go to bed." She didn't sound assertive at all, but hopefully, it would come before the girls grew older. Otherwise, they would run all over her.

She shut the door behind Tanner and turned the overhead off. The only illumination was a nightlight near the girls. Propping her shoulder on the wall, she watched the girls sleep. There were so many men in her life willing to help her, protect her, but the one man her heart yearned for didn't want her.

Her gaze landed on the bedside clock. Three hours until another feeding. She hurried over and flipped the lock on her door so she wouldn't be disturbed.

Her blood pounded in her veins as she trudged to her closet. It was a mistake. It had been a mistake the second she'd added the items to her packing boxes. But tonight, of all nights, she deserved to feel loved. In that first month, Rafe had doted on her. Colby wanted to believe that back then he'd even loved her a little.

She dragged the plastic container from the back of the closet and raised the lid. Three shirts, each in their own sealed bag to preserve the cologne she'd sprayed on them before leaving Rafe's house. What had possessed her to do it, she hadn't a clue. But she had needed something of his because as much as he hated her at the end—she had loved him. Still loved him, truth be told.

She took the T-shirt with the tech logo emblazoned across the front. The shirt was a garish green with white writing, and Rafe had worn it when he met up with friends to play basketball. It was the softest of the three and the most worn with a hole in the left armpit. The hem on the bottom of the shirt was falling apart.

Pressing her nose to the material, tears filled her eyes when she smelled his crisp aftershave. Rafe rarely wore cologne, but he used a crisp winter scent daily. Pine mixed with something that made her imagine a tundra full of snow and ice. Locking the plastic lid back into place, she stood with the green shirt and headed for her bed.

With a few tugs and a hard shove, she had a pillow filling the shirt. She laid it in the spot she wished Rafe had wanted and made her way to her side of the bed. Climbing onto the king-sized bed, she wiggled until she was snuggled against the pillow, her face smashed against the shirt. *I'm pathetic, wanting love from a man who screwed around on me and who only married me because of a damned contract.*

Frustrated, Colby rolled onto her back.

Jessup said he asked about me. But why? Too bad Rafe's mother interrupted before he could find out.

Maybe that was Colby's opening. Rafe had already discovered Chloe's dark side and left her. It could be he realized everything he ever needed could be found in Colby.

I doubt I'm that lucky. She ran a hand across the soft shirt. *And what, Colby? Do you think he's going to want you back after Harold spun so many lies? Will Rafe even believe you if you tell him you had no clue about the contract?*

Giving in to her desire, she rolled onto her side and opened the nightstand drawer. She didn't know what had made her move the two unused burners to her bedroom, but now she wouldn't wake anyone up taking a trip to her office. Her fingers traced the smooth surface. She snatched one up before she changed her mind.

Screw it. I need to hear his voice, especially after delivering his daughters.

Not that she would ever tell him that, but still. And she still needed to figure out names for the girls. Maybe the conversation would spark an idea.

She turned it on and dialed Rafe's number from memory.

"Rafe Martinez."

His smooth as whiskey voice made her close her eyes as so many erotic memories crashed through her.

"Hello?"

Jerking upright, she forced the memories away. "Rafe?"

"Elizabeth?"

"Yes," she bit off through gritted teeth as she barely remembered not to correct her name.

"Why are you calling me?" Defeat resonated through the line. "To gloat?"

"Hell, no!" She flinched at how harsh that had come out. "Sorry, no, I didn't call to gloat. I called to check on you."

A beat of silence followed that held so many feelings Colby almost ended the call.

"Why?"

"Because I care."

His answering snort was filled with derision. "If you cared, you wouldn't have done the same damned thing Chloe did."

"Cheat?" She gasped. "You think I cheated on you?"

But he didn't seem to hear her as he continued, "You know, when we became engaged, I thought 'Okay, the contract doesn't mean anything. It's just Elizabeth and Harold's way of ensuring her family line continues.' And hell, I got my grandfather's cabin out of it. But you couldn't even wait until we were married before you spread your legs—"

"What?!" she shouted only to quiet when one of the babies released a grumble. "What are you talking about?"

"Seriously? You're going to pretend you were faithful our entire marriage?"

She didn't have to pretend. She had been faithful. It was Rafe who had Chloe. Instead of pointing that out, she snarled. "Pot meet kettle."

"Oh, I was never unfaithful. Especially, not on our wedding day."

"What's that supposed to mean?"

"It means I have a picture of a disheveled waiter leaving your suite just before you walked down the aisle."

Disheveled waiter? Pinching the bridge of her nose, Colby struggled to keep her emotions in check. "You mean Armand?"

"Yes."

"First, he was the caterer, not a waiter—"

"And that makes it better?"

"Second, he wasn't disheveled because of me. He and the wedding planner are together, so they probably had a moment while I was changing my pantyhose." She remembered losing her mind because her pantyhose got caught in something of Marisol's. What? Colby had no idea. Then her backup pair hadn't been the right color, and Marisol had left to get help. Next thing Colby knew, the wedding planner was there calling Armand, asking him to get the emergency kit from their car. A few minutes later, she had a new set of hose in her hand and was pushed into the dressing room.

His sarcastic laugh was filled with acid before he snarled, "You expect me to believe that?"

"Nope. Just like I don't believe you when you claim you never slept with Chloe." Though a nugget of doubt had always been there because Rafe had never lied to her.

"Screw you, Liz." He snarled like an enraged beast. "I never cheated. I started seeing Chloe a month before I pushed for the divorce."

"Sorry." She smoothed her hand across his T-shirt and allowed him to calm down. If he thought Colby had cheated on him and then actually caught Chloe cheating, he had to be devastated. "I wondered."

"Yeah, well, we never did anything. It would have violated the agreement, and I'm not spineless and weak enough to lose my grandfather's cabin."

"So, who put you on to Armand?"

"My mother . . ."

Colby didn't hear anything else as the puzzle of how her and Rafe's marriage fell apart was laid bare. And wasn't that a blow? Not just Harold working against them with the contract but Marisol as well. Colby could see that now, looking back. Marisol had always been the one Rafe confided in and had lurked in the shadows, dripping her poison into his ear.

To say Marisol Martinez hated Colby would be an understatement. Hate wasn't a strong enough word. Loathe came closer as did despise. Colby was just beginning to see the utter destruction the woman had wreaked in Rafe's and Colby's lives.

"Right." She rubbed her throbbing temple. "Wait, was this the cabin you and your father used to meet your grandfather at to have men's weekends of fishing and stuff?"

"Yes, and the same one I lived in the year after my father was killed. Grandfather homeschooled me and helped me get my head on straight by taking me to counseling every week for almost a year."

Goosebumps blanketed her skin, and she shivered. *How had Harold gotten a hold of the one property that would push Rafe into that damned contract?*

"So, yeah, the cabin was pretty special."

"Your father's name was Juan, right?"

"Yes, but he went by John when handling business."

"And your grandfather?"

"Gabriel—"

"Is that why you're called Rafael, like a nod to him?"

"Yes." He released a deep sigh. "Why all the questions?"

"I don't know. We never talked about this stuff, and I guess I was just curious."

"More like you never had time to talk about this stuff."

She held the cell away from her ear and shook her head in disbelief before placing it back against her ear. "I had time to talk. You were always off gallivanting. The only times you made time to be with me were our nightly fucks. Did you make love to Chloe? Because you sure as hell didn't to me," she snarled.

"And whose fault is that?" he growled.

"Quite obviously, you think it was mine." She slammed out of bed and paced. "But let me tell you, it takes two people to tango, bud. And in our dance, I thought it was two, but came to find out it was a damned conga line."

"So I've been told, repeatedly."

She threw up her free hand. "What's that supposed to mean?"

"Exactly what you said. Our sex life apparently had a revolving door."

"Holy shit. There was more than Chloe?"

"There was only you, Liz. I thought even with that damned contract, we could build a life together. But I refuse to be one of many. I'm not made to share my woman."

"I never—"

"Save it. We both know you're a very adept liar. I mean, you were raised by Harold. So, to answer your question, Chloe and I are done. I touched base with Jessup to see if you were knocked up." His brittle tone made her wince.

"Nope, I'm not pregnant." Her gaze darted to the bassinet. *I'm not technically lying because I am no longer pregnant.* But the justification rang hollow as she soldiered through the painful call. *Why did I think this would be a good idea? The entire conversation is a minefield, and we both keep stepping on the mines.*

"Good, saves me from demanding a paternity test."

"Guess it does."

"Goodbye, Liz. Don't call me again."

The line cut off. Colby clutched the piece of plastic so hard it creaked in her hand.

Colby couldn't help but hear the underlying pain and devastation in Rafe's tone as he'd lashed out at her at the end. Like a wounded animal, he felt he needed to protect himself from her.

He'd never had to do that, not with her.

But now that Colby knew his mother had begun tearing them apart on their wedding day, Rafe wouldn't believe anything Colby said. It gutted her how much damage the woman had done.

With shaking hands, she popped the back of the cell and pulled the SIM card. Breaking it in half, she tossed it in the trash before pulling out the battery. After dumping the cell and battery in her purse so she could toss the items next time she was in town, she crawled back in bed. So many lies and so many people set against them from the start.

Should I even try to get him back after dealing with Harold and Megan? Something inside her refused to let him go. But to battle his mother's poisonous barbs that had formed deep roots after two years of careful cultivation, Colby wasn't sure she could rip them out. But maybe she could give Rafe the tools to kill the doubt himself. She didn't know how she would do it but damned if she wasn't stubborn enough to figure it out. With an imagination as thick as hers, Colby was sure she could come up with something. And if he chose Colby when he was free? It would be worth every bit of pain she felt now.

Chapter Nine

The sheer audacity of Elizabeth to claim she'd never cheated. Rafe slammed his cell on his desk. She was such a liar.

To even think he would sleep with Chloe with that contract in place was absurd. She knew if he cheated, it would void that contract forever, placing his grandfather's cabin out of his reach.

Too bad he hadn't thought to put the same damned leash on her.

But what if she's not lying?

A tiny voice of doubt niggled at him. He had trusted her until Harold had entered the picture. He shook his head; she had to be lying. If she wasn't, then Rafe was a total asshole.

I thought Chloe was faithful and trustworthy and look how that turned out. Could I have made a mistake? Damned woman is putting doubts into my head.

He flung open his office door, expecting to smell dinner. Instead, the house was cold, dark, and quiet. Too quiet.

Resolutely he headed for Rosa's apartment. Her door stood open, and he paused, brow furrowed in confusion at seeing her things packed up.

"What's going on?" He scraped a hand across the back of his neck.

"You dumped Chloe."

"Yes? But what's that got to do with you packing all your things?"

Red tinged Rosa's olive complexion. "She's the only reason I took this job."

Wait. "What?"

"Chloe is a saint that just needs a firm hand to curb her rambunctious spirit." Spinning to face him, Rosa jabbed a finger in his face. "Your ex, on the other hand, was a gold digger who needed to be cut out of your life."

"Cut from my life? How?" With sickening horror, Rafe stumbled away from the angry woman.

"By any means necessary." Rosa's angry hands flew around her the angrier she grew. "Elizabeth didn't even go with you to any of your charity events. My girl always made time for you. Mine."

"Chloe's your daughter?" Was that why Rosa made sure to tell him every time Elizabeth cheated? Or had *any means necessary* meant she'd stretched the truth?

"She might as well be mine. I raised her while her parents were off gallivanting around the world. I was the one who thought you two would be perfect for each other, and your mother agreed."

"My mother?" Rafe shook his head, unsure what his mother had to do with any of this. "And Elizabeth?"

"Never left the house. She was a homebody. I tripped over her every time I turned around." Rosa sneered. "I hated it; a woman so undeserving of living in the home that belonged to my Chloe."

"You're saying she never cheated?" Rafe asked, disbelief tearing through him.

"No, she did not, but you sure believed she did after I gave you pictures of her out to dinner with a few men and receipts from intimate restaurant dinners." Rosa smirked. "Did you ever smell another man's cologne anywhere in the house? Did you ever find masculine clothing that was overlooked but not yours?" She leaned in and added the sharpest jab. "And did the neighbors ever comment about all the strange cars parked overnight?"

Gutted. He was absolutely gutted as the truth was hammered home. How could he not have known?

A malicious twist of Rosa's lips turned her expression sinister. "You were so easy to manipulate because you wanted to believe the worst of her. She's Harold's daughter after all, who wouldn't? When you were gone on your business trips, she moped about the house. And she slept in your bed. It was the only time she broke the rule of not entering your room. You didn't want the truth with her. You hated her, and your mother hated her." Rosa's gleeful smile turned Rafe's stomach.

"My mother?" Rafe's entire body was numb as the betrayal tore into his heart. His only living relative had paired him with this viper?

"She's the one who convinced me to work for you. She's the one who wanted Chloe for you, but you were already with Elizabeth." Rosa paced toward him. "I wanted you for Chloe too, so your mother came up with a brilliant plan to make sure you didn't stay married to Elizabeth."

"You?" he asked hoarsely, reeling from his mother's betrayal.

"No, the cheating. It was all lies we told you in order to make sure you never fully accepted Elizabeth. So when that contract was over, you wouldn't go back to the bitch."

"Out! Get out of my house." With a roar, Rafe yanked her suitcases up and threw them into the hallway where they landed with a loud crash against the wall. "You're fired!"

"Please. I quit." She swung a bag across her chest. After grabbing the handles of the two large suitcases in the hallway, she sauntered toward the front door with Rafe dogging her heels.

He blocked the front door and invaded her space. Nerves showed in the fluttering pulse at the base of her neck as Rafe bared his teeth in rage. "If you spread any of your lies about my mother setting all this in motion, I'll spread some myself."

"Like what?" Rosa lifted her hand and rubbed the base of her neck.

"How you stole from me." He straightened and shrugged. "I mean, if you can lie and have my mother believing it, then I'm sure I can spread just as many lies and have everyone believing it."

"Chloe's family will defend me—"

"No, they really won't." He slid his thumb across his cell and opened the video he'd taken of Chloe. "Your precious Chloe will throw you to the wolves."

Rosa's eyes widened then turned frosty as they narrowed on him. "I won't say anything, not because of your threats, but because it would upset Chloe."

"Tell yourself whatever you want, lady, just get the hell off my property."

She stormed past him and out of the house.

Slamming the door, Rafe turned and punched the wall. Plaster crumbled to pieces as he yanked his fist from the hole. Blood and scratches dotted his knuckles, but he didn't feel them. Lies. He had believed all the lies.

He pressed his back to the wall and slid down to the floor, the pain in his heart more pronounced than the throb in his hand.

Why had he believed them? Was it because Harold had gotten involved? Or was it a flaw in Rafe's own character that he would automatically believe the worst in Elizabeth? Even his mother had been involved, the woman he'd trusted above all others since his father was murdered. She had helped tear his marriage apart as if Rafe's feelings meant nothing. Had she done it on purpose, or had she been as duped as Rafe?

Standing, he raced back to his office and snatched up his landline. His finger hovered over the unknown number Elizabeth had called from before hanging up the headset.

After all the things he said, he doubted she would believe his apology now. Falling into his chair, he cradled his head in his palms. He needed a plan to win her back. He had been his happiest with her until others started whispering doubts in his ear. If she truly didn't want him, he would find a way to move on, but if there was even a sliver of a chance, he wanted to grasp it.

Picking his cell up, he conferenced Tristan and Jackson.

"This had better be good, Rafe," Jackson grumbled. "We're in the middle of a horse giving birth."

"I screwed up big time, and I need you two to help me dig myself out of it." Wincing, Rafe soldiered on.

"Oh, Christ, I have bail money," Tristan muttered. "But I'm in Chicago, so it's going to take me a bit to get there.'

"I haven't been arrested, but thanks for the confidence."

"If it's not bail money, then what else do you need." Jackson chimed in.

Rafe laid everything he'd learned on his best friends. When he was done, he waited.

"So, what do you want us to do?" Jackson, ever the blunt one, asked. His job as Sheriff had made it to where he knew which questions would lead to the heart of the problem.

The silence was deafening as Rafe waited, for what he didn't know. Maybe for one of them to side with him and his mother. Rafe cleared his throat.

"Not sure what you want us to say here, Rafe?"

"I just can't believe Rosa convinced my mother Elizabeth cheated on me."

"Seriously? You believe Rosa fooled your mother?" Jackson asked.

"I don't understand."

"Did you not just hear what you told us?"

Rafe tapped his finger against his desk as he tried to organize his thoughts.

"With how long you're taking to answer me, I'm going with no," Jackson said in his blunt way. "Look, I love you like a brother, but you gotta listen to people when they actually tell you something."

"You mean when Rosa said my mother set the whole thing up?"

"Yes."

"She loves me." Rafe huffed a breath as he tried to wrap his mind around his mother deceiving him on purpose.

"Maybe, but she's also a cold-hearted, calculating manipulator," Jackson stated, raising Rafe's hackles in the process.

"Bullshit! She's just protective of me," Rafe shouted, his temper—already on a slow burn after dealing with Rosa—spiking at hearing Jackson's assessment of Marisol.

"Jacks, Rafe, look you two need to—"

"No, he needs to hear the truth, Tristan. Your mother loves herself. You were her golden boy. The only thing you ever rebelled on was Tristan and me, and trust me when I say if I didn't think of you as my brother, I would have dropped you like Obama dropped that mic."

Rafe fell silent as he remembered all the slights and slurs his mother had thrown at his two friends. How she always tried to steer him away from inviting them to his parties.

"And I'm gonna tell you something else you're not gonna like hearing, so you'd better sit your scrawny ass down," Jackson snarled. "I think your mom set my parents up to kill your dad."

"What?" Rafe's voice was barely a hoarse whisper before red hot rage poured into him, and he stood, his hand rolling into a fist. "Take that back!"

"No," Jackson said, his voice soft but deadly serious.

"Jesus, Jacks, now? You feel like now was the time to open that can of snakes?"

"Worms, Tris. The word you're looking for is worms," Jacks teased, though an edge of sharpness skated around his tone.

"Nope, I used the word I wanted to. Snakes. Between your parents and Marisol, that whole statement was filled with snakes."

"Jesus, Tris, you too?" Rafe rubbed a hand over his heart as the two men he called brother stabbed him.

"Sorry, but after hearing Jackson and Ray talk, I have to say I think your mother orchestrated it." Tristan sighed. "You know she's ruthless."

But not toward Rafe. And as much as he loved his mother, his father had been his world. They had to be wrong.

"Look, your dad was leaving your mom. And she wouldn't have gotten a dime based on the prenup they signed," Jackson's voice cut through Rafe's doubts. "My parents pulled that trigger, no doubt, but they were con artists, not killers. They claimed your dad was going to turn them in. My mom told me years later when I was curious as to why they killed him. She swears your dad brought the gun. To top that off, your mother was in the room tossing gasoline on the fire of their argument. Mr. Martinez picked up the phone to call the cops, and my dad picked up the gun and shot him."

"But he was cheating on her."

"He was. With a super nice lady that Ray interviewed. Then the lady was gone. The money your dad had was supposed to go to you, but your mom somehow circumvented the will and ended up with the money. And while you were at your granddad's house for that year, she liquidated everything. The house, your dad's vintage car collection, your dad's rare books, pocket watches, and so on."

"I didn't know that." He slumped back into his chair, the fight draining from him as the truth was slapped in his face. How could he have not known that? "Do you have any proof she was actually there?" His mother had maintained she had never been in the house when his dad was killed. If she had, she could have stopped it. "You never saw her in the house, did you?"

"No."

"So maybe she wasn't there."

"Technically, I only saw my parents in the house. I mean," Jackson huffed. "By the time I got to the kitchen and got your parents' housekeeper to come to your dad's study, no one was there."

"Exactly."

"Look, with the thin evidence they had and me as a witness, my dad only got manslaughter and my mom an accomplice. But I'm telling you, your mother was there. As for you not knowing your mother was capable of that? You were a kid who'd just lost his dad in the most violent way possible. Of course you never suspected your mother to be in on it." Jackson sighed. "I gotta say, I looked into it when I made detective, but your mom's good at hiding her tracks, and she had you sign away your rights to your father's money when you hit eighteen."

"I thought that was just papers to swap out brokerage houses." Rafe ran a shaky hand over his mouth in shock.

"Probably not," Tristan said. "If she consolidated it, all she would need was your signature either as Power of Attorney to act on your behalf or just having you sign it directly to her."

"Holy shit." *My own mother played me.* In his heart, he knew what Tristan and Jackson said was the truth when he looked back through the years. "What do I do?"

"What do you want to do?" Jackson asked.

"I don't give a shit about the money." He hated that he didn't have much in the way of his father's things. Looking around, he was glad his grandfather had put his father's furniture from the study, as well as a few odds and ends he'd thought Rafe would like, into storage before his mother got to them. Rafe remembered the vintage car collection. His dad had loved the old cars, but it was the pocket watches that Rafe was enamored with. He had wondered where they had gone, but his mother had put him off, claiming he was too young to have them. Eventually, he had forgotten about them.

"Okay, so you don't want to try to wrestle the money from your mother. Then what do you want?" Jackson asked in exasperation. "Because they need me to help feed the other animals while the horse gives birth."

"I want to win Elizabeth back." His mother didn't matter in the grand scheme of things. If she really had a hand in breaking him and Elizabeth up, then Rafe would find out and confront her. If she didn't, and wanted to be part of their lives, then Rafe would need to talk to her about his dad and how things had shaken out.

But he was sick of the secrets and lies that seemed to litter his life like so much garbage on the roadside.

"All right, bro! I'm proud of you for finally getting your head out of your ass," Jackson shouted down the line. "I liked Elizabeth, as you know. And I'm a damned good judge of character."

"Christ, Jacks." Tristan groaned. "Maybe instead of encouraging him with Elizabeth, we should set him up with someone else, because getting her back is gonna be close to impossible."

"Nah, just challenging," Jackson said. "Challenging, he can do. You know Rafe loves a good challenge."

"Really? Let's review what he just told us," Tristan growled. "Rafe basically left her for another woman. Another woman who ended up actually being the cheater. And then he asked Elizabeth if he was a baby daddy all in one conversation while also accusing her of sleeping around, calling her a liar, and wanting a paternity test. Did I miss anything?"

Rafe cringed at how horrible he sounded when Tristan boiled down the facts.

"No, you nailed it. Though, to be fair, sleeping around, the paternity test, and baby daddy can be grouped under one umbrella," Jackson said helpfully.

"That's what you got from my statement?" Tristan groaned. "You're a cop for Chrissake, and that's what you walked away with?"

"Well, you're an attorney, so I'd think you would want to make sure you had the facts correct."

"Guys," Rafe tried to interrupt, but Jackson was on a roll.

"Yes, but he didn't kill anyone, she didn't kill anyone, and there aren't any innocents getting dragged into the middle so they can start fresh. See, so it can be fixed." Jackson all but crowed near the end.

"Maybe. Rafe, let me and Jackson think about it, and we'll get back to you with some ideas. But don't call her." Tristan ordered. "No half-assed phone apology is going to cover this, and I have no idea if they have flowers that cover 'Sorry, I thought you were a whore. My bad.' No flower language would come close to touching that one I don't think."

"I agree with Tris, you're going to need to go big or go home," Jackson said.

"Hey, you told your wife you loved her and used her twin sister's name by accident when you did it. So, no throwing stones at me," Rafe teased, feeling more stable with his friends in his corner.

"Luckily, my wife is a forgiving woman with a heart as big as her damn animal sanctuary. Otherwise, I'd probably be at your place crying in my Fruit Loops."

"More like crying in *my* Fruit Loops, but okay. If you guys think of something, let me know."

He ended the call, still wrapping his mind around his mother's possible betrayal and Elizabeth's possible innocence.

There was one way he could definitely know if she'd cheated. Megan, Elizabeth's best friend, never pulled her punches. She would know who the men were in the photos Rafe had been sent, and she would tell him straight out if Elizabeth had slept around or not. Because she didn't care if Rafe's feelings were hurt. She only cared about Elizabeth, and with them being divorced, Megan wouldn't have any reason to lie.

With his friends willing to help him figure out how to mend the rift his assholishness had caused, Rafe had a chance. And since Elizabeth had called him, even though he'd been a grade-A ass, it gave him hope that she would be open to at least hearing his apology.

~ ~ ~ ~

Rafe scanned the coffee shop until he found Megan tucked in the back corner. Her copper-colored hair drew many an admiring gaze, which she ignored for her cell phone. She was dressed in a flowing navy pants suit with simple gold jewelry to match. Classy and elegant. With any other woman, Rafe would take a second and third look, but there had always been something that set his teeth on edge about Megan. He had written it off as slotting her into the category of Elizabeth's best friend, thus making her off-limits. But now that he was single, Megan still gave off that same odd vibe. One that gave him a shiver down his spine.

Catching her attention, he joined the line and placed his order. He took his coffee and muffin to the table and sat across from Megan.

"Thanks for meeting me." Rafe hated being indebted to this woman, but he wanted answers more than he wanted to keep his distance. With his mother abroad, he was unable to confront her about the pictures. And he needed to know if Rosa had been lying about Elizabeth the entire time before he tried to mend any fences with her.

Which was why he had reached out to Megan. Of everyone in Elizabeth's circle of friends, Megan was the one she regularly turned to for advice and to keep her secrets. Not that the woman did a good job, considering how much Harold knew about Rafe's and Elizabeth's sex life, but that might have been Elizabeth making sure the stipulations of the contract were met.

"I have to say, your voicemail was both unexpected and cryptic. Otherwise, I wouldn't be here," Megan said, icy disdain clear in her dark eyes. "The very last thing I ever expected was to receive a call from my best friend's ex asking me to meet him for coffee."

"Then why did you come?" Rafe asked.

"Curiosity." Megan wagged a finger between them. "But don't think I won't tell Elizabeth the second we talk."

"And Harold?"

"Pfft. As if I'd give that man the time of day. I only play nice with him to make things easier on Elizabeth."

"You know where Elizabeth is?" Relief flooded into him at hearing Megan didn't like Harold any more than he did.

"Of course, she's in Alaska." Megan all but rolled her eyes at him. "And you don't need to waste your time trying to get back in her good graces. After the whole Chloe debacle, Elizabeth wouldn't have you if you were dipped in dark chocolate and laid out for her pleasure."

"Only my sperm." Elizabeth was keeping secrets from her friend. Then again, after Rafe shot her down in a fiery fashion, he doubted she would want to share the humiliation with anyone. He was surprised she hadn't vented about it with her best friend though. Rafe would count himself lucky in this instance if it gave him the information he needed to make a decision.

Megan shrugged. "She's always wanted your children—no idea why, but there you are. I didn't say she was exactly sane during the divorce. The sperm is her guarantee to have the baby that was promised her."

"It doesn't matter. She has my sperm, but that's not why I asked to meet." Rafe shook his head and flicked a finger against the side of his cup.

"Then, why?"

"Do you know if Elizabeth ever cheated on me?"

"No."

"No, you don't know, or no, she never cheated."

"The latter," Megan answered.

He just couldn't believe he had been that wrong, but Megan had no reason to lie. At least not about this. Which meant Rosa really had lied. But did his mother know Rosa had lied? Or was his mother clueless and only snapped pictures of Elizabeth during seemingly intimate dates thinking she was doing Rafe a favor? His gut said Jackson and Tristan were right in their suspicions, but his heart had taken too many hits to give up on his mom. The second his mother returned home, Rafe planned on asking her. She couldn't keep up the pretense if he was looking into her eyes.

"You're saying she never cheated?"

"Not on you. At least as far as I know. Why would she? She loved you. Otherwise, she wouldn't have asked for your sperm." Megan leaned forward and tapped the table. "She only wanted your children."

"But the contract?"

"Was a ham-handed way to keep you." She shrugged one shoulder. "Not saying it was a good plan, but she only ever wanted you."

Rafe shifted his empty cup from one hand to the next as he mulled over what Megan had shared with him.

He flipped his cell over on the table and opened up the pictures his mother had shot him. "She seems awfully familiar with this guy." He enlarged it and slid it across the table toward Megan. "She's touching the guy's chest, and his arm is wrapped around her waist as she's laughing up at him." He tapped the screen.

Megan's gaze narrowed on the image. "I've never seen him before."

"How is that possible if you're her friend?"

She pushed the cell back at him. "I'm not her damned keeper, Rafe."

"Well, where is she? I want to ask her these questions."

"Like I told you before, she's in Alaska."

"Wait, you were serious about that? It's the dead of winter up there." Why would Elizabeth go to Alaska of all places?

"Yes, I'm serious. Why would I lie about that? Here, I'll prove it to you." Megan flipped her own phone over and swiped through several screens before holding it up for Rafe. "See? Barrow, Alaska."

"Like the vampire movie?"

"How the hell would I know? I don't watch horror. But she's been there since you dumped her, licking her wounds."

Rafe wanted to ask the woman how she knew the vampire movie was a horror but decided it wasn't important. "How are you tracking her? Isn't that illegal?"

"Hardly." She snorted. "We track each other in case we're nearby and want to grab lunch together."

"Oh, so she knows you can track her?"

"Of course, just like she can track me." Megan waved her hand between them as if it were nothing to be able to keep tabs on her friend.

Rafe shuddered. He wouldn't like someone keeping tabs on him. His gaze dropped to the ring Megan fiddled with, and he tried to remember if he had seen an announcement. When he drew a blank, he pointed to the ring. "Secret engagement?"

Megan jolted; her gaze dropped as her face flushed. "Oh, this?" She lifted her hand and flashed a large, emerald-cut diamond.

"Yes." Rafe leaned in for a better look.

"Oh, no, no engagement. This was my grandmother's, and it's a total knockoff."

"It's gorgeous." Rafe knew jewelry, had invested in two shops on the east coast. The diamond and sapphires she was flashing were not fakes. And the ring was strangely familiar.

"Thanks." Megan wrapped her fingers around her cup. "Everyone who sees it assumes I'm engaged to Harold."

Harold was not where his mind had gone. However, now that she mentioned the man, Rafe was curious and decided to poke. "You two attend a lot of social events together."

"God, yes," she chuckled. "But it's work. At least for us. I keep the sharks from circling him, and he keeps the assholes from getting close to me. It lets us both make the connections we need for business without the pesky questions about dates." She laughed again while rubbing the ring.

"I understand perfectly, and Elizabeth hated attending the events, so my mother usually went with me." Rafe tried not to appear as if he were scrutinizing Megan's ring, but he could swear it had graced Elizabeth's mother's hand years ago. It looked like the same setting Lillian had worn. It even had the three sapphires on either side like a triangle.

It had been a gorgeous piece and very distinctive, though he'd only seen Lillian wear it a few times. More than a little unsettled, Rafe discreetly snapped a quick photo of the ring.

"Well, I'm empty." Megan lightly shook her empty cup. "And I have another appointment I'm going to be late if I don't leave."

"I'll toss that for you, go on. I'd hate for you to be late." Rafe stood and took Megan's cup from her.

"Thanks," Megan patted Rafe's arm as she passed him.

Then she was gone, leaving him with more questions than answers. If he were speaking to Elizabeth, he would have shot her the picture of the ring and asked if it was her mother's, but he was sticking to Tristan's edict not to call her up for a half-assed apology. And a flimsy excuse would probably go over about as well as a fart contest at Christmas dinner.

Instead, Rafe checked the picture, and though it was a bit blurry, he could still make out the ring. With a nod, he saved the picture. His curiosity would probably be the death of him.

Chapter Ten

Colby pressed the button to turn the coffee maker on and began digging out the honey and milk she added to her coffee. She would need the entire pot after spending all day at the airport yesterday. But as Jessup continually reminded her, the movie execs were hot for her story now. She needed to meet with them as well as bait the trap for Harold and Megan. To do that, she had to be in California, so here she was.

Everything was in the same place it had been when she'd lived with Matt and Jessup for all those months. Or more like hid, terrified Harold would guess at her pregnancy. Not that she'd showed, but paranoia and protectiveness of the lives inside her had kept her living below the radar back then. So far under the radar she hadn't even gone to a doctor until she had settled into her new home.

But she wasn't pregnant any longer, and now it was time to deal with Harold. The plan to use Tanner as bait was solid. But that didn't mean she wasn't worried about the young man as much as she worried about her newborns. Were they still called newborns if they were three weeks old? She made a mental note to look that up as she poured her first cup of coffee.

Checking the time, she took the burner with
Hank's name on it and headed for the French doors,
stepping through onto the top tier of the multi-level
deck. She pulled her sweater tighter around her as her
house shoes slapped across the wood. When she
reached her goal of the small seating area near the grill,
she plunked down on the cushy black couch that sat
under a pretty slat ceiling with a large paddle fan in the
middle of it. This oasis near the cooking area was one
of her favorite places. The other was the swing on the
deck below. After setting her coffee on the large arm of
the lounge, she flipped open the burner and selected
the only contact programmed into it.

She sipped her coffee as she waited for Hank to
answer.

"Why are you in California?"

Colby grinned as the blunt man bypassed all
pleasantries and went right for the jugular. "I've come
for Harold."

"Oh. Do you need me to come?"

"No."

"You still using the kid as bait?"

"The kid has a name."

"Whatever."

"Yes, I'm still using him as bait. Jess and I will
go to meet the lawyer to release the trust—"

"Oh, that's gonna piss Harold right off."

"I know," she couldn't help the broad smile that
pulled across her face. *If only I could be a fly on that wall.*

"For an opening gambit, that's a good one.
Subtle, as you won't be the one announcing it to him,
and it'll give you a bit of time to get to Alaska and set
up."

"We're using the team I told you about." She took a sip of her coffee.

"Good. I didn't find any flags on them." He cleared his throat. "I saw you headed to California when I checked in on you yesterday, and since you don't need me . . ." He cleared his throat again.

She realized it was a nervous gesture and froze, unsure what was coming.

"Look, I'm at the ranch," he blurted.

"My ranch?"

Why is he at my ranch? She stood, ready to race inside and pack.

"Yes. I figured I'd keep an eye out."

"Are you on the ranch? Do you need me to talk to Mac?" She could picture Mac tying Hank up until he got answers as to why a stranger was nosing around. Those would be Mac's words.

"No. I'm not going to be running into any of the men unless there's trouble. I'm camping and shifting my camp around each day, so I can take it all in. I figured with the team in Alaska you didn't need me, but if Harold came here, then this group might."

"Thank you." She fell back into the chair, the liquid in her mug sloshing over the sides.

"You're a friend. I have few of those and will always take care to keep the ones I do have alive and well."

For the first time since leaving her babies behind, she felt like she could breathe. Mac and the men could more than handle trouble if it came calling, but Hank added a layer of security. Because if Harold somehow got his grubby hands on the twins, Mac might hesitate to shoot the man in case he hit a baby instead.

Hank wouldn't hesitate. He would pull the trigger, and as Casey always bragged about how his brother never missed, Hank would damn sure hit what he was aiming at.

"Just knowing you're watching over my girls will give me the peace of mind to stay focused on our end of the trap."

"Good," Hank said. "I've got this. Now, go make your bait look appetizing so we can get this over with. I'd like to see your ranch up close and not through my sniper scope."

He ended the call as abruptly as he'd answered it, but Colby didn't care. He was watching over her girls. All she had to worry about was herself and Tanner.

She closed the cell and grabbed the napkins from the drawer built into the coffee table.

"Who were you talking to?"

She yelped in surprise and almost spilled the rest of her coffee. Scowling, she mopped up what she had spilled before facing Matt.

He fell onto the couch next to her with his own coffee and, with a grin, took a loud slurp.

"Stop that!" She shuddered at the sound.

"Are you going to answer me?"

"Not if you're drinking your coffee like that, no. I'm going to leave you out here to bother the birds." She made to stand up and smiled when he gave a hefty sigh.

"Fine, no more slurping my coffee as long as you answer my questions."

"That's just wrong."

He smiled and shrugged.

"Fine, I was talking to a friend who's keeping tabs on where Harold is to see if our plan today works."

"Lord, tell me he's not going to your ranch too." Matt plunked his coffee on top of the coffee table and half-turned to face her with his ankle propped under his butt.

"Nope, not going to the ranch." She chuckled. "If another person shows up, Mac's liable to kill me."

"Or hurt himself tripping over all those guys that are already there watching the angels."

She tipped her chin in acknowledgment even as her conscience twinged at the half-truth. Hank technically wasn't on the ranch; he was just hovering around it. And it was true that he was keeping tabs on Harold's movements. Hiding her face in her mug, she drank her now-cool coffee.

"After this is over, are you going to tell Rafe about the girls?"

Choking as the liquid went down the wrong pipe, Colby hastily set the coffee on the table.

Matt was there in seconds, pounding on her back. "Sorry."

When she could finally breathe again, she waved him off. "I don't know."

"It's no secret that you love him, Col." He nudged her shoulder as he picked his mug back up to take a drink.

"Elizabeth. You have to use that name here, Matt. We can't screw this up."

"Sorry," he mumbled into his mug.

"The thing is," she huffed and grabbed her own mug so she would have something to keep her hands busy. Not that she would drink her now-cold coffee. She shuddered at the thought before leaning her head on Matt's shoulder. "I never stopped loving Rafe. But—"

"No, no buts."

"But he has been fed a lot of lies, and it's not like I can go up to him and say 'Hey, I never knew about the contract. Nor did I know your housekeeper fed you a bunch of crap about a revolving door to my bedroom.'" She rubbed her cheek on his shoulder. It hurt even now that Rafe believed those lies and hadn't spent time with her to form his own opinion. "With so many people telling him one thing and only me telling him another, it's like a whisper at a heavy metal concert. No one ever hears the whisper. They only hear the screaming and emotions from everyone around them."

"How can you still love him, though?" Matt plunked his cheek against the crown of her head. "After that phone call, you should hate his guts."

"No, I was pissed at him, but that phone call shed so much light on why he acted the way he did while we were married. Harold and the contract explained the rest." She shook her head as the memories rushed to the forefront. They didn't cut as deeply as they had in the beginning.

"I still can't believe they never thought to ask you if you were on birth control." Matt chuckled.

"Yeah, I didn't want to get preggers right out of the gate. I wanted to savor married life but after ten months it felt right. We both wanted a family." She spun the sliver of liquid around in the bottom of her cup around. "If I'd had any inkling of the contract, I would have never gotten pregnant."

"Yeah, but then you wouldn't have had those precious angels."

That was true. She loved those girls to the bottom of her soul.

"After Harold and Megan are taken care of, I'll go with you to talk to Rafe."

Colby bit her cheek to keep from smiling as she imagined her overprotective friend giving Rafe hell.

"Tell me about him."

"Not much to tell," she said, though there were a thousand little things she remembered about Rafe.

"Well, I know he's gorgeous."

"Matthew!" She gasped.

"Married, not dead. So, the beginning was different?"

"Oh, yes." She felt her smile stretch across her face at the memories that sprang to mind of that first month.

"Tell me."

She set her mug back on the table and turned to face Matt with her ankle tucked under her rear. "Okay, there was this one time he planned a picnic. He knew I loved daisies . . ."

She could still see that field he'd found in the
woods an hour drive from her home with Harold. The
sunlight had danced in the meadow and shone on
Rafe's dark hair. She had always called it black, and it
was, but there were threads of a deep red and brown in
the color. His shoulder-length hair had enchanted her
as she pictured a rogue pirate carrying her off to the
field to have his way with her. Unfortunately, he didn't,
though she wouldn't have stopped him.

"He took you to a field of daisies to eat?" Matt
sighed. "That's so romantic . . . wait." His brow pulled
into a deep V. "At your wedding, there weren't any
daisies."

"No. Megan and Harold planned that fiasco,
and there was no way a common plant was being put
anywhere in that over-the-top event. Harold said, 'I'm
not having some weed in these photos, Elizabeth.
They're going to be in the society pages, and we are not
hillbillies no matter what state you and your mother
came from.'"

"Jesus, he's a pompous ass."

"Hmmm." She couldn't refute that, but another
memory popped up, and she bounced on the couch to
draw Matt's attention. "Oh, and he took me to a few
musicals."

"Musicals? Willingly?" He wrinkled his nose and
puckered his lips in disgust.

"Not like opera. Like musicals. We saw *Cats*,
and that show *Wicked*." He had taken her to four of
them before Harold came into the picture. "Miss Saigon
was another."

The fourth was precious to her as it had been one her mother had loved. *Les Misérables.* Even now, the memory of sharing that with Rafe brought a sheen of tears to her eyes. She quickly looked down to hide the emotions.

"I love those kinds of musicals. But my favorites aren't usually on tours," Matt said.

Curious, she darted her gaze up to see him looking off into the distance. Not that there was much to see. The second tier of the deck held a small area they used as a dance floor, while on the opposite end was a swing with a few Adirondack chairs surrounding it. The bottom layer held the pool with a few shallow steps into their minuscule yard. Because their backyard was set on a hill, Jessup and Matt had had a designer come out to give them some ideas. The decks were the best design of all of them, and Colby had to agree, they were stunning but also welcoming.

"There must be a story there." She nudged him when he didn't finish.

"Jessup wooed me with DVDs of my favorites." He shook his head. "We couldn't afford musicals and such back then. He was paying off student loans, and I was working at the truck rental place with my uncle."

"Did he watch them with you?"

"Oh, yes. His favorite is *Oklahoma!* and *Meet me in St. Louis.*"

She bounced. "How about *Seven Brides for Seven Brothers?*"

Matt laughed. "Looks like we need to have a marathon."

"It's a deal." She hadn't met many people who loved the old musicals as much as she did. Most reverted to the *Wizard of Oz* or another famous one. Not many could name the lesser-known ones.

"By the way, Jessup and I were talking last night, and we were wondering what you thought of us moving to your town."

"Wait . . . what?" Shocked, she searched his face to see if he was joking with her but found only a pair of serious brown eyes staring back. "Oh, my God. Yes!"

He beamed. "Really?"

"Hell, yes!" She shouted, doing a mental fist pump at the prospect of having all her family nearby. Then it dawned on her what Jessup and Matt would be giving up, and she frowned at her friend. "But why? I thought Jessup was getting that promotion, and you own your own business."

He sighed and looked into his empty mug as if it would give him the answers.

"Matt?"

"A store owner was killed in a robbery gone bad last November. It was just a few blocks from me but could easily have been me if I had been open." He ran a hand through his hair. "And Jessup found out the promotion would entail even more hours of work and travel."

"He's barely home now."

"I know," he said in a soft tone. "It's not like we need the money. And Jessup loved helping Tanner last month—"

"Tanner loved sticking it to King, so that's a win-win for both of them."

"Exactly." Matt turned to face her; his arm propped across the back of the couch. "Mac said the attorney in town is ready to retire. Less hours, close to you, Seth is making noises that when he finishes his veterinarian degree, he wants to come work for you. Hell, even Ellis is talking about taking over the business piece so Mac can focus on the stock."

"So, all your family will be there."

He grabbed her hand in a tight grip. "Yes, and we want to come. I want to travel with my husband and spend time together while we're both healthy and can enjoy it."

"I think it's the best idea ever," Colby said. "You can stay with us until we find you a place. Or we can build something on the ranch . . ." She trailed off, imagining having those she now claimed as her family close to her and had to keep from rushing inside to help them start packing.

He laughed.

"What?"

"I was worried."

She tipped her head to the side.

"That you wouldn't necessarily want us there full time."

She jumped to her feet and slammed her hands on her hips as she scowled at the man she had adopted as her brother. "Screw you, Matt. Just for that, you're staying in the bunkhouse while I keep Jessup in my guest room."

"Now, Colby—"

"Elizabeth, dammit, and you gotta earn your way out of the bunkhouse."

Jessup's deep laugh drew their attention.

Colby snagged her mug from the table, and as she walked past Jessup, she pointed to Matt. "You need to do something about your man, Jess."

She darted inside with a squeal when Matt lunged for her. After dropping her mug off in the dishwasher, she hurried down the hall to her bedroom to get ready for her day. Even though today would be nerve-wracking, the beginning had been the best she'd had in a while. Especially if Jess and Matt really did move to her neck of the woods.

Now, she just needed to make sure she lived to see it.

Chapter Eleven

Rafe pulled open the door to his favorite Italian restaurant, ready to grab his to-go order and get home. The investors' meeting went longer than he'd anticipated, and he was more than ready for food, a beer, and the last half of the basketball game.

He automatically scanned the restaurant, always aware that his investors liked to be noticed while out and about. However, it wasn't an investor that caught his eye. It was Elizabeth. He froze halfway to the bar to pick up his order. His gaze narrowed on the man next to her. It was the man in the photos his mother had sent him.

Then his gaze caught on the man across from her. Jessup?

Was he on a double date with Elizabeth?

Rafe shook himself from his stupor and snapped a quick picture with his phone and shot Megan a text.

R: Look who's in town.

His cell chimed with a reply in seconds as he waited for his to-go order to be made.

M: Where are you?

Elizabeth and her group stood. Jessup made a comment that drew laughter from everyone as they gathered coats, purses, and briefcases. The man Elizabeth was closest to replied, drawing another round of chuckles, and Rafe took one more picture, curious as to who the man and woman were. Pocketing his cell, he hurried to the bar so as to not be seen by the group. Settled at the bar, Rafe responded to Megan's text.

 R: Picking up dinner at Antonia's. You see it's the same guy as before, right?

He and Megan had bonded over Rafe wanting to win Elizabeth back after he'd explained what Rosa had confessed and told her about all the rumors surrounding Elizabeth. Megan had finally understood what had prompted him moving on to Chloe. When Rafe had asked about the cheating rumors, Megan had no more of an idea of who had started them as Rafe.

What she did want was mini-Elizabeths to spoil, so she had hopped on board helping Rafe. There had been several conference calls between his friends and Megan before they had come up with a few scenarios depending on how receptive Elizabeth was to his apology.

 M: I see that. What are you going to do?

 R: No idea. I thought you would have given me a heads-up that she's in town.

He had counted on Megan knowing when Elizabeth would arrive and helping him separate her from Harold.

 M: I didn't know.

 Shit.

 R: What should I do? She's leaving.

Just as he typed it, the buzzer he had been given after placing his order flashed red and rattled next to him. He hopped up from the barstool, shoved several bills toward the bartender, grabbed his sack that held containers of food, and waved the change off before leaving.

As he headed for his car, he saw Elizabeth slide behind the driver's seat of a dark-colored rental. The bright yellow sticker of the rental company was easily seen on the lower left side of the windshield.

M: If she's alone, follow her and see what hotel she's staying at, then do what we planned. Get flowers, get the sweets, and then beg on bended knee for her to forgive you.

R: Okay.

M: I'll message her and find out what she's doing in town.

R: No, wait a few hours. Otherwise, she'll wonder if I hit you up first.

M: Good idea. You've got an hour.

Rafe chuckled as he set the containers of food in the passenger seat before responding.

R: Need longer than a damn hour to follow her in this traffic, then go and buy the stuff. Make it four hours.

M: Three.

R: Fine.

M: And no sex.

Like she needed to say that. Rafe wasn't stupid. He needed to prove to Elizabeth he was sorry, and then they could build up to the sex part again. First, he needed to regain her trust.

He would just follow the plan and pray it worked out. With that thought firmly in the forefront of his mind, he followed Elizabeth.

Starting his car, he fell in behind Elizabeth's sedan. It took twenty minutes before she turned into a circular drive with a colonial-style house set back from the street. He wasn't expecting her to go to someone's home.

Maybe she didn't have the money for a hotel. It wasn't outside the realm of possibility since Rafe had been the one to support her. And Harold had financed Elizabeth's spending before Rafe.

Everyone knew Elizabeth's father squandered her inheritance. She and her mother lived on the allowance Harold provided.

During the divorce, Rafe had briefly wondered why Elizabeth didn't press for alimony. He hadn't dwelled on it, too focused on getting the divorce finalized. Now, he worried Harold hadn't remembered to add her back to his accounts. If not, Elizabeth might have needed to stay with friends.

He drove past the house and down one more block before pulling into a random driveway and keying in the nearest grocery store. It being close to nine at night, he knew better than to look for an open florist shop. With the address of the nearest grocery entered into his GPS, he started his trip.

Travel in California was never quick. It took Rafe almost two hours to drive to the store, get the items he needed, and make the trek back to the house Elizabeth was in. Unsure if his takeout was toast or if he could salvage it, Rafe slid his hand through the plastic handles before grabbing the bouquet of daisies and the box of chocolate-covered cherries.

He closed his car door with his hip and headed for the front door. Within seconds of pressing the doorbell, the bright red door opened and Rafe's jaw hit the ground. "Jessup?"

"Christ, you must be the little bird."

"Dammit. I asked Megan to give me a few hours—"

"A few hours for what?" Elizabeth's soft voice asked from behind Jessup.

Jessup stepped to the side, and Rafe had his first view of Elizabeth since the divorce. She was adorable with her brown hair in a loose knot at the top of her head. A few unruly tendrils were loose and curled around her neck. He drank her in like a man dying of thirst finding an oasis. Blue and burgundy sleep pants hung on her hips, and a familiar long-sleeved navy shirt covered her torso, its baggy material tied in a small knot on the side of her hip. A sliver of skin between the shirt and the pants drew his attention. He remembered every inch of her soft skin. He craved to remap all of it and claim it as his, only this time it would be permanent. Once he had her in his arms again, he would never let her go.

"Is that my shirt?"

Her arms wrapped around her stomach, and her left foot came to rest on top of her right foot. The coral-painted tips matched her nails as he raised his gaze to tangle with hers. She shrugged, and the stretched-out neck of the shirt shifted to show part of her collarbone. "It is. Do you want it back?"

Remembering the flowers and box of chocolates, Rafe shoved them toward her.

"For me?"

"No, I mean, yes . . ." He huffed out an exasperated breath as he organized his thoughts. "No, I don't want the shirt back, and yes, the daisies are for you. As are the chocolates."

She lifted the box and grinned. "Dark chocolate cherries, my favorite."

Jessup clapped him on the shoulder and pulled Rafe across the threshold into the house. "Now you can tell us why Elizabeth is getting texts from Megan and how she knew where Elizabeth was earlier."

Rafe followed Jessup and Elizabeth deeper into the house, only to stop in the doorway, unsure if he should join them at the white-washed table near a pair of French doors or if he should use the kitchen to his right and see if his food was salvageable.

The decision was taken out of his hands when a man with a brush cut took the sack of food.

"I'm Matt."

"Rafe." Rafe pointed to the sack in Matt's hand. "I saw Elizabeth at Antonia's when I went in to grab dinner. Which is probably ruined by now."

"Meh. If it had seafood, then I'd say yes." Matt peeked into the containers and smiled. "But as Antonia would have sent the order to you fresh, and lasagna is pretty forgiving, I think it'll be okay. Especially since it's cold tonight." Matt moved around the kitchen, efficiently pulling out a pan and tipping the lasagna into it. Then he shoved it into the oven.

"That's good because I'm starving. I haven't eaten since ten this morning," Rafe replied, leaning against the big island that separated the kitchen from the rest of the open room.

While the man bustled around the kitchen, Rafe took in the rest of their home.

A fireplace with a comfortable-looking seating area was to the left, and the dining area was straight ahead, just in front of pretty, French doors. To the right was a hallway with a staircase at the end. Rafe usually preferred Mediterranean colors, but the gray, white, and black in this large room felt relaxing. Rafe attributed it to the family pictures of Jessup and Matt hanging from the walls. The couple radiated love as they were photographed at different vacation spots, sometimes alone and sometimes with two boys. But in all of them, they were smiling or laughing, except the one above the fireplace. In that one, they were dressed in monochrome tuxes, Jessup in black and Matt in white with a breathtaking view of the sea behind them. It looked to be from their wedding day.

So that wasn't a double date earlier.

Rafe wished he and Elizabeth had had something like the picture above their fireplace.

"I didn't know you and Megan were close," Elizabeth said, jerking Rafe from his perusal of the room.

"We're not, or weren't." He sighed and scratched the back of his neck. He hadn't felt this awkward since asking Suzanne Milner to their high school prom.

Elizabeth's chuckle made Rafe smile in return, and he moved to sit next to her at the pretty, white-washed plank table.

"I've never seen you nervous," she said before taking a sip from her wineglass.

"Never been this nervous." He shrugged.

"Why are you?"

"Nervous?"

"Yes." Her effervescent glow lit her from the inside and brought home everything that had been wrong toward the end of their marriage.

Neither of them had been happy at the end, but with Harold out of the picture, maybe they could find the happiness they had begun their relationship with. It had been a year since Rafe had laid eyes on her, and the impact she'd had on him the first time he had seen her slammed into him. Rafe thought he'd imagined his visceral reaction to her, but now he had to face reality.

He was in love with his ex-wife.

A hand landed on his shoulder, and Rafe bit back a surprised curse as he was caught staring at Elizabeth.

His gaze bounced around the room to land on Jessup's smirking face as Matt plunked a plate of steaming lasagna in front of Rafe.

"Ignore them," she said.

"Kind of hard to," Rafe teased. Then he sobered as he met her gaze and took her hand in his. "I'm not nervous because of them. God, Liz, I'm nervous because I owe you a huge apology."

She shook her head.

"Yes, I do—" Before he could finish, her cell buzzed, and her attention dropped to it. The smile that graced her lips slid into a frown as her brow pinched with worry.

Elizabeth glanced at her cell and winced. "It's Megan again."

"Gee, I wonder why she's calling," Matt said sarcastically as he scowled at Rafe. "You really stirred up a hornet's nest this time."

"Aren't you going to answer it?"

Elizabeth looked to Jessup as if seeking reassurance.

"We have a plan, so go for it."

Why do they need a plan to talk to Megan? And why is Elizabeth looking at Jessup to back her up? Rafe felt as if he had stepped into the middle of a play and the director was demanding his lines when he didn't even have a script.

Her cell quieted as it rolled over to voicemail before it started trilling again.

Jessup turned a sharp gaze on Rafe. "Don't say a word, just sit there quietly until we're done, and we'll fill you in after."

Rafe arched a brow, not liking being ordered around without a good reason.

"I'm serious. If you open your mouth, I'll have Matt toss you out on your ass and call the cops for stalking."

Seeing the seriousness in the man's gaze, Rafe mimed zipping his lips and locking them.

When Elizabeth's cell began trilling for the third time, she slapped the answer button and put the call on speaker. "Elizabeth."

"Jesus, I didn't think you'd ever pick up," Megan teased. "What took you so long?"

"I had it on vibrate for a meeting."

"Oh, is that what you're calling your dates now?"

"What dates?"

"The one you were on tonight."

"Who told you I was on a date?"

"A little birdy. The same one who told me you were in town. Which means we can hook up for lunch tomorr—"

"Whatever little vulture is spreading all those rumors, there isn't any way I can meet you tomorrow. I didn't tell anyone I was hitting town because I only planned to stay just long enough to get things squared away."

"Like?" Megan asked.

"Well, I'm not supposed to share anything since nothing is finalized." Elizabeth grinned broadly, but the smile never reached her eyes, nor did it stretch across her face in true happiness. Rafe had seen Elizabeth's many expressions but never one quite like this. It was almost as if she were in pain.

"Who am I gonna tell?" Megan teased.

"Harold."

"Pfft. Not in this lifetime."

Rafe straightened, his body on alert when he heard Megan's nervousness. Was she lying? But that couldn't be true. Megan hated Harold. Didn't she?

"Well, you and he are close. You go to all those events together."

"Because I don't want to have to bring a date, but it's crass for a woman to go stag at those events, and since I use them to drum up clients, I have to go. And Harold is still mourning Lillian, so I'm a buffer for him."

"Oh, I didn't think about that—" Elizabeth rolled her eyes and mouthed, "yeah right."

What does Elizabeth know that I don't?

"Yeah." Megan released a startled gasp. "Oh, my God, are you pregnant? Is that why you came back? To use the sperm Rafe left?"

Rafe's mouth dropped open in shock. Was she pregnant?

"First, ew on using frozen sperm from an ex who was only married to me because of a contract. Yeah, that's how I want to bring a child into the world," Elizabeth snarked.

His heart jolted at her words.

"You know about the contract?" Megan asked, surprised.

Rafe's brows crawled up his forehead. To keep from blurting out questions, he shoved the last bite of lasagna in his mouth.

"I found out during the divorce." Elizabeth dragged the clip holding her hair out and ran her fingers through the loose strands. "I can't say I was happy about it. Why Harold would force the issue, I'll never understand."

Holy shit. She hadn't known about the contract?

Rafe bit back a snort of derision. *Of course she knows about the contract. She signed the damned thing.* He froze. Unless Harold had forged Elizabeth's signature. Ice slid through his veins at the thought. Surely, Harold wouldn't have been that stupid. Rafe wracked his brain, trying to remember if he and Elizabeth ever actually talked about the contract.

He came up with instances where she'd blown him off when he tried to broach the subject, sending him to Harold instead. Goosebumps broke out across his skin as he realized they had never actually mentioned specifics of the contract. Hell, they hadn't even been in the same room when it was hashed out and later signed.

The lasagna sat like a stone in his stomach the more he thought about the agreement. Every memory he had regarding the contract only had Harold in the picture, never Elizabeth. His gaze lifted from his empty plate and tangled with hers. Her sapphire orbs held so much betrayal, devastation, and pain; it was a wonder she could even lift her head. The myriad emotions swirling in her eyes gave Rafe his answer.

Elizabeth had had no idea about that contract until their divorce. And he had been the one to mention it to her. Christ, he owed her a bigger apology than he had ever realized—more than flowers and chocolates.

He tuned back into their conversation.

"Besides, wouldn't you rather get the sperm direct from the source, aka Rafe himself?" Megan taunted.

"I don't know. He was by earlier to apologize." Her gaze warmed with a light of forgiveness as she mouthed, "trust me."

"Of course," he mouthed back. What else could he say? He had to trust her because now that the blinders had been ripped from his eyes, he saw they were swimming in deep waters without a life raft in sight. Until he knew what the hell was going on, he would follow her lead. His gut told him she at least deserved that much.

"He's gone?" Megan asked.

Rafe opened his mouth to say no, but Matt slapped a hand over it and shook his head.

"Yes. He apologized and left. I have no idea why he felt the need, but whatever." Elizabeth huffed in exasperation. "It doesn't matter because we're through."

Rafe wanted to protest but caught a glint in her eyes that let him know she would explain later.

"Just calm down, we don't want you in the middle of the shitstorm unless you choose to be there," Matt whispered as he took his hand away from Rafe's mouth. "Remember, no sound."

Rafe nodded and tuned back into the conversation while his mind spun. *What shitstorm? And why would I be in the middle of it?*

"That's not why I'm in town," Elizabeth's tone brightened. "I'm adopting."

"You're what now?"

"I'm adopting. I met this kid in Alaska—"

"Who wants your money."

Money? Rafe felt as if he were in an alternate reality. Elizabeth didn't have any money, at least as far as Rafe knew. He'd supported her when they were married. Before they married, Harold had grudgingly paid for everything Elizabeth wanted or needed and complained about every penny. *Why would Megan think Elizabeth had money?*

"No. They only know me as a struggling writer up there." Elizabeth's hand trembled as she tucked her hair behind her ear. He laid his hand on the table, palm up, and sighed in relief when she laced her fingers with his. "But I helped put together Christmas for the kids in foster care, and Tanner and I clicked. That's why I'm here, to finalize everything with my books and meet with Philip to free up the trust."

"What trust?" Rafe mouthed.

Elizabeth shook her head and held up her palm, asking him to wait.

"Adoption opens the trust?" Megan asked. "Wait. You have the trust open?"

Something in her voice raised the hairs on the back of Rafe's neck.

"I do," Elizabeth said.

"You must be alone to even bring it up."

Elizabeth freed her hand and tucked her hair behind her ears again. A nervous habit Rafe had picked up on early in their relationship. She always did it when something big was bothering her.

"I am."

"Tanner didn't come with you?"

"He did not." She crossed her arms, tucking her hands tight against her sides when she caught him watching her.

"Why not? If he was with you, I could meet him, and we could show him the sights." Megan sighed dramatically. "I mean, with you having access to the trust, the sky's the limit."

"He was in a four-wheeler accident." Elizabeth relaxed enough to trace the wood grain with her fingers.

"Damn, that sucks. He's in the hospital?"

"No, he has a busted arm and some cracked ribs. But since his cast won't be off for another few weeks, I thought it would be better for him to hang out up there so we wouldn't have to change doctors and complicate his recovery when it's not needed. And I could come down here for a day and get the trust handled as well as hold a few meetings about my books."

"Then you'll bring him down here."

"No." Elizabeth's fingers moved her hair behind her ears again as nerves got the better of her. "I'm setting him up to homeschool so we can travel. As soon as he has his cast off, we'll be headed out on a cruise to visit the Hawaiian Islands, then go from there."

"But that means you're going to be up there like two weeks—"

"Maybe three at most."

Megan huffed. "And if something happens to you, then what happens to the kid?"

Elizabeth pumped her fists over her head as she grinned broadly. It was an odd reaction to have about what would happen if Elizabeth died. Rafe didn't like thinking of Elizabeth being hurt, let alone dead, and for Megan to just toss that out there made him want to snap at her. But Elizabeth was happy about it. Why?

In a calm voice that held none of the glee Rafe saw stamped all over Elizabeth's face, she replied, "I have you and Harold sharing custody. I mean, he'll be Tanner's grandfather, and you'll be his honorary aunt. And with Harold traveling so much, I thought it was a good idea to split the custody."

"And the trust?"

"Oh, that goes with Tanner's guardians, of course," Elizabeth said, still in a quiet and solemn voice at total odds with her bouncing in her chair.

Even Matt and Jessup were tossing thumbs up at her.

Weirdest conversation ever.

"You really aren't coming back here?"

"No. But we can meet up somewhere when you take your vacation," Elizabeth said.

"Then why were you on that date?"

"You keep mentioning a date, care to explain?" Elizabeth raised a brow at Rafe, but before he could dig the picture from his cell, her cell dinged. She grinned and shook her head. "That's Chauncey."

"Your literary agent?"

"Yes, one of the YA books I wrote is being looked at for a television series." She shrugged. "Probably won't come of anything since they're scoping several stories, but they wanted to meet and get a feel for my process."

Rafe hadn't known she was a writer. He knew she dabbled, but he had never heard that she'd actually published her work. Instead of releasing a whoop of congratulations, he shot her a thumbs up, and she beamed with pleasure.

"That's awesome." Megan cleared her throat. "So, the trust? How close was I when we made that bet? Because I feel in my gut, I won it."

"I did." Elizabeth smirked, and her gaze darted between Matt and Jessup as she mouthed, "Got her."

Matt mouthed back, "Too freaking easy."

"No shit," Megan's voice went out on her.

"It's close to a billion. I guessed seven hundred mill when we made that bet."

Rafe didn't hear anything after that. His ears were ringing as if someone had shoved his head between his legs. When he finally had his equilibrium, the hands left his back, and Matt returned to his seat next to Rafe.

"Almost a billion dollars?" Rafe asked in disbelief. His eyes popped as they dropped to Elizabeth's cell. "Sorry."

"Oh, the call is done. Megan pumped me for all the information she needed," Elizabeth answered with a grin. "And yes, almost a billion dollars."

He shook his head, unable to wrap his mind around that kind of money. He was glad he wasn't the one who had to deal with the nightmare of figuring all the taxes and stuff that went along with it. He raised his gaze and met Elizabeth's. "Why did you lie to Megan? I mean, you were so serious with her at the end but celebrating in reality."

And why hadn't he known Elizabeth was richer than Croesus?

Elizabeth leaned toward him, all happiness wiped from her face as she took his hand. "Because Megan and Harold plan to kill me for that trust, and now they have three weeks to get the job done before I'm gone."

Chapter Twelve

Rafe clutched the armrest in reflex as the private plane he and Elizabeth were on slung itself into the sky. He barely remembered the trip to the airport, let alone climbing onboard the jet. With only a few hours of sleep, he was happy to still be upright instead of passed out along the divan he had slumped onto the second he'd stepped into the Gulfstream.

I can't believe Harold had Lillian killed. He snorted, his mind grappling with everything Elizabeth and Jessup had told him after ending the call with Megan. *Hell, I guess I'll know it's the truth if someone comes to kill Elizabeth.*

"I guess you will," she said, moving around the small galley across from the seat he'd taken.

"Did I say that out loud?" Rafe released the armrest as his gaze bounced around the small plane.

Four more seats were arranged to the right of him with a walnut-colored table polished to a glossy sheen between them.

Only Rafe and Elizabeth were in the back, but he could see the two pilots through the archway that led to the plane's cockpit. No one had introduced him, not as far as Rafe could remember anyway, but the way both of them had moved as they loaded the plane, they felt like more than just pilots.

"You did." Elizabeth plunked a soda mixed with the strong scent of rum into the shallow cupholder built into the armrest Rafe still clutched.

Jesus, he hadn't spoken his thoughts out loud like that since his father had died. His therapist claimed shock had knocked his filters out. It figured it would happen this time too.

"It's just hard to imagine Megan willingly killing you for a trust. Harold? Sure, if he would actually get his hands dirty, but you and Megan are best friends."

"I think Megan and Harold were involved before Mom and I came on the scene." Elizabeth opened the small refrigerator and pulled out a bottle of water.

"That's disgusting if it's true. Hell, she was a kid." Rafe tried to imagine it but couldn't picture even Harold crossing that line.

"It is." Elizabeth tipped her head to the side as she turned to face him. "When we moved here, Megan was already a fixture, and I just gravitated to her. It seemed natural since her parents lived next door to Harold's old house. We stayed in that house for three months before mother found the home she wanted for us."

"Why would a teenager hang around an old man's house?"

"For the pool her parents didn't have, obviously," Elizabeth teased. "In all seriousness, I never questioned why Megan was there, and I don't remember asking my mother either."

He sipped his drink. The alcohol burned a trail of fire down his throat, snapping him from his dumbfounded state.

"Something must have clued Mom in because the money Harold took from her, she didn't care about that. But him hurting a child? That I can see her screaming to the heavens about."

"And you think that's what got her killed?"

"Maybe. I'm not Harold or Megan. But Mom knew about Harold's gambling and made allowances for it." Elizabeth shrugged, sliding into the seat next to him. "Hell, she set up an account just for Harold to use to gamble and left in the will stipulations for that specific account. When she died, it had millions sitting in it."

"I just can't imagine anyone doing that. And especially a teenager. I mean, it's Harold." Rafe shuddered with revulsion.

Elizabeth snorted and then burst into laughter.

"What?"

"If you don't look more than skin deep with Harold, you have to admit he's got the whole Richard Chamberlain sexiness going for him."

He dumped the rest of his drink down his throat at that comment and did a full-body shudder while jabbing a finger at her. "Just hearing that is going to give me nightmares."

She grinned and took a sip of water.

"He's not that good looking."

"No, to me, he's not. But to other women, he is," Elizabeth put the cap back on her water. "It's just a fact."

"Thank God we never had kids." He thought he caught her flinching, but the plane hit a pocket of turbulence, so he wrote it off as that.

"You didn't want kids?" she asked, her face an expressionless mask that Rafe couldn't penetrate.

"Of course I wanted kids. I'm just glad we don't have any that are in danger."

"Except Tanner."

"Yes, except Tanner." He narrowed his gaze, worried. "You did fill the kid in on what could happen, right?"

"I'm not heartless, nor would I ever let someone walk around with a target on their back without a heads-up." She rolled her eyes and slumped back in the seat.

"Good."

He was ready to be done with all the talking about Harold and his machinations. Now that they had the secrets unearthed, he was ready for more with her. He moved his drink and lifted the armrest keeping her from him. "Now, let's get back to what brought me to Jessup's in the first place." He slid closer and slipped his arm across the back of the divan.

"And what was that?" she teased, tipping her face up.

"My apology." He cupped her cheek. "What about us starting over?"

"And do you?" She arched a brow as a feral light came into her eyes. This close, he could see every shadow in their blue depths.

"What, want to start over?"

"Yes." She nuzzled into his palm.

He traced each of her features with his eyes. Her pink lips, the top a little fuller than the bottom. Her nose that tipped up at the end. The dark lashes that framed wide blue eyes set in a heart-shaped face that made her look so innocent. Did he want to start over? God, yes. Especially if they dug Harold out of their lives. His decision made; he ran his fingers down her arms to her hands. Even through the long-sleeved shirt, his fingers tingled with the need to feel her bare skin. "I want a second chance."

"Do you think I'll forgive you just like that?" She snapped fingers as she leaned toward him.

"Maybe we should kiss and make up." He followed the statement up by claiming her lips.

The spark that had always ignited into an inferno was right there the second he touched her. He wanted her. No other woman had ever drawn this much passion from him.

When they broke for air, his fingers brushed across her cheekbone. Unable to stop touching her, he tucked a strand of silky hair behind her ear. Searching her gaze for doubts, he breathed a sigh of relief when all he found was a want so deep it seemed etched into her soul.

Before he could gather her to him, she boldly straddled his lap, laid her arms across his shoulders, and claimed his lips. Unprepared for the move, her taste exploded on his tongue. The heat skating beneath his skin burst. Warm and soft became hot and frantic. Before he became lost in the maelstrom, he caught her gaze. "More?"

"God, yes." She delved her fingers in his hair and dragged his mouth back to hers with a mumbled, "Don't stop."

Rafe growled and slammed his lips across hers. Her surrender was effortless. The way her body slotted perfectly against his was like coming home. Her taste was as intoxicating now as he remembered. She tightened her thighs as she ground onto his erection. He cursed at the barriers keeping him from her heat.

Realizing he was losing control, he pushed her back, keeping a hold of her upper arms, and gave her a chance to stop. "We should slow down."

"No." Her fingers were busy working their way underneath the hem of his Henley, and she had it up and over his head before his brain caught up with her words.

"No?"

Her fingers raked across the skin of his chest, scoring it with light pink lines. Any mark she wanted to leave on him, he would wear with pride because it would mean she chose him. Chose to forgive him and give him a second chance.

She grinned before tugging her own shirt over her head and tossing it aside. He grabbed her waist to keep her from toppling back.

"No." She leaned in and sucked his bottom lip into her mouth. A siren wooing him into temptation, but if he caved, it would be a disaster.

He wanted to prove he was better than he had been while they were married.

Her teeth trailed down the front of his neck and
grazed his pulse, and he froze. He was so hard he
wanted to throw caution to the wind. A touch and he
would blow. As if sensing this, she cupped his erection
and gave it a firm tug through the denim.

"I'm going to woo you." He gritted his teeth
and pictured every disgusting thing he could think of
while carefully untangling her fingers from his hair and
his dick.

"Need you." She whimpered.

He hadn't planned on it going this far; he'd just
craved a taste of her. To feel their connection was
healing. His plan had been to get everything out on the
plane ride, to have all his questions answered. However,
their ever-present chemistry was clouding both their
minds.

Yanking her to him, he breathed into her ear.
"Do you want to get off, Elizabeth?"

"Yes." She shivered in his arms; her nails dug
into his back as she clung to him.

"And for this, you'll give me a second chance?
Date me?"

"If you can find me, yes."

He ignored the last statement, unsure what she
meant and unable to wait for a second longer to feel her
come apart in his arms. "Then it's a deal." He captured
her lips as he unbuttoned and unzipped her pants.

The zipper bit into the flesh of his hand as his
fingers delved into her underwear. Christ, the scent of
peaches, the sweet taste of her, and the feel of her
heated skin were exactly as he remembered. So many
memories of their time together bombarded him. Her
writhing beneath him, meeting his every stroke while
demanding more. Him teasing her until she begged to

be filled.

He used it all. The sensitive skin behind her left ear received a lick. Her ear was nibbled, all while he brought her closer to the edge. He dragged her bra from her and bent to suck her nipple into his mouth. She convulsed on his fingers, and he raised his head to watch her release.

The walls surrounding his fingers gripped him just as he knew they would grip his dick in the tightest of heat. Milk him repeatedly as he gave her the baby she craved. The thought of her rounded with his child drew forth his own release. With a guttural growl, he unloaded into his boxers.

Slumping bonelessly into the divan, he cursed his hormones. He hadn't come in his pants since he was a teenager, and the feeling was as uncomfortable now as it had been back then. It was going to be an unpleasant trip even if he cleaned them up. But the second he caught her blissful expression, he knew it was worth it. *To hold her in my arms again is worth any irritation I'll feel for the next twelve hours.*

Pressing a kiss to her lips, he smiled, lifted the fingers coated in her essence, and sucked them clean.

She sank against him, her weight a welcome armful.

Slow, exaggerated clapping caused Elizabeth to jerk away from him and fall onto the cabin floor with a thump.

"Got to say, I haven't had that good of a floor show since I visited Vegas," the female pilot said, leaning against the doorway between the cockpit and the main cabin.

"There's a floor show?" the male pilot asked, craning his head toward the back.

"Knock it off, Ken. Focus on the sky while I finally get a chance to pee." The woman's dark eyes narrowed on them as she strode past, headed to the back of the plane where the bathroom was located. "Next time you two want to get your freak on, use the bathroom like everybody else."

"They got their freak on, and you didn't tell me?" Ken asked as he tried to twist to face them again while being blocked by his big pilot seat.

Rafe growled.

"I'm just going to focus on the sky," Ken said, snapping forward and facing the front of the plane.

When Elizabeth stood, Rafe caught a brief flash of regret move across her face before it was smoothed over. If he hadn't been watching her so closely, he would have missed it.

Guilt wound into him. He hadn't even coughed up a solid apology before losing himself in her. "Regrets?"

"About this?" Her gaze caught his.

He nodded.

"No, because I missed you. And yes, because . . ." She tipped her head from side to side. "This was always easy for us."

"It's about the only thing that ever works in our relationship."

"We don't have a relationship, Rafe, that's what I'm trying to say. After that first month, we never dated unless it was to attend charity events, and even those stopped after we married." She snatched her bra from the divan and slipped into it.

"And whose fault is that?"

"The way you're acting, I'm going with mine, but I have no idea why you would think that."

Unwilling to be the only one half-dressed, Rafe grabbed his Henley from the back of the divan and slid it on.

A throat cleared just as Elizabeth's head popped through the hole of her long-sleeved navy-blue shirt.

"I don't want to hear fighting the entire trip, so I'm going to cut to the chase for both of you and then let you two work it out from there—"

Rafe held up a hand. "Sorry, but I don't want to take advice from someone I don't even know."

"I'm Kennedy, and that—" She pointed toward the cockpit. "—is my twin, Kenneth. Now, can I offer you two facts?"

"Yes," he retorted through gritted teeth, doubting the pint-sized co-pilot had any clue as to what was going on.

"First, Elizabeth, you remember Jessup had us hack into Harold's electronics?"

Rafe jerked his head up in shock. They were hackers? Jesus, did they even have a pilot's license?

"Yes, we have a pilot's license. Now shut up and let me talk."

Shaking his head, he headed for the galley to make another drink. He was going to need a few if more information bombs were about to drop.

"Elizabeth? Do you remember?" Kennedy pressed for an answer.

"I do, but what does that—"

"So, while I was sorting the emails, I came across one that Harold sent to his assistant, Edith. It was about her receiving duplicate invites from Rafe to you, and she was told to decline them all until the system was straightened out."

Son of a bitch. Rafe turned and leaned back against the counter.

"Declined? I don't understand."

"No worries. Rafe's put it together so he can explain. Now, it's your turn, Rafe." Kennedy tilted her head so her gaze caught his, and he subtly tipped his chin to let her know he understood. "You thought Elizabeth knew about that contract, the romantic getaways, and all the other things you set up." She leaned toward him. "Letting you in on a little secret, Megan was groomed to be Elizabeth's best friend, among other things. Megan loved to do anything and everything Elizabeth wanted to do." Pointing at both of them, she headed with a determined stride back to the cockpit. "If you two start arguing, I'll come back here and put you in a damned time out. I'm not listening to fighting for twelve fucking hours."

With that, she slid into the co-pilot's seat and slapped her headset on.

Rafe arched a brow.

"I should probably tell you that the two pilots are part of our security team." Elizabeth tucked her loose hair behind her ears before folding her hands over her stomach.

"Well, that explains how she would be able to follow through on the 'time out' threat," he said, snagging his drink.

"Yeah." Elizabeth chuckled. "What did she mean about dates being declined?"

Rafe set his drink into the shallow cup holder and headed toward their carry-on bags. His only held a laptop, his cell phone, and the few gym clothes he kept in the back of his SUV. But when they stopped in Anchorage to refuel and stock up on supplies, he would make use of his empty luggage and fill it with arctic gear. Palming a clean pair of underwear, he snagged his cell. Within a few swipes, he had his calendar pulled up. It showed the first three months of their marriage.

"Red means the appointment was declined and never rescheduled. Yellow means it was moved, and blue means a new appointment." He handed her the phone. "I'm going to the bathroom to clean up."

Rafe needed some space as he came to terms with this new information. Each time he uncovered some new subterfuge Harold had instigated to separate him and Elizabeth, it felt like another gut punch. It began to dawn on him that their relationship had been doomed from the beginning. However, now that Elizabeth was willing to give him another chance, Rafe refused to make the same mistakes. Openness and complete honesty would need to be their new mantra.

Quickly cleaning up and changing his underwear, Rafe returned to the main cabin and slipped his soiled briefs in the pocket of his bag before zipping it closed. Turning to Elizabeth, he saw she was still studying his phone as if it held every secret that hung between them.

Exhaustion beat at him as he snagged his drink, then took a seat next to her.

Her fingers trembled as she swiped through the days of their marriage. Rafe knew what she would find. A sea of red and yellow.

"I've gone through these twice now, and I don't see that I've actually received any invites. Are you sure you sent them?" She held out her own cell as she compared the calendars. "I mean, if Edith was declining because of duplicated—"

"Click the appointment on my end, hon, and it'll open to who it was sent to." Rage at how blind he had been ate at him.

Rafe had already pieced together what Kennedy had pointed out. There were no duplicate appointments. The oddities of their yearlong marriage finally fell into place. It didn't make him happy to learn that even this Harold had somehow tainted.

The dates he made had never posted to Elizabeth's calendar. Even their six-month anniversary had been screwed up because Harold had demanded Elizabeth's presence at some fundraiser. That one had been the last straw that closed his heart. He had planned a sunset sail with dinner in the harbor. It was something Elizabeth had mentioned wanting to do on their first date.

Now that Rafe looked back, he could see the pattern.

"There are over fifty requests," she whispered, her fingers tracing the screen of his cell.

"The first few months we were married, I rearranged my life to make room for you . . ." He took a hefty sip of his rum and coke as the overall picture he was putting together sent a chill down his spine. "They were isolating you."

"Looks like." Her tear-filled gaze tangled with his.

He had the urge to gather her in his arms and comfort her but stifled it as he wanted everything in the open first. "I just don't understand why your personal assistant helped Harold—"

"I don't have a personal assistant." A deep frown pulled across her face. "Why do you think I have one?"

"Edith. You introduced her as your assistant at our wedding."

"She's Harold's personal assistant." Her gaze dipped back to his cell once more before she handed it back to him and sprang from the couch to begin to pace. There wasn't that much space, and her motions were jerky and agitated as she swung from one side of the cabin to the other.

"I don't understand why he would try to keep us separated since he was on board with me marrying you."

Rafe wanted her near him so he patted the seat next to him. With each truth they unearthed, he saw there was no way their marriage had any chance to survive. But they were being given a second chance and he was damned well taking it.

Her hands tucked her hair behind her ears as she gnawed at her lip. "No, I need—"

"To sit. You're shaking and probably got as much sleep as I did last night," he teased. "Which was none, am I right?"

She nodded and slipped next to him on the divan. He stood and hurried to the galley to grab her a fresh bottle of water as they sorted out what the hell happened. Her hands trembled as they wrapped around the bottle.

"I'm just going to lay out what I think might
have happened, okay?"

Elizabeth shrugged and twisted the cap off her
water bottle with a snap. He took that as a yes.

"I think Harold groomed Megan from the get-
go, and when he brought Lillian home, he put you and
Megan together as cover."

"Sounds about right. Megan was just always
there."

"Right. So, he puts you two together and
probably tells Megan, 'Do whatever Elizabeth wants,
like whatever Elizabeth likes, and in the end, we'll be
rich and can run off to live happily ever after.' My bet is
Megan never turned down anything you wanted to do?"

"No, she was always up for whatever I wanted
to try. If I wanted to go on a cruise, Megan would
rearrange her schedule and immediately come with me."
Elizabeth laughed, but it was wet and held a lot of pain;
he wished he could take it from her. "I just thought I
was lucky to have a best friend who was always there."

"I know, and with it happening for years, it was
habit, so you never looked too closely at it." Rafe
wrapped his arm around her and pulled her into his
side, offering what comfort he could. "My guess is,
Harold knew about the trust from the beginning."

"Oh, Christ, I was there when she told him."
Her voice gave out as she huddled against him.

"What?"

"I was there, Rafe." Elizabeth swung to face him. "He was worried about supporting me if something happened to Mom. Which was insane, considering how much Mom was worth, but whatever. She told him he never had to worry about me or my kids since the trust my however many greats set up took care of us."

Ice flowed into him. "That means Megan knew going in, to not only befriend you but make sure you didn't form other attachments so it would only be she and Harold who would need to split the money. And if Harold made it to where I was done with you too . . ."

"No one would ever look into any accident I had."

Rafe took the bottle from her shaking hands and set it in the empty cup holder next to his.

"I would never have suspected them, Rafe. If I hadn't seen them together that night, I would be dead by now, and you would still hate me."

"Shh, okay, we're taking a break." He pressed a kiss to her temple and urged her to lie with him on the divan. "You know, I don't think I've heard any stories about your dad. How about telling me some of those?"

A yawn cracked Elizabeth's jaw, and Rafe smiled. "Maybe they can be bedtime stories."

"Okay."

He held her until her voice grew softer and was replaced with soft snores. When the tension left her body, he relaxed and followed her into sleep. Determined to find a way to make Harold pay, but more than that, Rafe wanted to make Elizabeth his again.

Chapter Thirteen

The heavy weight of an arm around her waist was disorienting as Elizabeth cracked her eyes open. She had never been cuddled before, but when she remembered who held her, a smile broke across her face. Memories from the last few days filled her even as excitement spiked inside at feeling Rafe at her back.

This was the third time she'd woken to him holding her, the nap on the plane being the first. Each time was etched into her memory, never to be forgotten. First on the plane, then at the hotel during the layover in Anchorage to outfit Rafe for the below-freezing weather in Barrow, and last night after they finally arrived in Barrow was the third time.

Her eyes adjusted to the half-dark of the bedroom, but she wished there was sunlight to see by instead of the nightlight tucked in the far corner of their room. To watch those first rays of sun caress the burnished gold of Rafe's skin would be a dream come true. But she was out of luck, at least for now. The sun wouldn't shine again in Barrow, Alaska, until the end of January, and she wasn't hanging around for that long. She missed her daughters too much.

Instead of dwelling on those two, Elizabeth focused on the man behind her.

He wanted a second chance, and she wanted to give it to him. But concern ate at her happiness as she wondered what would happen when he learned about their twins. Pushing the doubt from her mind, she focused on the present. She had made her choices, and she would take the fallout from them later. If she lost Rafe because of her decision, then she would cross that lonely bridge when she came to it.

At the moment, she had the man of her dreams behind her and no interruptions in sight. There was nothing stopping her from reveling in the feel of him. She needed to take every opportunity she was given to forge a strong bond. When this was over, maybe he would be willing to forgive her for the secrets she'd kept and uproot his life to come live on her ranch.

Wiggling back, she grinned at his morning wood pressing into her rear. She'd often wondered if Rafe experienced it. He had never sought her out in the mornings, so she had thought it was a myth found only in the romance books she read. Elizabeth grinned. There was something else she had been dying to try but never had a chance. Rafe had always maintained control every night of their marriage when he took her. As if he needed to drive her to the brink over and over to prove a point. A point she understood now as him being in charge in the bedroom since he hadn't been in control of much else between them.

Now it was her turn.

Closing her eyes, she inhaled Rafe's rich masculine scent. Without his usual products covering it up, his smell was intoxicating. She wriggled back until her back was plastered against his chest, pleased when his arm tightened around her. Even asleep, he was still aware of her. The way his hand curved around her waist felt protective, sheltering, as if he cherished her.

The blackout curtains were drawn tightly closed, a precaution in case their enemies arrived earlier than expected. Kennedy had suggested Elizabeth and Rafe take the guest bedroom instead of the master. The closed shades gave their room a cave-like feel, with only the glow of the nightlight casting the softest of shadows.

The faint light allowed her to see him in the darkness. With a few careful shifts, she finally faced Rafe's sleeping form. She took advantage and freely explored his body without interference.

Any time she'd tried to learn him, he had stopped her. Now, she had a chance to memorize each part of him—the defined ripples of his stomach and the sleek strength of his arms. She paused to admire it all. Checking that he still slept, she became braver.

Curious about how the varying textures would feel on her tongue, she leaned in for a taste. His masculine flavor burst on her tongue. Craving more, she gently urged him to his back and kicked the sheets and blankets to the bottom of the bed. With him sprawled out at her mercy, she took her fill of him. Unlike his friend Jackson, who was built along the lines of a defensive lineman, Rafe had a sleekly muscled form, bringing to mind a slumbering cat. Even sleeping, he responded to her, arching into her touches.

He groaned as he woke up, and she sighed as her unhindered exploration wound to a close. His cock stood proud as it curved toward his bellybutton. Her gaze roved higher until it tangled with his heavy-lidded electric green eyes. Rafe had risen to his elbows and sat silently watching her.

"Look who's awake," she teased.

"I am now." He stacked several pillows behind his head and lounged back with a smirk. "It looks like it's my turn."

She shook her head, dragged the silky nightgown over her head, and tossed it aside.

His fingers trailed through the sparse hair on his chest, headed for his erection. She slapped his hand away with a firm, "No. You got to play for a year. Now, it's my turn. So, sit back and let me ride."

"I'm all yours." His smile broadened as he spread his arms on either side of him as if he were a sacrificial offering. But they both knew she would be the one to fall on his sword. His grin turned feral. "But just a warning, my patience will only last so long."

"If I do something wrong, you'll tell me, right?" She bit her lip.

He leaned forward and met her eyes. "Nothing we do in here is wrong. But if I don't like something, yeah, I'll tell you. Same goes for you."

She nodded. More confident, she crawled up his body and straddled his hips. Leaning over him until there was a hair's breadth between them, she cupped his jaw. "Did you and Chloe ever have sex?"

"No." His gaze pierced hers, and she knew he spoke the truth. He arched up, his lips brushing against hers as he asked, "And you?"

"Nope, I've never had sex with Chloe," she teased, loving this new facet of their relationship.

"Smartass." He nipped her bottom lip and gave it an apologetic lick with his tongue. "Have you been with anyone else?"

"There's only ever been you for me." She palmed his chest as she sank onto him. "And to answer your next question, I'm on birth control. The same one I was using for half of our marriage."

His dark gaze widened in surprise before drifting closed as she took all of him in. He gripped her hips, helping to steady her as she rose and fell—the ever-present fire overtaking her and muddling her thoughts.

"Liz."

Her name sounded like a plea from his sex-roughened throat as she slowly rode him. The more she learned, the bolder she grew and the more she relaxed. She became fluid under his fingers as they traced down her spine. His tongue licked across her chest as his gaze tangled with hers. He looked at her as if she were his greatest treasure. She gorged herself on him. His taste, his touch, his smell, and his sounds were hers to command in this moment.

His hand slid up her throat, and his fingers wrapped themselves in her hair. Or maybe her hair trapped his fingers. He dragged her down, covering her mouth with his. Even though she kissed him, he somehow took charge as he mapped every inch of her mouth, devouring her as surely as she took him.

Pleasure soared through her as a wave of ecstasy dragged her from the heights. Her entire body stiffened before collapsing on top of his heaving chest as she floated on the blissful waves left in the wake of her release.

"Jesus, hon, you can wake me up like that any time you want," Rafe said between panting breaths.

She raised her middle finger and flipped him off, unable to speak just yet. His torso jiggled as he laughed, dislodging her from her comfortable perch. Groaning, she rolled off him and stretched out on her side. She leaned on one elbow and propped her cheek on her palm.

"Give me a few, and we can go again." He tucked her hair behind her ear and trailed a finger down her cheek.

A hard bang on their door made her fall off the edge of the double bed.

"Rise and shine, campers," Kennedy shouted. "We need to get a schedule down, and then Kenny and I need to show you where all the cameras and listening devices are."

"You okay?" Rafe's face appeared above her.

"Yep." She stood and rubbed her rear. "Can't believe I fell off the bed."

"We need to find a room with a bigger bed."

She sighed because the only room with a bigger bed was in the damned master suite, which had way too many windows and only regular curtains keeping out prying eyes.

Elizabeth padded to the attached bath, calling out to Kennedy, "We'll be down in a minute."

"Okay."

"Come on, Rafe, unless you want the twins to break in here and drag us from the shower."

"Dammit." He muttered, storming into the room behind her. "You hit the shower first, and I'll grab it after you're done."

"We can go together." Elizabeth flipped on the knobs until a steady stream of water poured from above.

"If I get in there with you, we'll be in there for a while." He dumped toothpaste on his toothbrush and pointed to the shower. "Go on, I can at least enjoy the show. Maybe tomorrow we can take one together."

She grinned, liking that idea. But as she began to clean up, running the rag over her stomach, her smile turned to a grimace as she noticed her barely-there stretch marks. They were slowly fading, but in the bright light of the bathroom, Rafe would have definitely seen them. Growling, she dragged the rag over the rest of her body. Elizabeth hated lying, even by omission, but her babies were too vulnerable to be discovered. They were the whole point of this cat and mouse game she and Tanner were playing up here.

She wouldn't give up her time with Rafe, but she would need to be careful until she could tell him the truth.

~ ~ ~ ~

After cleaning up, Elizabeth headed for the kitchen where the aroma of freshly brewed coffee and scrambled eggs teased her nose. Entering, she smiled at seeing the table set and Kenneth moving food from the stove to the dishes laid out on the kitchen table. As comfortable here as she was on the ranch, Elizabeth gathered mugs, cream, honey, and sugar, setting them on the table before taking one of the seats.

The kitchen was homey with its French Colonial glass-front cabinets and white and light wood accents. Just as Kenneth dished up the last of the eggs into a large bowl in the center of the table, Rafe joined them, taking the empty seat next to Elizabeth. She felt as if she were living inside a dream. This was the first time they had ever eaten breakfast together. Granted, they had company, but Rafe was actually beside her, his arm brushing hers as he doctored his coffee. It was surreal.

"So, the reason K woke you up was so we could briefly brief you." Kenneth snickered as he shoveled grits onto his plate.

"Forgive the big lug, we're punch-drunk since we've been setting up perimeter alarms and testing the cameras inside to make sure everything is in working order before we sleep." Kennedy lightly smacked Kenneth on the bicep. "Knock it off and fill them in."

Elizabeth wondered if her girls would have this kind of rapport. A bit of sibling rivalry with a lot of love in the mix.

"In all seriousness, we set up the perimeter alarms, so if anyone comes in by foot or by car, we'll be alerted in the guest house and this cell," he slid a cell toward Elizabeth, "will alert you two, so keep it charged and on you at all times."

"The perimeter alarms are going to tip our hand." Rafe snagged a biscuit from the basket in the middle of the table.

"How so?" Kennedy asked.

"Those red lights will glow in all this darkness."

Kennedy frowned as she shared a confused glance with her brother before turning back to Rafe. "Red lights?"

"Yeah, like you see in all the movies."

"Jesus, we're not in the movies, nor are we amateurs who use cheap crap off the internet. The sensors don't have lights on them." Kenneth tapped the cell. "The alarms sync up to our tablets, so we know where they are."

"Oh." A blush stained Rafe's cheeks. "Well, even the ones online—"

"Like I said, we don't buy them online, so don't worry about it." Kenneth shoveled a forkful of eggs in his mouth, chewed, and swallowed. "We also wanted to let you know, Tanner lands in Anchorage tomorrow."

"And he has security?" Elizabeth had been worried about the kid being caught alone.

"Yep. Two guys, Luke and Rob, are with him. With you, Rafe, and the kid awake during the day, you can sound the alarm for us. At night, us four will set up shifts to scout the outside as well as keep an eye on all the perimeter sections and the indoor cameras," Kennedy said as she pushed aside her clean plate. "We also want you two to make a habit of checking the back cabin."

"Why?" Rafe asked, stacking his own clean plate on top of Kennedy's and taking them to the sink.

"Because at night I want you three to sleep there and let us have the house. I think they'll hit then. We'll leave one of the bedrooms open for you, and the kid can have the spare bedroom," Kennedy replied. "We'll keep the path there and back clear so we can move between houses easier."

When she put it like that, Elizabeth could see Kennedy's point both about the path and keeping Elizabeth and her family out of harm's way.

"And where are you all going to sleep?" Rafe asked, turning and leaning against the countertop.

"We can alternate sleeping on the couch in the cabin or grab a bed in here. It will be better to discuss it when Tanner's security team is here. I have some ideas, but I'd rather discuss it when everyone's together."

Just as Elizabeth pushed her cleaned plate away, her cell trilled from its charger on the countertop. It was Megan's ringtone. Every eye in the room jumped to the ringing cell.

Kennedy was the one who broke the deafening silence. "Probably should get that."

"Yeah." Elizabeth stood and hurried to the cell. Swiping the screen, she set it on speaker. "Jesus, Megan, I haven't even had my morning coffee yet."

"Well, I was worried," Megan stated in a sharp tone.

"Why would you be worried?"

"Maybe because you're in Barrow when you're supposed to be in Anchorage until tomorrow? Call me paranoid, but when I see that my bestie isn't where she says she's going to be, I wonder if she's been kidnapped or if her cell has been stolen."

Elizabeth winced. She'd never hated that damned tracker more than she did at this moment. "My location shows in Barrow?"

"Yes," Megan growled.

"Weird, since I'm in Anchorage. Tanner and I are waiting for the doctor's office to open so he can be cleared to go to Barrow for the last two weeks of wearing that damned cast." Elizabeth did her best to project confusion and irritation over her cell phone's location misfiring. She sucked at lying and could feel her face heat in embarrassment as she tucked her hair behind her ears.

"You're in Anchorage?"

"Yes. We don't leave for Barrow until tomorrow."

"Weird."

"Exactly. Maybe the cell is just plotting my last location when I was up here, and it'll settle down in a few hours."

"Maybe."

Megan didn't believe her. Elizabeth could hear it in her voice. To screw up all their carefully laid plans because she forgot the damned tracker . . . Elizabeth wanted to rage. Instead, she turned the tables. "Why are you tracking my cell anyway? It's not like we're close enough to grab a bite to eat or a drink to bitch about work."

"Why am I tracking you?" Megan asked, her tone holding a note Elizabeth had never heard before. If she didn't know better, she would swear Megan was nervous at being asked the question. But the feeling passed as Megan's own irritation bled through. "Because my best friend flew off to Alaska to adopt a freaking teenager neither I nor Harold have met, and yes, I asked him after you flew away—"

"Great, he's going to be blowing up my cell next."

"What the fuck do you want me to say, Elizabeth? I was worried. He's worried. You're not acting at all like yourself."

"What?" Elizabeth frowned, pissed at Megan for spilling the beans to Harold. Then she remembered this wasn't her friend. The reminder helped break her from falling into old patterns. Hard on the heels of that thought, Elizabeth remembered Megan had more than shared every detail of Elizabeth's life with Harold. Not only that, but this was also the woman who'd worked with Harold to kill Elizabeth's mother. "Why am I not acting like myself? You and Harold both knew I wanted a family. You both knew I was ready to start one—"

"With Rafe."

"Right, well that fell through—"

"He wants another chance."

"And I'll probably give him one, but I love Tanner like the little brother I never had. I want him in my life, and in order for me to have that, I need to adopt him." Elizabeth slapped her hands on her hips and narrowed her gaze on her cell, daring Megan to say one more negative word. "And if Rafe won't accept Tanner, then he can take a long walk off a short pier for all I care."

"Okay, calm down."

"Yeah, well, I'm sick of everyone telling me what to do. I'm an adult. I don't depend on Harold for shit except to be my family." Elizabeth threw her hands in the air as if Megan could see her, so caught up in her tirade. "And you're supposed to be my best friend and on my damned side."

"I *am* on your side, Liz." Megan's tone softened. "I was just worried about where you were, that's the only reason I tracked your cell. You were flying up there alone, and you usually call me when you land."

"Well, forgive me for letting you sleep since I didn't land until three a.m. your time."

"Okay. I get why you didn't call now."

"Sorry," Elizabeth swallowed her ire as she tried to play the role Megan expected. "You know I would have called as soon as I woke up."

"I do. I was just worried. Especially when you weren't where you said you would be. We're both tired, which is putting us on edge." Megan's deep sigh drifted over the cell. "So, Tanner's with you now?"

"Yep, he's sawing logs like a chainsaw in the next room." Elizabeth bit her lip as she pushed the lie a bit more and hoped to smooth out the rough edges the argument stirred up. "He told me last night that he can't wait to meet you after all the stories I've told him."

Megan laughed, and Elizabeth relaxed. They were back on familiar footing. At least for now.

"Tell him I'll fill him in with the truth since you dragged me into more mischief than I ever pulled you into."

"Hey!" Elizabeth teased, glad Megan was allowing the app tracker subject to drop.

"When he wakes up, maybe we could talk."

"If he's up to it. He's been super cranky with his cracked ribs and broken arm." Elizabeth looked at the group around the table. Rafe's thumbs up boosted Elizabeth's confidence and let her know she was handling Megan perfectly. Being so close to the situation, Elizabeth had wondered if she came across as false in her reactions. It was good to have someone outside with a level head, letting her know she was making the expected moves so as not to tip their hand.

"My bet is if the doctor gives him the all-clear in a few weeks, he'll be in a better mood," Megan mused. "But that doesn't mean I don't want to talk to him."

"Sure. How about when he and I hit the Barrow house we call you? That way, he's rested after the travel and not cranky from the doctor poking and prodding."

"Sounds good. Oh, and Elizabeth?"

"Yep."

"Reboot your cell so that tracker app resets. I hate not knowing where you are if I need to send a rescue party."

"I'll do that as soon as I hang up." Elizabeth shivered and rubbed her arms because she knew if Megan had her way, it wouldn't be a rescue party that would be arriving to help Elizabeth. Instead, it would be someone to kill her.

"Talk to you later." With that, Megan was gone.

The second the cell disconnected, Elizabeth flipped it off and stumbled back into a solid chest. In a panic, she almost slammed an elbow into the solar plexus behind her, only stopping when Rafe's scent wrapped around her. She sagged against him, cold to her core as she huddled into him for warmth.

"Well, that was not only interesting but a surprise," Kennedy said in a brisk tone as she pushed away from the table. "Here's what you're going to do. Leave the cell off and give it to me. I'm going to grab my go-bag and fly with it to Anchorage to wait for Tanner."

"I'll stay here and prep the master suite. If she's keeping that close of a tab, they're definitely planning to make a move." Kenneth stood, but Elizabeth waved him away when he began clearing the table.

"Go get some sleep. And Kennedy, maybe you should get—"

"I went a lot longer without sleep than this when I served in the Air Force. Her calling like this shows they're seeing the end in sight and getting impatient for it." Kennedy grabbed a thermos from the cabinet next to the fridge and dumped the remainder of the coffee into it. "You need to ask Jessup to get that forensic accountant looking at your trust to be safe."

"I'll call him," Rafe said before Elizabeth could answer. "How about I grab my cell, and we can call him together while we clean up in here."

She nodded. Everything was moving so fast, she felt as if she were about to fly apart. Rafe was the only thing anchoring her right now. His strong arms wrapped around her waist helped ground her so she didn't crumble into a pile of emotions.

Then Kennedy and Kenneth were gone, and it was only her. Finally, Rafe returned with his cell phone, but he didn't immediately call. Instead, he turned her gently toward him and pressed a kiss to her forehead before cuddling her into his chest.

"Are you okay?" he asked, his voice whisper soft as if he were gentling one of Mac's cantankerous mares.

"Not really." How else was she supposed to answer? The end was coming fast, and either it would be her end or Megan's and Harold's. She hoped they all survived. But if anyone died, she didn't want it to be her or anyone she considered her family.

"We can wait—"

"No, we can't." She nuzzled into his chest, absorbing what comfort she could from him before pulling away. "Let's get it over with."

"If you're sure."

Squaring her shoulders, she met his gaze. "I am."

While he contacted Jessup and set up the speakerphone so she could follow the conversation, Elizabeth began clearing the table.

Chapter Fourteen

Movement from the corner of her eye pulled her from the fantastical world she was building for her next YA story and returned her to the present. Sighing, she made a note of where she wanted the scene to go, saved her work, and shut down the laptop before turning to face the man not far from her thoughts. He was propped in the doorway with an affectionate smile on his face. Standing, she stretched the kinks out of her back and stepped toward him.

"Are you at a stopping point?"

"Never, until the story is done, and if the characters are willing to share their stories, I try to catch as much of it as I can before they go quiet." It was hard explaining her process. Creativity wasn't something set in stone, nor was it always there when she tried to capture it for her scenes. It was a savage mistress, and Elizabeth was its humble servant. Whenever it beckoned, she dropped everything to at least make enough notes to remember what was about to happen so she could capture the emotions later.

"Well, it's lunchtime, and I've been listening to your stomach growl for the past five minutes," he said, holding his hand out for her to take.

Just as she laced their fingers together, her stomach released a loud snarl. Heat filled her face, and she ducked behind her hair in embarrassment.

"No worries. While you were working, I scrounged up some food for us." He led her toward the den.

She gasped at the romantic setting he had put together for them and was almost tempted to write romance so she could immortalize it in a story.

Fire danced in the stone fireplace with tapered candles on the coffee table and end tables. The flames cast a golden glow over the picnic he had prepared for them. A dark burgundy blanket was spread on the cream-colored carpet, directly in front of the fireplace. The blanket was set with a charcuterie plank filled with delicacies; they could feed each other by hand. A cheeseboard and a platter of Bruschetta were nestled between the candles on the coffee table. An open bottle of wine with delicate wine glasses standing next to it completed the look.

"You did this for me?" Her gaze tangled with his.

"I did."

Then she remembered the cameras and bugs; her gaze bounced around the room, trying to pick out the microscopic spies.

"Hey." He jiggled her hand until her eyes met his once more. "You trust me, right?"

"I—" Did she trust him? With everything in her. Settled, she smiled. "Yes."

"Good." He led her to the blanket, but she still couldn't help glancing around when his back was turned. "Kenneth turned the cameras off after I told him this was an idea Kennedy gave me."

"Oh, she would get him back so hard if he messed up one of her plans." Elizabeth smiled, finally relaxing.

"She would, but I didn't fully trust him, so I covered all the cameras just to be safe. And I'll ask Kennedy to double-check the feeds when she gets back."

"Check the feeds?" Elizabeth asked in confusion.

"And I plan on making love to you in front of the fire," he whispered, his heated breath ghosting over her ear as he leaned in to nuzzle her neck.

She whimpered and shoved a piece of cheese in her mouth to stifle the sound. He smirked as he lifted a remote and hit a button. Soft jazz filled the room. It would muffle any sounds they made in case Kenneth had left the mics on. This was why she adored Rafe. Why she knew she could trust him even with their babies' lives. However, she could not chance word of their daughters reaching Harold's ears. And she knew Rafe would feel the same, especially with how concerned he was about Elizabeth's and Tanner's security. She had caught him quizzing Kenneth several times about camera placement and reminding the man to check the sensors. If she hadn't loved him before, his actions now would have sealed the deal. He was safeguarding her even though he had no definitive proof she was telling the truth about Harold and Megan wanting to kill her.

When this was over, she would share their daughters with him. Elizabeth wasn't sure he would forgive her for a secret that big, but she hoped in the deepest part of her soul he would understand.

She folded her legs to the side and took the glass of wine he passed her. As they ate, they exchanged bits and pieces of themselves. Nothing earth-shattering, just favorite movies, favorite songs, favorite books, and other things couples told each other at the beginning of their courtship. Years from now, Elizabeth would never recall what they'd talked about, but she would always point to this moment as being when she began to believe that Rafe cared for more than just her body.

When they had finished eating their fill, Elizabeth watched the muscles in Rafe's arms ripple as he shifted the leftovers from the blanket to the coffee table. She drained the last of her wine as he lifted the glass from her fingers and placed it next to his own.

With the blanket cleared off, Rafe took her in his arms and laid her across the blanket as if she were a precious treasure.

His mouth slid over hers as he stole her breath with languorous kisses. The edges of reality blurred until she only saw him. She only felt his touch.

Somewhere between one breath and the next, her clothes melted from her as his lips and hands reclaimed every inch of her. From the crown of her head to the tips of her toes and everything in between, all were given attention. Not a piece of her was missed. He never rushed.

It was like nothing she had ever experienced. Most of their couplings had been him pushing her over the edge several times to show his dominance before he followed her over. This was him joining her in learning what they could become together. It was more than making love. It was a merging of souls.

Until they both broke at the same time and with the same breath. For her, it felt precious and magical. And as their gazes met and tangled together, she realized it was soul-bearing as she saw the purest love in his green eyes and knew the same was reflected back at him.

It didn't matter that there were still secrets to be shared. It didn't matter that she might die when Harold and Megan came for her. All that mattered was, in this moment, she held Rafe's heart, just as he had captured hers.

Then he rolled to the side and grabbed the throw draped across the ottoman. Once he'd spread the beige fleece blanket over them, she nestled against his side, her head settled near his heart.

"This is what our marriage should have been like all along." His hands petted her back.

It was the perfect opening for her to share some of her secrets. Taking a chance, she whispered, "I think so too. But, Rafe, neither of us will be able to go back."

"No, but when we return to California, I want you to move back in with me."

She shook her head and hugged him closer. "I'll never live in California again."

"You've been living there since your mother and Harold married."

"I left." She knew she was making a hash of explaining things, but it was harder than she thought. She was terrified of telling him where she lived. What if Megan and Harold didn't come to Alaska? What if Rafe let slip where Elizabeth had run to, and Harold and Megan came for her at the ranch?

"Liz, are you saying you bought a place somewhere that's not in California?"

"Yes." She sighed when he gently urged her to sit up. Feeling vulnerable, she snagged her long-sleeved shirt and dragged it over her head before meeting his gaze.

"Would you be willing to move back?" he asked.

"To California?"

He nodded.

"God, no." She shuddered at even the thought of it. "Not with what I know now. It's toxic for me there, Rafe. The entire state. Harold's ruined it all for me by spreading vicious lies. I don't have any friends because I only ever needed Megan."

"We can change that . . ."

"No, we can't." She knew they couldn't; she had just been too blind to see it before. "Any committee I'm on, whenever I say 'I have the funds,' or 'I'll contribute such and such,' they always call Harold."

"But with Harold arrested and gone—"

"They'll call you." She ran a hand through her hair. "You didn't even believe I had any money until a few days ago. It's a nightmare, and there were always comments, but I never knew they were pointed at me until I found out Harold had allowed everyone to continue to believe I'm broke. Even after my mother died."

"Comments?"

"Yes, about why I wasn't asked to lunch with the others since they were going to some five-star restaurant they doubted I would be able to afford. No one said it to my face, but I was the committee member they were discussing. You know, the one someone else needed to pay for." Her face flamed at the memory. "It was embarrassing when all these little digs finally made sense. I'm not sticking around in California."

"Then where will you go?"

"Back to my ranch—" She gasped and slapped a hand over her mouth.

"Harold doesn't know you have a ranch?"

"No one here does. It's a safe haven I've used the past year while trying to figure out how to lure Harold and Megan out." She laid her hand over his thigh. "But I trust you, Rafe."

He smiled.

"I probably should tell you I've changed my name to Col—"

He covered her mouth and shook his head sharply. "Don't."

Confused, she frowned at him.

"No one except Tanner knows your new name and new address, right?"

She nodded.

"Don't tell me. The music should drown out the bugs in here, but I refuse to chance your safety like that."

Her eyes popped wide. She had forgotten about the bugs.

"Do you understand?"

Her heart melted at seeing his tender side peek out.

She nodded again, and he removed his hand.

"So, you changed your name."

It wasn't a question, but a statement and the sparkle in his eyes were mischievous as if he loved sharing a secret with her.

And though he didn't ask, she felt the need to try to explain. "Elizabeth felt like a name for a fool after everything came to light, and I wanted a new start at a new place with a new name."

The sparkle brightened, and a smile stretched across his face. "After this is over, I'm going on a treasure hunt."

"Wait. What?" *What the hell is he talking about? I just told him I changed my name and moved to a whole new state, and he's talking about treasure hunts?*

His palm cupped her cheek.

"I have the best idea. When we're done in Alaska, I need to go home, and you're going to return to wherever your home is—"

"But—"

"Shh, let me finish." He placed a gentle kiss over her lips.

She reluctantly motioned zipping her lips and tried to keep quiet even though she wanted to protest. They had just found each other, and now he wanted to break up?

"We're not breaking up, so get that look off your face. But my mother comes back from her trip abroad in February. I have several trips planned for a venture, opening their business in February. But the most important thing is," his earnest gaze tangled with hers. "I want to find you. I've been trying to think of a way to apologize for all the bullshit you went through and show you that you can trust me. That I'm not going to let you down again, and this is it."

"I don't understand."

"I'm going to find you. Each day we're separated, I want us to talk either by phone or by text. If I'm listening, like I should have been from the beginning, you'll give me hints to where you live now, and I'll use those to find you."

"Holy crap. You want to stalk me like prey." *And why does that turn me on?* Heat curled in her at the thought of having his undivided attention focused on tracking her.

"I do. I want you to know I'm paying attention. So, don't say 'this is your hint for this week.' Just toss something in during our normal conversation—"

"To show you're actually listening to me." Like he hadn't during their marriage. To be fair, she hadn't paid enough attention either, and she would need to own that.

"We both need to work on our communication, and I think this will do it." He pulled her into his lap and held her close. "I love you. I've been in love with you since the second you tripped over the sidewalk trying to rescue that kid's dog."

Her face heated to scalding as she remembered that coffee date. The poor little girl was almost in tears trying to catch the puppy before it darted into traffic. Elizabeth had just barely snagged the ball of fluff before it jumped the curb. Unfortunately, she had tripped over an uneven paving stone, but she had still caught the dog. "I didn't know you saw that."

"I did. It was one of the reasons I knew you wouldn't back out of the contract when Harold presented it. That maybe we could have made it work." He tightened is arms as if to feel she was actually there. "Little did we know, we were doomed from the start."

"Why? Why would that be the tipping point?"

"Because you were stubborn enough to forget about breaking your fall. Instead, you grabbed that mutt and body-slammed the concrete."

"Yeah, I have to say, that hurt like hell." She nuzzled into the hollow of his neck and sighed. He really did love her. They had just gotten sidetracked for a moment. Just as she was about to suggest another round, heavy footsteps traveled to them, and she scrambled from his lap. "Kenneth."

"Sounds like he's awake."

"Shit." She snatched up her clothes and raced for the downstairs bathroom, glad she had at least tossed on her shirt, even though it only reached the top of her bare thigh. Lying around half-naked with Rafe was one thing, but she would never live down her absolute embarrassment if Kenneth caught a glimpse of her naked ass.

~ ~ ~ ~

The afternoon passed in a blur, from helping Rafe clean up from their impromptu picnic in front of the fireplace to snuggling with him on the couch to finishing the bottle of wine while chatting. It was easy to be with him. Easy to share pieces of her past. And it was exactly as she had always imagined their downtime could be.

When both their stomachs began growling, they migrated to the kitchen. She dug out a frozen lasagna from the deep freeze in the attached garage and popped it in the oven. "The lasagna will take at least an hour to cook."

"Shower, then we can put together a salad and some garlic bread to go with it?" Rafe asked, setting the timer on the stove.

"Sounds good. I'll take the guest bathroom, so we don't get distracted," she teased, and he swatted her ass as she raced by him.

All cleaned up, she was heading for the kitchen when she heard the burner cell she had set up for Kennedy ring. Hurrying to the enclosed porch where she had been writing, she snagged her cell from next to her laptop and swiped it. "Kennedy? Is everything okay?"

"It's Tanner."

Her heart dropped on the way back to the kitchen, and she froze. "Tanner? Why're you using Kennedy's phone?"

"Because Mac thought it was a good idea not to bring mine, just in case. I wanted to let you know I got here okay, and Kennedy needs to talk to you."

"You're still coming tomorrow, right?"

"As far as I know. But I think they want to set me up with warmer clothes. Which isn't a bad idea, because holy crap is it cold outside," he said with an overdramatic shiver to his voice, making her laugh. "Okay, here's Kennedy."

When she entered the kitchen, Rafe turned to her with an arched brow.

"Kennedy," she whispered to him.

He tipped his chin and began pulling ingredients for a salad from the fridge.

"Elizabeth," Kennedy said.

"Yep."

"Have you checked the app I installed on your laptop that syncs up to your cell lately?"

"No," she said, snagging a piece of cucumber from the cutting board Rafe was using and shoving it into her mouth. "Why?"

A frustrated sigh passed through the speaker. "Because you need to check it asap and then call Megan."

"Not until after we eat. I'm starving, and the lasagna is sitting there smellin—"

"Fine, but you need to call because Megan spilled everything to Harold."

"Shit." Elizabeth's gaze darted to the porch, but she knew if she went in there, it would be a few hours before she was done. Especially if Harold now knew the trust was open.

"When you talk to Megan, I want you to do two things," Kennedy ordered. "Are you listening to me?"

"Yes, two things."

"Good. The first is, you're going to tell her Rafe is in Anchorage because he thought it would prove that he was serious about his intentions. And the second, you make sure you're angry with her for telling Harold since it wasn't his business and refuse to let her speak to Tanner because of it."

"She'll want to make sure he's here."

"I know, but that buys us tomorrow to get the kid set up in below zero weather gear. And I want you and Rafe to move to the cottage behind the house."

"What?" She shook her head. "No, that leaves Tanner—"

"With me and Luke, who has a similar look and build to Rafe." Kennedy huffed an exasperated breath. "Look, it'll be easier for us to watch the kid if we can actually be in close proximity, and if they come to kill you two, then they'll be coming for Luke and me."

"So instead of three targets, you're looking at one target with two people who can trap them." It was a good plan, at least by Elizabeth's way of thinking.

"Yes, so make damn sure those blackout shades are taped down tight, so no light peeks out from them. Button the entire guest house up so she thinks you're only using the main house."

"But what about the pathway we shoveled between the houses?" Elizabeth asked.

"You all need to deal with that tonight since the forecast claims another snowfall after midnight."

"Okay, I'll get with Kenneth and Rafe."

"Good. I'm going now because the kid has been whining about food for the past thirty minutes, so we'd better feed him before he starts gnawing on us."

Elizabeth chuckled as she hung up.

"Well, that can't be all bad," Rafe said, and she jumped, having forgotten for a moment that he was in the room.

"Not too bad." She rubbed her aching head. "Megan told Harold about Tanner."

"Shit." He wrapped his arms around her and hugged her back to his chest. "Do you need to deal with that now?"

Shaking her head, she set her cell on the kitchen counter. "After dinner. I want to fill you and Kenneth in so you two can add your two cents before I call, and we need to get the house and cabin prepped to Kennedy's specification."

"Okay, but you should call Harold too, so all of it's handled in one fell swoop."

"Yeah, that's what I was thinking." She didn't want to deal with the man. It had been heaven only responding via texts, but the time had come to confront him on some of the hell he had brought into her life.

After dinner, Kenneth helped them clear the table.

"I'll start shoveling the pathway and then tape those blackout shades down," Kenneth said.

"If you wait until tomorrow, we can help you with the shades," Rafe stated, bringing in the last of the dishes.

"No, I don't want to be rushed. That way, we can really check to make sure no light shows. And the pathway won't take any time at all since it's basically just a small trail that we've stomped between the two houses."

"I think it's overkill." Elizabeth filled the sink with soapy water. "I don't think either one will do much recon."

"Better safe than sorry," Kenneth replied and headed for the back door.

"Go call Megan and Harold. Don't forget to record the call like Kenneth suggested." Rafe nudged her side.

Elizabeth dried her hands on the towel, hanging it on a hook above the sink before slipping out to the enclosed porch where she felt most at home. Her fingers trembled as she fumbled the headset out of her briefcase and plugged it into her laptop. She tried to settle her nerves since she wasn't sure how bad the conversation would go. Oh, Harold was pissed. Elizabeth got that from the texts, but she felt nothing. It was as if she were encased in a numb bubble. The feeling wouldn't last, but she hoped it at least it held out through the phone call to Harold.

That was the call she needed to be very careful with as her temper was flaring at how he had manipulated not only her mother but her as well. She was livid at how he had nearly cost her Rafe. Hell, Harold *had* cost her and Rafe the precious moments they should have had during her pregnancy. Instead, she would be forced to show the man pictures of that time and pray he didn't leave her because she'd kept the girls from him.

Shivering with dread, she slipped the headphones over her ears and settled the mic close to her mouth. With everything in place, she hit the record button on her screen and then hit Megan's contact via the app Kennedy had set up. The app was a godsend, as it popped up Elizabeth's cell number on Megan's phone.

Nerves wound in her, and it dawned her why Kennedy had emphatically stated for her to be angry. She needed the reminder because, right now, anger was the furthest thing from her mind. She was worried, nervous, and most of all, terrified of what would happen now that Harold knew the trust was open.

Oh, God, Harold knows the trust is open. Elizabeth rubbed her churning stomach as bile rose to the back of her throat.

Warm hands settled on her shoulders, and she leaned into Rafe's touch, drawing courage from his solid presence.

It felt like years before Megan answered, but based on the recording, it wasn't even a full minute.

"Hey."

"That's all you have to say to me?" Elizabeth asked, forcing herself to sound pissed when all she wanted to do was grab Tanner and run back to her ranch. "You told Harold about Tanner."

"I did," Megan snarled. "He deserves to know. He's the kid's grandfather, after all."

"Bullshit, he's nothing to me, and he's nothing to—"

"He was—"

"Nothing." Elizabeth had had no idea there was so much anger inside her. It was as if a bottomless well had opened, and every bit of rage came pouring out now that she had a target. "He never wanted to be my family. Only my mother's husband."

"Because he cared about your mother, but constantly supporting you two was draining."

"Wait, what?" Elizabeth pushed toward the screen, wishing she could see Megan. Not only see the woman but jump through the internet connection and strangle her. "You believe those lies?"

"They aren't lies, Liz. You've never lived on your own. The credit card you have is tied to Harold—"

"Bullshit!" she yelled. "His is tied to mine. Jesus, Megan."

"What else am I supposed to believe? Seriously, Liz, you've constantly had to use Harold for his money and standing. I thought when you married, you'd have shifted everything over to Rafe, but nope. And then, after you got pregnant, I thought the trust would open, and you could quit leaning on the man. But that didn't happen either."

"How the hell do you know I didn't swap my accounts to Rafe?" Elizabeth couldn't believe this woman, to whom she'd lamented every bit of heartache about being stuck with the stigma of being called poor, actually believed Harold's lies.

"I'm Harold's date to the charity events, and he mentioned it. Then there were rumors—"

"Exactly. Rumors." Elizabeth threw her hands in the air.

"The ones about how much money you and your mother had traveled from North Carolina with. There has to be a kernel of truth there. Besides, I thought you would do everything in your power to open that billion-dollar trust. But instead of getting pregnant with the man of your dreams, you go out and adopt some gutter rat!"

"I don't get it. You were always talking about only liking Harold because of me. Yet, you chatter away about me at the events you go to?" Elizabeth wanted to go further by pointing out how far Megan had betrayed her, but Rafe's fingers digging into her shoulders reminded her not to tip their hand. It wasn't in Elizabeth's past nature with Megan to look too closely at the inconsistencies.

God, I was blind.

"When I'm trapped in a limo with him, we talk. You should know that." Megan huffed. "I felt it wasn't fair for him not to know about Tanner in case he ended up needing to support the kid. It would be the same if you had Rafe's kids. I would have shared that too."

"You shared that with Harold but didn't think to tell me that Rafe knew I was in Alaska?"

"He's there with you?"

"Yes, in Anchorage. Thanks for that, by the way," she spat through gritted teeth.

"Who're you talking to, hon?" he asked as they had planned at dinner.

"Megan."

"Oh, well, Tanner's hungry, so I'm going to finish getting dressed, and we can go grab dinner," Rafe chimed in, helping to break through Elizabeth's anger and put her on more even footing.

"Okay." Elizabeth pressed a kiss to his hand in thanks for being there with her.

"What the hell is he doing there?"

"He said something about a big apology, and that you had mentioned me being in Alaska when he met up with you for coffee. I happened to run into him at the hotel—"

"Shit. Look, I'm sorry. I didn't tell him so he could go up there. I told him because I assumed he already knew where you went for peace and quiet." She sounded as if the argument drained her, but Elizabeth highly doubted that was why Megan was sorry.

"It's . . . well, it's not fine, but it is what it is. I've got to go and call Harold—which is going to be super fun," she snarked.

"Just a suggestion, but maybe offer him half of the trust since he supported you and your mom all these years," Megan said softly.

"Bye, Megan." Elizabeth slapped the disconnect button with her mouse and fell back against the chair, shaken at how blind everyone around her had been to the truth. No one had looked beyond the rumors to see Elizabeth.

Rafe wrapped his arms around her, and she slumped against him, wishing she could crawl into him and live for a while.

"She believes the same lies you and everyone else did, even though she's supposed to be my best friend," Elizabeth whispered. "Harold really did isolate me."

"I don't believe them anymore, and I never should have. I should have made up my own mind and been more confrontational instead of just shutting down until the contract ended." He kissed her temple. "I won't make the same mistake twice."

"I won't let you shut down again, either." She lifted her face and claimed a chaste kiss. "Now that I know what went wrong before, I'm going to make damned sure we don't stop talking again."

"Sounds good." Rafe lifted her laptop and shifted it closer to the cushioned hanging swing in the corner. "How about I hold you while you talk to Harold?"

She nodded. His call would be bad but not as bad as the one with Megan. The pain at realizing she and Megan had never been friends at all was still tender even after a year.

Harold was another story. It had been easy to come to terms with him hating Elizabeth and wanting her dead. He had always been distant, never wanting to be called father or any other name denoting their relationship. Elizabeth was only ever allowed to call him Harold. And yes, his betrayal had hurt, but in the beginning, it had been Rafe's and Megan's betrayal that laid waste to her soul.

Megan was a lost cause. Elizabeth just needed to mourn the ending of their friendship. However, she wouldn't be able to do that until everything was settled.

Selecting Harold's contact, she braced for the worst.

"About time you called me."

"I wanted to wait until we reached Barrow before I hashed this shit out with you."

"Really?" Sardonic disbelief dripped from Harold's voice.

"Yes."

"But you weren't going to see if I agreed about you adopting some homeless kid?"

"Screw you, Harold." She was sick and tired of everyone assuming the worst about Tanner. "I don't need your permission to do shit."

"No, but you'd think you'd check in with your only living relative."

"You are not my relative."

"I'm your stepfather."

"When it's convenient."

"And inconvenient," he snarled.

"Exactly. You never wanted me, but I came with Momma, so you sucked it up." She snorted. "I mean, let's face it, the only reason you even married Momma was for her money. Even though you made damned sure to tell everyone we would ever come in contact with how poor we were."

"Your mother thought that was a good idea."

"I bet she did," Elizabeth growled.

"She thought it would keep gold diggers from hounding you."

"Uh-huh, and I suppose the contract you had Rafe sign was to protect me as well?"

"It was."

"I don't believe you. Especially since you went behind my back and forged my damned signature." She shook with anger.

"Who told you about the rumors? Rafe?"

"Megan and Jessup helped me piece it together.
Then I remembered weird stuff Momma would say
whenever we were forced to wait for you to come to us.
Say, for example, my school when they needed to
confirm payment."

"Well, it kept the money grabbers away—at
least until now."

"Tanner isn't a money grabber. He's a teenager,
and I love him like a little brother."

"Until he finds out you have a fortune. You
need to sign that back over to my firm. We at least have
to get it set it up so he doesn't go through it like water."

"No."

"No? You need to come to your senses, girl.
You didn't even mention this adoption to me. If
something happens to you, I don't want to raise another
kid."

"Another kid? You never raised one before, and
if you think that was me, let's get your facts straight."
She pushed up from the swing and began to pace as far
as the chord tethering her to the laptop allowed. "You
refused to let me use any kinds of terms that related to
being my father—"

"Because I was younger than your damned
mother."

"By a few years, not decades. You made sure to
ground our reputation beneath your heel before we
ever moved to California. You made damned sure my
marriage to the man I loved fell through. And then, to
add insult to injury, you forced that same man to
donate fucking sperm to humiliate him, knowing I
would: One, never know about it. And two, would
never in my life use it even if I did know about it
because why I would want to make a child with

someone who threw me away?"

"You're being overly dramatic. And for the record, I have my own money that I know how to manage. You and your mother had no clue."

"Again, I call bullshit. You were in dire straits when you married Momma. If she hadn't poured millions into your investments, you would have lost everything. And don't try to lie to me. I know she set up fifty million for you when she died. Specifically for your gambling habits. And that didn't include her paying off your house and leaving you enough to live on for the rest of your life."

"And she left the rest to you," he snarled. "You got the rest dumped into that damnable trust all for your children. I got nothing. Then I hear from Megan it's worth a billion? And it's open? Is that why you adopted? So you could get your hands on it? Because that's the only reason you would have a child. For that money."

"You don't know shit about me, Harold." She lost the reins of her temper. "But now that I know your and Megan's thoughts, I'll be having my will changed the second Tanner is free of his cast. I'll tell Jessup to draw up the paperwork, and I'll name Rafe as Tanner's guardian if something happens to me. You and Megan can go to hell the way you've talked about that child. And you especially, to have been so insecure as to drag my mother down the toilet so you could look like a hero is sickening."

"Elizabeth—" His tone held a warning that she ignored.

"No, you don't get to speak to me anymore. Don't call because I'm not picking up for you or her anymore." She slammed the mouse button so hard to disconnect the call, the wireless mouse flew off the table and landed on the floor with a loud clatter.

She yanked the headset off and tossed it on the table with a sob. Then Rafe's arms were around her, holding her tight.

"I'm sorry, Rafe. You don't have to actually take Tanner. I can get Jessup—" She could barely push the words out. They were a lie because she desperately wanted him to protect her family if something happened to her.

"Shh. I would be honored that you trust me enough to look out for him if something ever happens to you. And I can't wait to meet the young man that you defend so fiercely." He rocked her gently from side to side. "I'm so proud of you for standing up to Harold."

"I lost it. I think I told him more than I should have." She couldn't remember half of what she'd said because she had lost her head. Then she remembered the end of the call and shivered harder.

"What's the matter?"

"Oh, God," she couldn't stifle the whimper that escaped. "I told him I was giving you guardianship of Tanner."

"So?"

"That means they have to make a move before Tanner's cast comes off next week."

Chapter Fifteen

Rafe hefted the last piece of luggage out of the back of the SUV and trailed Kennedy into the main house. He hadn't met Tanner yet, but questions circled in Rafe's head like a record stuck on repeat. Mostly he wanted to quiz Elizabeth about her mother leaving Harold all that money. *Why would anyone do that? And why would Harold need even more now? The man shouldn't have gone through fifty million that quickly.*

Nerves wound tighter in Rafe as the time drew closer for Tanner to show up. This teenager was important enough for Elizabeth to make him family, and she cared for him. Which meant Rafe needed the kid to at least tolerate him. He hoped they could form a friendship.

Would Tanner like him? Would he like Tanner? Did Tanner know everything? Or had Elizabeth tried to shield him from some of the harsher aspects of Harold's machinations?

Voices broke into his meandering thoughts, and Rafe followed them up the stairs and into one of the guest rooms as he pushed away his nerves.

"Why are we up here?" Rafe asked, dropping the heavy suitcase just inside the door.

"Because Kennedy and Kenneth thought this would be the best place to protect Tanner." Elizabeth smiled, her arm draped around a tall, lanky teenager's neck. "They figure whoever is sent to kill us will start in the master suite first."

Rafe tipped his chin in agreement. It made sense unless the person came in through one of the upstairs rooms. Figuring the security team would know the weak spots, Rafe left it in their hands and took his first look at Tanner.

A beanie was pulled tight to the teenager's skull and over the tops of his ears, hiding his hair. His bronze skin gave Rafe pause as he wondered when Tanner had a chance to hit the beach in January. But then Rafe took in the chiseled features and onyx eyes and realized the young man was part native American.

"Shit. So, like Kennedy and Kenneth really are supervising our security team?" Tanner asked, his eyes popping wide.

"It doesn't bode well that you didn't pick that up." Elizabeth shook her head in exasperation.

"No, I mean, they act like kids. And Kennedy? She's all of like five foot and a hundred pounds soaking wet. She looks like a pint-sized Tinkerbell if Tinkerbell had black hair." Tanner waved his hand around as he tried to backpedal.

Rafe stifled a chuckle by pretending to cough.

"And can probably take you out with her pinky," Elizabeth teased. "She's ex-military, and with her twin at her back, she's lethal. Whatever you do, don't let her hear you compare her to some kind of tiny fairy."

"Got it. Don't mess with the pocket rocket, or she can make me disappear." If possible, Tanner's eyes became wider. "I wonder if she disappears her victims with fairy dust—"

"Usually, I use a plastic sheet and a shovel," Kennedy said from behind them.

Rafe had trouble hiding his laughter at seeing both Tanner and Elizabeth jump in surprise as guilty expressions pulled across both their faces.

"And never refer to me as a pocket rocket . . . That's supposed to reference a penis, not a person." Kennedy punched Rafe on his shoulder as she pushed past the two troublemakers with the last of their luggage before pointing at Tanner. "Please tell me you knew that was a penis reference, because if not, then you need to turn in your man card. Because I heard that shit all the time on station." Her amused gaze landed on Tanner, whose jaw opened and closed as he worked to form a response.

"Quit messing with the newbie, Kennedy, and come help me unpack all this shit we just unloaded."

"Some-damned-body better have some food ready, or I'm going to show you what a pint-sized fairy is capable of," Kennedy huffed and stomped back into the hallway.

"I have chicken and veggies in the crockpot since I wasn't sure when you all wanted to eat," Elizabeth called out.

Kennedy popped around the doorjamb with a smile. "Thanks!" Then she raced away with a yell of getting "shit done so they could eat."

Grinning at the mouth on the woman, Rafe held his hand out to Tanner. "Don't worry too much about Kennedy. She's pretty laid-back. I'm Rafe."

"Tanner." Tanner shook Rafe's hand. Calluses scraped across Rafe's palm and told him the teenager was a damned hard worker.

"Why don't you go check the food?" Rafe suggested with a hand on the small of Elizabeth's back.

"Oh," she looked between them. "I planned to help Tanner get settled."

"Nah, it's good. Me and your ex need to talk." Tanner smirked.

"Fine, do the guy thing. But if I hear any fighting, I'm getting a bucket of water." She rolled her eyes, and Rafe smiled.

Tanner patted her shoulder. "No fighting. Got it."

"Good. I'll meet you two in the guest house."

Rafe watched until Elizabeth had descended the stairs before returning to the guest room with a suitcase one of the twins had left at the top of the stairs. "I think this is the last of your stuff."

"Thanks." Tanner grabbed his backpack and tossed it on the far bed before hefting the suitcase Rafe had brought up and laying it on the dresser.

The room was basic, a nightstand between two twin beds with a matching dresser to the right and another door that opened into a small closet.

"Expecting to be here longer than a few days?"

"Not really." He turned to Rafe, a determined look in his onyx eyes. "So, you're the ex."

"I am." Rafe readied himself for the inquisition.

"And you decided you'd what? Come ride in on your white steed and be the hero?"

"No, I . . ." He scrubbed a hand over his face. "I just want to make sure she's okay."

"Do you believe her?"

"I don't know what to believe. The better question is, do you?" On the one hand, Rafe knew Harold was capable of anything if it furthered his goals. Hell, the man had even forced Rafe into that damned contract. Megan, he was having a harder time wrapping his head around. But murder? That could land the man strapped to a gurney with a needle in his arm, and Rafe didn't think Harold would take that kind of chance.

"Yep." Tanner snatched the beanie off his head, revealing hair blacker than night in a surprising brush cut. It was nothing like how a teenager would style their hair.

"Why?"

"Because I know people." Tanner propped his hip against the dresser. "Elizabeth doesn't lie."

Rafe's eyes widened in shock that Tanner knew Elizabeth so well and trusted her implicitly.

"Annoying, isn't it? A seventeen-year-old knows more about your ex-wife that you ever did." The kid smirked.

Rafe flinched at that statement as it hit close to the mark.

"The question is, are you up for changing it?"

"If she's willing to let me." Rafe raised his gaze.

"She's in love with you. Of course she'll give you another chance." He hooked a thumb in the direction of the guest house. "She'd walk across fire for you. How do you feel about her?"

"I care about her—"

"Love?"

"Yes." He had no problem telling the kid how he felt since he'd already said the words to Elizabeth. Not that she had returned them, yet, but Rafe had hope.

"I won't keep pressing you, man."

Deciding a change of subject was in order, Rafe latched onto the imminent threat. "Do you really think Harold will come up here?"

"Yes."

"And you think being up here like sitting ducks is the way to go about this?"

"I do. She has no proof to take to the cops. Hell, she wasn't even going to go after the trust until me, Jessup, and Matt cornered her at Christmas." He threw his hands up, and Rafe took a step back.

Rafe's gut clenched. He could have missed her altogether, never had the opportunity to actually have a second chance with her if she hadn't come back to California to open that trust. "Why?"

"Because she hates confrontation." Tanner began to pace. "Why do you think she ran from you and them instead of confronting all of you about the ridiculous contract Harold made you sign? She never would have fought for that trust."

"What changed?"

"Me. I've already got a target on my back with King . . ."

"I heard about him."

"Yeah, so there's that, and I've lived on the streets more than in foster homes pretty much all my life. Always with a target. Whether it's because I'm half Native American and got beat for not being white enough or because I'm half-white and got a beat down from other Native Americans. Hate's hate, no matter how you slice it." Tanner stood tall. The young man had balls of steel. "And they haven't won. I won't let them win. I don't want Elizabeth to let her bullies win either, and if I have any way to help with that, then I'll do it."

"But why not confront them in California, where she has others to back her up?"

"It's their turf. This is her turf. She comes up here a few months every year to write and knows this place better than any other spot. And they don't because Harold never comes, and Megan hates the cold."

"She's putting herself in danger up here."

"Look, I love Col—" He cleared his throat, red creeping into his face. "I mean Elizabeth, and we have a plan."

Rafe frowned as his gaze bounced around, looking for bugs. He didn't want Elizabeth's new name exposed to anyone in case Harold and Megan didn't come for Elizabeth. But he didn't see anything out of place. Kennedy swore Tanner's room was bug and camera free as he was a minor, and she didn't want any legal crap coming back to bite her in the ass. And as spartan as the room was, the small pieces of equipment would have been easy to locate now that Rafe knew what to look for.

Rafe tuned back into Tanner.

"She's the big sister I never had. So, I want this resolved. If me hanging a target around my neck does it, then bring me paper and some markers, and I'll draw the damned thing myself." Tanner pushed into Rafe's space, his voice dropping. "Because the only thing Harold understands is money and power. Lock him up, take away that trust, and he's nothing. Just another inmate. Megan too."

"Know a lot of inmates?"

"Yep, my dad's one," Tanner snarled. "So, are you in the game, or are you still tying your shoes on the sidelines?"

"I'm here, aren't I?"

"Seems that way, but we'll see where you stand when one of the crazies comes after us." Tanner shrugged.

Rafe shook his head. "I'll stand in front of her, protecting her."

"Good. As long as you don't leave her."

"*She's* going to leave me, you know."

"Yep," Tanner said. "And I know if you want to keep her, you'll have to find her." His onyx gaze bore into Rafe. "You better make sure you want to keep her because there won't be a place on this earth that I won't find you if you hurt her again. Now, get out of here so I can use the bathroom and wash up."

Rafe tipped his chin in acknowledgment and left Tanner to follow when he was ready. He wanted to tell Tanner not to worry, that he planned on finding Elizabeth just as he'd promised. But words were meaningless. Instead, Rafe would find them and prove he wanted to be part of their lives.

As for the teenager, he liked him. Tanner wasn't at all what Rafe expected. He was stronger than Rafe had thought in spirit and body. Whereas Rafe had expected someone meek and easily cowed with how badly Elizabeth and Matt had said the kid had been beaten. Add in living on the streets, and Rafe was shocked Elizabeth had been able to break through the shield Tanner must have had up. But then again, Elizabeth had been surprising Rafe constantly now that he had his full attention focused on her.

~ ~ ~ ~

Elizabeth smiled at how easily Tanner and Rafe got along after their confrontation in Tanner's room.

She shouldn't have eavesdropped, but she'd been worried. The second she heard the guest room door close, Elizabeth had hurried back up the stairs to make sure two of the people she loved didn't tear into each other. She'd been so worried that Tanner would rip into Rafe, that the teenager would forget his promise and mention Elizabeth's babies to the man. Alternately, she had worried that Rafe would lose his temper as Tanner knew how to push people's buttons. Living on the streets had given Tanner a sixth sense about what pissed people off, and he used it to his advantage.

But none of that had happened. Instead, they'd somehow bonded. Tanner had sounded more grown-up than Elizabeth had ever heard him, and Rafe had opened up to show the young man he was here to stay. Satisfied, Elizabeth had rushed away before the door was ever opened. She had been doing a good job of dodging Rafe's questions last night about the money her mother had left Harold.

Her mother had drilled it into Elizabeth that no one had taught Harold how to manage money, and that's why they needed to take care of him. Little did either of them suspect how ruthless the asshole truly was. If Elizabeth hadn't heard him with her own ears, she wouldn't have believed him capable of setting not only Elizabeth up to be killed but her children as well. Luckily, Tanner understood the stakes, unlike a baby. When Harold and his goons came, Tanner would be able to run and hide if he needed to until the security team got to him.

As for Rafe, he'd been amazing with the teenager, treating him more as a young adult rather than the seventeen-year-old he was. It made her want to share their girls with him even more.

With Tanner being in the foster care system since he was a child, he was by no means an average teenager. A wise soul peered from behind his eyes more often than not. But on the ranch with Charlie, Tanner had recaptured a small piece of his childhood. Though Charlie had been a foster kid too, he hadn't gone into the system until he was seventeen, so he hadn't built up a lot of defenses. And as the family who had taken him in had never changed, he also didn't have that added hardness of being unwanted. Tanner's hard shell, formed while being rejected and moved so much when he was younger, left him unwilling to depend on anyone. Elizabeth and her crew had slipped beneath his shield when they had saved him and then taken him in.

The adoption had helped Tanner lower his defenses even more. But the biggest piece was Charlie befriending Tanner as it had further reinforced that Tanner had found his forever home with all the family he could ever want surrounding him. No one could stay stoic around Charlie—the kid had too much joy at the simplest of tasks. And Tanner's interactions with Charlie and Elizabeth's babies proved Tanner's time on the streets and in crappy foster homes hadn't completely hardened him.

The chicken she had made was cooked to perfection as each of them dug into the various bowls filled with glazed carrots, green beans, and the basket of drop biscuits. This was also one of Tanner's favorite meals, which was why she had gone to the trouble since this would be the only meal they shared while in Alaska.

"I didn't know you played chess," she said, interrupting their animated conversation on some chess competition they had both watched last week.

Tanner shrugged and shoved a bite into his mouth. After chewing and swallowing, he dug his fork into a red potato she had cooked with the roast.

"It's not a big deal." He sighed and met her gaze. "When I was in my first foster home, it was in Philly . . ."

He trailed off as if waiting for Elizabeth to pepper him with questions about Philly, probably since they had met in North Dakota, but she refused to interrogate the kid. Knowing he would tell her when he was ready, she dipped her roll into the sauce from the roast and bit into it before motioning for him to continue.

"Okay, so yeah, I was in foster care in Philly. The first home wasn't so bad. I mean, there wasn't a ton to eat since they used the money they got for me on booze, mostly. They at least didn't beat me." He shrugged again. "The man thought he was a fu—I mean freaking genius and would drag me to the park to play chess there."

She hid her anger at his casual mention of not being beaten as an endorsement for living in a solid foster home. Instead, she focused on how hard Tanner was trying to clean up his language for his little sisters and shot him a look of approval, which brought a small smile to his face.

"And was he?" Rafe asked when Tanner didn't continue.

"Was he what?"

"A genius?"

Tanner snorted and shook his head. "Not even close, guy was dumber than a sack of rocks. The chess guys would hustle him. The guys were good at stringing my foster dad along too, letting him win a few but not by so much as to set off alarms. When the chess guys won, again, it wasn't by enough to make him stop going back for more."

"How long were you with them?" Rafe asked, curiosity burning in his emerald gaze.

"About a year."

"And they just dumped you?" Elizabeth couldn't stop that question from bubbling out of her lips.

"Nah, the wife got pissed because foster dad kept taking more than half the money. She said if she had to put up with a foster kid and get less than her share, she'd leave and get the full amount. Mostly because it's rare for them to give single men foster status. It's either married men or single women." He scratched his cheek. "At least that's my experience. The second foster home was for shit, and I bailed on that one. Rambled around a bit, went into the system when I was caught and ran when it was bad."

From a child until seventeen, you were alone? Elizabeth wanted to ask but knew it would shut Tanner up quicker than duct tape slapped across his mouth. He became prickly if he thought anyone pitied him.

"And you ended up in North Dakota."

"Yeah. Fu—I mean freaking small-town police got nothing better to do than hassle the homeless." He shoved another bite in his mouth, and based on the glint in his eyes, Elizabeth knew the conversation was done as far as his foster care situation was concerned.

"Well, when I find Elizabeth again, we'll have to have some real chess matches," Rafe said, breaking the uncomfortable silence. "But I'll want a good opponent, so I'm going to give you some books so you can read up on strategies. And until I get to wherever you all are, we can play virtually." He pointed to Elizabeth. "She has my number, so just shoot me a text."

"Cool. After this shit is done—crap. I meant crap." He made a frustrated noise in the back of his throat. "Cleaning up my language sucks donkey balls."

Elizabeth patted his leg, glad Tanner hadn't lost all his fire after his beating by King's men. She loved seeing the confidence building up in the young man and was doubly glad Kennedy had allowed her and Tanner to have this time alone with Rafe while the security group met at the main house to cover all contingency plans and fill the new guys in on what they'd set up so far.

"I hate not being able to hang out here with you guys," he mumbled.

"I hate it too, but the second this is over, we'll catch up," Elizabeth said.

"Not with Rafe."

"No, not with me, but you know I need to earn that time first," Rafe said.

"I guess." Then Tanner did the most unadult thing Elizabeth had ever seen him do—he bounced in his chair. "Oh, by the way, I downloaded your books and started reading them."

She groaned, sopping up the last of the juice on her plate with the roll.

"The pirate story is shit. I hate sci-fi crap. Why Seth thought I'd like that, I've got no idea." Tanner shoved the last potato in his mouth with a frown.

"Probably because it's YA, which is your age range."

"Screw you," he snarled, tossing his fork on his empty plate. "Age is just a number."

"For you? Yes." She could barely refrain from rolling her eyes.

"But that safe book . . . Holy shit." He pushed his plate away and leaned toward her. "Seth said he and Ellis met the guy that helped you with that one."

"Safe book?" Rafe interrupted, turning a confused gaze on both of them as he pushed his plate away too. "You know about safes?"

"Oh yeah, and she knows how long the air lasts in them before it kills a person."

Rafe's jaw fell open, and Elizabeth dropped her face into her hands.

"What the hell do you write?"

"What do you mean, 'what does she write?' Only the coolest books ever." Tanner jerked back with a frown.

"I thought she wrote romance."

"Ew, no. No way in hell I would read romance." Tanner scrunched his face up as if he smelled something foul. "She writes crime thrillers and FBI catching serial killer books."

"What's her pen name?" Rafe frowned.

"Lucy Stridell."

Rafe choked on the tea he had been sipping, and Tanner pounded his back while Elizabeth winced.

"Really?" Rafe's wide eyes held shock as he wiped his mouth with a napkin.

"You know, I've never been a blip on anyone's radar until this past year," she muttered and stood, snatching her plate and Tanner's to take them to the sink. "And yes, really."

"Jesus, I've read your books. I've pre-ordered Abduction."

"Oh, that one was . . ." She trailed off, unsure that Rafe really wanted to hear how emotional that book had been to write. It was also the most satisfying. She'd met with several trafficked victims and asked what they would do to their captors for vengeance as that was the primary theme of her books. They had been creative with their punishments, and Elizabeth had used a lot of their ideas in her book, hoping she could at least give her survivors not just vengeance but closure too.

"Was hard to write." Rafe finished for her, proving he was coming to understand her.

She tipped her chin in agreement, setting the dirty dishes on the counter. Placing the stopper in the sink, she filled it with warm soapy water.

Just as they set the last dirty dish next to the sink, her cell rang with Megan's ringtone.

"Shit," she said, drying her hands and grabbing her cell. "It's Megan."

"Put it on speaker," Rafe said as he packed up the leftovers.

Tanner stood with his arms crossed, a mulish expression on his face.

"Megan."

"You have me on speaker," she said.

"I do. Tanner's here, and Rafe's in the other room." Not technically a lie since he was in the kitchen area.

The mom-in-law cabin situated behind the rambling main house was an open floor plan with two bedrooms tucked into the back and a bathroom in between. It was perfect for a dual family vacation. The real estate agent had pointed it out as being nice for teenagers or for adults with no kids since there was a hot tub on the back deck.

"The kid is there with Rafe?"

"Not a kid," Tanner snarled.

Elizabeth cut her eyes to him in warning.

"Fine, the almost adult—"

"I have a fucking name." He huffed in irritation. "You know what, I'm going to see if Rafe has the chess game set up in the other room yet."

Tanner stomped off to the other side of the cabin with a smirk. Oh, the little shit knew how to push buttons.

"Great, now he hates me and likes Rafe."

"Rafe doesn't call him a kid. Besides, what does it matter? You and Harold both have made it abundantly clear you don't want anything to do with Tanner, even if something were to happen to me. Oh, and before we leave for our cruise, Jessup is meeting us in Anchorage to change my will—" Elizabeth rolled her eyes, knowing Harold had already passed the information along to Megan.

"He is? Wait, Anchorage?"

"Yes, so neither you nor Harold will have to worry about Tanner anymore." Elizabeth reiterated, going with Kennedy's idea of Jessup meeting them in Anchorage instead of them going to California. It was logical since Elizabeth had made such a big deal about not missing their cruise and it would put more pressure on the duo to come here instead of waiting for

Elizabeth in California.

She just hoped the gambit worked.

"Quit lumping me in with your stepfather. I never said I wouldn't take on the kid, and I would be better at it than Rafe since he dumped you at the drop of a hat."

"Well, you don't have to worry. I plan to live a long time, so no one will be the guardian of Tanner except me." Elizabeth sighed, already exhausted from all the subterfuge. "Is that why you called?"

"No, I just wanted to know you made it to Barrow okay."

"Yep," Raising her voice as if she were talking to Tanner, Elizabeth made sure Megan could hear her. "Tanner, before you get immersed in that game with Rafe, did you put your stuff up?"

"Yes, ma'am. I took the first room up the stairs since Rafe has the one next to you." Tanner caught on quick and winked at her while answering.

"Rafe's not sleeping with you?" Megan immediately took the bait, drawing a triumphant smile from Elizabeth.

"Not yet. Maybe after we get our bearings. Right now, he's in the room next to the master suite."

"Look, I'm sorry for how I reacted to the news of Tanner." Megan sighed. "I really am glad you found someone that you consider a little brother, and I'm hoping I can meet him soon."

"Thanks for that, Megan, and maybe we can meet up like we planned at one of the ports on the cruise," Elizabeth said, forcing herself to remember all of this was an act.

"Call me later."

"Sure." But Elizabeth knew she wouldn't because they weren't friends, so why would she waste her time? But she couldn't say that. Instead, she ended the call and tried to breathe through the panic stuttering in her chest.

"When Kennedy and Kenneth lift the lockdown protocol, do you think we could go look for the Sasquatch?" Tanner nudged her shoulder, drawing her out of her spiraling thoughts with his ridiculous request.

"Where the heck did you even come up with that?" Elizabeth squinted at the kid.

"Seth."

"Figures." She pinched the bridge of her nose and mumbled.

No way would she venture into the barren wasteland of Barrow to hunt some huge hairy beast in the dark. Nope. Not happening. But when she met Tanner's excited gaze, Elizabeth caved like wet toilet paper.

"Maybe we should plan a trip for all of us, including Seth and Ellis, so you all can go look for the Sasquatch." *And I can stay in the cozy warm cabin drinking a glass of wine in front of the fire.*

"Seriously?" His face lit up at the thrill of the adventure being presented.

"Yes."

"I'd actually enjoy coming on that trip." Rafe tossed her a smirk over his shoulder. "A couple of my buddies might like to come too."

Tanner released a *whoop* paired with a fist pump before bopping over to help Rafe with the dishes.

If a hunt for bigfoot brought Tanner this much joy, she would make it a point to bring all of them here so they could traipse through the wilds of Alaska looking for the imaginary hairy monster.

Watching Tanner and Rafe interact tugged at her heart. She could picture him fitting seamlessly into her new family. Would Rafe be this easy-going with his daughters when they reached Tanner's age? And would he ever forgive her for not telling him about the girls as soon as they reconnected?

Chapter Sixteen

They had been in Barrow for almost two weeks, and nothing. Even her writing was suffering with how on edge Elizabeth was. Setting their afternoon snack of brownies on the stove to cool, she sighed as she listened to Rafe voice his doubts. Not that she needed more stress dumped on her, but she couldn't fault him for his logic.

"Maybe you misheard them, hon," Rafe said as he finished making the coffee. "Megan apologized the next day, just like I remember her doing whenever you two argued. And Harold said he was sorry last weekend and invited you and Tanner to dinner when you got back from your cruise. I mean, if they were coming, they would have already been here, right?"

Elizabeth could see why Rafe would ask that since they were scheduled to go to Anchorage tomorrow to have Tanner's cast removed. This was the last night for Megan and Harold to act. If they didn't come tonight, she didn't know what she would do. If this plan failed, what else could she do?

"I get how this looks. But I swear to you,
Megan and Harold are planning on killing me,"
Elizabeth stated in a whisper, doing her best not to
wake up Kenneth and Rob since the two men had been
out in the biting cold dismantling the perimeter alarms
most of yesterday and then on patrol last night. "When
they make their move, you'll have your proof."

"If they make a move. It's been two weeks—"

"As if they would just jump the second they
knew we were vulnerable? They're smarter than that."
Elizabeth cut the delicious chocolate goodness and set
the brownies on the platter she had pulled from the
cabinet. "At least Megan is, she'll get the lay of the land
first."

Except Megan wouldn't have taken two weeks
to watch them.

"If that were the case, why are you and Megan
exchanging texts constantly?" Rafe ran a hand over the
back of his neck. "Based on your tracker app, she hasn't
even left California."

Just as the words left his mouth, her cell chimed
with an incoming text. Flipping it over, she sighed and
shot back a text that the latte artist was talented, and
she didn't know glitter could be added to a drink.

"Exactly like that. You two are acting like best
friends again."

"And that's all it is, is an act." Elizabeth
narrowed her gaze on him. But before she could lay out
all the evidence, Rafe shook his head and tossed the
towel on the counter.

"We'll see," he said cryptically and stalked to the
enclosed back porch.

Why hadn't Megan or Harold come yet? Elizabeth worried her lip. Then she snagged her burner and called Hank while gathering the milk and honey together to make her coffee.

"What?" he growled.

"Has Megan left California at all?"

"No, I would've called you if she had," he grumbled while wind whipped in the background before abruptly cutting off as if he stepped into his shelter. "Neither her nor Harold have left California. And from what I'm seeing, Harold's been in several meetings and has another one set up for today."

"Megan?"

"No, at least none since the day before yesterday. She's been mostly at her house, the coffee shop, and running what looks like random errands."

"It's the last night—"

"I know." He huffed. "I just don't get it. Everything is set up perfectly for them to come take you both out. Or at least you. But there's nothing."

"Maybe it's too perfect." Elizabeth rubbed her pounding temple. "Should I have agreed to meet them in California?"

"No. That's putting you on their turf, and that's not a good position to be in. Here, you control the area. They may be letting the argument die down so nothing comes back on them if the cops get involved."

Elizabeth sighed. "Maybe."

"Look, here's what we're going to do: First, you leave exactly as planned—"

"But they think I'm going to—"

"Second, you text them after Tanner gets his cast off that Jessup's running behind and you need to catch the cruise ship at the next port."

"What good will that do?"

"It will give us a chance to place someone else on that cruise for you. If they don't make a move before you meet with Jessup, they might try while you're both out to sea or at port, where you go off on your own."

That made an odd sort of sense. Worry ate at her. "But if they do that, we'll never catch them."

"You don't worry about that. You just worry about getting to the ranch safely so we can all regroup and figure out another plan."

It sounded good, but she didn't know what 'other plan' they could possibly come up with.

"You know, I could just kill them."

"Hell no," she shouted before catching herself so as to not wake up her housemates. "No. You're out of that life, and I will not drag you back into it."

Especially since it had taken a lot of time for Hank to relax and not look over his shoulder constantly. His last job had almost killed him, and it had taken three weeks in the hospital and months of physical therapy before he could use his left arm again. Then there were the psychiatrists he had gone through. Fifteen in all, by the time Hank had found one he trusted enough to talk to. Elizabeth had heard all this from Casey. So no, she refused to be the reason Hank stepped back into that world.

There had to be another way. They just had to find it.

Giving in to the inevitable pissed her off. She wanted this settled because she was ready for the next part of her life to start. But she couldn't start anything with Megan and Harold hanging over her like the blade of Damocles.

"Fine, we'll do it your way."

"Good. Get some rest, and if anything pops, I'll call you." Hank ended the call as abruptly as he'd answered it.

"Tanner's going to come over, and we're going to play chess with the actual board," Rafe said as he laid the board on the coffee table.

The two screens attached to a laptop still held rotating images inside the main house. Those would be taken down tomorrow morning as Kennedy and Luke packed up and put the house back in order.

"Is that okay?" Rafe asked.

"If Kennedy says it's fine, then I guess it's fine." Elizabeth's stomach churned. Should Tanner be here? Hell, if she knew. It felt wrong not following protocol, but it was almost three in the afternoon and their last night here. The last night Rafe and Tanner could bond in person instead of through their cells. The last night Elizabeth could play at having a family.

"Kennedy says she doesn't see a problem as long as he stays here for the night."

Screw it. It isn't like we won't have some warning if they come. Which is looking more and more unlikely.

"He can sleep on the couch." Elizabeth checked the hall closet. "And there are extra blankets and pillows in here."

"Great." Rafe tossed her a grin. The first one she had seen in two days.

She jumped when the front door was thrown open, then released the breath she hadn't realized she was holding as Tanner stomped into the room.

"Get ready to be beaten in real life, old man."

"Bring it, brat," Rafe snarked back as he waited for Tanner to take off his jacket and snowshoes.

Hours later, they were still battling it out.

Dinner was a quick meal of sandwiches; no one wanted to cook since they were all focused on the game.

Elizabeth tried to follow the moves, but she had never mastered chess. Instead, she enjoyed watching Rafe and Tanner interact. They exchanged smack talk while also tossing out questions. She learned Tanner was a fan of the Three Stooges, and there was a heated discussion on Shemp vs. Curly. It was unexpected to find a sixteen-year-old who had actually watched the show and knew the characters.

In between watching Rafe and Tanner, she kept an eye on the monitors that panned through the house.

"We're headed out to finish grabbing the last of the perimeter alarms and then packing up," Kenneth said, tapping Elizabeth's shoulder as he and Rob headed out the back door.

~ ~ ~ ~

It was close to midnight when Elizabeth cut into the game. "Time to call it quits."

"I'll grab a pic so we can keep going tomorrow on the plane."

"Good idea." Rafe took a step back while Tanner snapped a picture of the board.

Done, the two began cleaning up, and Elizabeth pulled the blankets out of the closet to make up the couch for Tanner.

After she checked that Tanner had everything he needed, she took her turn in the bathroom. A soft rap on the door had her hurrying into her nightgown and opening the door to find Rafe leaning against the doorjamb.

"Look, I'm sorry if it seemed I doubted you earlier—"

"No, I get why you think I might have misunderstood what Megan and Harold were saying that night." She sighed and turned back to the bathroom counter to finish packing her things up.

"Maybe they found out you were there and changed their plans," Rafe said, joining her. "Or maybe you didn't hear everything."

"Maybe." She shrugged. "I'm going to make sure I have everything packed up since we leave early tomorrow."

Rafe waved her out with his toothbrush before loading it down with toothpaste and cramming it in his mouth.

"That's way too much toothpaste." She shivered with disgust when Rafe tossed her a foam-filled smile. When he lunged at her with a growl, she squealed and raced for their room. Still laughing, she headed to their room for one more check of the chest of drawers and closet. Her mind turned back to the trust and Harold and Megan.

It was possible they'd caught on to her being there that night. She had no idea how, but it would explain why they'd left her alone. Whether they had discovered her being there or not, she knew she hadn't misunderstood them. Nightmares still haunted her from that conversation as well as her biggest fear. There would have been no witnesses if they had caught her and killed her that night. No one would ever have been the wiser, not even Rafe.

Of course, Harold would have lost out on the trust entirely since, in the wake of her death, all that money would have been dispersed into non-profits.

Elizabeth hated that damned trust. It'd brought
her nothing but trouble, and she wished she had just
signed it over to those charities. But since it was now
the bait to bring Megan and Harold out into the open,
she had kept it like Jessup suggested.

Except it hadn't worked. Instead, Elizabeth was
like the boy who cried wolf, and now she had pointed
everyone toward Barrow with nothing to show for it.

Habit sent her back to the computer screens for
one last check of the house. The clock over the
fireplace rang out over the soft snores drifting from the
guest room where Kenneth and Rob were sleeping.
Tanner was buried under the blankets, already sacked
out.

She wiggled the mouse to wake the monitors
up, her mind churning with ideas, hoping to land on
something else she could use to trap Harold.

Motion on the far corner screen caught her
attention before the video flashed to the den.

I'm probably just seeing what I want to be there. But
she refused to take any chances as she pulled the
keyboard from under the monitors. Growling in
frustration, Elizabeth hovered her fingers over the
keyboard as she tried to remember how to take control
of the cameras.

"Liz, quit looking at that thing and come to
bed," Rafe said, shuffling into the room in a long john
shirt and flannel pants.

Movement in the hallway leading to the master
bedroom had Elizabeth snatching up her cell as she
pointed to the guest bedroom. "Wake Kenneth.
Someone's in the house with Kennedy and Luke."

Rafe's eyes widened, and he darted to the room
that Kenneth and Rob slept in.

"What?" Kennedy's sleep roughened voice came over the cell, reminding Elizabeth of the danger the woman and her partner was in.

"Wake up. Someone's heading your way." Elizabeth clutched her cell as she watched Kennedy bolt upright in the bed and shove Luke awake with a quick hand motion.

Elizabeth disconnected the call just in case any sound alerted the intruder that Kennedy was awake.

Guilt gnawed at her. The others could be forgiven for doubting Megan and Harold would attack them. None of them had been there to hear the couple's confession, but Elizabeth had. She knew what lengths the two would go through to kill her, and she had let her damned guard down. If Kennedy and Luke didn't get to their weapons on the dresser, they would be sitting ducks, and Elizabeth was not naïve enough to think the killer would wait for a fair fight.

Kenneth was the first of the security team to hurry into the room. Elizabeth had expected as much since it was his twin in the crosshairs. Elizabeth hovered behind him as if she could keep the two in the house safe.

Shifting from foot to foot, she wondered if she should change out of her nightgown and into her snowsuit in case they needed to run. But she forced the feeling aside since she was better protected here with security around her than in the wilderness of Alaska that held bears and wolves, to name just a few of the untamed animals roaming the forest behind them.

Kenneth's fingers danced across the keyboard, and the screen flickered through the various video feeds until he found the camera he wanted and stopped. One half of the master suite was shown, with Kennedy and Luke near the dresser slipping the comms into their ears before palming their weapons and melting into the shadows on either side of the room.

"Looks like someone finally decided to pay you a visit, Elizabeth."

Elizabeth watched the monitors and knew it was Megan based on the way she moved. Having known the woman almost her entire life, Elizabeth could easily see it was her ex-best friend stalking toward the house. "It's Megan."

"Talk about waiting 'til the last second. Huh, all I'm seeing is Megan," Kenneth said when none of the cameras showed any sign of Harold.

Elizabeth shifted for a better view of the screen and frowned as she realized neither Kennedy nor Luke wore their vests. They had been sleeping in their vests every night . . . except the last two.

Jesus, I should have pitched a fit about how lax we've all become.

Maybe Megan would turn tail and run when she realized the couple in the master suite were armed. Elizabeth hoped the woman would run instead of shooting.

"He might be waiting in case she needs backup." Kenneth slapped several keys to pull up the entire array of views each camera captured, but none showed movement except the one that had Megan. Meanwhile, Rob quietly relayed where the intruder was to Luke and Kennedy.

"How did she get into the house so fast?" Rafe asked in a murmur next to Elizabeth.

"She must have a key." Elizabeth pointed. "And the alarm code."

They all saw the solid green light on the alarm panel. But how had Megan gotten those things? Elizabeth hadn't a clue, considering the woman who'd rented her the house had left the garage door openers and keys with the Sheriff before she headed south for the winter. Elizabeth had picked them up on the way in.

"She's just passing the guest bathroom, Kennedy," Rob said while he dressed behind them, sliding his bulletproof vest over his flannel shirt before putting on his winter gear. "I'm heading out to do a perimeter sweep in case Megan's backup is in a car, Kenneth, you're on comms."

Kenneth shot Rob a thumbs up as he slipped through the door but didn't stop following Megan's trip down the hallway toward the master suite.

Elizabeth was glued to the monitor as if she were watching a horror movie. "She has something on her face." Elizabeth squinted. "What is that?"

None of the cameras caught a good view of Megan's face as she slipped from shadow to shadow, but even with her face distorted, she still knew that was Megan on the screen. In one motion, Megan had the suite door open and her gun lifted. Bullets ripped through the bed, but at seeing it empty, Megan's head pivoted around the room.

Kennedy raised her gun before she opened her mouth to tell Megan to drop her weapon, but Megan pulled the trigger as she turned. Kennedy slammed into the wall. Megan ducked back into the hallway and fled.

Elizabeth gasped when she saw Kennedy crumple to the floor.

"Kennedy's down, and Megan's headed out of the house," Luke shouted over their coms.

Kenneth grabbed his cell and slapped the screen. Within several heartbeats, he began snapping out information to what sounded like emergency personnel.

Anger flooded into Elizabeth. She stormed to the front door, pausing just long enough to grab her rifle.

No one had put together that the rifle belonged to her. The security team assumed it was Rafe's, and Rafe assumed security had brought it. Elizabeth hadn't fully trusted either one, in the beginning, so she hadn't filled in anyone on who actually owned the gun.

The weapon was as familiar to her as her own hand. Her father had purchased the rifle for her, taught her to shoot at the age of eight, and had her kill once, so she understood the power behind the weapon as well as the weight of having a life in her hands. Her kill was a buck, and her father had taught her that if she ever hunted, she needed to use every piece of meat and the hide.

And though he'd probably never meant for her to use what he taught her in this manner, she was thankful she'd had the lessons and had continued them the second she'd set foot on her ranch.

Hefting the weapon to her shoulder, she rolled her neck before looking through the sight. Within seconds, she spotted Megan. One breath in and a slow exhale as she pulled the trigger and her bullet found its mark in Megan's leg.

Megan fell into the snow, and Elizabeth raced toward her with Rob coming from her left and the others at her back.

Rafe caught up to her and then pulled ahead. Megan rolled to her back, her gun still clutched in her hand as she smiled, aiming for Elizabeth. Elizabeth froze and winced when she heard the gun's rapport, cursing herself for leaving the cabin without a damn vest. But she never felt the fiery pain of a bullet tearing through her. Instead, Rafe slammed into her and grunted as he toppled them both into the icy snow.

Sitting up, Elizabeth swept a hand over chest and arms, but there wasn't any blood. No bullet holes. Nothing. She swung her gaze to Rafe to see the white snow beside him stained red.

"Dammit!" She rolled him over and saw him holding his arm.

"Screw you, Elizabeth. At least I had a vest. You just ran out of the house with nothing," he snarled, cradling his bicep.

She flinched, knowing she had reacted instead of stopping to think it through. "If you think getting shot will make me take your raggedy-ass home and nurse you back to health, you've got another think coming."

"As if I would go. I told you I'd find you." He snapped. "Besides, it's a graze, not even bigger than a paper cut."

It was then Elizabeth heard Megan's whining as Rob flipped her to her stomach and slid a pair of cable ties, like the ones cops used, onto her bony wrists.

"Tanner, get over here and help Rafe."
Elizabeth scrambled to her feet, rage warming her to
the point she didn't feel the biting cold through her
nightgown or the icy, wet snow soaking into the thick
socks covering her feet. Stomping over to Megan,
Elizabeth grabbed the woman's hair and yanked her
head back. When their gazes clashed, Elizabeth shoved
her face into Megan's. "When the Sheriff hauls your ass
away, you will make a deal, and you will tell them
everything."

"I don't know what you're talking about," she
growled.

"Bullshit." Elizabeth saw the wound and smiled.
It satisfied something dark in Elizabeth to have Megan
as helpless as Elizabeth had been when they had
destroyed her life. "You will tell them how you and
Harold murdered my mother, how you planned on
getting me pregnant. How you two planned on killing
me and gaining custody of that baby. And how you
both planned to steal my child's inheritance. If you
don't, next time I won't aim for your damned leg." She
leaned close to Megan's ear and whispered, "And I
won't wait for you to come to me. I'll hunt you like my
dad taught me before he died. I was an exceptional
student." Elizabeth pulled away and dropped Megan's
head. Ice-cold determination made her expression hard
as Megan ducked away from her gaze.

Standing, Elizabeth swayed on numb feet. Just
as she stumbled back to Rafe, the yard and driveway
began to fill with emergency personnel. Not many as
there was only a skeleton crew left in Barrow during the
darkness of winter. But there were two paramedics that
split up, one helping Rafe back to the main house while
the second examined Megan.

"We have a wounded person in the master suite that needs you more than I do." Rafe waved the paramedic toward the main house. "Go tend to her, and I'll wait for you in the kitchen."

The paramedic watched him for a few seconds before racing to the house, calling out as he entered with the sheriff's deputy on his heels and Kenneth bringing up the rear.

The sheriff made a beeline toward Elizabeth and Rafe but kept quiet until they reached the kitchen of the main house.

Rob and Tanner pushed Rafe into a chair, and the Sheriff began peppering them with questions. While Rafe was trapped, Elizabeth hurried to the smaller cabin to change before her own interrogation started.

Chapter Seventeen

Elizabeth woke slowly. Long arms wrapped around her held her close to Rafe's chest behind her. She blinked her eyes at the sight of the generic hotel room, and then the past several days flooded back to her.

Capturing Megan, being forced to hop on the puddle jumper to avoid the storm front moving in, and the FBI meeting them at the small airport in Anchorage.

But all that dimmed in the light of Rafe leaving today. Her gaze jumped to the clock. Its red numbers read 8:13. She winced. Only a few hours, and he would need to be at the airport for check-in, without her or Tanner.

The FBI had asked them to remain here for another few days while they confirmed their story with Barrow law enforcement. Unfortunately, the storm in Barrow was wreaking havoc with communication, but it was expected to clear up tomorrow morning. Megan wasn't talking. Not even when they patched her up. And because Elizabeth had been the one to shoot her, she had to wait for the sheriff up there to tell the FBI they had the evidence and coordinate sending it down here. What pained her more was she had been forced to leave her rifle with the sheriff.

Rafe's arms tightened. "You awake?" he asked in a sleep-roughened voice that sent a shiver across her skin.

"Again?" Arching back into him, she felt his hardened length nestled in the small of her back.

Her body ached in the most pleasurable way, but she didn't think she could make love with him again. He had been a demanding lover from the time Kennedy took Tanner yesterday afternoon and all through the night, repeatedly bringing her to the edge only to hold her there for what felt like an eternity before flinging her into the abyss. Then starting over.

"No, I hate to say it, but you wore me out last night and this morning," he teased while nuzzling the nape of her neck.

She was split on whether she was glad he was worn out since her entire body ached in places that hadn't been used that well since reuniting in Barrow, or sad since this was their last morning together.

"Are you okay?" he asked, his hand unerringly finding and kneading a spasming muscle.

"I think you had a good idea with no more sexcapades." She rolled over to face him.

"You're saying I wore you out too?" He grinned like the cat that stole the cream.

"Maybe." She mock-frowned at him, and he leaned in to nibble her lips, stealing a kiss before she pushed him away. Her fingers traced across his brow. "Why the frown?"

"Just wondering if those agents will actually explain why they're interested in Megan . . ."

"And me?"

"Yes."

She didn't know. Their roundabout questions were odd, and as her cell had been dead when they landed, she had left it on the charger in the hotel room all day yesterday. Rafe had suggested, after she had been cooped up for most of the day with the feds, that Sunday be a family day. So, he had herded Elizabeth and Tanner out to explore Anchorage.

It had been the best day of her life. Rafe had arranged a helicopter tour, then they had checked out the local museum and received a guided tour of the Oscar Anderson House. The day had ended with watching the Northern Lights. A sight she would never tire of seeing.

"Do you think Megan's talked yet?" he asked, pulling her from her memories.

"I don't know." She rubbed a hand across his shadowed jaw, loving the scrape against her palm.

"Why don't you see if the feds have left you any messages while I get cleaned up."

"Okay." She sighed, hating that reality was intruding on them yet again.

She stayed put as he disappeared into the bathroom. The flex of muscles under his skin made her want to say to hell with responsibility and join him to watch the water slide across his tan skin. The pink line where Megan's bullet had grazed his bicep was healing with no infection.

But she enjoyed checking his wound to make sure it was okay, preferably with her fingers and tongue. That would be much more enjoyable than anything Megan or the feds could offer her. Megan was lucky. Between the scratch on Rafe and the shoulder wound on Kennedy, it could have been much worse. If Kennedy hadn't ducked when she had, Megan would have riddled her chest with bullets. Elizabeth thanked God Megan was not as good a shot as she was, or they would have been bringing home Kennedy and Rafe's bodies.

Elizabeth, however, made damn sure to hit what she was aiming for as her daddy had taught her.

While her primary cell booted up, she decided to check her burner, knowing she needed to fill Hank in on what had transpired. She should have done it the second she and Rafe shuffled into the suite, but Tanner and Rafe had stayed up rehashing everything that had happened in Barrow. Then they had slept in, and the day got away from her.

The three missed calls all from Hank sat on the burner felt like a rebuke.

Ducking into the bathroom, she raised her voice to be heard over the steady drone of the shower. "I'm going to run downstairs and grab us some coffee and breakfast. Is there anything specific you want?"

"Bacon."

"Duh. Anything else?" She smiled and shook her head.

"Nope." His head popped out from behind the curtain. "But if you think you've gotten enough bacon, add a few extra strips just to be safe."

"I'm going to put you on a turkey bacon diet." She pointed as she stepped back, narrowly dodging the water he flung at her.

"Blasphemy!"

She laughed and headed back into the main room to toss on clothes. When she left the suite, the smile slid from her face as she hurried to the stairs leading to the lobby. It didn't matter that they were on the ninth floor and the elevator would be faster; she needed the privacy.

With trembling fingers, she hit Hank's contact. He answered within two rings.

"Where the hell are you?"

"Anchorage. The feds—"

"I know. I've been trying to reach you."

"It's been a shitshow. Megan showed up but not Harold." She sank onto the top step and raked a hand through her hair.

"And the feds? Why are they involved and not the sheriff?"

"I don't know. I've wracked my brain, but I've got nothing."

"You haven't talked to them?"

"Once, and they asked the weirdest questions." Elizabeth's stomach dropped just thinking about it.

"Questions? Like?"

"Like if he showed more interest in me than Mom. Or if I noticed anything unusual between him and any of my friends." Elizabeth knew what they were implying, but Harold couldn't be that much of a monster. Her mother never would have married him if he was.

"Shit." Hank fell quiet, but there was rapid tapping on a keyboard before he began cursing in what sounded like Arabic.

"What?"

"I had a feeling about Megan, but I never pursued it because, by the time she came for you, she had already made her choice. And I never suspected Harold had lined up a replacement for her."

"Are you saying he really was with Megan when she was a teenager?" Elizabeth's blood ran cold.

"I think so, but I can't be sure because he was smart in making it seem as if she were with you at any event. Shit." The typing came to an abrupt end.

"You found another one, didn't you?" Bile rose to the back of Elizabeth's throat, and she swallowed convulsively to keep from gagging.

"Yes," he hissed, barely held rage pouring through the line. "Except the girl is tied with a woman, Harold is actually wooing the woman."

"That's not possible. He gave Megan an engagement ring. He's still attending charity events with Megan," Elizabeth rasped through a constricted throat as she worked to keep from screaming. Then another, viler, thought hit her. One she didn't want to voice yet because she wasn't sure she wanted Megan to get off after almost killing Rafe and Kennedy. But Elizabeth was nothing if not honest with herself. Megan had pulled the trigger, but it was Harold's machinations that had pointed Megan and that damned gun toward Elizabeth.

She would need to ask if there were other girls before the call ended. If there were more victims out there, it would establish a pattern for Harold. And if there was proof, Elizabeth would bet every bit of her trust that proof would pry Megan's mouth open and get her to spill everything.

Shaking off her thoughts, she homed in on the information Hank provided as if this were just another story she would be writing. She would fall apart later. Right now she needed to prepare for whatever the feds were about to rain down on her.

"Smoke and mirrors. I bet he used that fake engagement to get her to come kill you, and then he planned to kill her." More typing on his end. "It would explain why she was sent, in case she was caught. She would be expendable, and as long as he made a show of supporting her. . ."

"She'd keep her mouth shut." Her cell dinged with an incoming file, and she flipped open the picture Hank had sent. The teenager looked eerily like Megan at that age.

"You have to admit the man has a type," Hank said.

"I want him buried, Hank. I want him destroyed." Rage consumed her at seeing Harold's fingers on the girl's shoulder and his arm wrapped around his new girlfriend's waist. It looked to have been taken around Christmas. Did that mean he hadn't been with Megan during the holidays? Or did he blow off the new girlfriend just after taking this picture in order to keep Megan happy so she would kill Elizabeth?

"That means you've got to get Megan to flip on him," Hank stated.

"Send me everything you can find. We both know there had to be more between Megan and this girl." Elizabeth ground out. "And I'll get her to flip. When she finds out he lied to her about their happily ever after, she'll tell the feds all of Harold's secrets."

"If she knows them."

Megan would know them. Harold always liked to brag. And who better to brag to than the brainwashed woman who would do anything for him, even kill?

"She knows them." And Elizabeth knew Megan. Her ex-friend wasn't stupid, and she sure as hell didn't trust easily. Elizabeth bet Megan had proof tucked away somewhere.

"Okay, give me a few hours to dig everything up, and I'll send it all over to you."

"Thanks, Hank."

"Yep."

Elizabeth stood and slid the burner into her pocket with a shiver. Her mother had married a monster. That had to be why Harold had really killed her, not for their money. Lillian didn't care what Harold spent. She must have found out he was a pedophile, and she was planning to burn his world to the ground.

How would Mom have found out? Elizabeth hadn't a clue. But if there was any scrap of evidence out there, Hank would find it. With a sigh, she pushed it all away and focused on the last bit of time she would have with Rafe. All of this would still be there after he left. But God, did she want to beg him to stay and help hold her together if what she and Hank suspected was true.

Shaking the thought away, she jogged down the stairs to get Rafe his massive amount of bacon he requested.

When she returned, she was just in time to watch him shave. The act had become one of her favorite things to see. She was racking up a pile of favorites now. Being held by him all night was the first. Enjoying a cup of coffee with him every morning was another. Talking to him about anything and everything that came up. And watching the razor as it dragged across his skin was an intimacy a wife would have the privilege of enjoying.

"Bacon delivery," she said as she rolled the cart carrying plates filled with their breakfast and coffee service into the room.

The few precious hours she had left with Rafe flew by as if they were seconds. Then they were downstairs with him, loading the rental while Tanner shuffled up next to them. She expected Tanner to climb into the backseat. When he didn't, she stepped over to him with an arched brow.

"I'm not going."

"Why not?"

"You and him need to be alone for as long as you can."

"But you're going to miss him too."

"Not like you will." He waved his cell in front of her. "And I'm still playing chess with him, so we'll stay in touch that way."

A little more time with just her and Rafe sent a shaft of joy into her. Smiling that the young man read the situation so well, she quickly hugged him while whispering, "Thanks" before leaving him with Rafe for their goodbyes.

The silence stretched between her and Rafe like an elastic band full of tension, not comfortable like it had been in Barrow. Elizabeth fiddled with her seatbelt, unsure what to say to break the silence. Just as she opened her mouth to fill the car with something other than quiet, her cell buzzed several times. Curious, she lifted it from the center console to see several emails from an unknown address. Clicking one, she winced as she realized Hank had sent her the information.

"What's going on?"

"Nothing," she said quickly and grimaced. "Just Kennedy reminding me that I need to meet with the FBI this afternoon."

The appointment with the feds was the only truth in that statement, and guilt wound into her. But what was the point in telling him what Hank had found since she didn't know what it was yet? All the information would do was guilt Rafe into staying another day, maybe two. And for what? He had meetings he couldn't miss. He had a mother due home from Europe soon. His place wasn't here right now. And though she hated admitting that, she forced herself to face the truth.

"Megan still not talking?"

"No." Elizabeth set her cell back into the cupholder. "She's not said a word."

His hand landed on top of hers before she could set it back in her lap. "I'm sorry I doubted you."

"It's fine." She flipped her hand over and laced their fingers together. "To be honest, I doubted myself there at the end."

"You did?" He frowned and slid a quick glance her way.

"Oh, I never doubted for a second they wanted to kill me. But . . ." She tugged at the toque Rafe had insisted she wear to stay warm. "I thought maybe Barrow would prove to be too far out, and they would try to do something on the cruise."

"Are you still going on the cruise?"

"No. I was never going unless this didn't pan out." Even then, she hadn't planned on going, but there was no need to explain her convoluted thinking.

"Why do you think the feds are involved? I mean, they didn't kidnap anyone. They attempted to kill you in just one state. So why the feds?"

"I've got no idea," Elizabeth said. She suspected it had to do with what Hank had uncovered. If they were right, that meant there were more than two underage girls. A lot more, for the feds to be involved. But she wasn't sure since she hadn't opened those emails. "Maybe they'll tell me this afternoon."

"Hopefully." He took the turn into the airport parking structure. After getting the ticket and parking, he swung toward her, his face set in a determined grimace. "Will you tell me what they say?"

"Of course," she said, taken aback that he would think she would keep something like that from him.

Seeing him vacillate as his gaze darted from the airport back the way they'd come, she knew he was debating leaving her to deal with the fallout from Megan by herself.

She placed two fingers over his lips. "I swear, the second I know what's going on, I'll tell you."

"Okay." He pressed a kiss to her fingers and tossed her a wan smile.

They untangled themselves from their seatbelts, and she helped him wrangle his luggage into the airport. Unwilling to just drop him off, she stood with him as he wound through the line to check in his baggage.

After getting most of his bags checked, Elizabeth clung to him like a barnacle, watching as the clock counted down the time until he would leave her.

Would it be for good? Would his doubts eat at him when she wasn't right in front of him? Would his mother finally drive that last bit of a wedge between them? To keep his mother's love, would he choose someone else?

Every fear Elizabeth had about letting Rafe go played in front of her as she watched the steady hand of the clock tick another second off their time together. Then it was time for him to leave her as he entered the security checkpoint.

Her gaze clung to the long-sleeved black polo he wore as he moved through the line until he finally disappeared from her sight as if he had only been a mirage in the desert.

Sliding into the SUV minutes later, Elizabeth stifled the sob that wanted to break free. She wrapped her fingers around the icy cold steering wheel to anchor her in the car when her heart begged her to race inside the terminal and drag Rafe out with her. Begged her to tell Rafe how to find her so they wouldn't be separated any longer than they needed to. And begged her not to let him go again. Tears tracked down her cheeks. Annoyed, she swiped them away with trembling fingers.

If he had wanted to stay with me, he would have. The real question is, will he really try to find me?

Her fingers brushed her cell as she wondered if he would call her just to talk. Or was it something he'd said so she wouldn't beg him to stay? Was this the end of them?

Frustrated, she snarled at herself. She needed to trust him. That was the whole problem with their relationship, trust. Until Rafe proved he was untrustworthy, Elizabeth needed to put her faith in him.

It would be a few days before they could touch base again. Between his flight and then the travel to his house, it would take him easily eight to ten hours total. By then, she expected to leave with Tanner, headed back to the ranch while Kennedy and her team returned to California.

Unable to control Rafe's decision to return to her, Elizabeth firmed her resolve. If she couldn't be with Rafe right now, then she would go harass the feds; hopefully, they had made some progress with Megan.

~ ~ ~ ~

With traffic, it took Elizabeth twenty minutes to arrive at the FBI satellite office in downtown Anchorage. Since her appointment wasn't for another hour, she headed to the coffee shop a few doors down to begin digging into the files Hank had sent her. She hated being forced to wade into the sewage her stepfather had entangled her, but if she didn't figure out what she was dealing with, she wouldn't know how to bring him down. For that, she needed every scrap of information she could get her hands on.

It took close to the hour she had left to read everything. Once finished, Elizabeth felt colder than she had standing outside in Barrow's snowy winter in only her nightgown.

She desperately needed a shower and brain bleach. If Harold was actually doing what Hank suspected and Agent Porter had hinted at with her questions, then the monster needed to be put in prison.

Elizabeth trusted Hank's sources. Harold was neck-deep in a swamp of sickness, and Megan was just one in a long line of girls Harold had preyed on. Before she blew Hank's cover, Elizabeth shot him a quick text getting permission to share the files with the feds.

His "duh" reply made her roll her eyes.

She should have expected that answer. A glance at the time had her hurrying to toss her empty coffee container and muffin wrapper. Swinging out of the coffee shop, she headed down the sidewalk and into the Alaska field office.

After giving her name and ID to the receptionist, Elizabeth was shown into what she thought would be a conference room but turned out to be an interrogation room.

A table with a metal bar attached to it stood in the middle with two chairs facing a blank wall and the chair closest to the metal bar facing a mirror. Elizabeth knew the mirror was as fake as the smile Agent Porter wore when she entered the room. However, the two additional people trailing the woman drew Elizabeth's attention.

"This is Agent Hunt and Agent Laramie. They'll be taking over your case," Porter said, waving to each person in turn.

Agent Hunt reminded Elizabeth of the woman from the Syfy series who was a secret government agent, only that woman traveled around commandeering strange artifacts that held power. Agent Laramie reminded her of an indulgent uncle from his thinning brown hair to the slight paunch that his jacket did nothing to hide.

Before Elizabeth could greet them, Porter added, "I'm leaving you two to sort everything out and handle the paperwork to transport the prisoner to your jurisdiction." She looked pointedly at her fellow agents. When they nodded in agreement, she continued. "Okay, then I'm off to Fairbanks on another case." Thrusting her hand toward Elizabeth, Porter pumped hers twice and tossed her one last smile. "It was nice to meet you, Ms. Harrison, and if there's anything you need that these two can't answer, please feel free to call me."

With that, Porter spun on her heel and left Elizabeth alone with the two new feds and a lot of questions.

What the hell have I gotten tangled up in?

Elizabeth took a seat in the lone chair, leaving the other two across from her empty. After laying her keys, cell, and knit beanie on the metal table, she folded her hands together and waited on the two agents to join her.

"Ms. Harrison, thank you for coming in to talk to us," the male agent said, taking the seat across from her.

"It's Elizabeth or Ms. Sutherland." Elizabeth smoothed her fingers over the soft material of her heather-gray woolen beanie.

"But it's really not. You changed your name," Laramie looked at an open file he slid onto the table. "To Colby Harrison."

"And why is my name change relevant? Better yet, why are you even involved in this at all?" Elizabeth scowled. "I mean, you're federal, not local or state, and Megan tried to kill me just the once, here. So again, I'm not sure why you're involved."

"Because your father—"

"Harold?" They couldn't mean her birth father.

"Yes, Harold Moore." The man looked in the file again, but Elizabeth slammed it shut with a snap, jolting both agents.

"You know his name as well as you know mine. What you're doing is stalling, and it's annoying." She folded her hands together and set them on top of her beanie. "Tell me what's going on, or I'm walking and you can talk to my lawyer."

"We're not trying to stall. We're trying to figure out what you know." Laramie scrubbed at his thinning hair.

Elizabeth arched a brow.

"Look," Hunt broke in. "We know Megan was sent by Harold."

"If you knew Megan was going to kill me, then why the hell didn't you warn me?" Anger sparked in Elizabeth as she tapped her finger on the metal table.

Hunt shrugged. "We didn't know your mother had left the proof with you."

"Proof?" The anger was quickly replaced with confusion. "About the trust?" That didn't make sense. Harold already knew about the trust.

"No, about the trafficking ring." Hunt leaned forward as if trying to peer into Elizabeth's head.

"What trafficking ring?" Elizabeth shook her head in frustration, feeling as if she and the agents were on two different wavelengths. "Harold sent Megan to kill me because I opened the trust my mother left me."

"Okay." Laramie lifted his hands up and patted the air. "I think we're both talking in circles.

"Told you, Laramie. You've been behind the desk for too long." Hunt sighed.

"Or you've gone to too many of those training sessions about getting people to talk, which are crap." He turned the frown on Elizabeth. "We've been following leads ever since your mother came to us almost twelve years ago."

Silence descended as Elizabeth absorbed the shock of that bombshell. Her mother had been killed on Harold's order around that time.

Frowning, Elizabeth shook her head. "This has nothing to do with the trust?"

"No, we thought Megan was coming to kill you because of the proof your mother had found that tied Harold in with a trafficking ring." Laramie turned to Hunt. "As for the trust, it came up in the original investigation when we were trying to follow Harold's money, but as it was only tied to you and had nothing to do with Harold. I didn't look closer at it."

"That makes sense," Hunt said before turning back to Elizabeth and opening the manila file folder. A photo was laid in the middle of the table. "Do you know this man?"

Elizabeth didn't want to look at photos. She wanted to know about the trafficking ring but caved when the agent tapped her blunt nail on the photo. Sighing, she dropped her gaze to the picture and gasped as she lifted them by the edges.

"This is Chris Bradshaw." Carefully laying the photo back down, she smoothed her fingers over it. "He's Harold's bookie and the main person who sets up the high stakes gambling weekends for the whales that Harold circulates with."

"He's not a bookie. That's what we thought too until your mother called us," Hunt said. "But the day we were supposed to meet up with whatever proof she collected, she had an accident."

Except it hadn't been an accident. Not wanting to get the agents sidetracked yet, she kept quiet.

"Anyway, based on the little your mother told us, we started looking harder at Bradshaw and found out he heads up an escort service with his girlfriend, Danielle. We also suspect they run a trafficking ring," Laramie said.

"And you think what?" Elizabeth opened her arms and slumped back in the chair. "That I'm involved?"

"No," Hunt stated, her angular face pulled into a frown. "No, we searched you thoroughly, and you have nothing tied to your stepfather. And none of your money is flowing into any odd places."

"Okay, then why did Porter ask if Harold seemed more interested in me than my mother? If he ever planned special trips for just him and me?" Spitting those words out left a bad taste in her mouth, and Elizabeth wished she had brought a bottle of water in with her. "I mean, if Chris is part of an escort service, what's that got to do with me?"

Did that mean Harold wasn't a pedophile? Maybe he was just a run of the mill cheater, but then where did the trafficking ring fit into all this? Elizabeth scraped a hand over her face.

"Because Chris and his girlfriend don't just pimp men and women but underage kids too."

Elizabeth wrapped her arms around her stomach as her blood froze in her veins. Christ. She knew in the darkest part of her soul Harold was a monster. If her mother had had actual proof of Harold's involvement with underage girls, that would explain why she was now dead.

Was that where the fifty million her mother had left Harold disappeared to? A trafficking ring? God, this just kept getting worse and worse.

"I don't understand. Why would Harold chance this? And why would you ever suspect that my mother or I would help him?" Elizabeth snarled, anger at them suspecting her mother in covering up for Harold warming her. "She wouldn't have done that."

"But she left him fifty million in her will."

"Because she didn't have time to change it." Elizabeth leaned forward into Hunt's face. "She died the day she was coming to see you two, which means she didn't have time to change her will before she died. And can't you trace that? Hell, she was coming to meet with you to give you proof, or so you claimed. Why would she do that if she were involved?"

Gambling was one thing, but this . . . her mother would never condone this. Elizabeth knew it with every fiber of her being.

"No, he's liquidated almost his entire fortune. The problem is, the money he's pulled out of all his accounts is nowhere. Neither here in the US nor offshore." Hunt's brown eyes frosted. "But we did find a sliver of a pattern that led us to Megan."

"What pattern?" she asked but wasn't entirely sure she wanted to know.

"A pattern where he seemed to have purchased extravagant gifts specifically geared for a teenage girl. Like one purchase was a new red Mercedes-Benz which we thought was yours but wasn't . . ."

Elizabeth's stomach dropped to her feet. The car they were talking about was gorgeous—candy apple red with a soft-top convertible and a light gray leather interior. Fully loaded with a custom-designed stereo system. And it had been Megan's gift. Megan had never explicitly stated that her parents had bought it for her when she'd showed it off to Elizabeth. And at sixteen,

Elizabeth hadn't thought to ask where it had come from since it was Megan's birthday present. She had just assumed the car was a gift from Megan's parents.

"You're saying he's been with Megan for . . ." It was one thing to suspect how depraved Harold was when talking to Rafe. But to have it confirmed beyond a reasonable doubt made bile rise in the back of Elizabeth's throat. Goosebumps broke out over her skin as she struggled to push the words past her lips. Words that she couldn't bring into the light of day.

"Years." Laramie scrubbed a hand over his brush cut which matched his military bearing. Though the man's overweight appearance spoke to him being long out of the armed forces. "We think so, and we think she's outlived her usefulness to him."

"I think so too." Elizabeth shook her head. It meant Harold had his filthy hooks deep in Megan so deep the woman might not turn on him. Unless . . . Elizabeth knew Harold had already chosen Megan's replacement, but Megan would never believe her. She would, however, believe the agents if they had enough evidence to back up the claim.

"You also said Chris's girlfriend is involved, but Chris never shows up to the social events with the same woman twice. And come to think of it, there were a few where he brought men as his guest." Elizabeth rubbed her arms, wishing now she had begged Rafe to stay.

"That's because those are his escorts. He's showing them off to build a client list specifically for them. This—" Hunt pulled another picture from the folder and laid it on the table between them. "—is his girlfriend."

"Holy shit," Elizabeth whispered.

"You know her?"

"No." Elizabeth tipped her head from side to side. "But I've seen her before." Lifting her cell, she flipped open the picture Hank has sent. The woman posing with Harold and the teenager wasn't the teenager's mother as Elizabeth assumed. It was Danielle. Passing the cell to Agent Hunt, Elizabeth hoped they would be in time to save the girl from whatever hell she was in.

"Where did you get this?"

"Before I get into that, I think I need to tell you why Megan was actually trying to kill me, so you have a complete picture of what's going on." Elizabeth scrubbed a rough hand over her face as pieces of the puzzle started falling into place.

Now that she understood all the moving parts, she spilled everything, from the day she'd overheard Rafe and Harold arguing up to the files Hank had sent her. After she left, she would be calling Hank to see what could be done to rescue the girl and whoever was trapped with her.

"You have files?"

"Yes, and if you have access to a computer and a printer, you'll have the leverage you need to make Megan talk. Because the picture of that other little girl looks an awful lot like Megan, and I think Harold's going to her to groom to take Megan's place." Elizabeth rubbed at her pounding temple. Megan could have come to Elizabeth and told her what was going on. *I would have helped her, dammit.* "Also, the ring Megan was wearing when she was arrested. It was my grandmother's. I want it back."

"That shouldn't be a problem. If you can provide a picture documenting it, we'll be more than happy to send it to you." Hunt stood and opened the door. "There's a computer and printer in Porter's office. Do you want something to drink while we wait for the files to print out?"

"Please." Elizabeth stood and followed Hunt, with Laramie a looming presence behind her. She was determined to put Harold behind bars no matter what. Hopefully, he spilled his guts on the way to prison, and then Laramie and Hunt could take down Bradshaw too.

When all the emails and files were printed and labeled, Agent Laramie crossed his arms over his chest, straining the seams of his blazer as his dark gaze landed on her. "I have a few more questions, and then you can leave."

"Shoot." It wasn't as if she had anything else to hide.

"We've looked over everything your security team gave us as well as everyone's statements."

"Okay."

"My question is this, how did Megan get a garage door opener and a key to the house?"

"I have no idea. Like I told you both, the only keys I have are the ones I get from the Sheriff."

"Why?"

"Why only those or why the Sheriff?"

"Why the Sheriff."

Elizabeth rolled the bottle of water between her hands and shrugged. "Barrow has almost no people during the winter months—"

"Which begs the question of why you continue to go up there."

"Oh, that's easy. I tried writing in Anchorage, but Megan would drop in at unexpected times and mess up my workflow. I made a comment about it at one of the coffee shops, and they put me in touch with . . ." Elizabeth's eyes widened as the puzzle piece clicked into place. "Christ." She lifted her hand to her mouth and swiped across it as she began to shake.

"What?" Hunt cut into Elizabeth's spiraling thoughts.

"Megan was with me when I talked to the realtor here in Anchorage almost ten years ago. That's the realtor who put me in touch with a woman who rents the house I stay at every year. Only during the dark winter."

"Why only then?"

"Because it's scary as shit out there, and it helps keep me in character when I'm writing my mysteries." Elizabeth waved that away. "But that's not important. What's important is that first time, the lady from Barrow—I forget her name because I've never actually met her—anyway, she sent the keys and garage door openers and everything down to the realtor in Anchorage. I had Megan's name on file with that realtor because I had to have a secondary contact before they would rent the house to me."

"What's this realtor's name? Would she still have duplicates to the house?" Laramie spouted off questions as Hunt lifted the landline.

Elizabeth reached for her pocket where her phone rested. "Isabelle Hess is her name, and I have her—"

"No need, I've got her business number right here," Laramie said, looking at his cell as he rattled off the number to Hunt, who jabbed it into the landline. While his partner dealt with Isabelle, Laramie turned his attention back to Elizabeth. "One last question, and you can go."

Elizabeth nodded and tucked her cell back into her coat pocket.

"How did you get this information?" He pointed to the stacks of papers they had just finished printing.

"From a friend who's been digging into Harold for me." She leaned forward and tapped her finger on the papers. "I bugged all of Harold's devices specifically for my friend to dig into him."

Technically, she had just asked Hank to handle it, but no way would she tell the feds that Hank had hacked Harold.

"You know that's against—"

"Nope. Not against the law since I was technically allowed access to each device by Harold." Especially since it was she who had upgraded Harold's electronics the year before. "Maybe a gray area but not illegal." She stood and grabbed her things from the top of the desk. "If that's all?"

She needed to be done here. All the information was beginning to hit her, and her insides felt as if they were going to shake apart. Elizabeth refused to be that vulnerable around these two.

"Make sure to leave contact information with our receptionist in case we have any more questions." Laramie nodded and waved her away.

"Will do." Elizabeth hurried to the small waiting area. As she pulled on her gloves and tugged her knit beanie over her head, she recited all her information for the receptionist.

Finally done, she stepped into the biting wind, which helped steady her, and made a mental note to call Hank and fill him in on this meeting.

Hell, Hank would probably find it entertaining if the agents tried to track the origins of the files. Not that they would get anywhere since the man always covered his ass.

Elizabeth's hope was that the information would pry Megan's mouth open and spill all of Harold's plans as well as why Elizabeth's mother had been killed.

Chapter Eighteen

Rafe stepped into the stale air of his home, glad to be done with that long, hellish flight. Leaving his luggage at the back door, he palmed his cell as he made a beeline for the kitchen and the ice-cold beer stocked in the door.

The woman with the kid who kept kicking the seat Rafe was in had driven him nuts since she wouldn't, or couldn't, control her kid. Hell, the terror had gotten gum stuck in another passenger's hair. How? Rafe had no idea.

It had been a nightmare flight. One that, on any other day, he would have ordered a scotch to numb himself with, but he didn't trust that the kid wouldn't do something horrible. So instead, he had kept a careful eye on the brat. Mostly because he didn't want to be digging gum out of his own hair. Any kid he and Elizabeth had would learn manners. Luckily, Tanner already had manners, so that was another plus in the teenager's column. Though his smack talk needed some work.

A quick swipe of his thumb had the texting app pulled up, and he shot off a text to Elizabeth.

Hey, cariña, just got home. Let me know when you land so we can plan our first phone date.

Smiling at the thought of wooing his ex-wife, Rafe opened his refrigerator and snagged one of the bottles rattling in the door. Only condiments and beer graced the inside of the fridge, and he made a mental note to pick up a few groceries. Just as he closed the door with his hip, his cell chimed with his mother's ringtone.

A quick flick of his finger, and he answered while twisting the top off his beer. "Mom."

"Where are you?"

"I just got home. Why?"

"I'm coming over." The line went dead, and Rafe scratched the back of his head. *Guess I'll find out what she wants in person.*

Unsure if there would be actual conversation involved, or if his mother was just dropping something off that she had picked up on her travels, Rafe hurried around the house and opened the windows to air out the rooms. Then he dragged his luggage upstairs to the master bedroom. He didn't want to deal with his mother; he wanted to use the bit of time he had before Elizabeth and Tanner's plane landed to get his work sorted. He grinned as he remembered Tanner catching Rafe before they separated at the hotel.

Knowing the teen wanted to pass along information about Elizabeth, Rafe had clapped Tanner on the shoulder. Then he had stopped him from sharing the information. Though Rafe appreciated the vote of confidence, he refused to allow Tanner to break Elizabeth's trust by giving Rafe a leg up. Rafe would find Elizabeth. But it had warmed a place deep inside to know Tanner trusted him enough to want Rafe in their lives. It was the equivalent of the teenager's seal of approval.

Now, Rafe just had to buckle down and find her in between catching up on his business meetings and getting his house packed up and ready to move. Because it would be him going to her and not the other way around.

He wanted to locate her before the summer. They had already missed Christmas, New Year's, and Valentine's Day would fly by in his round of travel for his business.

If he didn't miss her so much, Rafe would draw out finding her, but the second he had boarded the plane, he knew he'd made a mistake. He should have followed Elizabeth to the FBI meeting and then home with her.

He hated being apart. Being unable to touch her was wearing on him. Especially when he was constantly reaching for her to find the place next to him empty.

Finished moving his luggage from the foyer to the master bedroom, he moved back through the downstairs to shut those windows. His mother hated open windows. It was her biggest pet peeve, and as he still needed to fill her in on Elizabeth returning to his life . . . Rafe didn't want to push any more of his mother's buttons than he had to since he wanted answers to questions of her role in his father's death as well as lies he was fed about Elizabeth..

Just as he latched the last window, the doorbell rang . . . and rang and rang. A scowl pulled across his face as he stomped to the door, wincing with every step as the doorbell continued to peal through the house as if the person on the other side was jabbing incessantly at the button. Yanking the door open, he snarled, "What?"

"My key doesn't work." His mother pushed past him and marched directly to his office. Shoulders back and spine straight, anger vibrated like angry bees buzzing around her.

He followed her and watched as she trailed tentative fingers over the elaborate pen set he had placed front and center on his desk. She turned to look at the pictures he'd hung on the far wall.

"I haven't been here since you moved." Sadness muted her anger. "I didn't realize you pulled your father's things out of storage."

"They were collecting dust in that old place, and besides, I like having reminders of him around me." Rafe took the chair behind his desk while his mother shed her calf-length cream coat and placed it and her handbag on one of the two guest chairs.

She smoothed a manicured hand across her beige pants as she sunk into the other chair. After tugging the cuffs of her red silk blouse into place over her wrists, she faced him. Pink tinged her cheeks, alerting him that anger yet simmered just below the surface. Even pushing sixty-five, his mother was beautiful with her cafe latte complexion with only a hint of wrinkles and coal-black hair that she kept shoulder length with a hint of curl.

His mother had found a classic, ageless look and stuck with it. Based on all the suitors she had falling over themselves at the club to share her time, the look worked for her.

"Where's Rosa?" His mother's gaze bounced to the door before settling back on him with an arched brow. "I could use some tea if it's not too much trouble."

"I fired her."

"What?!" Disbelief turned to laser-like focus. "Why would you fire your help, Rafael?"

"Because she lied to me."

"Excuse me?"

His skin flushed as he remembered everything he'd uncovered about Rosa's duplicity. Needing a few minutes to control his rage, he stood. "I'll get us some tea."

His mother sniffed and stood to look at the rest of his office. He left her to it since everything important was locked up. It took him a few minutes to locate the packets of tea in the cabinet, but when the kettle whistled, he set a selection of tea choices and the pot on the tray next to the honey, tea mugs, and spoons. Ready, he lifted the tray and froze as he realized this was the first time he had ever brought tea to his mother. Shaking off the odd thought, he hurried back to the office to see his mother dropping his cell on to his desk.

"What were you doing?"

She frowned as she took her seat. "I heard it chime and wanted to see if it was important. But it was just a text from an unknown number."

He lifted his cell to see a response from Elizabeth's number, glad now he hadn't added her name to it yet.

Just boarding the plane. Lots to talk about after meeting. Will call when we land.

His fingers itched to call her. She was supposed to be halfway home by now. Which meant something had happened at the FBI office that delayed her trip. Instead, he would have to wait another fourteen-plus hours before he had any answers, depending on where Elizabeth's home was.

Placing his cell on the charger, he settled back into his chair, determined to focus on the woman in front of him and not the one circling his thoughts.

"Now, tell me why in the world you would fire Rosa." His mother stirred in a few drops of honey before taking a sip of her tea.

"She lied, and I will not have someone that I not only pay but who lives in my home lie to me." The hair on his jaw rasped as he dragged his palm across it.

"How did she lie?" Marisol asked, her tone silky smooth.

"You already know." Rafe could see the wheels turning in his mother's head. "I can see your mind working from here, so let me stop you now. I know Chloe has already filled you in on Rosa's departure, just as I know you and she worked together to destroy my marriage." Pain at this woman's betrayal hit him harder than anything Chloe or Rosa had done. "Why? Why would you do that?"

"Because you fancied yourself in love with her," she sneered, the teacup rattling as she all but slammed it on the table next to her. "A penniless gold digger, and you welcomed her with open arms—"

"She's none of those things. Harold's the one who's broke."

"Bullshit. You might not remember since you were busy securing jobs for your broke friend and palling around with that other friend who got your father killed, but I remember." She jammed a finger in her chest. "I remember when Harold came back and bragged about his gorgeous new wife and her daughter. I remember how he put the fear of God into anyone who even thought of demeaning them for having no money. And I remember when they moved here how little they brought with them."

"Of course they didn't bring much with them. Harold had a fully furnished house. The rest of it was lies." Rafe shook his head in disbelief.

She sniffed. "But it wasn't, Rafael. Even now, your precious ex-wife is swimming in debt."

"*Harold* is in debt."

"I'm telling you, that woman is bad news. She's in debt up to her eyeballs."

Could Elizabeth be playing me for a fool? Is she the one in debt? No, Rafe knew her. Trusted her. And he'd seen the truth when Megan had shown up to kill Elizabeth and Tanner. Shaking the doubts off, he focused on everything his mother had said.

"How? How do you know this?" Rafe forced the anger at how his mother wouldn't listen to him deep inside. He would deal with it after he got to the bottom of whatever vicious rumors Harold had spread this time.

"Besides Megan sharing it with a friend who told me?" Marisol leaned toward him; her onyx eyes flared like burning coals. "I had a background check done."

"What?" His voice gave out on him, and the question didn't come out as strong as he wished. Disbelief at how far his mother was willing to go to destroy his chance at love made his muscles tighten to the snapping point.

"Oh, yes, I did. I used the security firm Chloe's father uses."

"And you believe them?" Rafe asked. As if the man didn't want back into Rafe's good graces. Chloe's father needed Rafe's money to shore up his own crappy investments, and Rafe refused to be the man's piggy bank.

"Of course I do. They aren't going to lie to a paying customer."

Rubbing the back of his neck, his frustration only grew the more he heard.

"I'm protecting you now like I couldn't when you were younger." She crossed her arms and tipped her chin at a defiant angle.

"Younger? What do you mean?" A sick feeling twisted in his gut at the guilty look that flashed across his mother's face. "Mother?"

"You know what I mean." Her voice rose as she tapped her foot in agitation. "I did everything I could to break up those ridiculous friendships of yours, but you were too stubborn to—"

"Tristan and Jackson? Those friends?" *My best friends? She tried to run off my best friends? Why didn't they say anything to me?*

"Of course, those friends. It was bad enough Jackson got your father killed—"

"Jackson had nothing to do with Father's death. He was twelve," Rafe roared, half-standing, his rage barely contained. It took several heartbeats before he slumped back in his chair, exhausted at beating back his anger. His throat hurt with how he worked to keep from screaming. It made his voice rough as he repeated, "Jackson had nothing to do with Father's death. He was an innocent bystander who happened to witness the murder."

"Bah!"

"Not, 'bah,'" Rafe spat through clenched teeth. "He saw them. He called the police. And he told them everything. Then he had to do it on the stand in front of God knows how many people. If he hadn't caught them in the act, no one would have known who was to blame."

"Always so ready to defend him." She huffed and shook her head.

"And Tristan?" He ignored her barbed retort, more curious as to what she had against Tristan. The man was a lawyer who had graduated at the top of his class. Rafe was lucky to have his friend working with him to watch his back on some of his trickier real-estate deals.

"Poor, white trash who was only able to attend that school because his mother had a job there as a cafeteria worker." She smoothed a hand over her knee, a small smile touching her lips. "I offered the woman a hundred thousand dollars if she would move her son to another school and keep him from you."

"I bet she told you to go screw yourself." Rafe snorted. Amusement curled into him. More than likely, Anne Barrett had used more colorful language as she had no patience for snobs.

"It didn't work, no." His mother's smile broadened. "At least not with them. It did, however, work with Elizabeth."

His fingers curled into fists. Was this what Elizabeth had been fighting against since they married? *Not just Rosa and Harold but my own mother?*

"So, where have you been?" Her accusatory tone tore into him and put him on the defensive as he struggled to keep his roiling emotions in check.

"Away." He crossed his arms and propped them on the desk. "Why? You've never cared where I've gone before."

"You went to her." Her eyes narrowed to slits. "After all I did to get rid of that gold digger, you went back to her?"

"All you did?" His mind scrambled as the puzzle slowly came together. "You willingly sold the cabin to Harold." It was a shot in the dark, but the slight twitch at the corner of his mother's eye told him he was on the right track. "Why? Why would you do that?"

"Why? Because you wouldn't listen. For an entire month, you swanned about with her on your arm, never listening to anything I had to say." The smile on her lips firmed into a flat line. "Harold came to me about the cabin. It was already on the market, what did I care who bought it? And it made you warier of that gold-digging whore."

"What did you care?" Rafe snarled. Unable to rein in his anger any longer, he shoved the chair back so hard it slammed into the wall as he stood. "Because I loved that place. Because that was where Father and I would go once a month to bond with Granddad. Because that's where you sent me after Dad's death, to stay with Granddad." Tremors raced across his skin as he worked to get control of absolute fury. "I wanted that place, and you told me the bank had foreclosed on it due to Granddad's debts. Which I didn't know he had or I would have paid off."

"A miscommunication." She waved his words away with a swipe of her hand as if they were discussing the pesky changes in the weather.

"No. Another lie." He growled, slamming his fists on his desk. Rafe's gaze narrowed on his mother. "Were you there when Dad died?"

"What?" Her hand rubbed at the base of her neck, but her blank mask gave nothing away.

"Were you there?" He loomed over her. "Because, thinking back, you were always home that day of the week, and father was usually traveling on business."

"More like traveling to his whore's house." She snorted in derision.

"You knew about the other woman?"

"I'd always known about her." His mother shrugged carelessly. "What did I care what he did with trailer trash?" Then her eyes took on a dangerous tint. "However, deciding to turn that trash into a respectable wife to replace me?" She sneered. "Not going to happen."

"You helped kill him?"

"No, but I made sure he knew Jackson's parents were con artists, and I made sure Jackson's parents knew your father was ready to back out of the deal." Her smile held a deep satisfaction. "It all worked out in the end."

"Jesus, mother. They killed him."

He almost blurted out that Harold wanted to kill Elizabeth, but now that he knew what his mother was capable of, there was no way on earth he would give her that piece of ammunition. It would be like aiming a loaded gun directly at Elizabeth, and she had enough of them pointed her way.

"But I didn't lie to him."

"No, but you did lie to Elizabeth and to me."

"For your own good."

"No, for yours. That's all you, Harold, Megan, Chloe, and Rosa have done was work to tear me and Elizabeth apart." His anger at the duplicitous woman sitting in front of him swirled like a storm-swept sea. If Harold hadn't bought Rafe's grandfather's cabin, there would have been no contract. If Rafe's mother hadn't sold the snake the cabin in the first place. She had set Rafe up from the beginning, even knowing how much he cared for Elizabeth. His fingers curled into fists as he stood, keeping his desk between them so he wouldn't strangle his mother.

"Wasn't a very strong marriage if what we said did that much damage." She gave another careless shrug as if she hadn't cared one way or another about the lives she'd wrecked.

"Get out!" he roared, taking great satisfaction in seeing her jump and her face pale.

He strode to his office door, wanting her gone. Jerking it open, he snarled as a deep pain radiated to his very soul at the deception that continued to bombard him.

She rose and put on her coat, taking her time to settle it just so before picking up her purse. "If you marry her again, I will cut you out of the will."

"I don't need your money, and neither does she. So, go ahead, cut me out." He grabbed her elbow, needing her out before he did something he would regret. Reaching the front door, he all but tossed her from his home.

"If you do this, I won't speak to you again until you come to your senses." She spun on the sidewalk leading to the circular driveway and faced him, her own fury matching his.

"And if you come to your senses, I expect you to apologize to Elizabeth before you're allowed near either of us." He towered over her, his blunt nails digging into the palms of his hands. "As a caveat to that, I think you owe Jackson an apology as well."

"As if." She sniffed and marched to her car.

He stood on the stoop of his front porch, shaking. Adrenaline pumped through his veins with nowhere to go and no one to punch. A few seeds had been planted as he reviewed what his mother had said. Had their marriage been so weak as to succumb so easily to rumors?

Then he remembered that this campaign to malign Elizabeth began long before she ever arrived in California.

We never stood a chance back then. But I'll be damned if I'll allow lies to tear us apart now.

Determination filled him, and he swung back into his home. The door fell shut behind him as he headed back into his office to start clearing his agenda, so when Elizabeth called, he could begin the task of piecing together where she lived.

Now more than ever, he needed to prove his faith in her. And the first step was to find her as he'd promised.

Chapter Nineteen

Steam wafted from the lavender-scented water as Colby placed the bottle of wine and her half-filled glass on the lip of the tub. She had at least an hour before her call with Rafe, and as she already showered, this was strictly to help her decompress from the stress of the past few weeks.

The twins had been particularly fussy with ear infections. So, she had been up day and night with them. Not that she could explain that to Rafe since he still didn't know about their daughters' existence. And not that she could tell him about the girls since the FBI still didn't have enough evidence to arrest Harold yet. Though Megan was fully cooperating after seeing the pictures Hank had dug up.

Of course, after Jessup heard everything, he'd asked one of the trial attorneys at his firm to handle Megan's case. Which had piled even more stress on Colby. Not that Colby begrudged Megan the defense, but she worried Jessup would decide to become actively involved in the case.

Megan might have been a victim, just like Colby's mother. However, Colby's mother had died trying to do the right thing while Megan had tried to kill Colby, had shot Rafe, and had almost killed Kennedy. So no, Colby didn't want those she considered her new family tangled up in Megan's drama with Harold.

Not having Harold in custody was proving to be frustrating and a hindrance to her ranch. With it being spring, Mac and the men were walking the pens checking for anything that might poison their alpacas, so Colby had been dealing with the babies by herself.

She needed help with the girls so she could focus on work. The men needed help, especially in another month, when spring hit them full force. Yet, they couldn't bring anyone new to the ranch because they didn't know who they could trust.

To help Colby relax, Mac and the men had taken the twins to the bunkhouse for the night. In return, the men had the weekend off to relax and blow off some steam. Colby was footing the bill so the men could stay in town instead of driving an hour one way and then worrying about them getting back if they'd had one too many at whatever honky-tonk they landed at.

It was a solid compromise, in her opinion.

Hopefully, the FBI would have Harold squared away soon so they could all move on with their lives.

Colby checked that the burner phones were in the small basket near the tub in case anyone called with information regarding Harold; she didn't want to have to race from her soak to answer it. Seeing that everything was where it needed to be, she shed her robe and stepped into the water.

A sigh passed her lips as the hot water wrapped around her as she slid into the large garden tub. The lavender bath salts caressed her skin as she luxuriated in the first bath she'd had in what felt like forever. Tension she hadn't even realized she was holding in her muscles rolled out of her as she sipped the deep burgundy wine, letting it warm her from the inside out even as the hot water warmed her skin and delved into her taut muscles.

One of the phones in the basket released a garbled trill, and she groaned in frustration. Leaning over, she set her wine glass to the side and dug into the basket. *Dammit.* The burner for Rafe was the one making the noise. Just as she flipped open the phone to answer it, the call rolled over. Within seconds, it was ringing again, and she pressed the green button.

"Hello, *cariña.*"

"You're early." She shivered at the endearment Rafe had given her as she laid her head back. Water lapped the sides of the tub at the disturbance.

"Do you want me to call back?"

"What? No." Startled, she sat up.

"Liz, are you by chance, bathing?" His voice deepened to a growl at the end of the question.

"Maybe." She smiled and trailed her hand through the water, holding it aloft so the liquid dripped noisily back into the tub.

"Dammit, Liz."

She flinched. Feeling vulnerable at the bite in his words, she curled her knees toward her chest.

"I didn't want these phone calls to turn into sex." The last ended on a grumble as he went on, oblivious to the pain he was inflicting. "I wanted to prove we had more than sex . . ."

"Wait." The pieces fell into place, and she cursed herself for the careless words she'd tossed at him on the plane all those months ago. "Is this because I said this was always easy for us?"

"A bit, yes. Because you're right. The physical part of our relationship has always been easy, *cariña*." The squeak on the end of his line let her know he'd sat on the edge of his hotel bed. "I wanted to show you I care for more than your body."

"I know you do. But this piece is also a huge part of us because we've always meshed so well." That was putting it mildly. More like exploded, but Colby kept pushing forward. "I miss you. I miss your scent. I miss your arms around me. I miss the warmth of your chest behind me as we sleep. And I definitely miss you taking me and imprinting your claim on my skin." Her courage built with each sentence. "But most importantly, I miss being able to tell you I love you."

"For crissake."

"Sorry, I've been holding that in for a while. I didn't mean to blurt the words out, especially over the phone. I wanted to tell you in person, but your slow ass hasn't found me yet," she teased, not at all sorry to spill her feelings. He had already told her in Alaska, but she hadn't been ready to trust him with her heart again. At least not back then. But all these phone dates had showed her he would take care of her heart this time around. Especially since he hadn't missed a one. It helped her believe she could rely on him now.

"I love you too, Liz."

"Quit calling me that." Colby stepped from the tub and into the shower.

"Sorry." He sighed. "I love you, *cariña*. There, how was that?"

"Better, but I wish you'd use my new name."

"No, not until I'm there with you."

"Have you made any progress?" Lifting the nozzle from its holder, she quickly rinsed off before stepping from the shower, careful not to get any water on her one connection to Rafe.

"Oh, *cariña*, I've made quite a bit of progress. But I'll get to that in a second." There was more squeaking from his end of the call as he settled on the bed. "Now, did you get into that bath to tease me?"

"No. It's been a stressful week." She sighed as she dragged the bath sheet over her skin before her voice dropped, imagining all the ways she could work her stress out if Rafe was here with her.

"Damn, *cariña*, you make it hard to be good."

"I said that out loud, didn't I." She smiled.

"Yes."

"Sorry, I'm out of the bath now and just heading to bed." She hung her towel up and stepped into the darkened bedroom. sliding onto the cool sheets, she grumbled. "I hate being good."

"I can tell," he teased. "But just for a bit longer, hmm?"

She shivered. She didn't want him to think of her as good; she wanted to be desired with no holds barred. It had been too long since she'd felt his skin sliding against hers. Too long since his fingers caressed her, dragging pleasure from her and dammit, she missed it. She missed him.

"I have good news and bad news." He cleared his throat, and she knew he was trying to keep his word to not degenerate their phone call into sex.

Sighing, she snuggled into the pillow that wore his shirt. She answered grumpily, "Bad news first."

"I've got to travel to Australia."

"What?!" She pressed her lips together to keep from bombarding him with questions. The primary one circling her thoughts was when the hell was he actually going to come for her?

"It's only for a month at most, but . . . do you remember the fires?"

"Of course I do."

"Well, I invested in four startups and one expansion there. The expansion and one startup were set to begin construction right when the fires hit near Bairnsdale and Batemans Bay."

"I don't understand. Do they not want to build there anymore?"

"No, it's complicated. One of the men who wanted the expansion has lost everything and isn't sure he can expand while rebuilding his home base. The other passed away—"

"Because of the fires?"

"No, he was older and had a heart attack. But the fires probably didn't help his stress levels. Anyway, I need to go and talk to the other guy and find out what we can do to help get him back on his feet. Then I'm meeting with the deceased's heirs to see if they still want to open the other restaurant."

What could she say? This was Rafe's business, and even if he moved to her ranch, he would still make this trip. She felt bad for both of the men Rafe had mentioned. Colby knew what it was like to lose everything. And where she willingly walked away from her life, the man Rafe was talking about had absolutely no choice in losing all his material possessions as well as the memories his home had to have held.

"I'm not sure what your money situation is, but if the man wants to rebuild, I'd be willing to help him with his future," she said.

At hearing Rafe's gasp, Colby smiled.

"You would?"

"Yes, I know you probably have to answer to investors and such. So, if needed, we can buy the investors out, and it will be just you and me."

"Okay." He coughed. "If we go that route, then I'll get everything drawn up through Tristan and have him send it to Jessup to look at."

"What's the good news?" Ready for the heavy subject to be dropped, Colby trailed her hand over the soft material of his shirt.

"The second I'm done in Australia, I plan on coming to your ranch in North Dakota."

She jerked upright; the blankets pooled around her as her skin pebbled in the cool air. "You know where I am?"

"Yes." He rattled off her address.

"Did you cheat?" She frowned.

"Nope."

"Then how the hell do you know the exact address?" She had only expected him to have the nearby city in his sights. And if he had guessed the city, she planned to call it good and meet him in the center of it and drag him to her ranch.

"It was the alpaca comment combined with Mac working a month on an alpaca farm in Alabama."

"I forgot I mentioned that." Him remembering a small comment she had no recollection of sharing sent a shaft of joy shooting into her like the warmest sunlight.

"I didn't. It took a lot of phone calls to find the one where Mac had worked and also to find that Mac was buying a group from the man. It was a bit more digging to find out where he was having them delivered to." Glee filled Rafe's tone as if he were pumping his fists in the air in victory.

"Australia's, what, like fourteen hours ahead of us, right?" But where he seemed happy to have that victory, sadness wound through her at having to spend more time apart.

"Something like that, yes." He fell silent as if he realized they wouldn't be able to talk as much as they had been while he was in the States and Canada. "I plan on us talking at least once a week. I'd prefer every other day like we've been doing, but I want both of us to make an effort to talk once a week."

"I'd like that."

"And we'll trade texts." He sighed as silence fell between them. It stretched until he finally broke it. "You were going to tell me that Jessup set up Megan's defense, weren't you?"

"Yes?" Colby flinched as her answer sounded more like a question.

"Is that a question or an answer?"

"I was planning on talking to you about it in person." She plucked the bedding. "I just hadn't figured out . . ."

"How you feel?"

"Sort of." She huffed. "I'm glad he found someone to handle her case, but I don't want her to get off with just a slap on the wrist, either."

"Based on what Jessup said, Harold's been working on Megan since she was eight."

"I know." Colby rolled her head on her shoulders as tension crept back into her muscles. "He brainwashed her. I know she didn't have anything to do with my mother's death except to tip Harold off by accident."

"Exactly, your mother made Megan jealous when she asked about Harold and other women. And then your mother showed Megan the proof to try to help her."

"Right. Instead, Megan ran straight to Harold and confronted him." Colby knew all this; Jessup had come to the ranch two weeks ago and laid it all out for her while Matt and her men went to look over their new home to see if anything else needed to be changed before the construction crew began later this month. "Her big mouth got my mother killed. But that's not all, she could have chosen to turn state's evidence against Harold. Instead, she came to Alaska to kill me and probably Tanner too." Anger thrummed through her. "She shot you, shot Kennedy, and only after the FBI gave her irrefutable proof that Harold was grooming another girl to take her place did she finally pull her head out of her ass and turn on him."

"She loved him, hon." Rafe sighed. "I wish I was there to hold you."

"She might have loved him, but she knew what she did was wrong."

"I know."

"Are we done?" Colby needed to be done rehashing Megan's choices. If the woman gave the feds enough to hang Harold, more power to her, but Colby was a long way from forgiving her. "I'd rather talk about you not forgetting me while you're in Australia."

"Not gonna happen." Rafe snorted.

"Hey, they have sexy accents over there."

"I'm not going to forget you, *cariña*, and I'll damn well prove it when I come for you. And my accent is sexier." He growled playfully.

"Your everything is sexier." She smiled, hugging the pillow with his T-shirt tight to her chest. The scent of sandalwood, cedar, and other exotic spices made her hunger for him.

"Are you listening to me?"

"Of course," she said, struggling to focus and not shove her nose into the pillow that smelled of him.

"No, you're not. What are you doing?" he asked suspiciously.

"Nothing." Her face flushed, and she pushed away from the pillow, shoving it under the covers as if to hide the damning evidence of her obsession. She still couldn't believe she had sprayed the intoxicating scent on his T-shirt.

The everyday scent, yes, as that was the primary one Rafe used. But the one she had sprayed on this shirt was darker and called to her erotic core.

"That moan wasn't nothing."

She groaned. "Oh, God. I moaned?"

"Yes, now tell me."

"Crap." She huffed as she uncovered the pillow. "I might have stolen three of your T-shirts."

There that should hold him.

"The bright green one I liked playing basketball in, the yellow one I wore to lounge around in on Sundays, and the navy shirt you had on at Jessup's."

"How the heck do you know that?"

"I wore the yellow one every Sunday."

"No. You stopped wearing it two weeks after our one-month anniversary."

"Huh." He grew quiet. "I didn't realize that."

"And the green and blue you wore sometimes, but you favored a red one you got from a landscaping company."

"Oh, yeah. I did change over to that one." His voice turned pensive.

"So?"

"I don't know, I just noticed they weren't there anymore after you left and figured you threw them out."

"I didn't."

"You're wearing it?" His voice deepened, turning rougher.

"Not exactly." Her face heated as if it were sunburned. The green and blue she had sprayed with his everyday cologne. But the yellow . . . she hadn't been able to stop herself from spraying the special cologne on that T-shirt. The cologne Rafe only used on certain occasions.

"No one else better be wearing it."

"No. Dammit." She growled when she realized she was going to have to share her secret. "I have a pillow stuffed in it, and I might have sprayed that cologne you wore whenever you had to attend an event."

"Sex Magic?"

"What?" she squeaked, bolting upright. How did he know it made her remember every intimate moment they shared? "What the hell are you talking about now?"

"The cologne, it's called Sex Magic by House of Matriarch."

"Are you kidding me?"

He laughed a full-throated affair that she adored drawing from him. It was so rare that she kept count of each instance.

"No, I'm not kidding you."

"I don't think I like knowing you wore sex on your body." She flopped back in the bed with a grumble.

"*Cariña*, I only wore it because your eyes would turn molten and you all but plastered yourself to me at those events." He sighed. "I don't think I've worn it since the second month we were married because—"

"I stopped going to the events with you." She winced as the memory dug into her head.

It had been the whispers of her only using him for his connections and money and Rafe not defending her that had made her withdraw. She should have kept going and ignored all those vicious digs. But without Rafe's support, she hadn't felt strong enough to do it. If they had only talked more.

"Yes," his clipped reply dumped her back in the present.

"Jesus, Rafe, we really screwed up that marriage." Worry drained the happiness from her.

"We're not those people anymore," he snarled. "And that's why I will not have these calls turn into sex. I am damn well going to woo you."

The worry dissipated like fog in the sun. He was right. They were both working hard to overcome their pasts. Drawing strength from his voice, she smoothed her palm over his stolen shirt. "Okay."

"Now, tell me why you've been stressed this week."

She flinched, knowing she couldn't tell him about the twins, and she didn't want to discuss Megan and Harold anymore. Instead, she settled on the stories she could share about the men on the ranch and the help they needed.

She lived for these nightly conversations. The secrets she and Rafe shared felt intimate. More intimate than any sex they'd had. This was them wanting to be there for the daily grind. Wanting each other to be informed of the tiny details only spouses and significant others knew. Little details she had craved to learn and now gorged herself on during each phone call.

So, she settled in and listened to his worry about the families in Australia and made plans to help him any way she could. All while counting down the time he came for her.

Chapter Twenty

The ranch had shaken off the last of the freezing weather as they moved into spring. The one month Rafe had promised had turned into two months and a day.

Colby was on pins and needles. It was all she could do not to call him and tell him she was coming to him. But she held back. She wanted him to come to her. Maybe it was selfish since he still didn't know about the twins, but she wanted him to prove himself. She wanted him to prove he cared. But most of all, she wanted him to prove that he could keep his promise.

They'd had all of five phone calls over the course of the two months Rafe was in Australia, and Colby cherished every one of them, hoarding each whispered conversation like precious gems. Oh, there had been a lot of text messages and several photos she'd sent filled with satin and lace that she had draped across a black sheet and snapped pictures. The photos held a promise of what was waiting for Rafe at the end of his trip.

And though she was tempted to don the pieces, she refused to take a chance on those photos being stolen and slapped up on various internet sites.

Sighing, she pulled on her lightweight jacket and proceeded to buckle the twins into their stroller.

The one phone call that had troubled her was when Rafe had filled her in on his mother's visit and subsequent demand of dumping Colby. It hurt that he'd felt he needed to keep the conversation secret, even after he explained that he still couldn't believe some of the things his mother had told him. But other truths had come to light since then. Marisol had all but admitted to buying the gun that had ended up killing his father.

It gutted Colby that Rafe had to deal with all of it alone, and it hurt more that his mother blamed their rift on Colby. She hated being the reason Rafe and his mother were on the outs. But if Rafe had asked, Colby could have told him that Marisol had always hated her with a passion.

But in all the back and forth with Rafe, she missed him like a phantom limb, and her soul felt barren. Empty.

Their time in limbo marched on, and days turned into weeks and weeks into months.

Colby slapped her Stetson on her head, stomped her feet into her boots, and triple-checked the twins were buckled securely in their stroller before pushing them onto the porch.

The ramp Mac and Russell had built for her girls' double-seated stroller was a godsend as she easily rolled the monstrous contraption down it and onto the pebbled path. All the spring improvements came in handy now that the rain had finally let up.

"Here, let me help you," Charlie darted from behind her, and she waved him off. "I've got it."

He fell into step next to her.

"Aren't you supposed to be with Mac and Russell?" Colby manhandled the stroller over the dirt-packed drive toward the barn. The twins gurgled happily to each other, not minding the bumpy ride a bit.

"Nah, they're using a tractor to prep the fields for planting. I've never worked with a tractor, so I stayed here to check over the fences and replace the lock on the far side so the alpacas can't escape again."

"We really need help." She was happy Mac had Russell to help him with the big projects, but if they were going to handle a herd and become self-sustaining, they needed more than just the four men they had now.

"We do." Charlie shuffled his feet. "Russell said he might have an idea, but he has to check some things."

"I don't know how that's going to work out with Harold still on the loose and King stirring up trouble every chance he gets." Colby huffed in exasperation as her mind spun with ideas.

"Well, maybe you could check with Jessup about doing a background check or something."

"Maybe." She could ask. If the FBI would just arrest Harold, it would make all this moot. King was another story, one she could tackle after Harold was in custody.

"Mac wanted me to mention something else," Charlie said, crossing and uncrossing his arms before shoving his hands into the pockets of his worn Levi's and rocking back and forth on his feet.

"Why you and not him?" She stopped before the open barn door and faced Charlie. The teenager was as nervous as a long-tailed cat in a room full of rocking chairs.

"He said 'maybe she'll listen to some sense if it comes from someone other than me.'"

"I listen to him." Colby huffed and rubbed her palms over the handle of the stroller. Okay, she listened to him sometimes—most times. When Charlie's silence drew on for too long, she caved, "Fine. What is it?"

"Well, there's a woman, she's eighteen and has a baby now. She needs a job, and I know when we finally get up and running with more fields and more alpacas, we'll have more people—"

"Charlie, get to the point."

"I want to give her a chance like you all gave me." Charlie dug the toe of his shoe into the gravel.

"Doing what?"

"Well, you're gonna be gone next January when they start filming your book, and if we plant more fields and get more men, then she could cook for them like you're doing now."

"Why? Why her and not someone with more experience? What if she goes back to her baby's daddy? And how do you know she's safe?"

He ran a hand through his shaggy brown hair, and Colby made a mental note to round Charlie and Tanner up to get their hair trimmed. When the silence stretched, she arched a brow. "Charlie?"

"Okay, don't be mad, but I asked Jessup to run background on her, and she's not got any ties at all to Harold. And look, she helps at the shelter cooking, so she could handle our small group." His teeth dug into his lip as his eyes met hers. "And well . . . She'll never go back to the baby's father because it's her father."

"Wait. What?" That made Colby gag in disgust and dredged up memories of what Megan must have gone through with Harold.

"Okay, not her actual father because her mom remarried when Dana was just a baby. It wasn't until the asshole started sexually abusing her that he informed her they weren't related. She escaped with the help of the social worker at the hospital and ended up helping at the homeless shelter. But he's looking for her, and I thought she would be safe out here." His gaze begged Colby to give his friend a chance.

"You like her."

"Yes, I like her. She's not ready for anything, but I can be her friend until she is ready for someone to love her." Red covered his face as he ducked his head. Then he straightened and met her gaze with determination. "But put my emotions out of it, she deserves this."

"I'll give her a chance, but she probably doesn't want to cook as her forever job." Colby smiled at the young man willing to go to bat for the battered woman.

"She likes math, so maybe she could study something like that after she gets settled." He shrugged.

"Maybe. You can ask her when you give her the good news." Colby was so proud of the young men for volunteering at the shelter. They embraced helping others, working to pay forward their own good fortune.

Charlie bounced on the balls of his feet and grinned before frowning at Colby. "What about you? How're you holding up?"

Colby ran a hand across the back of her neck as she scanned the area for Tanner. "Isn't Tanner supposed to be—"

Charlie nudged her side. "No changing the subject."

"I'm sick of waiting, and I'm tempted to go to him. If I trusted that Harold wouldn't somehow trace my movements, I'd do it." She sighed.

"You think that's possible? He didn't trace you from here to Alaska."

"Alaska was carefully planned. This would be me darting away trying to get to Rafe without a fallback." A cold pit formed in her stomach as she remembered the anger stamped on Megan's face as she lifted the gun to shoot Colby.

"Okay, I get how that's different, but we could plan it."

"Ask me that next week, because if he's not here by then, I will have changed my mind." She fiddled with the girls' canopy to make sure they were out of the sun.

Charlie turned to face away from her as he gazed hard at the driveway with a hand shielding his eyes. "Someone's coming. Go get in the barn."

Just as she headed for the side of the barn, she cursed herself for not having her rifle with her. Not that she brought it out of its case with the girls nearby. Then Rafe's face came into view behind the windshield, and her smile broadened.

"Wait, Charlie, it's Rafe." She stepped around the corner, and Charlie shouted for Tanner before tapping her on the shoulder.

"We've got the herd covered." As he reached the door, he spun back around. "By the way, have you told Rafe about the girls?"

Colby froze as panic seized her, tightening her skin. She had thought Rafe would call before coming, that she could ease him into it. Sweat slicked her palms where they gripped the handle of the stroller as she shook her head at Charlie.

"Shit. Okay, me and Tanner will stick close in case you need us."

This was her mess, so she shook her head again. "No, he'll be surprised, but after the shock wears off, it'll be okay."

She hoped. Pushing the buggy to face the barn, she watched Tanner pause, and Charlie flagged him into the barn. He would explain everything to her adopted son, and she would focus on making sure Rafe didn't run.

She turned to watch Rafe as he pulled to a stop in front of her. The nondescript dusky gold rental was almost a match for the dust that swirled beneath its wheels.

Her heart raced, and cold sweat trickled down her spine as nerves twisted in her gut. Had she lied to Charlie? Would Rafe walk away from them? Would he walk away from her and try to take the girls?

But what else could she have done? In Alaska, there were too many strangers, and she didn't trust them to keep the girls a secret. It would be so easy for Harold to get to one of them when they returned to California. Or if one of the security personnel trusted the wrong person like Colby had trusted Megan. Hell, Rafe had betrayed her before he had known the truth. One word would be all it would take, and Harold would tear the earth apart to find the twins.

Even when she and Rafe were alone those few days in the little cabin, everything was so new that she'd refused to put her faith into them as a couple. Especially with the life of her babies on the line. No, there hadn't been any time nor a lot of trust back then. Now she trusted him with her whole heart and hoped he would understand her reasoning.

Rafe stepped from the car and lifted his aviator sunglasses to the top of his head. His shaggy black hair curled around the gold frames. A dark green Henley brought a richer hue to his cat-like eyes, and his worn jeans drew attention to his muscled thighs and long legs. Every bit of love he felt for her was revealed in his gaze as it meshed with hers. Joy, at finally having him on her ranch, burst through her, and she ran to meet him.

Her hands landed on his solid chest before traveling up and linking behind his neck.

"You kept your promise," she whispered.

"Of course, I did." He smiled gently.

Rolling to her tiptoes, she eagerly met his descending lips. Callused hands cupped her face as if she were a precious treasure. His thumbs stroked her cheekbones, then she felt nothing but his lips. His familiar taste was a flavor she reveled in as she tangled her tongue with his. Blood heated in her veins, and she arched into him, needing to be closer, preferably with fewer clothes on. He broke away from her with a startled gasp.

It was then she heard the stomp-stomp-stomp of feet as her three troublemakers hummed in varying keys behind her as they approached the girls.

Frustrated, Colby spun to face the troublesome alpacas and lifted her booted foot to gain their attention. Slamming it down as hard as she could, she jolted when her booted heel hit something soft instead of the hard concrete, she was expecting it to meet. Rafe released a yelp of surprise and tripped as he stumbled back, falling to his butt on the drive in a cloud of dust and dirt.

Face heating with embarrassment, Colby hurried to help him up. This was not the way she'd planned to introduce him to her ranch, the alpacas, or the girls.

He waved her off and pointed to the girls with a note of panic. "The llamas are going to eat the babies."

"They aren't going to eat the babies because they aren't llamas. Not that llamas eat babies——"

"Fine, the furry beasts are going to eat the babies."

She huffed in exasperation at how off track his welcome had gone. "The furry beasts are not going to eat the babies. They're alpacas, and I was late getting the twins to their play area so the alpacas could visit them for their allotted time."

"You don't keep them penned?" he asked in disbelief.

"Of course I keep them penned."

"I think my foot is broken." He started limping toward the beasts.

"Your foot isn't broken."

"Jesus, how many do you have? Is the barn like a clown car where you can cram like a hundred of the beasts in there?" he asked as three more strolled out of the barn.

"I have six in all." She released a heavy sigh. "Though sometimes it feels like a hundred."

Then she caught the glint of amusement in his eyes and narrowed her gaze on him, daring him to keep poking her.

He ignored the hint. "You know, one of them is darting for the grass, and I think the other one has flowers in its mouth."

"I see her." She caught one of the alpacas dancing around in the grass and rolled her eyes.

"And that one looks like they're preening." He chuckled as he drew closer to the stroller.

She threw her hands up, having lost all control. "The three humming at the girls are Fee, Fi, and Fo."

"Jack and the Beanstalk? It's because of the stomping, isn't it?"

She nodded, and he tossed his head back and laughed.

"The one darting for the grass is Cinderella, Cindy for short as she absolutely hates concrete and loves to steal shoes. But never in pairs, just one at a time."

He grinned broadly, his eyes dancing with mirth. "And the flower guy?"

"That's Phillip."

"Sleeping Beauty? Classic. And the last?"

"Charming."

"Because he preens?"

"Yes, and because when he wants to, he can be a charmer," Colby said.

"They won't bite, right?"

"Nope. Not unless you piss them off."

"Do you have more animals?" Rafe lifted a hand, and Charming was right there, shoving his head under it, begging for attention.

"Not yet." She wanted to adopt a few dogs and already had the names chosen for the fairies that protected Sleeping Beauty, figuring the dogs would do a good job protecting the herd.

"I think I detect a theme here," he teased.

"I like fairy tales, sue me."

Before he could continue to tease her, Charlie and Tanner raced from the barn with panicked expressions.

"Treats!" Charlie held a sack aloft and shook it.

The alpacas turned as one and ran after the young man as he disappeared back into the barn.

"Sorry about the furry welcome. They got away from us," Tanner said sheepishly.

Colby knew that was code for "Charming had figured out the new latch on their gate and opened it." It was his fourth one; the escape artist was good at freeing himself and his friends when they felt the need to roam outside the pen.

"About time you got here, man." Tanner held out his hand, and Rafe immediately clasped it as they did a quick guy clench ending with a back slap.

"Yeah, sorry for the delay. I decided I didn't want to have to leave again," Rafe's gaze darkened as it returned to her. "So, I stopped off in California and signed the paperwork, selling my house."

"Seriously?" Colby gasped, her hand covering her mouth as tears pushed against her eyes.

"Yes." Rafe raked a hand through his hair, sending his sunglasses askew. "That's okay, right?"

"God, yes!"

"So, I'll go help Charlie with the chores while you two catch up." Tanner took a step back and hooked his thumb toward the barn.

Colby tipped her chin at his subtle head tilt toward the girls.

"We don't want the alpacas breaking out again, so let's get the girls settled." Gathering her courage, Colby grabbed the handlebars of the stroller.

His hands slid around her waist, and his mouth nibbled at her neck, sending liquid heat pooling low in her stomach as he nestled in behind her. "Why don't you call the babies' mother instead and tell her you need some time alone because I've finally tracked you down." He placed a kiss behind her ear. "Then we can have a chance to talk. Preferably naked."

"As much as I would love to do that, I need to talk to you about the babies." She pressed a hand to his linked fingers and squeezed. "Now, come with me."

Worry and fear began to form cracks in the joy she had felt at seeing him arrive and discovering he already planned on moving here. His fierce frown wound her nerves tighter as they arrived at the small area set up for the girls.

Mac and the men had done a fantastic job with the play area. Wooden slats painted a washed-out white acted as a barrier to keep anything wanting to get to the girls out and would wrangle the girls when they began to walk. A rainbow-hued nylon canopy shifted above them, keeping the twins safe from UV rays while allowing them to enjoy the outdoors. It was simple, with no other structures cluttering it, almost like a giant playpen. The fence to the pasture was lower than the panels painted white, allowing the alpacas to stick their heads over and coo at the babies.

"This is nice," Rafe's gaze scanned the large square area.

"It is." Colby toed off her boots, and Rafe followed suit. "Mac and the men built it big enough for the girls to grow into it."

Rafe bent and swept his hand over the foam puzzle-like pieces done in primary colors that made up the ground cover. "This is similar to kids' play areas I've seen in fast-food restaurants."

"Here," she passed him a gray fleece blanket. "Lay this out near the section close to the pasture so the fur babies can visit the girls. Then we can talk."

"That doesn't sound ominous at all." While he laid out the blanket, he continued to tease her.

She flinched, but as she was bent over unstrapping the girls, he didn't notice as he continued, "You can't be hiding anything else from me. Because we covered everything in Alaska." He took a seat on the blanket and met her gaze, his brow furrowed. "We did cover everything in Alaska, right?"

"There's one thing we did not cover." She passed him the now freed baby and lifted the other from the carriage before joining him on the blanket.

His eyes widened and shifted from the baby he held to her before landing on the one cradled in her arms. "No." Realization dawned, shadowing his green eyes. "You didn't tell me?"

She dropped next to him. Carefully setting the baby on the blanket, she curled her fingers into the green and gray flannel shirt she wore over a gray T-shirt and folded and unfolded the hem.

"Why the hell didn't you tell me?" His voice was as sharp as the rebuke the question held.

The accusation slammed into her like a fist to the gut as her own anger burned off her nerves.

Sensing the rising tension, the baby he held scrunched up her face and began to fuss. His eyes popped wide, and he murmured, "Don't cry. Please, don't cry."

"Here, set her by her sister," Colby directed, urging Rafe to lay the little one down.

The second she was near her sister, the babe calmed and began to burble. Immediately the alpacas filled the section of fence, peeking their heads over the slat and humming. The distraction helped Colby calm her temper and soothe her frayed nerves.

She lifted her eyes to his and saw anger and betrayal in his stony expression as he asked again, "Why didn't you tell me?"

Taking a chance, she folded her hand over his where it rested next to the girls' heads. "Do you remember when I told you I came to surprise you and Harold and heard the argument that ended our marriage?"

"Yes." His mouth pulled down in confusion.

"Why do you think I came?"

"I thought you wanted to take us to dinner for something or another." He shrugged.

"I had never done that before, so why would I do it that night?"

"You came to share your news." His eyes fell to the twins.

"Our news, yes."

"Oh, Christ, and you heard that I didn't want you." He gripped her hand. "Is that why you left? Why you didn't confront me?"

"Not just that, Rafe. If it was only about you leaving me, I would have dragged you kicking and screaming to stay in our girls' lives. But you told me in your study that if there was a child, you still wanted to be—"

"Part of their life. I remember that."

"Right, but what you aren't putting together is that's the same night I heard Harold and Megan talk about needing our babies to open that damnable trust."

"Dammit," he whispered. "I've been so focused on finding you and confronting my mother, I forgot about that piece."

"That's also the reason I didn't say anything. I wasn't chancing me being murdered and Harold stepping in to gain custody of them. Back then, he would have told you the girls weren't yours, and you would have believed him."

"But you could have said something in Alaska."

"Rafe, do you honestly think I would put the two most important people in our lives in danger in order for you to know about them?" She jutted her chin out because no way would she have endangered her babies. "No, we were in Alaska to catch Harold. The rooms were bugged. We had security people everywhere. Strangers that could be bought. Would you have chanced that? You know what Harold's capable of, the lengths he went to in order to separate us while getting what he wanted." She didn't add that they now knew what Harold did to girls that weren't his. It wasn't needed as she met Rafe's gaze and saw the anger in the depths of his eyes.

"No, I wouldn't have chanced them. But the few days we were alone—" He wiped a hand over his mouth.

"We were a minute old. To top that off, you weren't even sure Harold was really after me." She cut him off with a huff of exasperation and a slash of her hand.

"Okay, you've made some valid points." The last of his anger left him as he slumped back onto the white slats of the fence.

"I'm not trying to make a point. I'm just trying to explain." Colby gestured at the two squirming girls kicking their legs as they talked gibberish with their furry friends. "They're innocent. Hell, it was Tanner's idea to use himself as bait to bring Harold out in the open, but it didn't work."

"No, it didn't work, but Megan has turned her evidence over to the feds. She wasn't as trusting of Harold as he thought, so it's just a matter of time before Harold's behind bars and no longer a threat." He tugged at his ear. "How many know about the girls?"

"Just the men on the ranch and Jessup and Matt."

Surprise widened his eyes. "That's it?"

"That's it." Colby leaned toward him. "Megan finally turned over evidence to the feds? Was it actual evidence or just her word?"

"Actual evidence. She had recordings, videos, she had even cloned his cell."

"Holy shit. If Harold finds out . . ." Colby trailed off with a shiver as if someone walked over her grave.

"He'll kill her. But she must have been worried he would burn her for your murder."

"Jessup hasn't shared that with me."

"Jessup might not have heard yet. I'll enjoy one-upping him." He smirked. "The reason I know is, I had Jackson keeping an eye on Harold after Alaska in case he did something odd so we would have some warning. With Jackson's connections, he got called when Megan's information dropped, and he immediately called to warn me to watch my back."

"You were keeping me safe." She smiled.

"I was. And it seems I was keeping these two safe too." He touched one of the babies' feet. "How old are they?"

"Six months." She watched as he interacted with the twins.

"Did you name them?"

"Yes, it's kind of a requisite since they wouldn't let me get away without naming them for six months." She chuckled.

"What did you name them?" His gaze held so much love it almost bowled her over.

"The one who has your finger is called Johanna Gabriella . . ."

Tears sheened his eyes as they fell back to the girl. "After my father and grandfather."

"Well, I sure wasn't naming her after your mother," she said, crossing her arms. "She hates me."

"Sorry, hon, but she really does."

"I know." Colby shrugged, and it shouldn't hurt, but it did.

"She's not going to interfere with us, and I swear I'm not going to tell her where this place is until I feel like she's accepted you."

"You do know that probably won't ever happen, right?"

"I know," he said with a deep sigh.

"Even with you moving here?"

"Even with me moving here. I won't have her bringing any poison to the sanctuary you've built." He leaned over and pressed a kiss to her lips before sitting back down and tugging on the other baby's foot. "Now, what's this one's name?"

"Lily Maxine." Colby ducked her head, worried that he wouldn't like the name.

"For your mother and father?"

She nodded and peered at him through the veil of her lashes.

"Their names are perfect. Hell, they're perfect. Too bad we can't go and celebrate me finding you and the babies." The leer he tossed her way let her know he meant preferably naked in bed.

Tanner and Charlie popped up between the alpacas, startling Colby since she hadn't heard them enter the paddock. But she quickly forgave them when Tanner's tipped his head at the twins. She knew then what he was about to offer.

"We can watch them while you two . . ." Tanner looked at Charlie, unsure how to finish that statement.

"Reconnect." Charlie waggled his eyebrows.

"Come on, Rafe. We need to hurry before they change their mind." She laughed and grabbed Rafe's hand, tugging him toward their home.

~ ~ ~ ~

The second they crossed the threshold of the house and the front door shut, Colby's back hit the door and her hat fell to the floor as Rafe kissed her. Every bit of emotion she felt for him, she poured into the kiss. Jumping, she wrapped her legs around his waist while separating for a breath. He gently set her on her feet and grabbed her hand.

"Where's the bedroom?"

"Down the hall." She pointed toward the hall opposite the fireplace and followed in Rafe's hurried wake.

When they arrived at the master bedroom, Colby pressed the door closed and flipped the lock. Her heart lurched at the sight of Rafe slipping out of his clothes. To see him finally in her room drew the breath from her body.

Within a few steps, Rafe was in front of her, whispering her name and gathering her in his arms. The second his arms closed around her, she knew she was home.

Between kisses, Rafe slowly slid her clothes from her, christening each inch of skin revealed with a press of his lips.

Impatient, she took Rafe by surprise and tipped him onto her bed. She didn't want slow. There would be more than enough time for them to take their time later. Now, she needed to feel him. To know this wasn't a dream. To know he was actually here with her. To know he was in her bed, wanting her as desperately as she craved him.

Straddling his lap, she paused as a shudder ran through her. This felt so right. More so than Alaska or their entire year of marriage. Looking into his eyes, she saw them filled with love and want, no more shadows, and no more secrets hidden within any parts of their depths. His hands ghosted across her skin; she shivered as he drew her down and whispered, "You're perfect."

"No, I'm not." If she were perfect, she would have told him about their daughters before he was blindsided.

"Hush." He pressed a kiss to her lips. "For me, you're perfect."

"Then why are we still talking?"

He laughed and flipped her under him. "How's this?"

"Better." She lightly dragged her blunt nails down his back and arched into him.

He growled as he took control, nipping and tasting and driving her to the brink over and over as he branded himself on her skin and in her heart.

Colby writhed under Rafe. "Please," she whimpered.

Releasing a deep groan, Rafe pushed into her with barely a pause as he sealed their mouths together.

When they broke apart, Rafe's dark gaze met hers. "I don't think I can be gentle."

"I didn't ask you to," she moaned. "I need to feel you, Rafe. I need to know you're actually here with me, and this isn't a dream."

"*Cariña*," he moaned as he gripped her thighs, lifting her into his thrusts.

The tight grip would leave bruises, badges she could look at and touch later, all while remembering it was her who had made him lose control. Every other instance in their marriage, he had been in control, all smooth seduction and languid heat. But now, he was a warrior bent on staking his claim for her.

She clung to him, the only harbor in the storm that raged around them as they reclaimed each other. Her lungs burned for air and her heart raced as her soul cried out for more. For the connection that had spun until it was as translucent as gossamer during their months apart but was still there during each text and each heartfelt, whispered word that passed between them. When their gazes tangled again, she found the connection in the love pouring from his gaze and returned it tenfold.

He had etched his place so deeply it was burned into her soul.

Wrapping her arms around his neck, she pulled him back to her and uttered the words she had longed to say for what felt like years. "I love you."

He gentled his possession, as if something had snapped in him.

His mouth brushed over hers, soft as a feather, his lips forming the same words, "I love you" against her lips, stealing her breath even as he gave her his own.

They moved in perfect synchronicity, and when she was pushed over the edge, she saw bursts of stars as she clutched him tighter, anchoring herself to him. Rafe growled her name as he followed before collapsing on top of her, a welcome weight she held close, never wanting to let him go. She didn't know if it was minutes or hours before they came down from their high.

Needing to hide, she crooked an arm over her eyes. God, she was flayed open. If he looked into her eyes, she knew he would see her every emotion, and she wasn't ready to be that vulnerable.

Though he had sold his house, he hadn't said he was coming here. And what about all the travel he did for work? Would he expect her to go with him?

Nothing was settled. They had immediately jumped into bed . . . again.

"Hey," he whispered, gently nudging her arm away from her face. "Look at me, Liz."

Swallowing convulsively, she shook her head. "It's not Liz or Elizabeth. It's—"

"Colby," he finished for her. "I know."

She opened her eyes to find him peering at her, his soul as bare to her as hers was to him.

"There you are." His hands cupped her face as he smiled.

"This is so easy for us, Rafe." She nuzzled into his palm. "It's always felt so right."

"Making love?"

She nodded while her fingers toyed with tucking his thick, sweat-soaked strands of black hair behind his ears. He pressed a kiss to her forehead.

"Do you want to know what I think?"

"Always."

"I doubt that, but with us clicking in the bedroom, I think it was our souls finding their mate but us being too blind to see it until now."

"We probably weren't ready to see it."

"More like both of us had challenges to overcome. For me, it was my preconceived notions and realizing everyone was lying to me. And you, standing up for what you wanted." He pushed the hair out of her face. "And I would say, I completed the first of several challenges with flying colors. I found you."

She sighed as her mind turned to his mother.

"What's that sigh for?"

"Your mother."

"Ew. No bringing a parent into the bed with us." He flinched away from her and rolled to his back.

"Especially when we're naked," she teased while smoothing a hand over the silky skin of his chest in apology.

"Okay, yuck." He huffed before gathering her to his side. "And why are you thinking about my mother when you should be thinking about us?"

"It's about us in a roundabout way." She propped her chin on his chest and met his gaze. "Are you really going to disown her?"

"Yes." His elegant fingers wove into her hair. "She lied about you. She lied about my father. And she sold Harold my grandfather's cabin that instigated this entire mess."

"Jesus," Colby mumbled. "I didn't know about the cabin.

"I know, *cariña.*" His gentle smile let her know he didn't blame her. "She isn't at all who I thought she was. Jackson thinks she might have even set my father up to be killed."

Colby gasped and wrapped her arms around Rafe. Pain flared in his eyes, turning them to a dark, shadowy green of a forest floor. What could she say to that? Before she could muster a response, he was already filling the silence.

"I don't want to believe her capable of that, but he said when he delved into the mess surrounding his parents and my father's murder that there were inconsistencies. And that my father planned to leave my mother."

"She wouldn't have liked that at all." Colby's mind raced. Not liking it was an understatement. Marisol would have been livid.

However, even though he had cut ties with Marisol, Rafe's entire business had been based in California for almost fifteen years. All of his contacts were there. Would he really leave?

To top that off, his mother was his last living relative, surely Marisol would eventually cave to Rafe's demands. Oh, Colby had no doubt Marisol wouldn't say anything bad about Colby or the girls to Rafe's face, but the woman would still tear Colby down behind Rafe's back. And Colby did not want the woman here, to have her one sanctuary turned into a war zone where poisonous barbs flew at the drop of a hat. She shivered at the thought.

And what about the girls? They would want to meet their grandmother even if said grandmother hated Colby. "Were you serious about California?"

"About not going back there?" he asked with raised brows.

"Yes."

"Yes, the place is toxic for both of us and holds too many painful memories," he replied, his gaze tracing each of her features. "Which is why I hired movers, put my house on the market, and left Jessup with a power of attorney so he could handle my affairs out there."

"But your business?"

"Can be run anywhere in the world since I have to travel to the sites for the openings."

"But your mother. . ."

"Has a choice and has my phone number. She won't be getting this address until Harold is behind bars. And only if she has a change of heart about us." He pressed a kiss to her temple. "If I change my mind and want to see her, I can always go there, but . . ." He released a hard breath. "She was as toxic as the rest, and she set me up to believe the lies. I mean, I trusted her, and even when I tried to explain and show her the truth, she refused to hear it."

"It's because she hates me."

"Well, I love you, and I choose you and the girls. I won't have them attacked by my mother. And I sure as hell won't have them poisoned against you by

my mother nor by that entitled crowd out there."
Worry stole the light that shone in his eyes. "Unless
you're asking in a roundabout way for me to only visit
you until we're more solid . . ."

"No!" She clutched him to her, alarmed he
would try to leave. "I want you here." The first tendrils
of hope wound into her. "But are you sure?"

"Oh, I'm more than sure," he stated, the smile
returning as he relaxed into the pillowtop mattress.

"Oh, my God." Colby delved into the electric
green of his eyes, searching for the truth, and found a
bedrock of determination. "You're moving here."

Bubbles as heady as champagne burst in her as
the dream she had always held in the deepest part of
her became reality.

"Most definitely." His expression softened as a
warm light filled his gaze, and he rolled on top of her,
trapping her beneath him. "Don't get too excited. I'll
still need to travel for work, but I can do the rest of that
from here as easily as I can from California. Your home
is here, and my home, I've discovered, is you."

Tears overflowed as she dragged him back to
her with a wet laugh. She might even have a solution
since Hank was a licensed pilot. Not that Colby knew
where he was at the moment, but she was sure she
could convince him to come here and be just as isolated
as living on his mountain. At least if he traveled with
Rafe, Hank could not only keep an eye Rafe, but Rafe
could keep Hank out of trouble.

It wasn't until Rafe tried to roll off her that they
both realized they were a sticky mess. He smiled as she
groaned from muscles that hadn't been that well used
since Alaska. With a chuckle, he climbed out of the
king-sized monstrosity.

"Quit smiling and help me up." She held out her hands, and he pulled her from the bed. The satisfied smirk never left his lips. "We need to get cleaned up before the girls start screaming for food."

"And I was hoping to try out that tub you teased me with not too long ago."

Heat flared within her, but she shook her head. "After we put the girls to bed. I'll take you on an extended tour of the bath and the shower."

"Sounds promising, *cariña*. We could start with a shower and soak in the bath after." His smile turned into a leer. "Better yet, we could shower together now and conserve water."

His gaze roved over her, turning heated in its intensity. Her body warmed under his perusal. If they showered together, it would be another hour before they left their bedroom. Giddiness bubbled into her at the thought that this would now be their room. A smile bloomed across her face before she shook her head. "No, you take the master bath, and I'll shower in the guest bath."

"Ah, no fun."

"If we shower together, we'll never leave here. And in all seriousness, I like to help feed the girls." They were growing so fast, and Colby wanted to savor every second of them before they were gone.

"I want to help. I want to get to know my daughters." He sobered at the reminder of the twins.

"And I want you to know them. Which is why you're going to help me feed them. And I'm getting pictures when they spit strained peas at you." She laughed at his slack-jawed expression before he spun and headed for the master bath, his chuckles trailing like the happiest of music in his wake.

She slid on her robe and all but danced to the den to grab his bag. Setting his bag on the bed, she gathered her scattered clothes and hurried to the guest bath, happy that her family was finally whole and together.

Chapter Twenty-One

Colby moved from the stove to the table as the eggs, biscuits, and bacon filled the spots between the grits and ham. As Charlie, Tanner, and Russell took their seats, the chairs scraped across the wood floor, and Colby snagged the coffee carafe and joined her family.

The last month had fallen into the perfect pattern. Rafe woke early with Colby, and while she prepared breakfast for all of them, Rafe handled getting the girls changed and to their highchairs so they could eat with everyone. Then Rafe fed one while Colby fed the other between eating themselves. Normally, after breakfast, Charlie or Tanner would clean up while Colby and Rafe went to the play area with the girls so they could play with the alpacas. When they returned to the house, they fed the twins and Rafe spent a few hours alone with them while Colby worked. In the afternoons, Colby watched the girls while Rafe worked. As his clients were in different time zones spread around the world, he needed to wait until they were in the office before calling.

The only fly in the ointment was Harold still roaming around California. And with spring in full swing, they needed help desperately. She was behind in edits and writing. Mac was constantly complaining about needing more men to help repair fences and set up paddocks so they could go to the stock sales and start prepping for a herd.

Settling into the chair near Lily, Colby spooned up a bit of baby cereal and fed her little girl while the men dug into the meal. The only one missing was Mac. He had been on a phone call when Colby called them in, so she expected him any minute. Just as she spooned up Lily's food, heavy footsteps tromped across the back porch and into the kitchen.

Mac snatched his cowboy hat off his head and slapped it against his thigh with a muttered curse as he set to pacing, his boots clomping over the thick oak planks as he walked from the large fireplace that was shared with the main room to the back door.

The kitchen wasn't small by any means, but a six-foot-plus muscled cowboy in a fit of temper sucked up the extra space fast.

Lily started to fuss as Mac continued his muttering until Colby huffed and pointed at the empty chair. "Sit down and tell us what's going on."

"Fu—freaking King." He hooked his hat on one of the two spokes on the back of the ladder-back chair as he took his seat.

"King?" she asked. The spoon full of baby cereal hovered just out of reach of Lily's open mouth.

They hadn't heard from King in over a week. Not since some of his herd broke through one of their fences and trampled a paddock they'd planned on using to plant the feed for the alpacas.

Of course, the sheriff wasn't any help since neither she nor anyone here could prove King's men had damaged the fence and driven the herd onto her property. As far as the evidence the sheriff and his deputies had collected, it looked as if the fence had a weak spot. It was just happenstance King's cattle had broken through. Not that Colby or her men trusted the sheriff, considering he was related to King.

Lily's hands slammed on the tray, jolting Colby. Hurrying to get the spoonful of food into Lily's mouth, Colby waited for Mac to fill them in. When the silence stretched, she realized Mac wasn't done thinking about the issue, and the others were scared to poke the bear. Rafe was the only one who didn't seem bothered by Mac's quiet; instead, his emerald gaze held a spark of simmering anger with a heavy dose of determination. Unsure what Rafe was thinking, Colby focused on Mac slathering his biscuit in butter.

"Well, since you're not yelling at the men to come help you gather up King's herd, I'm assuming the call was about something else," she said, hoping to prompt the taciturn man.

"King's herd done broke through one of the fences on Cutter's homestead." Mac bit off a chunk of the drop biscuit and chewed voraciously.

Colby could tell Mac was at the end of his rope. His accent had thickened, and he gnawed on his food as if it had picked a fight with him. She waited for him to swallow before quizzing him further. "Which fence?"

"The one their temporary hands triple-checked a few days ago."

"You think the hands messed with it or something?" Russell asked tentatively.

"Hell, no. They was cursing up a storm in the background when Cutter called me to see if King had been after us the past week." He shoved the rest of the biscuit in his mouth and took a sip of his lukewarm coffee.

Colby kept a wary eye on the man in case he choked.

"Shit," Russell muttered with Tanner and Charlie bobbing their heads in agreement.

"Yep," Mac said. "I'm gonna head up after breakfast and see iff'n I can help them."

"The Cutters? They're to the . . ." Rafe trailed off, waiting for them to fill in the blank.

"To the north. We bought the homestead to the west of us, and that's the house Jessup and Matt are gonna live in, so we ain't gotta worry about it too much. King has the land to the east and south of us," Mac said. "And he wants Mr. and Mrs. Cutter's homestead, but they only wanna sell their land, not their home."

"So, he'll basically surround you," Rafe said.

"Yes, sir, that's what he's tryin' to do," Mac answered.

"Why not buy the Cutter land yourself, *cariña?*" He looked at Colby as he wiped Johanna's face and hands before turning to Lily and doing the same while Colby finished eating.

"Because we don't know about crops. The Cutters' place is set up for farming, not cattle, and we don't know anything about that." She would jump on their land in a heartbeat but had no clue about gardening or farming. And Mac had only ever dealt with animals.

"Okay," Rafe tossed the rag in the sink. "Here's the thing. This is what I do for a living—"

"You farm?" Charlie asked, his face scrunched up in confusion.

"No, I put businesses together with people and invest in the business so I can help monitor and guide the outcome."

"I've got no idea what that means," Charlie replied while his gaze bounced between Tanner, Russell, and Mac as if they had the answer. Russell was his usual reticent self, but Colby knew he was paying close attention and would chime in if he didn't agree with whatever was said.

"It works like this. Mac, tell the Cutters my soon-to-be-wife and I want to purchase their land. We also want an agreement drawn up regarding their home and the land it sits on that states they are allowed to live there for the rest of their lives, but upon their deaths, it reverts to Colby. Furthermore, I would like to contract with Mr. Cutter to take an apprentice on to learn his farming techniques." Rafe leaned against the counter, his hands braced on the edge behind him. "I would recommend Russell hold that position and, in a few years, take on the role of foreman, or farmer, or whatever the title is for that and having Mr. Cutter move to an advisory capacity."

Colby's eyes widened at how much Rafe dumped on them, but one thing stood out above the rest. "Soon-to-be-wife?" she asked.

"Yes."

"You haven't even asked me yet."

"We did the big extravagant proposal the first time around, along with the over-the-top wedding," he said, crossing his arms. "I don't want that this time. I don't want to wait a year for you to wear my ring, and I definitely do not want to wait a year for us to be tied together."

"Agreed. But still, asking is always nice. And a ring to go with the question is even better," she stated, watching his muscles bulge under the navy Henley hugging his chest. Her gaze drifted down his frame and over the blue jeans that were still stiff enough to be new but relaxed enough to mold to his thighs and legs. He was a distraction she didn't need if he expected her to think through the rest of his proposal.

Peeling her eyes off Rafe, she turned back to Mac as she ran through everything. "As for the rest, I agree with what Rafe just proposed." Looking to Russell, Colby arched a brow. "And you, Russ? Are you okay with farming, or would you prefer to work with the animals?"

Russell drank the last of his coffee before setting the empty mug down. "I actually prefer gardening over animals." His gold eyes darted to Rafe before jumping back to her. "I mentioned to Rafe last week how I missed working in my grandmother's garden, that maybe we should start our own. If Mr. Cutter is willing to teach me, I'm more than willing to learn to do that on a bigger scale." He puffed out his chest, and his onyx eyes sparkled with pleasure. She could tell he was proud that they had this much confidence in him.

"Good enough. But we can't do nothin' til we get more people," Mac stated emphatically, tapping his finger on the table as he made his point.

"I know." She sighed as she lifted Lily from the highchair and passed her to Rafe so they could get the twins cleaned up and out to the alpacas. "I'll call Jessup today and see where the FBI is on—"

"Maybe some of my family could move up here and help us," Russell said.

"That's a good idea, Russ," Rafe said. "But first let's figure out what the FBI is doing about Harold. Then we'll need to sit down with you and Mac to determine how many people we need and what else we need, and if your cousins would even want the jobs we have. If not, one of my other businesses might work better for them."

"That would be great." Russell beamed as he stood and began clearing the table.

"You finish eating, and I'll call Tristan to see what we would need to do to help the Cutters." Rafe clapped Mac on the shoulder.

Colby mouthed *thank you* to Rafe because they both knew Russell wanted to move his two younger cousins out of the poor area he and his mother had lived in that was mostly run by gangs. And if they could not only help the Cutters but figure out a way to incorporate their land with the ranch, Colby would be ecstatic.

Rafe helped her get the girls back to their bedroom then left her to get them ready while he called Tristan.

"Daddy might have just solved all of our problems, girls." Colby slipped the cow print top and bottom onto Lily before setting her into the playpen and picking up Johanna.

The giraffe print was just as cute as the cow print, and Colby wished she had gotten the rest of the animal prints for the girls. In another month, they would have outgrown them, but next time she found something this adorable, she was buying them in larger sizes and the entire collection.

Just as she slid the shoes on Johanna's feet, Rafe joined her and handled Lily's shoes like a pro. She couldn't tear her eyes from him as he interacted with the girls. The twins ate up the attention, turning adoring gazes up to their father as they babbled in their secret language about how amazing Rafe was. Each facet she uncovered of the man made her love him even more.

"You're not upset, are you?"

"About you stating we were getting married without being asked?" she asked.

"Not about that."

"Then what else would upset me?" Confused, she turned to meet his gaze.

"About me jumping in and saying we'd look into buying the Cutters' ranch."

"God, no. I'm glad you can not only help them but us too. I'm not sure how you thought of it, but if you can make it work, I'm one hundred percent behind you on buying their farm."

"But you're mad about me not asking you to marry me." Lily looked so natural nestled against his chest as she gnawed on her fist.

"Frustrated." She headed for the front door. "I don't need the extravagant proposal, and I don't need the big wedding, but . . ." She sighed as she set Johanna into the stroller. "I would like to be asked, and I would like a ring that shows we're serious."

"You mean like this one?" He held out a velvet box with a solitaire nestled in it. The white stone sparkled in a brilliant array of colors offset against the black felt. The ring was nothing like the platinum wedding set she'd had before. This ring was simple—a plain burnished gold band with a single diamond in the center.

She finished buckling the baby into the stroller before reaching for the case. Rafe tucked Lily in the seat behind her sister, then turned to Colby.

"Why don't you make sure it fits?" he said, holding her hand in his as he plucked the solitaire from its case. The ring slid on her finger as if it were custom made just for her. "Perfect." He lifted her hand and pressed a kiss to the band.

"But you still haven't asked me."

"Will you join your life with mine, Colby Harrison? Will you make us a family again?" he asked, all the love and devotion he felt for her in the sparkling green depths of his eyes.

"Yes." She placed her palms on his chest as his arms wrapped around her waist. Rafe pulled her against him and bent to claim her lips.

Before the kiss could turn heated, the front door slammed open, jarring them both as they spun to confront the intruder.

"Sorry, sorry." Charlie shuffled into the house, his face beet red and his gaze turned to the chocolate-colored carpet. "Mac suggested I come help you with the girls while him, Rafe, and Russell go talk to the Cutters."

"Good idea." Colby stepped away from Rafe and pushed the stroller toward Charlie. "I still need to dress." She gestured at her pajamas she'd donned before leaving the bedroom. "And I'll be right there."

"Take your time. Tanner's out there trying to teach the alpacas tricks."

"Lord," Colby said. The last thing they needed was the alpacas getting even smarter.

Charlie darted away with the girls, and Rafe pulled her back into his arms for a more heated kiss. Breaking apart, he ran a hand down her back. "I've been trying to figure out a way to keep King off our borders for the past few weeks. I've had Tristan working on it as well. So, this takes care of the north border, and with Matt and Jessup west of us, you're as protected as we can make you."

"True. North of the Cutters is the nature preserve, and the west piece abuts the utility station. Now if we can just keep King from breaking our fences."

"I have some thoughts on that as well, but I need to talk to Mac and the Cutters to find out the regulations. And I'm probably going to need to get Jessup and Tristan involved."

"Oh, you're going to attorney him to death," she teased. "That's the best idea ever."

He lightly swatted her rear. "No attorney'ing him. Jesus, is that even a term?" He shook his head.

"Well, just be careful, the sheriff is related to King, which is why shit doesn't get done to the asshole. No matter how many times we involve the law, there's never enough evidence."

"Or so he claims."

A loud banging on the door interrupted them as Mac stood in the doorway and pushed his tan cowboy hat up on his head. "We're heading out iff'n you still want to come."

Rafe pressed a quick kiss to her lips before grabbing his lightweight jacket and following Mac. She watched Rafe jog down the porch steps as he slipped his sunglasses over his eyes and gestured as he talked to Mac about whatever Tristan had said. Mac listened intently, head tipped to the side, his cowboy hat doing a good job shielding his eyes from the bright sun.

She and Rafe had been dealt a raw hand in the beginning, but he'd done everything in his power to show how much he regretted what had happened as well as prove his commitment to her and the girls. He could have walked away at any time when he uncovered all the drama that had become her life. Instead, he'd stood beside her as she faced each obstacle. Not only stood beside her but discussed each decision with her so they could make them together.

Just as she entered their bedroom, one of her burners trilled from her nightstand. They had been eerily silent the past month, so to have one ring now was jarring. Her muscles tensed as she fumbled open the drawer to see Hank's cell dancing in the bottom.

Trepidation danced down her spine as she lifted the rattling cell. It fell silent, and she hoped maybe Hank had butt-dialed her. But every instinct told her he was calling with bad news.

If it were good news, Jessup would have phoned her. If it were good news, the FBI would have called to tell her Harold was in custody. If it were good news, Harold's face would have been plastered all over the news.

Instead, there was silence.

She held the cell, watching and waiting to see if Hank called back. Just as she gave up and started to call him, the cell jolted in her hand. She startled, almost dropping the phone before flipping it open.

"H-hello?" her voice gave out on her as her throat was dry as dust.

"Colby?"

"Yes."

"Harold's escaped," Hank said.

There was no lead up as the world went out beneath her. Falling onto the bed she and Rafe had made love in this morning, she snatched his pillow up and hugged it to her chest. His lingering scent comforted her as she found her footing.

"Colby, are you there?"

"Yes, sorry." She cleared her throat as her mind came back online. "You said 'escaped.' Does that mean Harold was in custody?"

"No, they lost him." He heaved a deep sigh. "And it happened two days ago."

"Two days?" She grappled to keep from screaming for Charlie to bring her girls back into the house as she worked to figure out why no one had called her. "You just found out?"

"Yes and no," he snarled into the phone. "Yes, I just found out because the person I had tracking the FBI and the other who had hacked Harold's accounts left messages for me—"

"When?"

"Two days ago."

"Jesus, Hank, why didn't you call? We could have—"

"First, I didn't call because Casey's wife has been in ICU the past two days from gunshot wounds inflicted in a convenience store robbery. She threw herself over her two kids when a junkie went nuts and started shooting up the place because it didn't have any more Oatmeal Cream Pies. At least that's what your goddaughter said to the cops while they wheeled her mother away in an ambulance—"

"I didn't know." Colby rubbed a hand over her eyes to try to clear them; it was then she realized she was crying.

"I know. I'm not angry at you. I'm just pissed at everyone right now," he growled.

"But she's out of the ICU?"

"Yes, in a room. And Casey's done with the locksmith business as well as the other. He has a year left before he can touch the money safely, but I told him that place was dangerous. Hell, he was robbed once at his storefront and keeps a gun under the counter now." He cleared his throat. "Anyway, that's not why I called. I don't know where Harold is, and since Tracey is out of the woods now, I'm on my way to the airport to get to you."

"No."

"Oh, hell, yes," He stated emphatically. "Because Megan turned up dead yesterday."

"What? How? She's in WITSEC."

"Not yet, she wasn't. They had to take her to the Cayman Islands to get her recordings because she wasn't as stupid as Harold thought she was. She didn't trust him not to be able to get into any safe deposit box she had in the States. I don't know how they got to her because she was under FBI protection, but they cut out her tongue."

Bile rose to the back of Colby's throat as she shivered.

"And I will not let that happen to you or your family. So, I'm flying out there."

"Okay," she whispered.

"If Jessup or anyone else calls to tell you these things, act surprised. Now, I'll be watching you in a few hours. Just stay safe until then."

Hank hung up before Colby could tell him that he could stay at the main house. Imagining Megan's murder, Colby bolted for the bathroom and lost her breakfast. Sitting on the cold tile of the bathroom floor, she wished she wrote romance instead of murder mysteries. Maybe then she wouldn't be able to picture Megan's last minutes on earth as the scene spun in her head like a broken record.

To kill Megan was one thing, but to come after Colby and the girls? That didn't make any sense. What did she have that he would want now? All the money was set up in various foundations with the rest in an account collecting interest until the Harold mess was settled. She had no proof of anything he was up to, only Megan and Lillian had had that evidence.

Colby had nothing to tie Harold to anything. No, he wouldn't come for her. He would run like the coward he was.

~ ~ ~ ~

"Are you insane?" Matt screeched over the speaker of Colby's cell, making Rafe wince.

In any other situation, he would have smiled, but not now. Rafe had talked until he was blue in the face before giving up and calling in reinforcements in the form of Jessup and Matt. Rafe was still angry that Colby hadn't told him about Harold slipping away from the FBI until after they had put the twins to bed. Then she had told him some man from her past was coming to help keep watch, not that she expected anything to happen.

Even after meeting the man, Rafe hadn't stopped worrying until Hank took him to the barn and explained some of what he had done in his past life. Hearing about Hank's past helped Rafe to understand why Colby trusted him. She had saved the man's life, and it was a debt Hank said could never be repaid.

However, it was Hank's steady presence and calm that let Rafe know the man would do whatever he had to in order to keep Colby and the girls safe. But it was Colby's blind insistence that Harold would not come for her that pissed Rafe off.

She refused to take the threat of Harold seriously. Instead, he found her in the paddock with the alpacas, checking fences. In Matt and Jessup's house, following up with the construction crew on the remodel. Or in town helping at the shelter. It was a nightmare keeping track of her.

As for Hank's claim of being a contract killer, Rafe hadn't believed him at first. The man looked nothing like a hitman. He wasn't thuggish; he also wasn't plain enough to blend into the background.

No, Hank looked like a carefree aristocrat or a rich playboy who enjoyed a life of leisure with laugh lines bracketing his mouth and eyes. Thick layers of dirty-blond that hair hung in waves to his shoulders, a perfect white smile that sparkled in his tan face, and gold eyes that warmed to honey when they landed on Colby. The affection glinting in the gold depths set Rafe's teeth on edge.

Nothing of the man said he was willing, or able, to kill someone until he'd had Rafe cornered in the barn. All warmth had fled his gaze. Instead, the hardest of amber lit with determination told Rafe that Hank would do whatever was needed to protect Colby and her family. The easy-going persona Hank had wrapped himself in had disappeared, and Rafe saw all the sharp edges of the man when Hank swore he would kill anyone who even thought to hurt his friend or her family.

"Then we're on the same page," Rafe had said before stepping toward the barn door.

"Good, I'll meet you at the back of the property for shooting practice tomorrow," Hank said with a clap to Rafe's shoulder. "Now, you just need to convince Colby to keep her damned head down."

Rafe snorted. "First, I have to convince her that Harold really will come for her."

"Oh, that's a given."

"Not to her," Rafe had answered as he ushered Hank to the bunkhouse and then left to deal with his fiancée.

But had she believed him? No. Which was why they were in Colby's office two days later listening to Matt lose his shit.

"He's not after me, Matt. Harold has no reason," Colby shouted into the receiver.

It was the same thing she had told Rafe, Hank, Mac, and everyone else who'd voiced their concern.

Every point Rafe tried to make, she steamrolled over with her emphatic statement that Harold had no reason to come for her now, that his entire focus would be on escape before those metal handcuffs decorated his wrist for the rest of his life.

Now, Rafe watched the woman he loved argue with the man she considered her older brother. It was easy to think of her as Colby on this ranch. Elizabeth had been polished to a high gloss in California. Her hair had held blond highlights, and she'd rarely worn jeans. Here, he only saw her in jeans. Her brown hair—which she considered the color of mud—held red and copper highlights that shone like fiery beacons under the sunlight. In California, her skin was a creamy white;

here, it was sun-kissed and rosy.

Elizabeth peeked out now and again, but not often. Only a few mannerisms lingered, like tucking her hair behind both ears if she was nervous or gnawing on the ends if she was in deep thought. And her manicure was long gone, her nails clipped short with a coat of clear nail polish.

In California, Rafe had been drawn to her shy smile and warmth. Here, he had fallen in love with her all over again, with her confidence and how she stood toe to toe with him as an equal. But what won all his heart was her laughter. Here it was carefree as she threw her whole body into it. He had never seen her laugh like that before and never wanted to lose it.

Before the argument could degenerate into an all-out screaming match, Jessup took control of Matt's side of the conversation, and Rafe laid his palms on Colby's shoulders to soothe her.

"He's not the enemy, hon," he reminded her with a gentle squeeze as he draped over the back of the visitor's chair she sat in.

"I know. I'm sorry," she sighed, leaning into his touch. "But I had planned on us going to the pound today. We've been talking about it for weeks, and now this." Her dark blue eyes, the color of sparkling sapphires, lifted to his in a plea. "I really don't think Harold is coming here, Rafe. If I did, I'd never set foot off this ranch."

"And that's why I called them . . . well, Jessup anyway. He's the logical one, and if he had said you weren't in extreme danger, I would have dropped it." He pressed a kiss to the crown of her head and coaxed the tension from her shoulders with gentle rubs.

"He convinced you—"

"That Harold will come here." Rafe didn't add that Hank coming should have been enough to alert her.

Colby arched a brow, and Rafe tipped his chin toward her cell.

"Okay, I'm listening, Jessup. What makes you think Harold's coming here?"

"The trust—"

"Which doesn't exist any longer."

"No, but the money still does," he retorted, calm, and controlled.

"Right," Colby leaned over the cell, a frown marring her brow. "And it's in a secure bank that has no ties to Harold."

"So? You still have access."

"He knows I won't give him a dime."

"Unless he has one of your daughters," Jessup stated in a flat tone. "Would you give him money for your girls? Or Tanner?"

Rafe would kill Harold before he would let the pervert anywhere near his kids. Or die trying. After Jessup had filled him in on Harold's sick games with Megan, the man would have to kill Rafe before he could come anywhere near any of Rafe's girls. That included Colby. Tanner was at least being smart and made sure he was never alone. Mac, Russell, and Charlie were sticking close to the house, at least for the time being, but Colby was hellbent on following her own schedule of what needed to be done.

Colby's gasp and jolt pulled Rafe's attention.

"I'm going with yes on that."

"But even then . . ." Her voice gave out, and she cleared her throat. "The government tracks transfers over a certain amount."

"Not to mention the FBI would probably freeze your assets if they even thought you would pass money to Harold." Jessup fell silent as Colby scrambled to think of other options. Rafe would have done the same thing, worked to find other alternatives if one of his family was taken.

"So," Jessup continued, "your assets are frozen, and Harold still has one of your girls. Or you transfer the bare minimum to him, which would take years to drain the accounts. Do you want your daughters to grow up with a man who grooms little girls so he can molest them when they hit puberty?"

"What?!" Colby swung to face Rafe. Her gaze held confusion and terror. "They're his granddaughters!"

"They really aren't, though," Jessup continued digging into her weak spot. "You're not related to Harold. Hell, he didn't even like you enough for you to call him Pop or Dad or any other father-like moniker."

Colby's face lost all color as she slumped into her chair, trembling.

"Or am I wrong?" Jessup asked with a hint of a bite.

"How do you know he would do that?"

"Because that's what he did to Megan. She knew him since she was three. She started having sex with him at fifteen. The sex dwindled the past six months—"

"How could you know that?"

Jessup heaved a deep sigh, and there were murmurs so soft they barely breached the cell phone's speaker. He finally took a stuttered breath and answered. "Because, after some of the things you said when Megan was arrested in Alaska, I asked one of the attorneys working in my office to represent her, remember?"

"Yes."

"Well, I kept checking and got the entire history between her and Harold." His tone was tinged with sadness. "I didn't tell you everything because you didn't need to know. None of it changes her coming for you. And frankly, Megan needed to climb out of that pit on her own, or she would have gone back to him."

Tears tracked down Colby's cheeks that she swiped away with an angry huff. "You lied to me."

"No, I just didn't tell you every detail," Jessup retorted.

Rafe winced. He had demanded every bit of detail Jessup had held regarding Megan and Harold as long as it didn't break client confidentiality. Seeing as Megan had told Jessup, he was free to tell Colby; it released the man from the legal binds that generally would have tied his mouth shut.

As for the anger and devastation swimming in Colby's wet eyes, Rafe hugged her to him. He had the same visceral reaction, though he landed on angry more than sad. It was unimaginable, someone being evil enough to warp a child's affection and twist it into a demand for sexual favors.

Rafe wanted to help Megan after hearing everything, but only to a point because for her to truly be free she had needed to find the courage to help herself.

But seeing the pain and rage in Colby's gaze, Rafe knew Colby would have dove right into the middle to act as a shield between Harold and Megan. Which was why he was glad Jessup had given Colby a CliffsNotes version of their disgusting history.

"You should have told me." Colby pushed away from Rafe and hovered over the cell. "I could have helped her."

"No, you couldn't have, Colby. That was just the grim truth of it. However, you need to face facts. If Harold gets his hands on your daughters, he will not think of them as blood." Jessup huffed. "They'll be groomed just like Harold twisted Megan and like he planned to groom the other girl in those photos."

Bile rose to the back of Rafe's throat at the imagery Jessup was painting. Colby sprang from her chair and raced out of the room.

"Colby? Colby?" Jessup called from the speaker.

Rafe heard her retching in the bathroom. "She's gone."

"Dammit. Is she okay?"

"Yes," came the tentative reply, and Rafe swung toward the doorway to see Colby wiping her face with a damp rag. "I get it. We'll stay close to home until Harold can be found."

"Thank you," Matt said, his voice soft as if worried he would send her off the rails. The call disconnected, but Rafe knew to expect the two men the second Jessup could free up his schedule.

"We all love you, Tanner, and the girls, and we all want you safe." Rafe gathered her in his arms and tucked his fingers under her chin. Her beautiful, tear-filled eyes met his.

"I love you too," she whispered. "Help me to forget what Jessup said about Megan and Harold."

He cradled her in his arms and carried her to their bedroom. Rafe had all morning to love her so much she wouldn't even think about Harold, at least for a while, and with Mac and Tanner watching over the girls, Rafe would use every second of it.

Chapter Twenty-Two

Colby sifted through all the papers Rafe had laid on her desk. Shocked, she lifted her gaze to the man she loved. The man she was so glad to have a second chance with had given her the best almost wedding day present in the world.

"The town is ours?" she asked, lifting the file folder that held notarized deeds.

"Not all of it, but most of it, yes."

"And you didn't want to wait to give me this present on our wedding night?"

"I did." Rafe shifted in the visitor's chair across from her with Russell taking up the other one. "But I needed your signature on the contracts with the business owners. I also wanted you to know in case King stirs up a hornet's nest and I'm not here to put out the fire."

"King? Why would he be involved?"

"Because the majority of the land belongs to us now, and the rest is owned by the people running their own businesses."

"And none by King?"

"No, he hasn't bought up any of the property in the town. This is why I wanted to alert you, in case any of the other property owners start getting pressured and they come to you. You can step in and buy them," Rafe said, worry sparking in his bright green eyes.

"Because if I hadn't known, I would have wanted to talk to you first." Colby signed the last page of the contract.

"Exactly."

"Why hasn't King bought any of the property?" She frowned because that didn't make sense from what she knew of the dictatorial man.

"He's stretched pretty thin from what we've heard, buying up any farm near him."

"Except the ones we now own."

"Yes."

A smile stretched across her face as she squealed with happiness. She'd wondered why King hadn't purchased any of the land the town sat on, but if Rafe was right and King's finances were tight, it made sense he wouldn't turn his sights to a town that sat an hour away from them. And now it didn't matter because Rafe had gotten to them first.

"You're not mad at me for doing this without checking with you first?" he asked.

"Definitely not mad." Colby leaped from the chair. Falling into Rafe's lap, she rained kisses on his face.

"The other reason I couldn't wait is. . ." He turned to Russell with a raised brow, as if asking if he wanted to tell her or if Rafe should fill her in.

"I talked to my mom, and she said she wasn't the only one who wants out." Russell ran his fingers along his bearded cheek.

"What's that mean?" Colby asked, her gaze bouncing from Rafe to Russell.

"It means Russell gave me an idea," Rafe said, pressing a quick kiss to her lips. "He's going to help his mother and cousins pack up to move and talk to the others that want a new start away from that gang."

"But . . ." Worry gnawed at her as she met Russell's gaze. "How do we know they want to leave that behind and aren't bringing it here with them?"

"That's where I come in. In the contracts Tristan and Jessup are helping me put together, it implicitly states no gang affiliation will be tolerated, nor any illegal activity or they lose their lease immediately." Rafe hugged her waist. "It should be common sense, but as these people are leaving all their community ties, we want to make sure they understand we won't allow them to be influenced into giving the gangs a toehold here."

"Okay," she nodded at Russell. "I trust you." Laying her head on Rafe's chest, she pressed a kiss to the hollow of his throat. "Both of you."

"Good, because Jessup is talking to people at the homeless shelters where he and your mother volunteered. Some of the people have just fallen on hard times, and he wants to give them a hand up." Rafe grinned from ear to ear. "And Tristan is checking in with people he knows in Detroit to see if any of them want to start over as well."

"So many changes." She hopped from Rafe's lap and returned to her leather office chair to flip through all the properties. "We'll need to get inspections and such."

And if they were surrounded by people they trusted, ones who owed them, then King wouldn't be able to influence them either.

"I'm working on it," Rafe said.

Before they could dig in further, Russell's cell rang. He frowned. "It's Mac." Sliding his thumb across the screen, he answered the call. "Mac, what's up?"

Russell sprang to his feet, making Colby's heart jump in panic. Her gaze darted to the windows facing the barn to see Mac jogging from the open doors to the truck parked to the side.

"I'm on my way." Russell hung up.

"Wait. What's going on? Is it Harold?" she asked, standing to go check on the girls.

"No, it's the Cutters. King's herd broke through, and while Mr. Cutter was busy keeping them from trampling Mrs. Cutter's vegetable garden, one of them got away and hit two of the hives. There are bees everywhere." He growled in frustration. "It's a mess."

"Okay, go. Help them."

"Ugh! But one of us should—"

"I'm here," Rafe said, herding Russell to the door. "And Colby's here. Hank's out there keeping an eye on us too, and Tanner and Charlie are in the barn, so we'll be fine until you all get back."

"He's right. We'll keep an eye out for trouble and keep the girls inside."

The alpacas wouldn't be happy that their schedule was disrupted, but they could be bribed with treats. And if she brought the twins out this afternoon, they would forgive her.

Russell slapped his hat on his head and left. Within a few seconds, she heard the slam of the front door and watched as Russell dove into the truck. Mac took off, his beat-to-hell truck kicking up a trail of dust the same shade as the truck, causing her to quickly lose sight of it.

"Are you really okay with everything?" Rafe asked as they returned to her office.

"I am." She swung toward him with a burst of joy. "I think our life is finally falling into place, and if we can help others . . . This is the best wedding present you could have given me." Lifting up, she met his descending lips and was consumed with heat.

His cell chimed, interrupting them.

"I've got to go if I'm going to make my conference call." He sighed and laid his forehead against hers.

"Okay. But remember, no matter what, we're getting married next Tuesday. And on the following Friday, we're having our Fourth of July barbecue-slash-reception, and everyone is invited."

"Only if—"

"No, we're doing it whether Harold is caught or not. I'm not allowing him to dictate this." She pressed another kiss to his lips and then stepped away. "Besides, it's been two weeks since Hank warned us. Harold is in some other country with no extradition, like I've said from the beginning."

"We'll argue about Harold after my call." Rafe pointed at her as he backed out the door.

"It's a date," she replied as he disappeared.

She settled back into her chair and lost herself to her writing. Just as she drew the scene to a close, Charlie bounded into her office and flung himself on the couch. Glancing at the clock on her computer, she saw it was almost time for lunch.

"Where's Tanner?"

"Putting the alpacas back in the barn so we can get lunch ready. Where's Rafe?" His eyes bounced around the room as if she had hidden Rafe somewhere, and then his gaze landed on her desk.

"Well, he's not under there." She gestured toward the ceiling. "He went up to his office for a conference call."

"Are the twins with him?"

"Yep, I helped him get them settled in the play area myself. Why?"

"We're not supposed to leave you and Tanner alone for long." Charlie shrugged. "I thought he would be in here with you."

"Why? What's going on? Have you heard something I haven't?"

"Russell said they were bringing in others besides his family, and . . ." He smoothed his hand over the armrest.

"You were wondering about Dana?"

He nodded.

"I haven't forgotten her." Shuffling the papers around, she grinned at finding what she was looking for and held it out to Charlie. "Rafe didn't forget either."

Charlie sat up and took the piece of paper that held a list of people coming to the ranch. The attached documents listed what jobs each would have and what buildings needed to be constructed to house them.

"This is awesome," Charlie all but bounced on the couch in excitement.

"When do you think Mac will be back?" Colby asked as she made sure her work was saved before shutting down her computer.

"No idea. Why?"

"Trying to figure out how many for lunch."

Charlie shrugged. "You know Mrs. Cutter. She's gonna feed Mac and Russell, so it'll just be us."

"Have you heard what happened yet?"

"Russell said someone cut the fences."

"King, of course, just like he messed ours up a few weeks ago."

Charlie grunted.

"If that jerk had an original thought, he'd be dangerous," Colby muttered, remembering the chaos King's herd had caused and the utter uselessness when Colby had called in the Sheriff, again.

"Or if he teamed up with that Harold guy," Charlie chirped as he laid the pages on her desk.

"Take that back," she growled.

"What?" Charlie's face scrunched up in confusion. "Why?"

"You don't put shit like that out there." Colby waved her hands around to encompass the world at large. "It jinxes us, so take it back."

"Fine, I take it back." Charlie's face was flushed, and his mouth turned down into a frown. "It's just an observation, not like it'll ever happen."

"Quit while you're ahead. And as punishment, you not only get to clean up after lunch, you get to help me make it."

"Dangit, I was just pointing out it could be worse," Charlie shouted as Colby left her office. A loud thump let her know he was up and following her as he muttered about stupid superstitions behind her.

Lunch was her, the girls, Tanner, and Charlie. With Rafe in the middle of contract negotiations, she had Charlie take him a plate of barbecue while Charlie and Tanner wrangled the girls downstairs.

~ ~ ~ ~

After lunch, Colby settled back at her computer to catch up on her emails. Seeing the email from her publisher about the next round of edits, she clicked it. Just as it loaded, Rafe strode in and sat on the leather sofa to the left of her desk. Fortunately, he'd chosen to interrupt her now instead of when she was neck-deep in edits.

"Where've you been hiding?" Colby met his gaze and smiled.

"Not hiding, watching you," he teased, leaning over her desk for a kiss. "And what've you been doing while I've been working?"

"Making lunch, cleaning up . . ."

"Sounds like you've been working hard too."

She chuckled. "True."

"With the girls down and my conference call finished, I thought we could have some uninterrupted us time. Then we can wake the girls up and take them out to play with the fur babies." His hooded gaze met hers.

"Oh, I love the way you think." She stood and was halfway around her desk when a shuffling noise in the hallway made her pause.

"No getting laid now!" screeched Charlie from the doorway, his eyes covered by his hand and face scrunched up as if he smelled one of the babies' dirty diapers.

"Dammit," Rafe growled as he adjusted the hard length she could see outlined through his jeans.

Her blood heated at the display of want. She loved how even the thought of her made Rafe horny. Of course, their chemistry had never been in question. As many times as he'd explored her body, and as many orgasms as they'd shared in the almost two years they'd known each other, he still couldn't keep his hands or his lust-filled gaze off her.

"What the hell, Charlie?" Colby growled.

Rafe's heated stare made her want to tell Charlie to get out of the office so Rafe could keep the promise his eyes and body were making her.

"Charlie, take your hands off your eyes, we're not naked. Hell, I'm not even near him." Instead, she slumped back into her office chair.

He lifted two fingers and peeked through them as if he were watching a horror movie. With a sigh and a sheepish grin, he lowered his hands and opened his mouth just as Rafe's cell trilled in his pocket.

"Dangit. It's Tristan. Probably wants to hash out something else about the new contract," Rafe said, crossing behind her desk and gently kissing her. "I'm holding you to that raincheck on getting laid, and don't call the Cutters. Mac will call you when he's done."

"As long as I get my reward later, I promise not to call Mac." She licked the taste of him off her lips and wanted to ask him to tell Tristan to call back later. Just as she thought that, his cell began trilling again.

"Deal." Rafe grinned, heading for the door.

"Okay, after the twins go down tonight. Then we've got a date."

"The second I finish with Tristan, I'll be back, so you're not by yourself for too long," Rafe said as he tucked a hank of hair behind her ear before stepping away.

"Hello, what am I?" Charlie asked.

"I don't know, chopped liver?" Rafe teased, loping toward the door. "I'm here, Tris, what's up?"

Rafe's voice faded away as he headed for his office.

"Hey! I'm more than cat food. I'll keep her company while you're gone."

"And I'm more than capable of watching out for myself without a babysitter," Colby said with a frown while trailing a hand over the gun she kept in a shoulder holster since finding out Harold had escaped.

"I know, but it never hurts to have backup," Charlie said, laying his head on the armrest.

"Fine." She sighed, giving in to the inevitable. She glanced at the clock and winced. "I have got to get these edits done today, so you either need to be quiet or go find something to do so you don't distract me."

"I'll grab my e-book." He stood, but instead of moving toward the door, he pointed at the window behind her. "The alpacas escaped again."

"Damn that escape artist. I thought you and Tanner fixed the latch." Colby swung around to look out the window and stood with a muttered curse.

"We did." He turned to the door. "They haven't gotten out in a week. Tanner must not have latched the second lock good enough."

"Look, Rafe will be finished with his conference call soon, right?" A niggle of unease skated down her spine, and she jumped around her desk to put a staying hand on Charlie's arm before he entered the hallway.

"Probably, why?"

"You stay with the girls. I'll go round the herd up and get them into the outside pen. When Rafe comes down, you and he can check the latch."

"You think someone's out there, don't you?"

The kid wasn't as naïve as Colby had been at his age.

"I don't know, but Tanner's not chasing after them." Which worried her since Tanner had gone out earlier with the lunch scraps to feed to the half-wild dog he was hoping to befriend. She headed for the front door.

Colby didn't think this had anything to do with Harold. However, this was right up King's alley. Especially if it caused one of her alpacas to get hurt. Everyone in the surrounding area knew how much the herd was doted on and treated more like favored pets than animals strictly raised for their wool.

"That's because he was trying to work with that wolf again."

She stomped into her boots and slid her .38 into the ankle holster inside her boot in case she needed a backup weapon. "It's not a wolf. It's a mutt with some husky, and I think German Shepherd mixed in."

Though the dog looked like a dark-coated wolf from a distance because of the breadth of its chest and the sharpness of its snout.

"Yeah, you keep telling yourself that." Charlie snagged the rifle from its rack next to the door and headed down the hall. "I'll hang at your office window in case you get into trouble.

"Tell Rafe where I've gone."

He shot her a thumbs up as he disappeared around the corner.

Under her breath, she muttered, "Should have named that damned alpaca Houdini even if it did mess up my fairytale theme."

She scratched her neck as she called the herd to her. "Oh, Aladdin was a thief. But Charming never steals anything; he just frees him and his friends. So that wouldn't work." She yanked open the barn door. When none of the alpacas followed, she groaned. It was going to take treats to get them in the dang pen.

The cock of a gun hammer froze the blood in her veins.

"I told you if you freed the things she would come running," a gruff voice stated behind her.

Slowly pivoted to face the threat, Colby scowled at seeing King and Harold both armed with guns trained on her. "It figures."

She would kill Charlie for putting the bad mojo into the air if she got out of this alive.

~ ~ ~ ~

The call with Tristan didn't take long at all. Rafe wished he'd just stayed in Colby's office so they could have been in bed faster, but as he wasn't sure what Tristan had needed, Rafe had gone to his office instead.

Heading back downstairs to check on the girls before luring Colby into cashing in that raincheck now. He grinned, thinking about his new life. The more time he spent with Colby, the deeper his feelings grew.

He loved living here. He loved how seamlessly he and Colby meshed in raising their girls and couldn't wait to have more with her. Here, he didn't feel the taint of poison spewing from the gossips they'd left behind in California. Nor did he have the memories of how horrible he had treated her slapping him in the face.

It was a new beginning for them as a couple, and it felt like a more solid foundation than the one they had tried to build on before.

Lost in thought, he almost fell on his ass when Charlie barreled into him. Grabbing the young man by his biceps to keep them both from falling, Rafe's gaze darted to the girls' room before glancing into Colby's empty office. "Is everyone okay?"

Charlie shook his head, followed by a shrug.

"Charlie, focus. What's going on?" Confused, Rafe shook him.

"I don't know. Colby left to round up the herd, but the herd is still wandering around out there, and Colby's nowhere in sight."

It was then Rafe saw the rifle clutched in Charlie's left hand. "Colby went out unarmed?"

"No, she has her gun and the one in her ankle holster."

"Go and make sure the girls stay safe. Lock and barricade that door. No one gets in until you hear my voice or the word spaghetti." Rafe snagged the rifle from Charlie's limp grasp. It had been the safe word Tanner and Colby had decided on in Alaska.

"What'er you gonna do?" Charlie gulped audibly.

"Go check on my fiancée." Rafe headed to the front door alone while Charlie's hurried footsteps raced into the twins' room.

Within seconds, Rafe had his boots on and the door open. When his gaze fell on Fi gamboling with Fo at the bottom of the stairs, he knew with a deep sense of dread Colby was in trouble. He jogged down the stairs, his blood pounding through his veins as fear and rage battled in him.

Is it Harold or King? My money is on Harold since the Cutters are dealing with King. But if it is Harold, how did he find us?

Rafe wasn't a religious man. He'd lost most of his faith after his father was murdered and the rest when he caved to that unholy contract. But with Colby in danger, he sent up a prayer with everything in him that he would be in time to save the woman he loved.

He slithered around the barn, staying out of any line of sight that might give away his position. It took him the long way around to the back side of the pens and through the pasture with its open gate, but he was thankful he'd done it when he heard Harold's silky-smooth voice drift out of the barn.

Blood pounded so hard in Rafe's veins his ears rang with the rage that roared inside of him as he peered around the barn door. His hand shook as he struggled not to rush inside and start shooting. Rafe had lifted the rifle and taken a step into the stall before he realized Harold wasn't alone.

King, in his tan-colored Stetson with its distinctive silver trim, stood next to Harold. But that wasn't enough to stop Rafe. No, it was the two guns. One Harold was waving around carelessly as he rambled, and the other King had pointing straight at Colby's head. King's hand was steady, his eyes dead.

Rafe stepped back to gain control of his anger. He needed all his faculties if he was going to get Colby out of this alive.

"How the hell did you find me, Harold?" Colby asked.

"How do you think?" Glee filled his tone, and he chuckled. "Rafe's mother. He told her where he was and who he was with, and she told me."

Rafe's blood turned to ice and his feet to lead as he strained his ears to catch any sound from Colby. Would she believe Harold's lies?

Rafe's stomach gave a sickening swirl when he realized he had believed every lie that left Harold's lips. Not only had Rafe believed them, but they had shaped his entire view of Colby over the past two years. His breath caught in his chest, and his vision blurred as he waited for Colby to rage at the betrayal.

It never came.

Instead, Rafe heard a snort, then chuckles that turned into belly laughs, and he took a chance to peek through the slats of the stall. All his nerves washed away like dust in the rain when Colby swiped beneath her eyes. "Oh, that's a good one, Harry."

"It's the truth," Harold growled.

"Puh-lease, Rafe would never betray me, and as many lies as you tell, do you honestly think I'd ever believe you?" Colby held up a hand. "Not saying Rafe's mom didn't tell you where to find me, but I know for a fact Rafe would never have told her."

Rafe slumped in relief, the clean hay a soft cushion underneath him, muffling any sound he made. A soft huff alerted him; he was no longer alone, and he raised his head to see Philip and Charming clomping around just outside the pen. His gaze darted between the alpacas and the gate that would let them into the main aisle of the barn.

Hoping Mac's fastidious nature encompassed the hinges and locks inside the barn, Rafe tightly gripped the rifle and slid open the bolt, keeping the furry beasts away from Colby. With a whisper of sound that was easily hidden among Philip's and Charming's shifting hooves, Rafe pushed the stall door open. The herd did the rest as they rushed through the opening into the barn and toward Colby, creating the distraction he needed.

"Goddammit! I should have shot the fuckers," King snarled as he trained his gun on the herd.

Before he could hurt the beasts, Rafe shot the man just as Colby shouted, "No!" The sound of a fist hitting flesh and a body slamming into the concrete drew Rafe's attention.

"I'll kill you!" Harold screamed, the barrel of his gun swinging in Rafe's direction.

Rafe hesitated at seeing Colby sprawled across the concrete, her Stetson skipping across the smooth pavement like a stone over still water. The bullet that whizzed past him kicked in his survival instinct. Rafe dove into the stall and crawled through it into the grassy pen outside. His quick reflexes kept him just ahead of the bullets pinging around him.

He clung to the grass as if the soft green sprigs would save him and Colby as silence descended behind him. Another shot ringing from the barn shook Rafe from his shock, and he rolled to his feet, looking for the rifle he'd lost when he fled the hail of bullets.

"Rafe, are you alright?" Colby's sweet voice called from the barn, and Rafe forgot about the rifle to race inside.

Seeing Harold and King on the floor, both with bullet wounds, settled the warrior inside Rafe screaming for the blood of their enemies. But it was Colby looking like a dangerous gunslinger from old that truly calmed him.

He needed to check to see if she was okay. Needed the clothes covering her gone so he could inspect every inch of her skin. The desire to check on her and return to hurt these two men faded to amusement as the two alpacas paced behind Colby.

A grin crawled across Rafe's face as Philip grasped Colby's Stetson between his teeth and trotted over to set it on her head. The hat perched precariously, tipping back and forth until with a huff, Colby helped the alpaca to settle it with a muttered "Thank you."

A pain-filled groan from one of the wounded men drew both of their attention and soothed the primitive part of Rafe that demanded payback. The sound also reminded him he couldn't rush Colby inside their house to do an up-close and personal inspection to make sure every piece of her was okay.

"I'm okay." His gaze darted back to her as he moved to stand next to her. "You didn't believe Harold."

"Of course not. I'm not saying your mother wouldn't throw me to the wolves in a raw meat coat, but you wouldn't have helped her strap it on me. Besides, she doesn't know where we are." She looked up and raised her voice. "Tanner, come on down, son. It's safe now."

"You're kidding me. We could have locked the barn doors and set the damned place on fire and been done with it, Harold," King snarled.

"Not worth it," Colby said as her hand landed on Rafe's arm, stopping him before he kicked the asshole.

"You're right. Let me get their guns and call the FBI to come take out the trash." Rafe loped to the discarded guns, growling when he noticed the one Colby kept tucked into her shoulder holster was one of the weapons lying on the floor.

He was glad now that Hank had demanded Colby carry a backup in her boot. Shaking at how close he'd come to losing her, Rafe carefully picked up the guns by their barrels and set them on the shelf at the back of the aisle. He spotted his rifle tossed in the corner of the stall and picked it up too.

"Don't bother," Tanner said. "I called Jessup. He conferenced the FBI in while I hid." His booted footsteps tromped down the small wooden staircase leading up to the loft.

"Good job." Colby tipped her chin at him, pride shining in her eyes.

"Way to keep your head." Rafe clapped the teenager on the shoulder. Passing him a hank of rope, Rafe pointed to the injured men. "Let's get them tied up, then you and Charlie can watch them."

Colby arched a brow.

"I need to look you over, hon. I heard the punch you took . . ." Rafe shook his head.

"I'm fine." Colby frowned, her aim never wavering from the two men. "Besides, I don't want both boys out here with us inside. It would kill me if they got hurt while we were busy checking each other over."

It made sense, though the decision did not make Rafe happy. She probably had a slight concussion with how hard Harold had punched her. Because it hadn't been a slap Rafe had heard, but a punch.

A slender hand gently turned him, and then his gaze was filled with the woman he loved.

"Give the rifle to Tanner and go check on Charlie." She rubbed at her temple, pain swimming in the depths of her blue gaze. "And we need to round the alpacas up."

"I can do that," Tanner shouted.

"No!" Rafe and Colby shouted at the same time. Rafe gently caressed the red of her cheek, already beginning to swell and bruise. He pressed a soft kiss on her split lip, then faced Tanner and pointed to Colby. "Your job is to keep her safe. If these two so much as twitch in her direction . . ." He handed the rifle to Tanner. "Shoot them."

"Yes, sir." Tanner snapped off a smartass salute before lifting the gun toward the men with a sinister smile. "I owe Mr. King here for the hospital stay, anyway."

Rafe left Colby to keep Tanner from shooting the two men since he couldn't care less if King or Harold were accidentally shot. As he headed for the house, he wondered if he could convince Colby to come with him the second the FBI was done with them. He rubbed his neck, already knowing the answer.

There wasn't any chance he would get her alone until after the twins were put to bed for the night. Sighing, he pushed open the front door and jogged down the hallway. Before he reached the door to the girls' room, he called in a loud voice, "Spaghetti."

And waited with his forehead pressed to the solid wood door separating him from his girls. The heavy drag of the dresser across the wood floor reassured him that Charlie hadn't taken any chances with the girls' safety. When Rafe finally stepped into the room, he relaxed even more at seeing the screen propped next to the closed window, as if Charlie wanted to make damn sure he had an escape route for them if it was needed.

"You did good, Charlie," Rafe said, clapping the teenager on the shoulder. "I need you to guard them a bit longer."

"What?! Why?" Charlie's shoulder tensed under Rafe's palm as his gaze bounced between the door and the unscreened window. "Did you not get Harold?"

"Oh, no, we caught Harold. Tanner and Colby are in the barn holding Harold and his buddy King there until the FBI comes."

"Thank God. King too?"

"Yes, they're both tied up in the barn with Tanner and Colby watching them."

"So, why do you need me here?" Charlie's muscles relaxed as he met Rafe's gaze.

"Because I don't want Harold anywhere near our girls. I don't want him even knowing about them."

"But King—"

"Might have seen the babies, but since none of us talk about who the girls belong to, he probably hasn't pieced it together. And I don't want Harold to until after he's locked up."

"Oh," Charlie turned toward the play area where the girls were babbling to each other as they crawled around the penned in space. "That makes sense. No worries, I'll keep them safe."

"Good man. Now, I'm going to wait on the porch for the agents to arrive and haul the trash out of our barn."

"That sounds like a plan." Charlie took a few steps toward the babies and sat down to play with them.

Rafe tipped his chin in acknowledgment before loping to the front porch to wait.

Epilogue

Rafe stepped onto the front porch and passed the ice-cold beer to his best friend and business partner, Tristan Barrett. The scent of barbecue mixed with fresh-cut grass as their ragtag group of friends and family gathered to celebrate his and Colby's new life.

"It's nice having you and your kids here. Kind of wish you and Jackson lived closer instead of several states away." Settling into the rocking chair, Rafe propped his feet on the porch railing and twisted open his beer.

Tristan's son and daughter had fallen in love with the alpacas, the horses, and all the other animals Colby had on the ranch. Charlotte, Tristan's daughter, had been begging for an alpaca of her own. Rafe had a feeling his friend would cave like crumpled wet toilet paper when the little girl batted her baby blues. But so far, the man had held firm.

"I appreciate you all making room for us, especially since I initially told you I couldn't come." Tristan picked at the label of his beer with this thumbnail.

The squeal of the kids running around the outside of the paddock filled Rafe with happiness and contentment. The sounds the children made were what he had to look forward to when his daughters grew older. It had been a rocky year but, with Harold and King taken care of, his family was finally safe.

"I still can't believe King was tied up in the trafficking mess, and that's how Harold found Colby," Tristan said. His gaze sought out his children as if needing to make sure they were still within sight and okay.

Rafe grunted in agreement. None of them had suspected King of hiding the newly kidnapped people in the buildings scattered on the far edges of his land. It explained why the man had been buying up the surrounding farms to keep prying eyes away.

When Megan had been captured, and Harold realized the entire Alaska trip had actually been a setup, he had asked Chris Bradshaw, the man behind everything, for help. It had ended with everyone Bradshaw dealt with receiving a picture of Colby, and King, of course, immediately identified her as his troublesome neighbor.

"I can't believe King and Harold are dead." Rafe shivered at how Bradshaw had eradicated anything that threatened him.

If King had told Bradshaw that Colby endangered their operation, Bradshaw would have sent men in a much larger force to kill all of them. Instead, Hank had incapacitated the few men King had brought with him while Colby, Rafe, and the alpacas had dealt with the two ringleaders.

"Speaking of Bradshaw, he turned up in the morgue last night," Tristan stated, his thumb smoothing over the torn label.

"Seriously?" King and Harold's deaths weren't a surprise after what had happened with Megan, but Chris's murder shocked Rafe. "What about his girlfriend?"

"Only Bradshaw was hit."

Panic blindsided him. Rafe jerked to the edge of his chair while his gaze swept the area for Colby and the twins. Spotting them at the far end of the pen, he released a sigh of relief.

"No one has seen or heard from the girlfriend, but her apartment was cleaned out when the FBI hit it." Tristan continued as if he hadn't just tossed a live grenade at Rafe as terror filled him that Colby would be taken from him. "You don't need to worry. Colby's safe here, and there's no reason for anyone to come for her."

Rafe nodded. It was true. With Harold's reign of manipulation in their lives over, and with King out of the way, it was peaceful here. Even King's brother hadn't been spared. His badge hadn't kept the handcuffs from circling his wrists when it came to light how much he had covered up for King.

King's daughter had been reunited with her mother, a woman the girl thought was dead but whom King had had deported back to Estonia when she'd threatened to blow the whistle on his operation.

"Seriously, no one is coming for Colby anymore." Tristan patted his shoulder.

"How can you promise that, Tris?" Rafe couldn't tear his eyes from his wife.

Colby's husky laughter blended seamlessly with the children and drew a smile from Rafe. She was gorgeous, her happiness glowing as bright as the midday sun.

"It's Jackson's promise."

"I don't understand. Jackson's promise?" Rafe asked in confusion since Jackson and Brianna were the only friends that hadn't been able to make Rafe's wedding celebration.

Rafe's second wedding to Colby had been as low key as the first had been over the top. A quick stop at the courthouse to seal them together, and it was done. The simple ceremony fit them so much better. It felt real while the first had felt contrived and constricting.

And now their second wedding reception was perfect in that everyone closest to their heart was here to celebrate, from the Cutters to Jessup and Matt, who were chatting with the local attorney, Mr. Thomas. They had become fast friends since Jessup was taking over Mr. Thomas's law office. The older man could finally retire, knowing the town he grew up in would be taken care of. Even Hank was in attendance, manning the grill with Russell. The two quiet men didn't pass many words between them but got their points across well enough to have Casey laughing as he unfolded the long tables for his wife to snap the red and white checked tablecloths onto them so they could start loading the food buffet style.

Jackson and Brianna were the only two that couldn't come due to Brianna's travel restrictions. But Rafe and Colby planned on taking a trip down to Alabama to see the small family during the winter months. Rafe tipped his head toward Tristan as the man laid out why Colby wasn't a target.

"Well, more like his take on things, and since he was raised by con artists, I'd say he can read people a lot better than us any day of the week and twice on Sundays."

"Maybe."

"Look, he's not pulled a con since before he was twelve and yes, that was well over twenty years ago, but he's been in law enforcement for almost as long as he was a con artist. So again, it's all about reading a situation and anticipating how a person will react. It doesn't hurt that Jackson's got a lot of contacts now that he's the sheriff as well as his old contacts in Chicago. All of whom confirm that no one is coming for Colby." Tristan waved his bottle around to encompass the group of people scattered between their front yard to the barn. "Colby doesn't know anything. If she had a shred of evidence, she would have died right along with Harold and King. She never had the evidence her mother had found or, again, she would have been relentless in pursuing Harold to the ends of the earth to make him pay."

"And you think that matters?" Rafe began to relax at each stated argument.

"Yes. This is a business for these people. Harold made it personal by going after Colby's money. He also tangled Bradshaw up in his scheme. How? I have no idea, but if I had to guess, it was the promise of some of that cash. Then there's King. Someone who probably saw an opportunity to rid himself of Colby while also currying favor with Harold and Bradshaw by revealing her whereabouts." Tristan ticked each point off on the fingers of his left hand. "During none of this was Colby actively going after Harold except in Alaska, and that was only to save herself. So yes, I think now that the higher-ups of the ring have severed their connections that were close to Colby, she's safe. And that was Jackson's point as well. They have no logical reason to come for her. Because her death, or disappearance, gains them nothing except more attention."

"Which is the last thing they want." With that last assurance, Rafe slumped back onto the rocker, his nerves settling at last. He hadn't realized how on edge he still was, still expecting an attack, but what Tristan said made sense. If Colby was kidnapped, or heaven forbid she died, Rafe and his friends would hunt the culprit to the ends of the earth and into hell itself. The group that coordinated the trafficking ring wouldn't want to draw even more attention than Harold, Bradshaw, and King had already garnered. No, they would lie low and methodically cut any ties that led back to them before resuming their operations. "You know they aren't going to stop."

"I know, and so does Jackson. We're going to help the FBI with their case any way we can, but we only know so much." Tristan rubbed a hand across his jaw.

"Give them access to any of our things they need, whether it's Harold's personal accounts or anything tied to Colby and Harold," Rafe stated. "And anything else you can think of. Those people need to be brought down." Rafe tapped the armrest of his chair. "I don't want to sleep in a warm bed at night while others are suffering when we could have helped stop it."

"We will," Tristan said. "There's not much we can give them, though. Although, when we bought King's ranch, Tanner remembered hearing about some sort of storm shelter out in one of the pastures. He's never been in it but says one of the foster kids talked about being locked in there for punishment. So tomorrow I'm taking Tanner with me to see if we can find it. Maybe there's something incriminating King kept hidden in there."

"Take Hank too." Rafe didn't think it would amount to much, but if it allowed the feds to move closer to the top of the ring, he wanted to help. As long as he could keep Colby and the girls safe, he would do whatever was needed to topple that trafficking ring. "So, are you going to tell me why you decided to come? Because when we spoke last week, you were still a solid *no.*"

"What's the deal with him?" Tristan quizzed, ignoring Rafe's question.

"Who? Hank?"

"Yeah."

"Just a friend of Colby's. She met him while researching one of her books." Rafe wouldn't betray Hank's trust any more than he would betray Tristan. If Hank wanted Tristan to know his story, he could be the one to tell it.

"And now he's your pilot?" Tristan asked.

"It's how they met, and since he's looking to move here, he volunteered to fly me to the various business meetings I'll have to travel to." It wasn't entirely a lie since Hank had flown Colby to some of her destinations, but it was definitely not the complete truth. However, that wasn't what caught Rafe's attention. He narrowed his eyes on Tristan. "Quit trying to change the damned subject and tell me why you and your kids ended up showing up at the last second. Because we both know something's going on." He huffed an impatient breath. "I've tried to not ask, but it's been two days, and you've not told me shit."

"Hank's brother and his brother's family are moving into one of the houses y'all are having built—"

"Tris!" Rafe snarled. "What the hell is going on?"

"I lost custody of my kids."

"What?! How? Why?" The breath whooshed from Rafe's lungs as if he'd been punched in the chest. "You'd better start explaining right the hell now."

"Like I just said, I lost custody."

"To your druggie wife? Seriously?" Rafe knew beyond a shadow of a doubt that Stephanie was an unfit mother with her drug abuse and her numerous stints in rehab starting at sixteen. But Tristan rocked fatherhood like he was born to it. He adored his kids.

"No, to her father." Tristan's eyes reddened as he fought the tears building in his eyes.

"How the hell did that happen?"

"I had too much on Stephanie. There was no way she would get custody, so she signed her rights over to her father. And I think Charles paid off the judge. He was awarded custody."

"What can we do to help get them back?" Rafe's head spun at the thought of losing his daughters like that. It had almost happened. If he hadn't followed Elizabeth to Jessup's house that night. If he hadn't given her a second chance. Or if Harold had succeeded in killing her and taking the girls. Anger like he'd only felt toward Harold and his machinations poured into Rafe on his friend's behalf, followed by determination to thwart whatever Tristan's father-in-law planned.

"I have no idea." Tristan shrugged and gave a choked sob he turned into a laugh. "I'm not home enough, or so the judge said. Not that Charles is home more, but he has a proven track record of raising his own kids somewhat successfully and he has a wife."

"Except for Stephanie." Rafe snorted.

"Yes, but her older brother and sister, Trey and Lesley, turned out well. Which was pointed out when I fought for them."

"You know how to remedy the situation, right?" Rafe asked. They both knew how to fix it, and that was to find someone to help shoulder Tristan's load.

Tristan hummed and tipped the last of the beer in his mouth before answering, "I don't trust anyone not to screw us."

"No one?" Rafe shook his head. "It's not about trust, it's about giving up control. You know I've hired a manager to do more of the traveling so I can stay here. We've agreed to try taking the girls with me when I travel during the winter months. But it's time to loosen up on the reins."

"Oh, god, another cowboy reference," Tristan teased, but the barely-there smile never touched his eyes.

"Look, talk to Jessup He can't help he has a lot of connections. He also has a sixth sense for whom to trust and from whom to run." First, they would get the custody issue settled, and behind the scenes, Rafe would work with Jessup to find someone to assist Tristan.

"Really? He'd be willing to help?" Tristan's expression brightened. "Because frankly, everyone I come in contact with knows Stephanie's family, and I don't want there to be any divided loyalties. Nor any information filtering back to Charles that could damage our business."

"Jessup is the perfect one to help then. He considers you and Jackson family now that Colby and I are married." Rafe nudged his shoulder as another thought brought a predatory smile to Rafe's lips. "Hell, if he can practice in Alabama we should get him to lead the charge in the next custody hearing. He'd tear Charles's ass up in court."

"Do you really think Jessup would go to bat for me?" Tristan straightened from his slouch, a real smile finally reaching his eyes, and Rafe was glad to be able to help the man he considered one of his brothers.

"Yes." Rafe scrubbed a hand over his jaw. "Look, he's here until Monday, and so are you, so how about you go enjoy your kids and ask him to talk after they're in bed."

"Sounds good, man." Tristan set his beer on the porch railing. "Thanks."

"Anytime," Rafe said.

"I'll go pet the llamas, but no matter how many times Charlotte begs me, we are not getting one," Tristan tossed the comment over his shoulder as he jogged down the steps.

"Whatever you say," Rafe called out. "And just a heads-up, those aren't llamas, they're alpacas."

Rafe chuckled at the finger Tristan threw up behind his rapidly retreating back. Rafe's snorted laugh turned into a smile as Colby spun and raced from the paddock at a word from Tristan as he joined Tanner in entertaining the kids and making sure the animals weren't overwhelmed. A quick sweep of the area let Rafe know everyone else was occupied as his wife joined him with a brilliant smile. Grabbing her hand, he'd no sooner tugged the front door open than several wolf whistles pierced the summer air.

"No disappearing from your own party," Matt shouted, his hands cupped around his mouth for extra volume. "You have guests."

Colby laughed as she turned and leaned her back against Rafe's chest; his arms enfolded her as she nestled trustingly against him.

"You're not guests," Colby called back in return.

"Oh, no?" Matt arched his brow. "Then what are we?"

"Family," she said, her smile bright and teasing. "Which means Rafe and I can sneak off for a few."

"Nope, grub's on," Charlie called from the side of the house as the screen door fell shut with a smack. His hands held a massive bowl that had to be Dana's infamous potato salad he'd been bragging about since the ranch's newest addition had agreed to make it a few days ago.

With the promise of food on the air, the adults began rounding up the kids. Tanner pushed the buggy with the twins in it toward the picnic area they'd set up earlier. Russell, Hank, and Chase added the meat they'd been grilling to the overburdened table while the kids tromped inside to wash up after petting the fur babies. Mac, seeming to have a sixth sense about when food was ready, strode from around the far-field that housed the horses brought over from King's ranch.

"Welcome to your new life, Colby Martinez," Rafe whispered in his wife's ear.

She turned gently, making sure not to dislodge his hold, and cupped his face. "*Our* new life, Rafe Martinez."

He pressed a kiss to her lips before more catcalls and demands for them to join the chaos spilling across the picnic area interrupted them again.

Nuzzling Colby's temple, a warm peace settled over Rafe. They still had challenges ahead with Russell's family moving next month and finding someone they could trust to move into the King ranch. Add in Tristan's problems with his kids, and Rafe knew they would in no way have a quiet life. But whatever life they had, it would be together, and it would be filled with love.

Printed in Great Britain
by Amazon